RIDDLE IN STONE

BOOK ONE

Liminal Books

Liminal Books is an imprint of Between the Lines Publishing. The Liminal Books name and logo are trademarks of Between the Lines Publishing.

Cover design by Morgan Bliadd

Between the Lines Publishing
1769 Lexington Ave N, Ste 286
Roseville MN 55113
btwnthelines.com

First Published: February 2026

ISBN: Paperback 978-1-965059-76-0
ISBN: Ebook 978-1-965059-77-7

No Artificial Intelligence was used in the creation or publication of this work.

The publisher is not responsible for websites (or their content) that are not owned by the publisher.

RIDDLE

IN

STONE

BOOK ONE

ROBERT EVERT

Chapter One

"Blood spurted out of him, saturating the ground where he lay crumpled in the bushes," Harden, the evening's hired storyteller said, his voice quavering with emotion. Standing alone on a long wooden table in the middle of the Wandering Rogue's crowded common room, he knelt in the circle of lantern light as if comforting a dying comrade. Around him, in the smoky dimness, nearly a hundred of Rood's townsfolk leaned forward, spellbound.

"And then my brother slowly opened his eyes, and he said to me with his last gasping breath, 'Harden . . . tell Rose, tell her I—'"

Harden sprang to his feet, his booming voice startling the audience. "At that moment, another of the goblins' accursed arrows tore into his chest! My brother's blood splattered across my face as I drew my trusty sword . . ."

From his usual spot in the far corner of the tavern, Edmund watched Molly wait on Bert the cooper a couple of tables away. She filled the elderly man's stein to the rim, smiled at him, and made her way to the next customer.

Quickly, Edmund drained the rest of his warm beer. Pushing aside the books he brought to read, he placed his glass in the middle of the table so she couldn't miss that it was empty.

Okay. Relax. Relax and try to sound confident.

"... with my dead brother still in my arms, the terrible goblin horde charged at us, waving their cruel scimitars over their heads and screaming as if they were possessed by the Evil One himself!" The speaker swung an imaginary sword over his head and shrieked a high-pitched war cry. Those around him covered their ears.

The people at the table behind Bert didn't require anything else to drink, so Molly continued along the aisle. One more table to go before she reached Edmund.

Relax. Just relax. Remember to breathe. And don't say anything stupid!

"... at least forty of the foul beasts stormed the hill upon which I and my three surviving comrades stood drenched in blood ..."

Molly filled the glasses of the customers in front of Edmund. When she looked up, her gaze met his. His heart thumping, he couldn't help but smile. She smiled, too.

Okay. Here she comes! Relax. And for the love of the gods, don't stutter!

As she approached, Molly playfully pretended she didn't see Edmund or his empty glass. She bumped into his shoulder.

"Oh, excuse me, my dear sir," she whispered in exaggerated surprise. "I didn't see you sitting here all by yourself. How could I've missed such a handsome gentleman?"

"... the first goblin fell dead at my feet," the storyteller went on, "my fine blade planted in its cloven chest ..."

"Hello, M ... M ... Molly," Edmund said, trying to remember to breathe.

Winking at him, she bent forward to retrieve his glass. Edmund's grin widened when he inadvertently caught a glimpse of her ample breasts rebelling against her tight dress.

What the hell are you doing? Chivalrous men don't leer! Look away! Look away!

Averting his eyes, he mentally reproached himself for what he was thinking.

Golden-brown beer rose higher in his glass as she poured.

Hurry! Say something. Compliment her. Women love that kind of thing!

"Uh . . ." Edmund struggled to find something to say. "Th-th . . . that's . . . that's a b-beaut-beautiful, a beautiful dress you're wearing."

"This?" She tossed her hips to one side, showing Edmund her profile. "A special man gave this to me for my birthday." She winked again.

"W-w-well . . . well, you look beaut-beautiful." He shifted his gaze nervously, unable to find a part of her that didn't make him babble like an idiot. "But it, but it . . . isn't, it isn't the dress that does it."

Should I've said that? Did that come out wrong? Oh, I'm so stupid! Damn it!

Putting her hand on his shoulder, Molly let it linger for a few seconds. Wonderful warmth radiated throughout Edmund's body. His ears tingled.

"Why, Ed, you're making me blush!"

However, it was Edmund who was blushing. He felt as if a burning light radiated from his face.

"Look . . . M-Molly. I . . . I want to ask you something."

Molly's eyebrows rose, a devilish smirk appearing on the corner of her red lips. "Oh?"

Edmund fumbled with his glass. "I . . . I was w-wondering . . ."

He spilled some of the beer. Molly quickly wiped it up before it could reach his books.

Breathe! Remember to breathe!

"I . . . I was w-w-wondering . . ." Edmund sucked in an uneven breath. "Well. That, that, that is to say . . . I was w-wondering if—"

"You!" The storyteller pointed at Edmund. "There in the corner!"

Jerking up, Edmund knocked his glass over, sending a wave of beer onto the person sitting in front of him. He glanced around, hoping the speaker meant somebody else. But everybody was looking at him, including the cursing customer drenched with beer.

"Yes, you," Harden shouted. "The fat fellow sitting by himself. You're interrupting me. If you have something to say, say it and be done with it. Otherwise, these good people deserve an uninterrupted tale."

Rood's townsfolk glared at Edmund.

Next to him, Molly knelt, wiping the beer dripping onto the floor. Edmund tried not to glance down her dress but kept failing miserably.

"Now, will you let me continue?" the storyteller asked. "Or am I going to have to give you the beating you deserve?" He clenched a sizable fist.

A sense of excitement rustled through the dark room. A fight was as good as a tale for entertainment, though it wouldn't have been much of a match given the speaker's young, well-muscled body versus Edmund's short stature and generous middle-aged gut.

Edmund glowered at the storyteller.

Go ahead. Show everybody what a fake he is! Him at the Battle of Bloody Hills? He doesn't know a damn thing about it. Ask him who his commanding officer was or what his company was called. Show everybody he's been making everything up. Go ahead!

The speaker hopped effortlessly from his makeshift stage. The benches screeched as they were pushed aside. A lane leading to

Edmund appeared through the crowd. Edmund's defiant expression faltered. He searched for Molly, but she was nowhere to be found.

Don't cause trouble. It isn't worth it. Don't say a thing.

"Well?" the storyteller asked, tattooed arms folded across his chest.

Edmund reached for his glass. Then he remembered all his beer was on the floor—and on the person sitting in front of him.

Everybody continued to stare.

The storyteller waited.

You need to say something.

Damn!

Focus. Nice . . . smooth . . . speech.

He took a deep breath.

"I—" Edmund coughed and prayed he'd get the words out intact. "I, I . . . I'm s-s-s . . . s-sor-sorry. Pl-pl-please . . . please go on."

The storyteller turned to the audience.

"Did you all hear that?" he asked in mock astonishment. "The fat fellow is s-s-s-s-sor-sor-sorry!"

Everybody laughed.

Edmund swore under his breath.

Nearly everybody from town was at the tavern. For years, they'd all come to Edmund if they wanted their children to learn their letters or if they needed a legal document read. They all came to him for help. But now they were taking the side of a complete stranger rather than defending him.

Ingrates. Where are you when I need you?

The speaker pointed to the kitchen door. "Why don't you g-g-g-get out!"

Tell him to go to hell.

By the glowing fire pit, a boy of eight years or so pretended to stutter. Several of his friends giggled.

Go ahead. Show everybody what a liar he is. Tell everybody he's been fabricating the entire tale. He doesn't know a thing about the Battle of Bloody Hills. You have the books and maps to prove it!

Slowly, Edmund got to his feet.

Some of the children snickered.

The storyteller took an angry step toward Edmund. Women on the far side of the room climbed on top of their benches, hoping to get a better view of the coming carnage.

"I said—" He jabbed a finger at the door to the kitchen again. "Get out!"

The room held its breath, waiting to see what would happen next.

Fight him! Punch him in the nose! You've come here every day for the past twenty years. You have every right to stay. Punch him in the nose and watch him—

The storyteller lunged.

Gasping, Edmund shot to the back door, nearly tripping over somebody's bench in the process.

There was an eruption of howling laughter and clapping. Somebody stomped their foot.

"And that, ladies and gentlemen," the speaker announced to an even greater avalanche of applause, "is how you deal with stuttering morons!"

Edmund tried not to run as he pushed through the Wandering Rogue's crowded kitchen, but he couldn't slow down. A serving tray crashed to the floor. Cooks yelled. He hurried outside through the servants' entrance.

Panting, he stopped and listened.

The storyteller went on with his story.

With a humph, Edmund sat on the tavern's rear steps and stared at the pale blue stars shimmering in the autumn night. They were of no help to him. He dabbed a silk handkerchief across his sweaty forehead.

Well, Ed. You've made a jackass out of yourself again. You'll never live this one down. You should've fought him.

He's a trained soldier! He would've cleaned the floors with me. Besides, there's no use fighting a man like that. They never change.

But at least you'd still have your dignity.

Behind him, the screen door creaked open. Edmund spun around, ready to run. But it was only Molly, silhouetted against the yellow lantern light streaming from the bustling kitchen.

She grimaced. "You okay?"

Edmund nodded.

"Should I bring your dinner out here?" she asked. "Or are you coming in?"

Edmund pondered his options. "I, I, I think . . . I think I'll go home," he said, although the thought of spending another night sitting alone in his empty house made his soul dim.

"All right. If that's what you want."

The storyteller addressed the common room in an embellished stutter. The crowd hooted and cheered. Edmund frowned at the ground.

"Look, Ed . . ." Molly said.

He waved his hand. "I, I had it c-coming. I disrupted him. I shouldn't have."

"Don't worry about him. He'll be off to Havendor in a couple of days, and all of this will be forgotten."

Havendor! He's half my age and has seen more of the world than I have. What I wouldn't give to see Havendor!

You'll go someday.

Knowing he wouldn't say anything clearly, Edmund nodded again.

Molly kissed the bald spot on top of his head. "I better get going. Gotta earn a living and all that."

Tell her!

"W-w-wait," Edmund said before she could disappear inside.

Molly's green eyes gleamed in the starlight. Her smile made his heart sing.

"I-I know you're busy with the, the throng and all. B-b-but I was hoping you could talk with me for a moment. I'll give you the b-best tip I've ever given you if you stay!" He put on a forced grin.

"I have a minute." She leaned against the door. "Maybe two if you keep me interested."

"Interested," Edmund repeated to himself.

Go on. Tell her!

"What do you want to talk about?"

"L-let, let me ask you something." Standing, he inched closer to her. "Wh-wh-why, why do you think I come here night after night? I mean, with my books and all. I mean, I could easily read at home. Why do you think I come here?" He longed to take her hand in his—but didn't.

"I'd guess for the same reason I come here."

Edmund's eyebrows rose in hope and anticipation.

"We're waiting for somebody to sweep us off our feet and carry us away from this horseshit of a town."

Edmund blinked at the uneven step he stood on. "Oh."

"Don't be ashamed. I know you're looking for a way out of here. Most of us are. Hell, I certainly am. This isn't exactly the most exciting place in the world. And no men here are knocking down my door no matter what I try."

I'd knock down an iron door with my bare hands for you.

Edmund played with his trouser pocket. "Wh-what makes you think that? I mean, about me wanting to leave?"

She tapped her temple. "A woman knows these things. Besides, on the rare occasion when a merchant or adventurer or government official comes through this place, you practically beg them to take you with them when they leave."

Edmund's eyes widened.

"Oh, I'm mostly teasing you," she said. "You don't actually beg. But everybody knows you want to leave. Heck, I remember when I was a little girl. You used to tell me how you were going to travel and see the world. You were quite the character—very unique, especially for this tiny place."

"Were? And, and, and . . . now?"

"You know how it is. We get older and stop acting like children. Dreams change. People become more predictable. More settled. You have to pay the rent, put food on the table, and all that." Molly patted his arm. "Speaking of which, I have to get going. I'll put that big tip on your account."

His eyes followed the gentle curve of her hips as she hurried into the kitchen. He wanted to say something. He wanted to stop her and finally reveal his heart. But, as usual, the words never managed to escape his lips. The screen door banged against its frame behind her.

You should've said something.

The timing wasn't right.

It's never right.

Edmund sighed.

Somebody in the darkness laughed. "Never in a million years."

Shaking himself out of his thoughts, Edmund sat on the steps, ignoring the smirking stable hand standing by the stable door.

"Not even if you were the head librarian of the King's personal library," the begrimed man went on.

"I, I don't know what you mean, Norb," Edmund said. "And I'm n-n-not, I'm not a librarian."

The stable hand sat beside him. The stench of his body odor and horse manure made Edmund's eyes water.

"Oh then, teacher," Norb said, "if librarian doesn't suit you. Heaven knows you've enough books in that house of yours to make a library. But don't go pretendin' you don't get me. Not you, Ed. You're a man and a smart one at that. I see how you look at Mol and those breasts of hers."

"I never!" Edmund said, his blood running cold.

"And you never will." Norb chuckled. "And it's not why you think."

Edmund didn't take the bait.

"It's not your s-s-stutter that gets in your way, my dear teacher," Norb said.

"S-s-scholar," Edmund stammered defiantly. "I-I-I'm, I'm a scholar. Not a t-t-teacher or a librarian. I'm a scholar."

Inside, the storyteller recounted how he singlehandedly fought three scimitar-waving goblins simultaneously.

"All right." Edmund gave in. "So, so, so what is it then, if not my stutter?"

"Oh, so the learned scholar is interested in what a lowly stable hand has to say, is that it?"

"Come on, out with it, Norb. Say what you want to say. I'm listening."

Norb leaned closer to Edmund. There was more than a hint of cheap alcohol on his breath. "As I was saying, the reason why you'll never, you know, with Molly there isn't because of your particular manner of speaking. It's because women don't dream about being with guys like us."

Edmund recoiled at being lumped into the same category as the skinny, foul-smelling, stable hand.

"You see," Norb said, "women always want what they can't have. And around here, they can't have men of adventure, men of glory. Don't believe me? Look at all the women drooling over this storyteller for the past week. Now, he's a good-enough-looking chap. I'll give him that. But put him in mended trousers and throw shit on his boots, and he'd look like any of the lads from the farms."

Edmund recalled the overabundance of women attending the evening's festivities. Most sat in the front rows. The mixture of their perfumes was practically overwhelming. He remembered how they hung on the storyteller's every word, giggling and crying out at all the appropriate moments. The girls approaching marrying age dressed in their best clothing and had their hair done up. At least three were holding bouquets of red roses, presumably for the storyteller when he finished.

"Your point?"

"Let me put it to you this way." Norb scratched his unshaven chin. "In all those books of yours, how many times has the beautiful damsel ever run off with the librarian? Or the stable hand? And how many times have they run off with the unknown stranger? Or the mysterious traveler? Or the lad returning from the big battle?"

He has you there.

"Go on," Edmund said.

"The qualities women want in a husband are: one—" Norb held up a grubby finger, its ragged nail gnawed to the quick. "Faithfulness. They want somebody who won't run out on them when they get old or somebody prettier comes along."

Nodding, Edmund motioned for Norb to continue.

A second blackened finger appeared. "Two. They want security. They want somebody who can buy them the things they want. And they want to know they'll never starve."

Again, Edmund nodded in agreement.

A third finger rose. "Three. They want something different than what every other woman around them has."

Raising his own well-manicured finger, Edmund tapped at the evening air. "I, I don't see your point there. We're, we're all different. No two women can have two identical men. It's an im-im-im . . . possibility."

Norb smiled sympathetically. "Boy, for as smart as you are, you don't get it, do you? Here, let me educate you about the fairer sex." He leaned closer to Edmund as if letting him in on a well-guarded secret. "Suppose the Rogue here is the Royal Gathering Hall at Eryn Mas. Each of the men inside is a tried-and-true warrior, rich, famous, and oozing with all that chivalry crap you're always spouting off about. Now, which one would be the most desirable to women?"

"You're talking nonsense. You haven't provided enough information upon which to—"

"I'll tell you who'd get all the ladies panting," Norb said. "The fella who's different from all the rest, that's who."

Edmund jumped when Molly appeared on the top step behind them. In one hand, she had a bottle of wine and a glass. In the other, she had his books.

"Here you go." She handed him his stack of books. "I don't want anybody spilling anything on your precious babies." She handed him the glass and the bottle. "Do you want me to bring you some steak? Bart killed a young heifer last night. I can give you the best cuts."

Edmund stammered. With no coherent words issuing from his mouth, he shook his head.

"Suit yourself," she said. "Don't let Norb here get you into any trouble, you understand? He's a rapscallion if ever there was one."

Norb chuckled. "Good evening, Mol." He inclined his head in a slight bow. "Sure lookin' pretty tonight, as always."

Grinning at the stable hand, she was about to respond. But somebody in the common room called for more ale.

"Gotta run!" She wiggled her fingers at them and disappeared inside, the screen door banging shut behind her.

Edmund blinked at the space Molly had vacated. Sighing, he said to Norb, "Go on."

"Finally, women want to live through their men. They can't go out and do what they want. They don't have the legal rights, or education, or the money. So, they live vic . . . vic . . . vicorously—"

"Vicariously." Edmund poured himself a drink.

Norb eyed the bottle. "Yeah, that's the word you use, 'vicariously.' They live through their men. They want excitement and passion and mystery and adventure. Let me ask you this. How exciting would it be to be married to a librarian? Or a stable hand, for that matter? What new stories could we tell them each night as they served us our dinner?"

"But, but, but that's where you're wrong." Edmund sipped the red wine with satisfaction. It was from the Hillcrest vineyard. Molly knew all his favorites. "You see, I have a world of st-st-stories. Stories from when humans first came to this continent." He stabbed his chin at the tavern and took another drink. "Stories far better than this imposter could ever tell."

"Yes, but those aren't your stories. They're the ones you've read about. Any woman can have their man read to them."

"Only if they're l, l, literate."

"Look. The reason why women like Mol don't go for fellas like us is because we're boring."

"Boring?"

You can't deny that. You've been bored your entire life.

Scowling, Edmund took another drink.

"Here, let me ask you this," Norb said. "How long have you dreamt about going to Eryn Mas and becoming one of the King's advisors? How many years have you dreamt about writing your own book? If a man doesn't follow through on his own hopes and dreams, how can a woman believe he'll help her achieve hers?"

Edmund drained his glass.

I'll do all of that and more when I have the time.

You always say that. Pretty soon, you won't have any time left.

"You're a good guy, Ed. But you ain't exactly exciting, if you don't mind me saying it." Norb flicked a manure-encrusted thumb at the screen door. The storyteller was now regaling the crowd with a comic rendition of how the goblin chieftain surrendered to him. "He, on the other hand, has gone places and done things we could only dream about—or read about in your books."

Edmund refilled his glass, trying not to show his growing anger.

You know what he's saying is true. You need to do something with your life. You can't sit here until you die.

"Let me ask you this." Norb licked his lips as he watched Edmund drink. "Could you honestly see yourself standing on a hill, leading a company of men against a single goblin, let alone an army of them?"

Edmund snorted.

"Now, all right, this young fellow might not have done that either," Norb conceded. "But it's easy to picture him doing it. He has that air about him, you know what I'm saying? It's the perception that's important. That's what makes the man. It's not what men do, but what women believe he can do in a pinch, if you get me."

Edmund emptied his glass in one long gulp.

"And, and wh-wh-what am I capable of doing, pray tell?" he asked.

Norb slapped Edmund hard across the knee. "Running and hiding!"

Bastard.

Edmund slammed the nearly empty bottle on the step between them.

"Don't get me wrong," Norb said. "I mean no offense. Like I say, you're a hell of a guy. You're kingly compared to the likes of me."

Then why do I always feel like a worthless peasant? I used to think I'd be somebody of consequence. Somebody who mattered.

"I guess what I'm trying to say is, you're a tough book to read. Women don't like that." Norb threw up his filthy hands. "But hell, what do I know? I go to bed alone every night, stinking of horseshit."

The back door swung open. Standing above them, Molly held a plate with a thick pink steak, steaming baby potatoes, and pickled cabbage. She gave it to the startled Edmund.

"In case you change your mind." She returned the way she came before Edmund could coerce 'thank you' out of his mouth.

The screen door banged closed.

When she'd gone, Norb said, "We've both known Mol since she was a squirt in pigtails. Do you honestly see her with a fella like us? Or do you see her more with a guy like this storyteller? That's all I'm saying."

You know he's right.

I don't want to hear this anymore.

Edmund shoved the plate into Norb's hands and heaved himself to his feet. He stomped off into the darkness.

"Where're you going?" Norb called after him. "Oh, come on, Ed. Don't go away mad. I didn't mean any harm."

Chapter Two

Strolling along the cobblestone lane bisecting Rood, Edmund sucked in the cool night air, hoping it'd revive his flagging spirit. But it didn't help. He still felt bored and old and empty.

Passing colorfully painted buildings, Edmund roamed Rood's streets. He considered going into the hills overlooking the cemetery where his parents were buried or maybe sitting in the ruins of the great watchtower along the East Road. But he'd been to both places more times than he could count. And neither held whatever it was his heart wanted. Hands in his pockets, he wandered along the village's dark streets, looking at the too-familiar sites bathed in the bluish glow of shimmering stars.

As he approached the town square, he tried to recall all the good times he had when he was a child, playing on the lawn or climbing in the red maple trees lining the way. But the memories of his childhood weren't all that happy. And those days seemed like a lifetime ago.

He glanced behind him at the Wandering Rogue. Light and laughter streamed out of its inviting windows, making Edmund feel even more lonely and depressed. Turning away, he crossed the village green, wondering what he should do. He couldn't take another night of sitting home alone.

He came to the news pole at the center of the town square. He often went there to read the various announcements. Sometimes, he helped the less literate make out what the postings said.

When he glanced at the pole, his stride faltered.

Something new was nailed to it—something with King Lionel's golden crest.

Situated in the Far North, Rood was a month's ride from the capital city of Eryn Mas and at least two weeks' ride to any other settlement bigger than a logging camp. Although technically in King Lionel's proclaimed kingdom of Arinóre, the residents of Rood hadn't felt the yoke of nobility for nearly three centuries. And most generally believed they were a land unto themselves. Consequently, royal proclamations from Eryn Mas were rarely seen. And when they were, they never boded well for the town's inhabitants.

Edmund read the announcement. Then he read it again.

What? This can't be right.

It's a joke. Lennart's son probably put it up. He's always pulling pranks like this.

Tearing the proclamation from the pole, he examined the paper it was written on.

It was parchment, expensive parchment at that. Further, the King's stamp was clear and unmistakable. Anybody making this good a forgery would undoubtedly be strung up.

Edmund reread the proclamation.

In big block letters, it said:

NOTICE!

BE IT KNOWN THAT WHOEVER LOCATES, ACQUIRES, OR OTHERWISE OBTAINS THE STAR OF ILIANDOR AND BRINGS SAID ITEM TO THE MAGNIFICENT AND BENEVOLENT HAND OF HIS MAJESTY, KING LIONEL IN ERYN MAS, SHALL BE GRANTED LORDSHIP OVER LORD ILIANDOR'S FORMER FIEFDOM WITH ALL POWERS AND RESPONSIBILITIES ASSUMED BY THAT HIGH STATION.

Edmund read it a fourth time, checking each word carefully in case Molly's wine was playing tricks with his eyes.

This can't be real.

But who'd post such a thing? Who'd risk their life pretending to be the king? People are beheaded for less.

He examined the golden seal again. It was clearly authentic. He'd seen it enough in his library to know it anywhere.

Lordship over the Highlands?

"The Star of Iliandor?" he said to the night.

Nearly five hundred years earlier, Iliandor was the beloved ruler of the territory known as the Highlands. He created many of the region's advancements—the roads, the walls around the settlements, the string of watch towers. He even saved his people by defeating the Undead King and his goblin armies in three hard-fought wars. To most people of the Far North, he was the greatest hero of the Elder Days, and his "Star," the blue jewel he wore on his forehead, symbolized his benevolence and the prosperity of the region's past.

After Iliandor's mysterious death at the end of the third and final Northern Goblin War, the star disappeared from history when bandits converged upon the caravan carrying Iliandor's belongings to Eryn Minor. Surrounded and outnumbered, only one person from the caravan escaped the massacre—a young squire named Isa.

Months after the slaughter, half-starved and delirious, Isa collapsed on the doorstep of a farmhouse outside of Rood, clutching Iliandor's personal diary. A message had been scrawled across its final pages. But it was written in the ancient tongue of Dunael, which nobody in Rood could read. Over time, the diary came to be owned by Edmund's grandfather, and then his father, and eventually by him.

Fortunately, from an early age, Edmund showed a peculiar gift for acquiring languages. He could read almost anything, including Dunael. As a result, he knew what the message said by heart.

It was an account of the bandits' ambush and how they surrounded the caravan in the ruins of a tower called Tol Helen. In fragmented sentences and hastily written words, it told how the knights guarding the caravan hid their precious cargo before the bandits closed in. Where they concealed it, however, the diary didn't say.

"The Star of Iliandor," Edmund said again.

Nobody knows where it is.

Neither do you.

Yes, but at least I have a clue. Considering the circumstances and the time they had to complete their task, the knights could've only hidden it somewhere in the tower or its immediate proximity. A little poking around. A little prying up loose stones. How hard could it be to find?

You aren't considering adventuring all the way to Tol Helen, are you? You've never been more than ten miles from the East Gate.

Suddenly finding what his heart craved, Edmund exclaimed, "Adventuring!"

No! Don't even think about it. Nothing good will come from you running off into the blue. You'll screw it up. You'll wind up dead in some ditch somewhere.

Nothing good will ever come from me sitting here, either.

If you go, you'll—

But Edmund had stopped listening. With the royal proclamation in hand, his feet started walking toward his house. Then, they began to run.

Chapter Three

Turning onto Healing Street, Edmund was immediately confronted by the formidable silhouette of his home—the old apothecary his father built for his mother shortly after they married. The more rational part of his mind seized control. His heart and feet faltered.

"This is stupid. I can't—"

But then the rest of him, fortified by Molly's fine wine, reasserted itself. He thrust his key into the lock, turned it, and threw open the door in triumph.

Familiar silence greeted him.

Fumbling in the darkness, Edmund felt for the oil lamp he kept on the table in the foyer. He put his fingers to the wick and, not caring if somebody overheard him, uttered the secret phrase his father taught him when he was a child.

"*Fyre av nå.*"

Nothing happened.

Cursing himself and the alcohol clouding his head, Edmund leaned against the doorway, closed his eyes, and tried again.

"*Fyre av nå!*"

A blue spark appeared, followed by a red flame creeping over the lamp's wick.

His body sunk deeper into grey weariness.

You're not doing this, are you?

Why not? How hard could it be?

Knowing the weariness from the spell would pass, Edmund stumbled into the living room.

You can't leave! This is your home. You're supposed to get married and raise children here.

Nobody will marry me. Besides, I want to see the world. I want to do . . . something, anything!

"It's now or never!" he declared to the house, surprised at how easily the words flowed out of him. "It's now, or I'll sim-sim-simply die of boredom and regret!"

He hastened to the storage room. There, he found a battered pack he always meant to put to use. Pack in hand, he bounded into the library. Thirty-three hundred and sixty-two books greeted him like trusted childhood friends—books of ancient mythologies and faerie tales, firsthand accounts of the initial human-goblin wars, priceless biographies of heroes of old, and other rarities that only he had ever read.

As if running into an invisible wall of cherished memories, he stopped.

If he went through with his plan, he'd never see his treasures again.

It's not too late to end this. Go to bed and sleep it off.

"I'm going!" Edmund announced to the books, his words echoing in the still darkness. He added as if in apology, "I have to."

The books didn't answer.

Storming to his desk, he searched the right-hand drawer. Sifting through scrolls and parchments, he took out a pouch of gold coins and several maps of the western foothills where the tower of Tol Helen lay in ruins.

He peered at the maps.

He had them memorized. He could close his eyes and visualize every road and every contour line. He stared at the books again. He had them memorized as well. He could recite each of them word for word, even those written in the languages of the Elder Days. Like a broken crutch, they were useless to him.

"A sword!" Edmund shouted, his soul leaping.

Rummaging through the contents of a nearby chest, he found his father's short sword wrapped in the remains of a moth-eaten blanket. He drew it from its sheath. Lamplight glinted dully off its smoke-colored steel. Edmund marveled at its edge. He hadn't touched the sword in ten, maybe fifteen, years. And the blade was still as sharp as a butcher's knife.

Be careful. You'll lop off an ear with that thing. Put it back. You're acting like a drunken fool! What will happen to the house and your books if you leave?

He hadn't thought of that. He couldn't simply abandon everything.

An idea came to him—a wonderful and inspired idea that would solve two problems at the same time. Delighted, he laughed aloud.

Snatching a piece of paper and a quill from his desk, he wrote a line, then another, followed by several more. Soon, he had the entire page filled. With an unsteady flourish, he signed his name at the bottom, adding an emphatic period at the end.

Are you sure this is wise?

She could use a decent place to live.

That's not why you're doing this. You're hoping it'll make her love you.

He imagined Molly's reaction to his gift.

You'll regret this.

Edmund fastened the short sword to his belt. Immediately, he felt half as old and twice as happy. He laughed again.

Now stop! Just stop!

Grinning ear to ear, Edmund hesitated.

Why are you doing this? Is it because of what happened with the storyteller? People will forget after a while.

No. It's not that.

Is it about becoming Lord of the Highlands? Do you really want to rule other people? Telling them what to do? Solving their problems? That's not what you want, is it?

It's not about becoming a lord.

Then what? Why are you throwing everything away?

Edmund fell into his chair with the thud of a man facing more problems than he knew how to handle. He thought for a moment, trying to piece together the emotions constricting his heart.

It's about . . .

What?

He sighed.

Hundreds of other adventurers will search for the Star—real adventurers, people who make their living rescuing princesses in tall towers.

Nobody ever does that!

That's not the point. They'll all be looking for the Star, all these respected men. Big, strong men. The best of the best! And it will be stupid, stuttering Edmund from Rood who'll find it. Me. It isn't about the Star. It isn't about becoming Lord of the Highlands. It's about . . . me.

The doubts in his head subsided.

I want to do something with my life. Otherwise . . .

He fiddled with the pommel of his father's sword.

Otherwise, everything would be pointless. Living with no purpose. Getting up in the morning. Moving around. Doing nothing of value. Going to bed only to do everything again the next day, and the next, and the next. It's a waste. I don't want to live like this anymore. I want my life to matter. I want to accomplish . . . something!

So, you're simply going to leave?

Why should I stay?

The question jarred him.

Why should he?

Nothing came to mind. Absolutely nothing.

What about Molly?

The doubt came flooding back. How could he leave Molly? What was he thinking?

But then he recalled Norb's words. "Do you honestly see her with a fella like us? Or do you see her more with a guy like this storyteller? That's all that I'm saying."

No. No, I don't honestly see her with me.

The realization wasn't nearly as painful as he thought it would be. Despite how he'd dreamed and wished and hoped and prayed, he knew Molly wouldn't be interested in somebody like him.

I'm too boring.

Maybe if I become Lord of the Highlands, she'll —

Forcing the thought out of his head, he glanced out the window. It was too dark to see anything, but he knew his backyard like his own face. In the blackness waited his garden, overgrown with weeds he always meant to pull, a broken bench he always meant to fix, and the flowering poplar tree from which he found his mother hanging when he was fourteen. He'd been alone ever since.

"Why should I stay?" he asked the house.

Silence answered him.

Chapter Four

Okay. Try it again. One last time.

Patting his sweaty brow with a damp handkerchief, Edmund took a deep breath. "Six sl-sl-sleek, sleek sw-swans sw-sw-swam, swam sw-sw-sw-i-iftly s-s-southwards."

How long have you practiced that? Thirty-something years? You'll always stutter like an imbecile.

Maybe it'll go away. I've read about instances where—

It won't go away. You're an idiot, like everybody says.

Edmund adjusted his pack again. Sweat dribbled into his eyes as he trudged along the road heading east, away from Rood. He'd only been walking for a few hours. It was barely midnight. But sharp pains stabbed at his calves, thighs, and lower back. His breath whistled when he inhaled. Burning sensations filled his lungs.

Maybe it's time to stop for a bit and eat something. You're starving.

Think about something else. Think about finding Iliandor's Star. Picture the faces of all those adventurers as I present it to King Lionel! Maybe after the Star, I could try to find the Lost City of Gold!

Swabbing his handkerchief across his face and neck, he surveyed his surroundings.

To his left, a peaceful meadow rolled like an emerald ocean, the smell of its wildflowers lingering in the autumn air. To his right, nestled between the arms of two hills, a lake shone in the soft moonlight, stars appearing to float in its still waters. He marveled at the scene.

It's beautiful out here. I should've left years ago.

But he didn't admire these sites for long. He knew a pause might allow cramps to set into his already aching legs. So, he continued heading east, the silver tip of his walking stick digging into the grey track with a determined thud, his sword swishing back and forth on his left hip.

The moon climbed higher into the black sky. Eerie shadows from tree limbs reached across the road. Chimney swifts and hog-nosed bats darted overhead. An owl hooted. Countless crickets chirped around him.

Edmund plodded along, his eyes affixed to the ground.

Behind him, something rustled.

Edmund froze, his body jarred by the sudden lack of movement. He listened.

He didn't hear anything.

It's only my imagination. I'm still by the farmlands. There's nothing to worry about.

If you're afraid now, wait until you get farther from home. Why not turn around? A hot bath would do your body a world of good right now. You probably stink worse than Norb.

He resumed his course eastward, trying to force his complaining legs into their previous rhythm. Then he heard the noise again, a crunching sound in the tall grass alongside the road.

Edmund quickened his pace.

So, too, did the noise.

Bandits?

Here?

It doesn't matter. Run!

Edmund ran, his arms and legs pumping wildly, his ample belly and pack bouncing. More sweat trickled from his already-matted hair. His breath came in thin wheezes.

Behind him, he heard pursuit.

Sprinting as fast as he could, Edmund turned to see how far behind his assailants were. His feet tangled, and he fell, tumbling end over end into one of the ruts in the road. Debris flew from his pack and scattered in the darkness. When he finally came to a stop, he found himself lying face up like an upside-down turtle. His head was bleeding, his clothes soiled and torn.

Somewhere in the blackness behind him, his pursuer stopped. However, Edmund wasn't going to take any chances. Gathering his wits, he threw his considerable weight to one side and rolled over. He was about to jump up and begin running again when he remembered his father's short sword.

Fumbling, he jerked it out of its scabbard. The blade glinted in the moonlight.

A dark figure crept closer.

"Who, who goes there?" Edmund called in a voice that was far less commanding than he desired. "Friend or f-foe?"

Silence.

The low black shape slinked nearer.

A wolf?

Struggling to his feet, Edmund gripped the hilt of his short sword with both hands. He shot a glance behind him. Where there was one wolf, he once read, there was always more. That was how they hunted. They formed ever-tightening circles and then attacked their prey from behind.

Keeping one eye on the figure next to the road, Edmund swung his sword around, attempting to look in all directions at once. He saw nothing but tree trunks wrapped in darkness and shafts of silver moonlight streaming through the branches overhead.

The figure came out of the grass, stepped toward Edmund, and—to Edmund's amazement—sat down.

His heart thudding, Edmund looked closer at the intruder.

What the—?

It was a dog, a black and white, long-haired mutt of a dog. Her mouth was open, her pink tongue hanging to one side. She tilted her head, thoughtfully studying Edmund.

Thinking he might be in some sort of bizarre trap, Edmund whirled around again.

Nonplussed, the dog also peered around and then returned her gaze to the spinning Edmund.

Satisfied they were alone, Edmund lowered his blade.

"Damn it! You, you scared the cr-cr-crap out of me."

The dog raised her floppy ears.

"Get going! Go! Yah! Get out of here!"

The dog didn't show any signs of going anywhere.

"Damn it." Edmund felt the blood pool above his brow. "Look what you made me do!"

Your first battle wounds! Maybe you could find a tavern and tell everybody your harrowing tale.

Shut up.

They might give you free food and drinks.

Shut up.

The women will hang on your every word.

Shut up!

Edmund considered the dog waiting in the middle of the road. "Wh-what, what are you? A, a herding breed or something? Are you from the ranches around here?"

She didn't answer.

"Go! Go back to whatever farm you came from. Go away!"

Bending over, Edmund picked up his things. He had his sword ready in case the dog attacked. But she didn't. She merely watched as he retrieved his belongings.

"Oh, great! Look at this." He held up his lantern and shook it at the dog. "It's dented. I bet it'll leak. I'll light it, and it'll burst into flames or something! Damn it."

She didn't seem too concerned.

"And this, this, this food is ruined!" Edmund gathered pieces of dried beef from the ground. He tried dusting the dirt off; however, he ended up wiping more dirt and blood on them. "Great. Just great."

He faced the dog. "I said, go!" He threw a strip of bloody beef the way they'd come.

The dog watched it sail over her head into the darkness. She turned to see what else he'd throw.

"What? Hey! That's, that's good meat. Go get it!"

Edmund contemplated throwing something else, but thought better of it. "Fine. Let some more intelligent animal eat it."

Satisfied he'd picked up everything, Edmund headed eastward.

Getting up, the dog followed him.

"Oh no. No. Go! Go home. Do you hear me? Go home."

The dog matched his pace.

"Go!"

She kept trotting behind him, her tail wagging.

"Fine. But you'll have a longer walk home later."

For half a mile, Edmund limped along, constantly aware of the dog a handful of paces behind him. Cramps pinched his legs. His knees felt like hinges rusting in place. Eventually, the stiffness in his lower back got so bad that he couldn't go any further. He halted.

"Well, I . . . I don't know what your plans are," he said to the dog, who appeared to be wondering why they'd stopped. "But I'm camping here. You go wh-where-wherever you like."

She watched as he untied his bedroll from the top of his pack.

"Go!"

She watched him unravel his bedroll and lay it on the ground.

"Fine."

Drawing his sword, Edmund drove it into the dirt. "That's a reminder in case you get any bad ideas."

Lowering himself, his body seemed to melt. He sighed in a way that he'd never sighed before.

Ecstasy!

Kicking off his boots, he let his throbbing feet breathe. Rubbing his tight calves, he inspected the dog. She lay in the middle of the road, facing him.

"Suit yourself."

Closing his eyes, Edmund felt his mind sinking into the embrace of a warm, pleasant dream, a vague image of the tower of Tol Helen rising in his mind's eye.

Leaping to her feet, the dog snarled at the darkness.

Edmund scrambled for his sword.

Wolves? Bandits? What—?

Up the road, a herd of whitetail deer broke through the trees and bounded across the open track. When they'd gone, the dog lay down again. Edmund collapsed with relief.

"Maybe you'll be useful after all."

Chapter Five

When Edmund awoke, he was beyond stiff. His body felt like month-old bread. Even his hair seemed to hurt. But his spirits were high. The word "adventurer" echoed in the recesses of his mind.

Sitting up with a moan, he stretched. Then he noticed the black and white mongrel lying next to him.

He didn't know what to think about that. For whatever reason, animals always liked him. When he was a child, birds used to land on his head and chirp away like in a faerie tale. More than once, squirrels scampered up his leg and tried to get into his coat pockets. Even fish schooled around him whenever he swam in the river outside Rood.

However, to him, animals were stupid, unsanitary creatures — dogs in particular. Every time they scratched, Edmund imagined fleas or ticks or other blood-sucking vermin burrowing into his skin. Dogs also stank.

Then again, it'd be nice to have a traveling companion. I could name at least twenty heroes of old who had dogs. Sandon had a dog. So did Ivan the Wanderer.

But they were all trained purebreds that were properly groomed.

He pushed the mutt off his bedroll.

She looked at him, annoyed.

"None of that," Edmund said. "If you're going to be tag-tag-tagging along, we best set some rules, and the first one is: you sleep on the ground. I don't expect I'll launder my things nearly as much as I should like, so I don't want your stench on them."

The dog sniffed Edmund's pack.

"Yes, yes. I'm famished, too."

Reaching for his pack, he stifled another groan. His spine seemed locked in place. Scowling, he stood, making various gasps and whimpers at each stage of the excruciating ordeal. Pinpricks of pain needled his feet. Pulling off his socks, he found his toes encased in puffy blisters.

"Damn."

Could be worse.

Could be better.

The dog pawed Edmund's pack.

"Hold on." He gingerly lowered himself to the ground. "You don't eat until I do. That's, that's, that's rule number two."

Wincing, he punctured the blisters with the tip of his short sword. Filmy pus oozed out from his incisions. Cutting his torn and formerly white shirt into thin strips, he wrapped his battered feet. The fabric felt smooth and oddly comforting. He wiggled his toes and smiled at the unimpressed dog.

"That will do nicely, don't you think?"

See, I'm not a complete failure. I can manage to live in the wild.

She blinked at the pack.

Edmund pulled on his socks and slid a foot into one of his boots. It got stuck halfway down.

Edmund withdrew his foot and examined the boot. It was the correct one. He examined his feet. They were both swollen.

"Damn it, Ed," he said aloud. "You should've known."

Rubbing his bloated feet, he considered how long it would take for the swelling to diminish naturally. The early morning sun was still climbing over the green hills to the east. However, he wanted to put some distance between him and Rood. He was still within a full day's walk from the surrounding farms. And the last thing he wanted was to run into somebody he knew, especially if he was hobbling along like a cripple.

Lifting a paw, the dog set it onto the pack. Her sad brown eyes drifted over her shoulder to Edmund. He ignored her.

You're only strong enough to cast your healing spell once a day. Best to save it in case you really need it.

Without the spell, I'll be sitting here until noon. I might as well use it now.

Suit yourself. But you better hope you don't miscast it. Or else you'll be lying here unconscious until nightfall.

I'll take that chance.

Edmund looked around, making sure nobody could overhear him. Putting a hand on each foot, he concentrated on the phrase he recited whenever he skinned his knees as a child.

"Smerte av reise."

The tenderness faded, the puffiness receded, and the flaps of loose skin hanging over his pierced blisters drew closer together.

Lying down, Edmund wondered if he was about to faint. When the tingling greyness in his head dissipated, he inhaled deeply and rubbed his eyes.

"I suppose," he said to the dog. "I suppose my mother was right." He got up and walked in a circle, testing his feet. "I, I should've practiced more when I was younger."

She always said you'd be a talented magic user someday.

Mothers always say stuff like that. It doesn't mean it's true.

Edmund sighed. "But I never saw the purpose, you know?" he went on. "I never thought such things were important. Then again, nothing seems important when you're young, and you have all the time in the world to fulfill your dreams."

He pulled on a fresh shirt. It was a thick wool tunic more suited for a cold winter evening than a hot autumn afternoon. But it was all he had.

You should've brought more lightweight clothes. You're going to sweat like a pig in that.

A little sweating will do me some good.

"All right then." He handed his companion one of the dirt- and blood-covered pieces of dried beef he'd salvaged from the road the evening before. "Here you go. Enjoy."

The dog looked at it, then at Edmund.

"Come, come. This is all you'll get until nightfall. We won't be stopping until then. And, if we make good time, we'll have something warm to eat, maybe by a nice, cheery fire. Sound good?"

Reluctantly, the dog took the sullied beef and held it in her mouth as if she were smoking a pipe.

"All right." Edmund shouldered his pack and bit into one of the apples he'd taken from his pantry. "Off we go. Onward to destiny and all that!"

Onward to the Star of Iliandor and my first glorious adventure!

They walked eastward along the overgrown road.

"I suppose you'll need a name," Edmund said after they had gone a mile. He hoped talking would distract him from his labored breathing and stiffening legs. Plus, he wanted something to do. Examining the trees as they passed only occupied his mind for so long.

"Do you have a name?"

The dog didn't answer.

"Well, you, you, you seem fit enough. You must have a home. Aren't you going to miss it?"

Aren't you?

The dog looked at him as if she were happy to be anywhere.

"Very well. Regarding a name. I need to call you something. The question is—what?"

Edmund pondered this.

There were many dogs in the books he'd read. But they were all large, wolfish animals. Some were even said to have had magic powers. And all of them always saved their owners in some absurdly spectacular way, usually at the expense of their own lives.

Perhaps that was why having a canine companion appealed to him. It felt right somehow. Plus, he didn't like the idea of sleeping in the wild by himself. A dog's quick ears could definitely come in handy.

He studied the black and white mutt as she trotted along beside him. She stared up at him. She appeared to wink.

"I'm not very good at this," Edmund said. "I don't know the f-first thing about animals. It's not my area of study."

She didn't reply.

"Or people, for that matter. Especially people. Sometimes, I think they're stupider than you are. No offense, I mean."

No offense seemed to be taken.

They followed the road around a hill crowned with oaks. Many of their red and orange leaves glided to the ground in the warm autumn breeze.

"One of the seamstresses in town, Hilde, had a dog once. It was a big drooling beast. You know the kind? It had all these folds around its face and these yellowish teeth jut-jut-jutting out from its lower jaw. Hideous creature. Its name was Wellington, if I recall correctly."

They looked at each other.

"You don't look like a Wellington, if you ask me."

The dog's furry head bobbed up and down, apparently agreeing.

They both fell silent for another mile.

"You'll need a name that will serve you well," Edmund said. "Something that will enhance you. Something that'll strike fear into people's hearts or give you authority. Not like 'Edmund.'"

There was no disagreement from the dog. She continued nodding, like a disinterested cleric listening to a confession he'd heard many times before.

"See those ruins?" Edmund pointed to the top of a craggy hill in front of them.

The dog examined it.

"That's Endris Haflen. Or at least it was. It used to be an important city in these parts. It had huge markets. People used to come from all around to trade there. But then the Undead King destroyed it. It was his la-la-last major victory before Iliandor turned the tide. I bet you didn't know that. Had Iliandor failed to check the goblin army's progress here, Rood would've been next. Not exactly a pleasant picture, though I don't know why. It was ages ago. Still, it's thought-provoking, don't you think?"

The unnamed dog sniffed an orange leaf in the road. Nearby, a blue jay screeched in the bright sky.

Edmund gestured to the branches reaching over their heads. "D-do, do, do you know the Undead King hung people from these very limbs? He used to torture anybody he captured, women, children . . . it didn't matter to him. He pulled out their intestines while they were still alive."

Edmund shuddered.

"In fact, during the wars, thousands of bodies lined this road. Most of them hung from these big hooks that were em-em-embed-embedded under the victim's jaw. They were left to die slowly in the hot summer sun. You can still find the hooks from time to time, rusting in the grass. Big grizzly things with barbed ends. Farmers use them to pick up hay bales."

Squinting at the trees, the dog moved closer to Edmund.

"At any rate," Edmund said, feeling compelled to go on, "that's a horrible name for a town, Endris Haflen. Rough-roughly, roughly translated, it means 'Hill of Protection.' But people often called it Endris Hedland. Which means 'Hill of Shit.'"

The dog looked at him, seemingly checking to see if she'd heard correctly.

"Actually, that's not quite an accurate interpretation. You see, 'Hedland' is a term for lands directly downriver from large cities, which is where refuse from sewers goes. Hence, the association with excrement. Which brings us back to what I was saying about the utility of names. You see, you need something good. Otherwise, your future will be limited. Heaven knows you don't want to deal with a bad name for the rest of your life."

They walked along in silence.

"How about . . . Trudy or, or maybe Glenda?"

The dog squatted, a yellow puddle growing on the ground beneath her.

"That bad, eh? Yeah, I suppose you're right. I can't imagine 'Glenda' charging up the Stone Heights to do battle, you know? And I've never heard of any ballads about a dog named Trudy."

More nodding.

Dry leaves crunched under their feet as they followed the grass-covered road. Above them, nearly bare branches swayed in the warm breeze.

"It's just that there aren't many female heroines in the old tales," Edmund said. "So, finding something appropriate is a bit ch-challenging."

The ruins of Endris Haflen loomed closer, the collapsed walls and towers of the fortress now in view. Edmund and the dog passed the hulking wreckage of siege engines and other rusted equipment of war. A flock of country sparrows nesting in the remains of an attack tower took flight as they strolled by.

"What about Arta? Athena? Anfala? Aubrey?"

None of these sparked a reply.

"Bashna? Betty?"

Betty got a wag of the head.

"Chelsea?"

Edmund climbed the steep hill, his hands pushing on his knees with every tedious step. When he approached its summit, he was on the T's.

"Taperall?" He forced his legs to keep moving. "Thorax?"

At Thorax, the dog barked.

"Really?" He panted. "Thorax? You sure?"

She raised her shaggy eyebrows.

"Well." He struggled to catch his breath. "It's not . . . it's not exactly a feminine name. Actually, it's not a name at all. Not a proper one, that is. I kind of threw . . . I kind of threw it out there, you know? Without thinking. But I'm certainly not going to argue with you. Thorax it is. Although I must say, you don't strike me as a . . . as a Thorax."

Edmund hung his pack on a broken hitching post outside of what used to be a smithy.

"I'll tell you what," he said when his heart stopped hammering his sternum. "Tell you what. Let's take a break here for a few minutes. We can eat a decent lunch and rest our legs in the shade a bit. It's going to be a warm one today."

Edmund filled his waterskins with the rainwater gathered in an old trough. He drank heartily. Thorax followed suit.

"Here." He handed Thorax another soiled strip of dried beef.

Thorax didn't take it.

"Oh. Sorry." He washed the beef and offered it again. "Here you go."

Thorax snatched it, her tail wagging.

"So—" Edmund ate a slice of cheese between two pieces of black bread. "This is pretty impressive, don't you think?"

He scanned the rows of burnt-out buildings around them. Rotting timbers protruded from their stone foundations like soldiers surrounded by the enemy. To their left, a grand tower rose above the desolation. Its western face lay in a heap in the grass. Croaking ravens flew in and out of the exposed rooms.

Thorax gnawed on her lunch.

"The t-t-tower here is much larger than the one we had by Rood," Edmund said. "This one once stationed nearly three hundred Knights of the North during its heyday. Its courtyards had room for enough livestock to withstand a long siege. Then again . . ." He paused, wistfully surveying the toppled walls around them. "I suppose they would've been better off fleeing westward. None of the inhabitants survived the Undead King's final assault. Only Rood and the surrounding farms remained after the end of the final war. All the other towns were destroyed. Still, it's interesting, don't you think? If we had time, I'd love to investigate. Who knows what's buried here or there? A manuscript or scroll or something. Maybe even a map. But they don't preserve well in the wilderness with the elements and all."

He slowly stood, his spine cracking.

"But first, let's, let's take a gander around and see what's what."

Cautiously, Edmund climbed a pile of crumbling rubble. When he turned east, his heart and shoulders grew heavy.

The road reappeared on the other side of Endris Haflen's ruined walls and wound its way over and around hill after hill after hill, neither the road nor the green rolling countryside ever ending. The hills got progressively higher as they marched toward the grey mountains forming the eastern horizon.

What did you expect? Did you think crossing a few inches on a map would be like taking a leisurely walk across town?

Edmund looked westward. Wisps of smoke rose from somebody's chimney in Rood.

Why not stop this foolishness and go home? You've had your fun. Go back and sit in a nice, hot bath. This will end badly for you if you keep going.

"Come on, Thorax," Edmund said with an effort. "Let's see if we can make it to those woods by nightfall."

Chapter Six

"Okay! Okay!" Edmund dragged his saturated sleeve across his purple forehead. "I know . . . I've . . . I've said it b-b-b-before, but . . . I swear . . . it's right . . . around . . . this . . . next . . . hill. Trust me!"

Baring her teeth, Thorax glared at Edmund's rear end as she plodded after him.

It had been nearly two weeks since Edmund left Rood, and they still hadn't found the tower where Edmund insisted the Star of Iliandor was hidden. Of course, the delay wasn't entirely his fault. If the weather had been hot before, it was beyond miserable now. In the narrow valley through which they were hiking, the air was heavy with humidity and as still as a rotting corpse. Even breathing was laborious. If not for the cool water of the River Celerin near at hand, they would've laid down and died.

"Come on, girl," Edmund said, not for the first time. "If we could . . . get . . . up . . . this . . . slope . . . and . . . around . . . this . . . damned . . . hill—"

A deafening explosion shook the ground. Thorax cowered against Edmund's leg.

"Oh!" Edmund lifted his sweat-covered arms to the sky. "Oh, thank the gods! Rain. Oh, blessed cold, wet, wonderful . . . rain."

Thunder pounded the forest-covered hills surrounding them.

They stumbled into a small clearing. Overhead, ash-grey clouds flew past. In the western sky, darkness tumbled toward them. Flashes of lightning stabbed the hills.

Edmund groaned. "That . . . that looks bad. I can't predict the weather like my father could, but I bet you, I bet you anything that'll, that'll be one nasty storm."

Now you'll wish you were home. Just a bunch of walking, eh? Easy as pie?

"We have to find shelter." His gaze flitted about the rocky cliffs lofting above them. "It has to be high up, or we're done for."

Thorax's ears perked, her head cocked to one side.

Edmund broke into a jog, his stomach and pack bouncing as he hurried northward.

He pointed to the white-capped mountains looming to their right.

"When those clouds hit those peaks, they'll drop their moisture . . . all of it at once."

Thorax examined the mountain peaks, puzzled.

"Flash floods." Edmund pushed northward with renewed vigor.

Thorax trotted after him.

"You, you see, those clouds contain a great deal of water, which will come down in all directions for at least fifty miles. These hills are mostly stone with little topsoil. They'll channel all that water to the lowest place possible." He nodded at the churning current a few feet away. "Which is where we are. In an hour, this river will expand t-t-ten, maybe twenty times its normal size. It'll rip away anything in its path. Trees, rocks—everything."

A fat raindrop hit the brim of his sweat-soaked hat.

They quickened their pace.

Another rumble shook the ground.

More raindrops pelted them.

The tops of trees crowning the hills swayed in the mounting wind, their branches creaking. Blackness engulfed the valley.

Edmund and Thorax hastened deeper into the foothills, the sheer cliffs rising even higher as they pressed closer to the river. The wind whined as it whipped through the jagged stone formations. Rain came at them horizontally now, stinging their skin.

Shielding his face from the onslaught, Edmund pointed to the hill to their left.

"What's . . . what's that?" he shouted through the gale. "Is that, is that a shadow or an, an opening? Up there, through the trees. See it?"

Thorax's gaze shot to where Edmund pointed.

A smothering blanket of rain battered them.

Lightning exploded, turning the wall of water a ghostly shade of blue.

The ground shuddered.

"We have to get out of here," Edmund hollered, bracing himself against the deluge. "I'll, I'll see if it's a cave." Grabbing a tree root, he scaled the practically perpendicular slope. "Stay here!"

Sopping fur plastered against her body, Thorax crawled underneath a buckthorn bush.

Trees reeled and lashed at the rain.

Upriver, a branch as thick as a man's neck snapped and slammed into the white-capped current. Where it hit, a fountain of water heaved up like a searching hand.

Seizing another stone outcropping, Edmund hauled himself higher, his muscles straining under the weight of his sodden pack. Lightning blasted overhead, wrenching apart the darkness. His feet slipped from their perch. Rocks, loosened by his kicking, toppled down the slope, ricocheting off tree trunks and crashing around Thorax a hundred feet below. Bolting from her hiding spot, she retreated to the bank of the swelling river.

Reaching, Edmund grabbed a clump of prickle vines. Their tiny thorns sliced into his skin as he pulled himself upward. Blood mingled with the rain flowing down his arms.

White lightning cracked.

The valley shook.

Somebody laughed.

Edmund looked up.

The silhouette of a hunched figure with an enormous head peered down at him. Lightning exploded, revealing the creature's grotesque face and bulging eyes. He laughed again.

"Don't like the rain?" it said through the howling wind. He reached for Edmund. "Then, by all means, come and join me."

Troll!

Raising his hands to ward off the troll's grasp, Edmund let go of his holds and plummeted down the incline, his body bouncing off the hillside. More rocks and debris cascaded around the scurrying Thorax.

"Run!" Edmund screamed as he careened off tree trunks and boulders. "Run, Thorax! Run! Troll!"

"Run! Troll!" the creature mocked. "Run, my plump little fellow. Run!"

Bruised and bleeding, Edmund landed headlong in the surging river. He got to his battered knees, water racing over and under him, blood dripping from his face and hands. Thorax licked his cheek.

"Run! Go! Save yourself." Edmund hobbled northward, pain wracking his body.

More laughter.

"Run!" the troll said from a ridge high above the valley. "Run!"

An explosion split the sky. The hills quaked. Rain pummeled Edmund with increasing intensity.

Drop the pack!

No, I need my gear!

It's slowing you—

"Run!" The troll's laugh reverberated through the black forest. It was getting closer.

Edmund found Thorax still next to him.

"You've got to run." He pointed downriver. "Run in the opposite direction. He can't, he can't go for both of us. Save yourself, girl. Run!"

Thorax regarded the blood trickling from Edmund's forehead, knees, and hands. She bolted southward.

Above, the troll lumbered along the hill, following a course that would intercept Edmund a couple hundred yards upriver.

"Run!" he hooted. "Run!"

But Edmund couldn't run. Holding his cramping sides, he gasped for breath.

A . . . a troll? They were . . . they were killed off!

Evidently, some survived. Now, think! You can't outrun him. He can cover at least three times as much ground as you with each step.

The troll drew closer.

Trying to breathe, Edmund doubled over. Rain cascaded over him. Droplets of blood fell from the tip of his nose. His hat flew off, whipping in circles above the raging river. Blue lightning cleaved the dark sky.

Do something!

The troll galumphed down the hill. "I'm coming!"

Sir Henry! Remember the Tale of Sir Henry? Hide where he'd least expect it! Hurry!

Exhausted, Edmund staggered to the hillside. Hand over bleeding hand, he pulled himself up the forested slope. Upriver, the troll reached the bottom of the hill.

Lightning detonated. The valley pulsated red and then vibrated.

"Hiding, eh?" the troll called, delighted. He sniffed the storm-ravaged air, a crude spear the size of a man in his gnarled hands.

Clinging to a stunted pine tree, Edmund's grip started to give way. He dug his fingers into the wet bark, praying the troll wouldn't look up. Fifty feet below, the troll stalked along the frothing river.

The troll sniffed the wind. "You can't hide for long!"

He stopped directly beneath Edmund.

Edmund's arms strained, his strength almost spent.

Somewhere downriver, Thorax howled.

"Ah ha!" The troll laughed and bounded after her, brandishing the spear. "You can't hide from me! Run! Run if you can!"

The troll gone, Edmund forced himself to resume climbing. His muscles quaking, he pulled himself onto a cliff and collapsed.

The sky flashed red.

A huge cavern yawned before him.

Hide! He'll never think of searching his own cave.

He will if he's heard of Sir Henry.

Edmund hadn't thought about that. Trolls weren't stupid, and the tale of Sir Henry's trickery wasn't a secret. What if he returned to his lair once he couldn't find Edmund in the woods?

You better pray there's another exit. Otherwise, you're done for!

I'll only stay for a few minutes. I'll catch my breath while he searches the forest. Then, I'll run in the opposite direction.

Downriver, Thorax snarled and barked. Edmund mentally urged her to run faster, using her small size to dart beneath the low-lying branches. Trolls were quick. But their enormous girth would slow them considerably if they had to fight through the undergrowth.

Hurry! Get out of view!

Wiping blood and rain from his eyes, Edmund got up and stumbled into the cave. Wind screeched. Rain stung the side of his face. Lightning slashed the sky. Something glittered on the ground. Thousands of coins, gems, and pieces of jewelry lay scattered about the cave's floor. He reached for it.

Leave it. It's bait! Don't you know anything? Remember what happened to Harlen in The Horrors of the Mountains? Hide!

Edmund limped into the tunnel's darkness, his hands feeling the cold stone walls, his boots crunching on the unseen riches. The stench of rot and decay punched his nostrils. He fumbled with the dented lantern hanging from his dripping pack.

What're you doing? You'll give yourself away!

The bend in the tunnel will block the light from outside. I need to see, or I'll fall into some pit.

Edmund touched the wick.

"Fyre av nå."

A small blue flame flashed in the darkness.

Edmund swept the light around him.

Hundreds of black rats with red gleaming eyes scattered in every direction. They were everywhere—on the floor, on the tops of boulders, along the ledges lining the cavern. Then, in a matter of seconds, they vanished in any of the countless cracks and holes pocking the walls.

His skin crawling, Edmund retched.

Pull yourself together. They're only vermin. Nobody has ever been eaten by rats. Catch your breath, then get the hell out of here.

Edmund forced himself to examine his surroundings.

He was in a cavern halfway up the hill. Water dripped from tree roots hanging like dirty spider webs from the ceiling. Bones, some still with traces of flesh and fur, lay in great heaps. Assorted weapons, armor, and broken wooden chests filled niches in the wall. One of the dented shields caught Edmund's attention. He gasped.

That's the emblem of Sir William of Endris!

Then he spotted shields from other heroes he'd read about—Sir Reginald, Sir Harris of Upshire, Sir Arlington, Sir Perris. Perplexed, he stared at them lining the cavern like paintings in a museum. Some had been sliced cleanly in two.

How can this be? They didn't die around here. They should be in the Hall of Heroes in Eryn Mas.

Thunder rattled the shields.

Come on! Extinguish the light and hide!

As Edmund turned, his lantern illuminated a narrow fissure. Inside stood a black book the size of a tall man's torso.

That must have over three thousand pages!

As if drawn by magic, he stepped toward it.

Don't be a fool. Get out of here. You've rested enough. Go before he returns!

He squinted at the tome's dark leather binding, unable to make out the faded gold lettering.

Remember the troll? Go!

Edmund reached inside the fissure. The book was heavier than he thought it would be. Grunting, he laid it gingerly on the ground. He blew the dirt from its cover. In the wavering lantern light, a single word appeared.

Kalvella?

What does that mean?

Who cares? Get out of here!

Taking care not to drip water on it, he opened the cover. An ink drawing adorned the first page. A hulking humanoid shape loomed over what appeared to be three sickly children, their arms upraised, their faces contorted in silent screams of horror. In the background, adult-sized figures lay in a pool of blood.

Edmund turned the page, the dry parchment crackling in his damp hands.

What is this?

He turned another page.

Maybe an epic poem?

But in what language?

He tried to decipher the spidery script.

It could be a derivation of the early languages. Some of these characters seem similar to Núvel.

Perhaps. Whatever this is, it's old.

He searched for a date but couldn't find anything he could read.

He turned another page.

He came to an ornate illustration of a dying man sprawled in a woman's arms. One of his pale hands lay limp at his side, the other clutching his chest, blood seeping through his fingers. His eyes were rolled heavenward, his mouth open. A weeping woman bent over him.

Beautiful composition. I wonder who did it.

He couldn't find a signature.

A flash of crimson light illuminated the entrance to the cave. A minute later, thunder rumbled.

Come on! Let's go!

In a second.

Edmund turned a few pages.

I wonder what this is.

He turned several more.

He looked up. Grey light shone into the cave.

Edmund sprang to his feet.

He'd gone through a quarter of the book.

How long—?

Get the hell out of here! Run!

He wrapped his arms around the tome.

Put it back!

No. It's too valuable.

You can't run with it, you idiot! Get out of here!

With the book pressed against his breast and the lantern swinging from his fingertips, Edmund waddled to the cavern entrance. He surveyed the ravaged valley.

Trees and branches lay across the engorged river like giant beaver dams. Muddy water streamed down the hillsides. To the west, the sun lingered above the horizon in an orange haze.

How long was I—?

Somebody swore.

A large shape splashed along the undulating river, its back bent, spear dragging by its side.

"Damn imp," he said. "Taunt me, will he? I'll get the bugger. The worm! When the blasted sun sets, I'll get him. I'll get him and squeeze his eyes out!"

Edmund flattened himself against the cave wall.

Too late!

Go back. See if there's a second exit to this place!

No, you'll get trapped. Get out of here and run. Run!

Edmund let the book slide from his grip and propped it against a boulder.

Blowing out his lantern, Edmund stalked along the cliff away from the advancing troll.

The troll plodded up the hill's eastern slope. "Curse the bugger. I'll get him. Then I'll make him squeak."

Edmund carefully descended the northern slope.

"Where was he heading?" the troll said. "He was heading upriver. Him and that miserable dog. Where was he going? Where?"

Edmund crept farther away.

"He didn't have a horse," the troll went on. "Would've smelled it. Only that damned dog!"

Edmund inched down the hill. His feet slid on the wet rocks. He lost his balance. As he grabbed a tree limb, the lantern slipped from his grasp. It bounced, hitting stones and crashing into tree trunks with ringing clanks. When it finally came to rest at the bottom of the valley, all was quiet. Clinging to the tree branch, Edmund listened, terrified.

"Maybe to the old mines?" the troll grumbled. "The old human settlement? Maybe the tower. He was alone. Maybe he's lost . . ."

Half sliding, half running, Edmund raced to where the lantern lay. He affixed it to his pack and turned.

Through a gap between two hills, he could see a broad, waterlogged glen. On the other side, a lopsided mountain stood. On its summit, stabbing at the underbelly of the late afternoon sky like a deadly spear, stood a tower. Staring at it, Edmund muttered its name in awe. "Tol Helen."

Finally!

Behind him, something moved. He spun around.

Thorax pulled herself out from under a bush, her mud-covered tail wagging.

"Hey!" Edmund whispered.

Running to him, she jumped into his arms. He hugged her.

"You look a wreck. Are you okay, girl?"

She licked him.

"Listen, we, we, we have to get out of here," he said.

Thorax headed north along the river.

"No," Edmund whispered. "This way! Follow me. I know where the tower is. See it? There through the hills? We're almost—"

A great shout shook the hillside. "Imp!"

Chapter Seven

Somewhere in the night, crossing the marshy valley behind Edmund and Thorax, the troll bellowed again. "Imp! I'm going to crush your miserable skull! I'm going to bash your brains into jelly! Do you hear me? Jelly!"

Covered in mud, Edmund collapsed onto rubble that once formed a wall ringing the now-destroyed city. Thorax thrust her nose under his arm, urging him onward. But Edmund swatted her away.

"I, I can't." He panted. "I can't."

She grabbed his sleeve in her teeth and tugged.

"No." He groaned. "No. Hon-honestly. I can't . . . I can't move anymore. I need . . . I need to rest."

Maybe a mile away, the troll roared. "You can't hide from me!"

He drew closer.

Thorax pulled harder, her eyes flitting to the road winding up the mountainside to the tower above them.

Maybe I can get up there and drop rocks on him—like what the Hillmen used to do to invaders.

You'll never make it there in time. It's at least another three or four miles to the top of the mountain. Besides, any rock you can lift will bounce off him like a snowball.

There has to be another way.

"Listen . . . listen to me," Edmund told Thorax. "You need to save us, girl. You need to . . . to save us."

Letting go of his sleeve, Thorax cocked her head.

Edmund gestured vaguely at the remains of the settlement on the other side of the ruined wall. "Some, somewhere, somewhere on the southwest face of this mountain . . . up, up from these ruins . . . somewhere . . . somewhere is a cave . . . a tunnel. It's small. Just, just big enough for a young boy to crawl through. You need to find it."

Thorax darted into the darkness.

You better hope Isa wasn't lying about how he escaped the tower.

The troll waded through the nearby swamp.

Edmund noted the gibbous moon shining silver in the blackness overhead.

It's after midnight. Maybe he'll—

What? Turn back at dawn? The troll will be here in ten minutes. It'll be all over then.

Scared out of the reeds, a flock of marsh wrens scattered into the night sky.

Maybe we can find someplace to hide.

Where? There is nothing but wreckage left. Besides, he'd sniff us out eventually.

Maybe try the road.

You can't outrun a troll. Isa's route is the only—

Thorax barked.

"Imp!" the troll shouted. "I'm going to rip off your stinking arms and beat your damn dog with them!"

Edmund clambered over the ruined wall, his legs quivering with fatigue and fear.

Thorax dashed to him.

"Did you find it? Did you find it, girl?"

She grabbed his hand in her mouth and pulled.

"Where?"

She shot off into the darkness.

Edmund stumbled after her.

Thorax barked again. But Edmund couldn't make his legs move any faster.

"Steal my things, will you?" the troll hollered. "I'll show you what I do to thieves!"

Edmund hobbled along a street heading toward the side of the mountain. Behind him, the troll climbed over the ring of stone upon which Edmund had rested.

Thorax reappeared.

"Thorax," Edmund said. "We don't have much time. If we don't make it . . . run. Okay? Head . . . head, head to Rood. Head home. All right? Don't worry about me."

Shooting off the road, she crawled under a thicket of overgrown scrub bushes. Edmund tried to follow but couldn't push through the mass of branches. He tried again but couldn't get more than a few feet into the entanglement.

Use your sword. Cut them down!

I don't have the strength to—

Just do it! You don't have time. He's coming this way!

Edmund drew his short sword from its mud-caked scabbard.

On the desolate street below, the troll pounded toward them.

It'll take an hour to cut all of this—

Hurry! Hack them down and get to the tunnel.

Edmund swung feebly at the first bush. Half of it teetered and then fell to his feet. He examined the inch-thick branch. His sword sliced through it like water.

Incredible!

The troll stormed along the road. "You can't hide from me, imp!"

Hacking at the bushes with renewed vigor, a previously unfelt power welled in Edmund's sword arm. He swung again and again, the dense foliage falling before him like grain ready to be harvested. Cleaving a path through the growth, he found Thorax standing next to a moss-covered boulder.

"Where's the tunnel?" Edmund asked. "Where is it, girl?"

She pawed the boulder.

"I don't understand. Where—?"

Behind the massive rock was a narrow opening, barely big enough for a thin man to crawl into.

It's blocked!

Somebody laughed.

Edmund turned.

The troll stood among the collapsed buildings at the bottom of the slope.

"Nowhere to run, thief!" he said.

Thorax nudged Edmund's short sword.

"Fight? He'll embed that spear in me before I—"

Thorax barked and dug frantically at the boulder.

She means use the sword to pry it away!

"This metal better be as strong as my father used to say." Slipping the sword's smoke-colored blade between the boulder and the mountain, Edmund pulled.

The boulder rocked forward and then rolled into place.

The troll strode up the slope. "Do you know what I'm going to do to you and your damn dog?"

Edmund heaved on the hilt again. The opening of a tunnel appeared. He threw his considerable weight backward. The boulder teetered and then toppled, gaining speed as it crashed down the mountainside.

Leaping effortlessly over the boulder, the troll laughed.

"Nice try," he said. "I'm going to take your tiny head and—"

Edmund pointed at the hole. "Quick Thorax, get in!"

She scooted into the darkness.

Seeing the tunnel, the troll shouted, "No!" He sprinted toward them.

Dropping to his knees, Edmund dove forward. But he couldn't fit through the opening.

Your pack!

The ground shook under the charging troll's weight.

Edmund slipped off one shoulder strap.

Eighty feet away, the troll raised his spear.

Edmund slipped off the second strap.

The troll threw.

The spear shattered against the mountainside inches from Edmund's left shoulder, splinters of wood and chips of stone spewing everywhere.

The troll roared.

Pushing his backpack before him, Edmund scrambled into the dark passage, his head scraping against the unseen ceiling.

The troll reached into the tunnel. Its long arm swatted behind Edmund's feet. "You miserable thief." He hollered into the small opening. "You like holes?"

The troll disappeared from the entrance. However, he didn't go far.

"Enjoy your grave, imp!"

There was a sound of smashing stones as the tunnel suddenly went completely black.

Chapter Eight

In the blackness of the crawlway, Edmund lay flat, his hands covering his head, fragments of rock showering him from behind. Then, a heavy silence settled around him from the surrounding stone.

Oh god. What have I done?

For many minutes, he trembled in the darkness, afraid of moving and finding he was in his own coffin.

Something licked his face.

Extending his fingers, he felt Thorax's furry neck.

"Thanks, girl. You . . . you saved us."

Maybe.

She licked him again.

"I-I . . . I suppose," Edmund said, "I suppose we should see if the old stories are true."

If they aren't, you'll slowly suffocate in here.

He swept his hands in all directions. The passage seemed natural. Its walls were rough, its low ceiling irregular, and its floor covered with sand and jagged stones. From up ahead, he thought he heard the splash of water. But his heart pounded too hard for him to be certain.

"Pray Isa wasn't prone to exaggerate," Edmund said, his voice echoing around him.

They crawled blindly, Thorax leading the way. Gradually, the sound of flowing water became unmistakable. Then, the tunnel widened, and the ground before them disappeared. Somewhere in the blackness, a waterfall splashed.

"Well. At least we haven't run into a dead end. That's something."

Fumbling in the dark, Edmund unhooked his battered lantern.

"*Fyre av nå.*"

He turned up the flame.

They were at the top of a deep grotto. Drops of water plummeted around them, falling like thousands of shooting stars into a shimmering pool below. To their left, a waterfall sent sheets of white water pounding against polished stone. To their right, a small stream flowed down another narrow passage. Above, reflections of lantern light danced among the countless cream-colored stalactites.

It's beautiful!

Edmund's heart quickened, his fear replaced by hope and joy.

This certainly seems to be what Isa described.

Then there should be a way out through the tower.

"Remember the boy I told you about—Isa?"

Thorax shook her head as drops of water pelted her brow.

"He, he . . . he was the boy who brought Iliandor's diary to the Hansen's ranch outside of Rood. Anyway, this must've been how he escaped from the bandits. He climbed to this shelf and crept out of the tunnel we crawled through."

Edmund surveyed the grotto in wonder.

"It's beautiful, isn't it? It's like walking into the history books. You know what I'm saying?" He sighed. "We're probably the only humans to come here since Isa fled."

A droplet hit the top of the lantern. The flame hissed.

"I still can't believe it," Edmund said after a few moments. "I honestly feel like crying, in both a good and bad way, you know? I mean, here we are, which is wonderful. Absolutely wonderful. It's heaven! Yet, it's sad. I mean, I . . . I wasted so much of my life sitting in that horseshit of a town, dreaming and waiting, when I should've been out here exploring and doing something of consequence. Who knows what I could've done in my younger days? Who knows . . .?" His voice trailed off, but haunting echoes lingered.

The lantern sputtered again.

Edmund got to his feet.

"Speaking of doing something of consequence."

He hoisted his pack onto his shoulders.

Thorax appeared puzzled.

"The Star is probably somewhere above us. And all we have to do is get it!"

And my first adventure will be over. I wonder what I should do next. Perhaps the King has other tasks he'd like me to perform.

A drop of water struck Thorax between the eyes. She rubbed her face with her front paws.

Edmund flicked his chin at the waterfall. "See that? That's where we're headed. Behind it, actually."

He climbed from the ledge onto a slender stone lip circling the pool.

"You know," he said, "in every story I've ever read, important things are always hidden behind waterfalls. I don't know why. It's kind of like how every barkeeper is portly, bald, and absentminded. It's simply how things are, I suppose."

He picked Thorax up and set her on the ledge next to him.

"It's kind of like how big battles are never fought during cheerful spring days," Edmund said. "They're always fought during a storm or at night or something dramatic. The black clouds roll in. Everybody fights. And then the clouds part, sending a shaft of bright light upon the victor. And they always fight in grim places like the Battle of Bloody Hills or the Battle of Deadly Dike. I've never heard of a battle fought in a field of fragrant wildflowers. But I suppose people wouldn't write about 'the Battle of Daisy Meadow.'"

He inched along the edge of the pool. Thorax followed, staying close to his heels.

"And another thing. Ever notice how princesses and queens are always beautiful? I mean, what happens to the ugly ones? Or even the plain ones? Why don't they end up in stories? I suppose it's all in the telling. The eye of the behold—"

Startled, he stared at the cavern wall.

"Look at this." He lifted his lantern. Its ruddy light shone off the bluish-grey stone.

"It's written in Dunael." Edmund touched the deep gashes forming the foot-tall letters. "Fortunately for you, I know it fl, fl, fluently."

He waited for the echoes of his voice to recede.

"Loosely translated, it says: '*The salvation of humanity can be found in buildings of wise men, doubly so in optimism of the learned, and in knowledge that is written on a daily basis.*'"

"It's true enough, I suppose," he said. "Strange thing to write way down here, don't you think?"

Thorax shook the water from her muddy fur.

"Whoever wrote it must've been a novice. He incorrectly capitalized 'knowledge,' 'buildings,' and 'optimism,' and several articles are missing. For example, it should be '*the* optimism of the learned.' Then again, that doesn't sound very good. The whole thing is a bit off. Good writing should flow effortlessly from the t-t-tongue."

Edmund studied the writing, then snapped his fingers.

"Maybe Isa wrote it! He was merely a boy when he fled the tower."

More drops of water pelted his damp hair.

"No. That wouldn't make much sense. After all, why would he spend time carving this when he was trying to escape with the diary?"

Feeling as though he was missing something vital, he touched the letters again.

How could somebody cut so deeply into stone?

Maybe the stone is softer than it looks. Maybe being wet for centuries has made it brittle.

He rapped his knuckles against the cavern wall.

It seems as hard as any rock.

It doesn't matter.

No. But it's curious.

Think about it later. Remember the Star?

"At any rate," Edmund said, "it's of no concern to us, now is it, mighty Thorax?"

Thorax scurried around him, trying to find shelter from the dripping water.

Edmund motioned ahead of them.

"See that opening? We need to push through the waterfall and go into the crevasse on the other side. There should be a stairway spiraling up through the mountain and into a secret room where the knights held their last stand. We'll search for the Star there. After we find it, we'll go to Eryn Mas and complete our first mission! Of course, b-b-before that, I'm going to sleep the sleep of the dead. I'm exhausted to my marrow."

Thorax watched the sheets of water pound the ledge.

"Oh, don't worry. You'll be fine. There's plenty of room. But be careful. After all, I wouldn't want you to fall into the pool. Strange half-blind creatures with long tentacles always live in subterranean lakes like this. At least, they do in the stories I've read."

Thorax eyed the pool.

"Ready? One . . . two . . . three."

Shielding the lantern with his body, Edmund ran through the curtain of white water. Seconds later, Thorax followed.

"See." Edmund brushed off the top of his pack. "That wasn't so bad, was it?"

They were in a deep cleft, barely wide enough for Edmund to slip through sideways. Inside, carved into the rock, was an uneven step. Beyond the step was another and then another, each winding erratically up in a roughly hewn fissure no more than five feet high.

Crouching, Edmund climbed the stairs, his bright lantern leading the way.

Thorax didn't move.

"What is it?"

Thorax peered the way they came.

"The troll? I'm sure he's still out there. They don't give up easily. He's probably waiting to see if we can dig our way out."

She glanced up the stairs.

"Oh, I see what you're getting at. I don't, I don't think he'll be waiting for us in the tower. How could he know about this passage? He probably thinks we're trapped in the tunnel."

He climbed the next step.

Thorax's nose twitched.

"Come on, girl. I'm exhausted and need sleep. Let's find the Star and lie down. I'll even give you half of the salted pork we have left if you don't dawdle."

Hunched forward, Edmund ascended the cramped stairs. Hesitantly, Thorax followed.

Chapter Nine

They scaled the narrow stairs for over an hour, turning constantly upward and to the left in a haphazard spiral. More than once, Edmund banged his head on the low ceiling, his curses reverberating in the damp closeness around them. Then, abruptly, the steps ended at a brick wall.

Thorax groaned.

"Not to worry." Edmund rubbed his throbbing spine. He tried to straighten it, but couldn't without cracking his head against the ceiling again. "We've finally made it." He patted the wall with a tired hand. "This, this is the secret door to the room where they probably hid the Star and Iliandor's other belongings. All we have to do is . . ." Edmund pushed on the bricks, but nothing happened.

"All we have to do is . . ."

He pushed harder.

What if some piece of debris is blocking the door from the other side? Or the masonry has settled? You'll be trapped in here.

There's a stream exiting the grotto. It probably leads out. But don't give up. Not when we're so close!

Setting the lantern on the top step, Edmund threw himself at the brick wall. A crack appeared. Thorax pawed his leg.

"I know, I know." He drew his sword. "I was about to get it. Thank you very much."

He slid the sword tip into the crack and pulled on the hilt. Inch by inch, the wall yielded. Its bottom edge scraped against a wooden floor emerging at Edmund's feet. When he'd gotten the opening wide enough for him to slide through, he stopped.

"See." His gasping echoed in the stairwell. "Nothing to it. Easy, easy as falling out of bed. Like I told you. Now... onto the completion of our first quest!"

Fresh air blew into the stairwell.

Growling, Thorax retreated.

Edmund leaned against the wall, panting. "Oh, c-c-come on, girl. Don't be so afraid of everything. It's, it's the air from, from outside. I'm sure there's an open window or something in the tower. Relax. Okay? Trust me."

Sniffing the air again, Thorax fled farther down the stairs, the hair between her shoulder blades stiffening.

"What is it?"

Reaching through the opening, Edmund set his lantern and pack on the other side of the brick door. He poked his head into the room beyond.

"There's nothing here. It's an ordinary room. I can't see everything, but it looks like it used to be a parlor or something."

He peered around the open door.

"There are pieces of rotting furniture and a few skeletons lying about. There are also several dead birds. That's probably what you smell."

Thorax growled.

"I'll tell you what. We can use the furniture to make a fire. I'll fry the last of the pork and have a bit of hot coffee. Okay? Sound good? But first . . ."

Lifting his stomach and twisting, he thrust himself through the narrow opening with a loud grunt. He beamed at his feat.

Squeezing through a doorway wouldn't be such an accomplishment if you weren't so fat.

The way I'm losing weight, I'll soon be thinner than anybody in Rood! In fact, by the time I get to Eryn Mas, I may be as muscular as that storytell—

"Well, well," a soft voice behind Edmund said. "Look what we have here, Mr. Gurding."

Edmund's heart skipped several beats, his grin vanishing.

Stiff with fear, he forced his reluctant body to turn.

Behind him stood two figures. They were small, even compared to Edmund. Their hunched backs made them appear to be the height of boys in their early teens. Under their oversized hoods, Edmund detected a hint of sickly white faces.

Monks? Here?

Relaxing, Edmund smiled. The two figures returned the smile, revealing many pointed yellow teeth.

Edmund retreated a step, his damp skin turning cold. "Goblins!"

"Oh," the first goblin said, disappointed. "We don't particularly care for that name, do we, Mr. Gurding?"

Producing a long knife from the interior folds of his cloak, the other goblin shook his head. "No indeed, Mr. Kravel. It makes me angry simply hearing it."

The one called Mr. Kravel stepped toward Edmund. "You see, the term 'goblin' is a bastardization of the word 'gobel,' which means 'children of Gob,' the evil guardian of the nether regions—in case you weren't aware."

"We're not children," Gurding said in a low, menacing voice.

"Well put, Mr. Gurding." Taking another step toward Edmund, Kravel cautiously scanned the rest of the empty room. "Nor are we evil. You see, it isn't as if an entire race of beings can be—"

Gurding whispered, "Perhaps we should take care of other matters before you continue." He nodded to the secret door.

"Right you are, Mr. Gurding. Right you are." Drawing a knife from underneath his robes, Kravel stalked to the edge of the doorway. "If you would be so kind, please tell the rest of your party to enter the light. We'd dearly love to meet them."

Edmund finally managed to swallow. "I-I-I-I . . ."

Kravel pursed his lips. "Oh, that won't do. That won't do at all, I'm afraid. Please comply with my request so we can proceed to the next stage of this joyous event."

Edmund swallowed again. He opened his mouth, tried to speak, and swallowed a third time. Knife in hand, Gurding came closer.

"I-I-I-I-I'm," Edmund forced the words out of his lungs in great bursts. "Alone! I-I-I-I'm . . . alone. I'm alone. Alone. Alone."

Kravel tutted. "You seem determined to make things difficult for yourself. Mr. Gurding, could you please compel our new friend to comply with my previously stated instructions?"

"Certainly, Mr. Kravel." Fingering his knife, Gurding strolled toward Edmund.

"Alone!" Edmund croaked, backing away. "I'm alone!"

"You disappoint me," Kravel said. "Why, only a few moments ago, Mr. Gurding and I heard you speaking with somebody. But no matter. We'll extract them from their hiding spot momentarily."

Like a butcher entering a pigsty, Kravel calmly took off his cloak, revealing a squat body with brawny arms reaching practically to the floor. He folded the cloak into a neat square and set it on the ground. Drawing a scimitar from his belt, he contemplated which hand should hold it and which should hold his knife.

Gurding approached Edmund.

Edmund retreated but found the space available to him rapidly diminishing.

Run!

To where?

Do something!

"A-a-a-a," Edmund said, his voice hitting ever-increasing high-pitched notes.

"Oh, stop your squeaking," Gurding said. "I haven't even started hurting you yet."

Snatching Edmund by the hair, the goblin placed his knife against Edmund's throat.

"For the moment," he said, "I'd prefer you remain quiet."

Edmund raised his hands in surrender, his body quaking. A shivering squeal continued emitting from his lungs.

"That isn't being quiet." Gurding's knife poked Edmund's neck. A drop of blood trickled down his convulsing chest. Edmund closed his mouth tight, but the squeal persisted.

"I'm afraid this is as quiet as he'll get," Gurding said to Kravel, who'd decided to hold his scimitar in his left hand and his knife in his right. "Shall I end him?"

"No, no," Kravel said. "No need to rush things. It doesn't really matter anyway, now does it? They know we are here. Whomever he was talking to isn't going anywhere."

"As you wish. I'll handle him while you take care of the others. Or do you want my help?"

"That's just like you, Mr. Gurding. Always being kind. But time will tell. Let's first determine what we have, and then I'll let you know."

Kravel peeked around the edge of the partially open brick door. A fierce snarling emitted from the darkness.

"There's a stairway here," Kravel said, nonplussed. "A stairway going down. Has such a feature been noted in earlier reports?"

"Not to my knowledge," Gurding said, still holding Edmund by the hair. "If you look at the door, it appears to have been constructed so it blends in. See what I mean? No handle. No hinges either. Perhaps the others have missed it."

Kravel examined the door more closely. "I believe you are correct as usual, Mr. Gurding." The corners of his thin, white lips turned upward. "You know, I have a very good feeling about this. Perhaps our new friend here has guided us to what we've been searching for."

Gurding grinned at the trembling Edmund. "If that's the case, I'll have a much better opinion of you."

Edmund squeaked.

"Tell me, Mr. Kravel," Gurding asked. "What's making that growling noise?"

Kravel stared into the darkness. "It appears to be a dog of some variety or other. Not very useful looking, I'm afraid."

Thorax snarled some more, the narrow stairwell magnifying the sound of her wrath.

"How many meals can we make from it?" Mr. Gurding asked.

Kravel scratched his bald head. "No more than two, I should think. Ask our friend how many non-canine creatures are down here if you would be so kind, Mr. Gurding."

Gurding poked Edmund with his knife again. "You heard what he said. So, there's no need to repeat it, is there?"

Edmund licked his dry lips and then opened his mouth. "I—" He took another breath and exhaled in uneasy fits. "I . . . am . . . alone. I . . . was . . . was . . . was . . . sp-sp-speaking . . . to . . . Thor-Thor-Thorax . . . the dog."

"Thorax?" Kravel glanced into the stairwell and then at Edmund. "Are you making a joke?"

Edmund's head twitched side to side.

"Kind of a stupid name for a dog," Gurding said. "Is it ferocious looking? Like a black wolf or something?"

"No," Kravel said. "In fact, it's a runt. For a moment, I thought it was a groundhog or a creature of that ilk. However, why he'd be traveling with a groundhog is beyond me. Here, look for yourself."

Releasing Edmund, Gurding went to the doorway.

Edmund clutched at his neck, trying to stop the bleeding.

Your sword! Your sword! Draw your sword!

No, you fool. Run! Get the hell out of here while you have a chance!

Peering through the opening, Gurding tapped his chin. "Not much of a dog. Some sort of herding breed, I would think."

"Quite possibly. Quite possibly."

"Still," Gurding said, "I believe you're right. It won't make much of a meal for both of us, not after it is skinned, gutted, and deboned."

"No, indeed, Mr. Gurding," Kravel said. "I do believe I overestimated its size during my initial assessment of the creature."

The two goblins stared into the darkness. Thorax continued growling.

"I'll tell you what I am prepared to do, Mr. Gurding. I'll make you a bit of a wager. Whoever strikes the animal with the killing blow gets to eat the miserable thing."

Do something!

"The entire animal?" Gurding asked.

"Of course," Kravel said. "It wouldn't be much of a wager with us splitting the reward for the winner's effort, now would it?"

"That's very generous of you, given that I'm far more accurate with knives. Now, had we our bows handy, I would've given you the advantage."

"Perhaps, perhaps. But I believe your recent string of successes has made you a tad overconfident. However, time will tell. Are you ready?" Kravel positioned his knife in his fingers, ready to throw.

"P-p-put . . . those . . . d-d-d-down," Edmund said in as commanding a voice as he could muster.

Turning, the goblins found Edmund with his short sword drawn. It was shaking.

"Interesting twist of events," Gurding said to Kravel.

"Interesting, indeed," Kravel said. "But not completely unexpected."

"P-p-p-p-p . . ." Edmund strained to get the words out.

"Put?" Kravel suggested.

"I'm afraid he's going to be rather frustrating to interrogate," Gurding said. "I wonder if he hit his head at some point. Perhaps when he was a child."

"Now, now, Mr. Gurding. Let's be pleasant. Our friend here is about to make a decision that will undoubtedly alter the course of his life for a very long time. Or at least until it comes to its eventual conclusion. Let's not sully the moment for him."

"P-p-put, put . . . y-y-y . . ."

"Yes, yes. You want us to put our weapons down. We understand," Kravel said. "Unfortunately for you, I'm afraid that won't happen. I will, however, propose a deal. You can concede defeat and give us your weapon. In which case, we'll take you prisoner and turn you over to the Questioners. They are not pleasant people, as a rule, you understand. Rather obnoxious and overpaid, as a matter of fact. However, you will be alive and can dream about escaping."

"You might even die of old age," Gurding said. "Though that might not be too far off, judging from the looks of you."

"Or," Kravel went on, "you can choose either Mr. Gurding or myself in a fight to the death. If you select this option, I suggest you opt for Mr. Gurding. He's not as skilled as he imagines himself to be."

"That isn't exactly polite to say," Gurding said. "You wound me."

"My apologies. Allow me to rephrase. Of the two of us, my colleague, Mr. Gurding here, is less skilled than I am in lethal combat with a blade."

"I'm not too sure I like that either."

"Th . . . Th . . . Thorax!" Edmund called. The snarling in the stairwell subsided. "Do, do, do, do what I tell you. Okay, girl? Do, do what I s-s-say."

"It's a girl?" Gurding said to Kravel.

Kravel shrugged.

"I-I-I want, I want you, I want you to run. Run. Go. Go now. Run!"

"I'm terribly sorry," Kravel said. "We can't allow that to happen. Mr. Gurding, if you please."

"Right." Before Edmund could say anything, Gurding spun and threw his knife into the stairwell. Thorax cried out, a pain-ridden howl that tore into Edmund's heart.

Edmund screamed. "Run! Run! Go. Run. Get out of here!"

"Did you succeed, Mr. Gurding?" Kravel asked.

"Well enough, I suspect," Gurding said. "Solid thigh strike. She won't go far. We can track her after we finish here if you wish. Or we can let her die on her own in an hour or so."

"Splendid. We'll decide later. First things are, as they say, first."

"You bastards." Tears pooled in Edmund's eyes. "You, you . . . bastards."

"It's only a dog," Gurding said.

Edmund's hands shook even more, a combination of fear and rage propelling them in spastic circles. He took a half step toward Kravel. "B-b-b-bastards!"

"Yes," Kravel said. "I suppose we're all bastards in our own little ways, aren't we? At any rate, let's refocus on the question at hand. Have you made a decision? Am I to have the honor of dismembering you?"

"You bastards," Edmund repeated in a weakening voice.

"I don't think he has much fight in him." Gurding pulled a small coil of rope from his pocket. "Fat humans never do. Too soft. No discipline."

"I believe you are right," Kravel said. "I say he'll give up. Shall we wager?"

Gurding formed the rope into a noose. "No. I concur. He'll say bastards a few more times, start sobbing, and then beg for his life."

"Bastards," Edmund muttered, tears rolling down his cheeks.

"Shall we wager on how many times he says that?" Kravel asked Gurding. "I say one more time."

"No bet," Gurding said. "That was going to be my approximation."

They waited for Edmund to say something else, but he only cried.

"Our skills are a bit off today, Mr. Gurding." Kravel strolled forward. "Here, let us move things along a bit quicker, shall we? Be so kind as to hand over your weaponry. It's always better to die another day. Wouldn't you agree, Mr. Gurding?"

"Absolutely," Gurding said. "After all, he may escape someday. Or perhaps die in his sleep, smothered by the Pit Dwellers."

Fight! Kill them!

There are two of them.

Then run!

"You are a hopeless optimist, my dear Mr. Gurding." Kravel plucked the short sword out of Edmund's hands. "It's one of the many things I like about you."

"Please," Edmund said, his voice cracking.

"And you have a nice way with words," Gurding said. "I've always appreciated that about you."

Kravel paused. "Mr. Gurding. Look at what our new friend has given me."

Gurding examined the sword over his colleague's shoulder. "Very interesting."

"Very interesting, indeed. Why, I haven't seen anything like this before."

"It looks sharp. He might've done you some damage if he had the mind."

"Quite possibly. Sharp and light. Feel this." Kravel handed Gurding the short sword.

Gurding balanced it in his pallid hand. His bony fingers squeezed the sword's black hilt. "Impressive. It looks like it's never been used."

They examined the sobbing Edmund and then the weapon.

"Quite possibly," Kravel said.

"Dibs on the sword," Gurding said.

Kravel sputtered. "What? You can't call dibs."

"Why not? I just did."

"Yes, but you did so improperly, as you are undoubtedly aware."

"How so?"

"For starters, our prisoner gave it to me. Hence, it is technically mine, and no dibs can be called."

"He would've handed it over to a corpse if we had one with us."

"Yes, but that is hardly the point I am making." Kravel took a deep breath through his crooked nose, then exhaled. "All right, Mr. Gurding. I see your perspective. To settle the matter, I'll propose a deal. I wager that our chubby friend here doesn't live more than, say, twenty days in the mines. If he does, you get the sword and everything in his pack. That's a potentially very lucrative arrangement, as I'm sure you'd agree."

Mines?

"You're kidding me, aren't you?" Gurding said. "After I agree, you could simply kill him right now and get everything for yourself."

"Very well, Mr. Gurding. Very well. You are quite the suspicious one today, aren't you? I shall amend my terms. I say that, barring the merry fellow forcing my hand in any way, he will die within twenty days of today with no intervention from myself—"

Gurding interjected, "But—"

"Or anybody acting on my behalf."

Edmund whimpered. "P-p-please . . ."

Gurding thought about this for a moment. "Show me your hands," he said to Edmund.

"P-p-p-pl—"

Gurding seized Edmund's wrists and twisted his palms up. Edmund sank to the floor, sniveling.

"Look at these," Gurding said, disgusted. "Not a mark on them."

"No, indeed," Kravel said. "They are soft as a baby's liver."

"He won't last a week in the mines if you ask me."

"Very well then, Mr. Gurding. Shall we reverse our positions? I think you are not giving our stout friend here much credit. He's a crafty one. I can see it in his cold brown eyes."

"What? Behind the tears?"

"Exactly, my dear Mr. Gurding. Why, I would stipulate that this fellow here is a seasoned warrior, back from some big battle way to the south. He has undoubtedly killed many of our kin's finest heroes. His tears and endless stuttering are merely a ruse to lure us into a false sense of security. Why, I wouldn't get too close to the old fellow if I were you. He may rip out your throat with his own, admittedly tender, bare hands."

"P-p-p-please . . ." Edmund sniveled.

Gurding examined the weeping Edmund and then his companion's face. "You're putting me on. I can tell."

"It's difficult to fool you, my friend," Kravel said. "Do we have a deal? I say he will last at least seven days in the mines, provided we apply the aforementioned stipulations to you as well."

Scratching his chin, Gurding examined the smoky steel of the short sword's blade. "Deal. What about what he has on him?"

"Perhaps we can incorporate those belongings into another wager. The length of his intestines, perhaps?

"Which intestines? The large or small?"

"Your choice, Mr. Gurding . . . your choice."

Chapter Ten

Someone yanked the foul-smelling hood from Edmund's head. He blinked.

Lying face down, hands tied behind his back, he was in some sort of underground complex several days' march from Tol Helen. At least thirty goblins stood around him, including his captors, Kravel and Gurding. Others rushed into the room. A variety of knives, pliers, hammers, and other instruments of torture gleamed next to a blazing firepit. On a stool sat a copper bowl full of coins.

A large goblin with a whip stood over him.

"What's your name, filth?" he demanded.

Edmund blinked at him.

"Your name?" the questioner repeated louder. "What is your name, filth?"

Edmund blinked several more times.

A boot kicked him in the ribs. Edmund grunted, the air driven from his lungs. He wheezed. "It's E-E—"

Another boot pummeled Edmund's side, propelling him closer to the crackling fire pit. The heat scalded his back. Another couple of kicks, and he'd be in the coals with several glowing pokers and branding irons. Edmund gasped for breath. The cords binding his wrists sliced into his skin.

"What is your name, filth?" the questioner asked again.

Despite the sharp pain shooting throughout his ribcage, Edmund forced himself to inhale. "M-m-my name, my name is . . . Ed-Ed-Edmund—"

"That's once!" a goblin called gleefully.

The other goblins hushed him.

Edmund's head snapped to one side, snot and blood flying from his nose, the dirty imprint of a boot across his cheekbone.

"P-p-please," Edmund begged. "Please! I-I-I—"

"What is your name, filth?"

In between sobs, more blood slid from Edmund's mouth. A long trail of it already connected his swelling bottom lip to the stone floor. His panicked gaze scurried over the faces in the crowd, hoping to find help, any help at all. The questioner nodded to one of the guards standing over Edmund.

Edmund's head cracked back again, pain exploding throughout his face. Fluid, whether tears or blood, he could not tell, flowed from his left eye. It pulsated and bulged. Through his tattered shirt, the dancing red flames burned his skin.

"What is your name, filth?"

Remember the tale of Markus of Anberry? Remember what happened to him?

The questioner nodded at the guard again.

Edmund girded himself for another blow.

Hurry!

"M-m-m-my, my name . . ." Blood pooled in Edmund's mouth. He spit, hoping to buy time for his head to clear. Several goblins leaned forward eagerly. "My, my n-name is, is . . . f, f, filth, sir."

There was silence. Then the goblins howled. Most were cursing, throwing pieces of paper on the ground. Kravel, however, laughed.

"See what I mean?" he said. "That is exactly what I was telling you all. If I am not mistaken, there is more to this chubby fellow than meets the eye. He's an extraordinarily quick learner for his kind, I dare say."

Kravel emptied the bowl of coins into a pouch. "Thank you all for doubting me. It truly has been a wonderful, not to mention exceedingly profitable, episode."

"Can we measure his intestines now?" somebody from the growing crowd asked.

"Patience," the goblin with the whip said. "First, I have some questions for Filth here. Where are you from? And what were you doing in the tower of Gara' Zen?"

Grovel. Show weakness. Do anything to appease them. Use your stuttering to make them think you're stupid!

"M-m-master . . ." Edmund said. "I-I-I-I . . . I am, I am, I am f-f-from, from . . . a t-t-town, a, a, vil-vil-vil-vil-village really, a vil-vil-vil-vil . . . village a-a-a-about, about, about a . . ."

The goblins shifted uneasily. Several grumbled.

"Told you he'd be frustrating to interrogate," Gurding said to Kravel.

". . . a vill-age a, a, about... may, may, maybe. . ."

"What the hell is this?" the questioner asked Kravel.

"He's been speaking like that since our initial encounter," Kravel said. "It seems to be his way of conversing, I'm afraid."

"Probably dropped on his head as a child." Gurding touched his temple for emphasis.

"At any rate," Kravel said, "we've found him to be more than willing to answer questions. Though it takes Filth here a great deal of time to answer to any degree of satisfaction or clarity."

"An excruciatingly long period of time," Gurding said.

The questioner groaned. "I don't have all day."

"Let's measure his intestines!" somebody shouted.

There was a chorus of agreement.

"Perhaps I can assist in making this ordeal less painful for all of us who have to listen to the chatty fellow," Kravel said. "During the splendid time we've spent with Master Filth, transporting him to his lovely new home, we have extracted a good deal of information from him—though the quality of said information may not be as stellar as what you would have eventually gleaned from him yourself had you been with us." He bowed to the questioner. "Perhaps you would like us to restate what he has revealed?"

The questioner exhaled heavily. "If you can do it with fewer words than his miserable human, go ahead."

Several goblins laughed. Most exited the chamber. Some inquired about other betting opportunities.

"Very well." Kravel cleared his throat. "And perhaps my esteemed colleague, Mr. Gurding, could add his own insights should any occur to him during the course of my recounting—"

"Brevity, Kravel!" The questioner rubbed his forehead. "Brevity."

"Of course. To begin with, Filth and his canine—"

"Thorax," Gurding said. "Her name was Thorax. It was a female."

A knot formed in Edmund's stomach at the mention of his companion's name.

Poor Thorax.

The questioner groaned. "Please, just tell me what I need to know. Where's he from? Is he a threat?"

"He says he's from a small settlement approximately two weeks' journey west of Gara' Zen," Kravel said. "It's in the old realm of the fallen northern human kingdom, it would seem."

"Two weeks?" the questioner repeated in disbelief. "What was he doing in the tower? And how did he find the passage you mentioned in your report?"

"From what the articulate Master Filth has revealed, he was attempting to become a famous adventurer. Evidently, he was hoping to find something of value so that he could buy the respect of his people."

"An adventurer? Him?" The questioner shook his head in disgust. "Never mind. Continue."

"So, he and his dog—whose name was Thorax, as Mr. Gurding has astutely indicated—

traveled eastward aimlessly, without any degree of thought or planning, hoping to find some self-respect."

"What does he do?" the questioner asked. "In his village, what's his occupation? Is he any use to us?"

"From the sounds of it," Kravel said, "he was a librarian of sorts. Read too many books and became enamored with faerie tales, it seems."

"A librarian?" The questioner shook his head. "Never mind. What about the tower? What was his interest there?"

"The day before we took him under our nurturing wing, a thunderstorm struck the region. He took refuge in a cave where a hill trog lived. In the trog's lair, it seems Filth came across this." Kravel gestured to the short sword in Gurding's hands. "The unnamed trog chased him to the tower, where he—"

"All right! All right! Tell me this. Is he a danger to us?" They all looked at Edmund as he lay sobbing at their feet. "What I mean is, does he have any knowledge of us that could put us in peril?"

"None that we could ascertain," Kravel said. "He's merely a foolish human who is entirely out of his element, ignorant of what is happening around him. As are most of his kind."

"Fine. Then I'll order the executioners to put the pig out of his misery. At least the wolves will have a good meal tonight."

Lifting his battered head, Edmund cried out. "P-p-please!"

Somebody kicked him in the ribs.

This is what you get for adventuring. You should've stayed home. You were happy enough there. You just didn't realize it!

"Actually," Kravel said, "Mr. Gurding and I have a bit of a wager on the eventual termination of Master Filth's existence. We'd be most obliged if you would sentence him to work in the mines. I'm quite certain they could use his skillful assistance."

"The mines?" The questioner snorted. "You're joking. Look at him! He wouldn't last two days in the mines."

Massaging his pouch of coins, Kravel grinned. "Care to make a wager on that?"

Chapter Eleven

A guard thrust the leather bag over Edmund's head again as somebody lifted him off the ground. For many muddled moments, they threw him about, throwing him from one set of hands to another. Several times, they dropped him onto the stone floor. Then, they carried him through the tunnels. Jeering goblin followed him, hitting him in the face, side, and stomach. When somebody struck him in the groin, a great cheer erupted as Edmund's bladder emptied all over himself.

Gradually, the sounds around him changed. There were still the harsh voices of goblins here and there. But these became fewer in number and less often directed at him. The beatings subsided, and he was left unmolested as they carried him to heaven only knew where.

In the distance, Edmund's bleeding ears detected something new, something even more unsettling than goblins. He heard the desperate wails of other humans, dozens of them. Their moans were all around him. Some laughed cruelly as he passed.

Eventually, his handlers stood Edmund on his feet. Cold steel slid along his wrist. There was a hard tug, followed by the cords binding his arms giving way. Edmund started to mumble, "thank you." But somebody pushed him, and he plummeted.

He landed face-first, the impact only slightly absorbed by his outstretched hands. Not daring to move, he lay motionless on a dirt floor, the foul-smelling bag still over his head, his eyes forced shut. The thought that he was in a dream, a very bad dream, once again entered his mind. But he knew the torment of reality when it kicked him. With what little strength he had left, he started muttering the words of healing he'd been using every day since being captured.

"*Smerte av—*"

Something behind him moved.

His eyes popped open. But he saw only the darkness inside the leather bag.

The shuffling crept closer.

"Is it dead?" a deep voice said, with no hint of compassion. "Are we supposed to eat it?"

Edmund sat up with a jerk. Tearing off the bag, he whirled around, prepared once again to beg for his life.

Two eyes stared at him through the darkness. They were wide, intense, and only a few feet from his own. They drew even closer.

"How're you doing?" the owner of the eyes asked in a perfectly normal, almost happy tone. "Doing okay?"

Edmund pushed himself along the dirt floor and backed into a rough stone wall. "Wh-wh-what? What, what did you say?"

"I said, 'How're you doing? Doing okay?'" a man with a black face said. Indeed, except for his eyes and his few remaining teeth, everything about him was as black as night. He smiled at Edmund. "So—how about it? Doing okay?"

Edmund's vision adjusted to the dimness.

He was in a deep pit, perhaps forty feet in diameter. Across from him sat three humans. They were covered in the blackest dirt Edmund had ever seen. Then the stench of human waste, sweat, and death hit him.

The man directly in front of him inched closer. He surveyed Edmund. "You don't look too bad. Not bad at all. Why, I've seen a great deal worse. You should consider yourself lucky."

"L-luck, lucky?" Edmund repeated in disbelief. He couldn't see out of his left eye. Two egg-sized bumps pulsated on his forehead. Sharp pains radiated throughout his ribcage whenever he moved.

"You're alive, aren't you?" the dirt-covered man asked. "Well, there you go!"

Edmund glanced around again.

Maybe one of those blows did something to my head.

"I'm Pond Scum, by the by." The man held out a black hand.

Out of habit, Edmund shook it. Then he examined his own hand. It was now covered in a muddy mixture of blood and black dust.

"Oh, don't mind that," Pond Scum said. "We were digging coal today. It coats you, inside and out. You'll see what I mean later. But don't worry. We get baths next week. If we achieve our quota, that is. Which I'm sure we'll do now that we have your help. Say, what's your name?"

Edmund felt his throbbing head. He peered across the pit at the other men. They seemed half-dead, staring with unseeing eyes at the walls, mouths hanging open as if they were too tired to moan. Even the giant figure across from him seemed only barely alive. All he did was blink. Pond Scum waited patiently.

"N-n-name?" Edmund said.

"Yeah. The one they gave you when you came in. You can't use your real name, the one your family and friends used to call you. If you do, the guards will beat the crap out of you. So be careful."

Edmund looked around again but found nothing in the pit had changed since the last time he inspected its contents. "F-F-Filth. They named me . . . they named me Filth."

Pond Scum chortled. "You must've had Questioner Bar'zal. Not very creative, that one. Everybody is 'filth this' and 'filth that.' Tell me, did he call you pathetic?"

Scanning the opening above him, Edmund wondered whether he could climb out. He nodded at Pond Scum.

"How about vile?" Pond Scum asked. "Did you get the 'vile thing' line? Vile this, vile that?"

Feeling his stomach, Edmund wondered when he'd eaten last. He nodded again at the oddly happy man.

"Exactly what I mean," the man said. "Now, I had Questioner Norvel. He's much more original. He puts some thought into it. There've been at least a dozen or so 'Filths' that have come and gone since I've been here, and not so much as one other 'Pond Scum.' Gives me a sense of identity. And identity is something you'll value after a while."

Edmund's attention drifted past Pond Scum. He peered at the other, less talkative, people in the pit.

"Oh. Right. Sorry." Pond Scum crawled to Edmund's side. His odor was worse than Norb's. "Let me introduce you to the rest of the gang."

"Gang?"

"The gentleman to our immediate right is Vomit." A nearly naked, bony man with a beard to his waist lifted his tired eyes and then stared at the floor. "He's number two in this pit. I'm number three. But I'll explain our rankings later."

He pointed to the massive man next to Vomit.

"The big fellow there, he's Turd, or Tiny Turd as the guards sometimes call him. Please don't upset him. He's number four, the newest here—that is, before you came. You're number five."

Turd didn't acknowledge Edmund's presence. He merely rubbed the palms of his burly hands and scowled.

"Continuing along to the far left," Pond Scum said, "is Crazy Bastard. His name used to be Vermin, but they changed it a while ago. They do that on occasion. I pretend I don't like Pond Scum, and they keep calling me that. I don't want a change."

Edmund's thoughts wafted to the skeletal figure sitting farthest from him. He appeared older than everybody else, though Edmund couldn't begin to guess his actual age. Unlike Pond Scum, Vomit, and Tiny Turd, Crazy Bastard didn't have a beard. He only had patches of short black hair on his head. Soon, Edmund understood why. As he watched, Crazy Bastard ripped out a portion of his remaining hair and shoved it in his mouth. He cackled, then slapped himself across his face.

That'll be you soon.

"By all rights," Pond Scum said, "Crazy Bastard should be our Pit Leader, being here longer than anybody, that is. But, given his mental state, Vomit takes care of us."

At this, Crazy Bastard sprang to his feet, screamed, and beat his bare chest like a gorilla. The old man's ribcage protruded through his taunt, coal-covered skin. Several ribs had been broken and healed at off-kilter angles. Edmund rubbed his own abundant belly. It rumbled with hunger.

"There you go," Pond Scum said. "Welcome to the family. Next," he went on as if mentally ticking off an item from a list. "There're a few things you need to know straight away. Things you need to remember. All right? First, never talk to a guard or any non-Pit Dweller unless spoken to first. Only Vomit, who is acting in Crazy Bastard's stead, can ever approach a guard. Got that? That's really important. If you approach a guard, or say something when not spoken to, or even so much as look at them in the eye—they'll beat the crap out of you or worse. And believe me, there's a lot worse than a beating."

Worse?

"Second," Pond Scum said, "that bag they put over your head. As of now, that's your most prized possession. You'll put your food in it when you get some. You'll also defecate in it, should you need to go while in the pit."

Edmund looked at Pond Scum, wondering if he was serious. Evidently, he was.

"This is also very important," Pond Scum said. "You don't defecate in our home." He motioned about the pit. "You go in the bag and dump it once we get into the mines. You understand? If you go in the pit, Vomit will levy a punishment against you. But let's not talk about that right now. I want your first day to be pleasant and all."

Pleasant?

"Let's see," Pond Scum said. "What's next?" He thought. "Oh! Never touch another man's bag. It isn't polite, and if you do, we'll beat the crap out of you. Just a friendly warning. Again, I want your first day to be a good one."

Good one?

Edmund's gaze drifted around him.

"This here is your spot." Pond Scum created an arc with his arms, showing Edmund the five-foot-wide area he meant. "Generally, we tend to keep out of each other's space. But I'm here because you're new and all."

Edmund's awareness floated to his assigned section of the pit.

Pond Scum tapped his bearded chin. "I'm sure I'm forgetting a good deal. But I don't want to overwhelm you."

Overwhelm?

"The main thing is to keep your head down, don't provoke the guards, and do whatever you're told without question," Pond Scum said. "And stay positive. That's my motto. That and . . . 'Don't get captured and thrown in a damn pit!'"

Pond Scum grinned, waiting for Edmund to laugh. But Edmund was incapable of such an emotion. He was beyond numb. Even the pain wracking his body somehow seemed distant and something other than his own. He felt as if he were sinking into cold darkness.

"You might want to get some rest," Pond Scum said. "Our shift begins in about four hours. We'll talk more then."

Heavy footfall and the clink of armor approached their pit. Pond Scum's smile vanished. He put an urgent black finger to his black lips and scampered to his spot along the wall.

Overhead, a bright light appeared. A helmeted goblin with a torch looked down at them.

"In honor of our new guest," he said, "Mr. Kravel and Mr. Gurding would like to give you all a present."

He dropped a pinkish mass. It landed in the dirt with a lifeless thud. In the dimness, Edmund couldn't make out what it was. Then, the goblin dropped the torch next to it.

In the middle of the pit was the skinned and gutted corpse of a headless dog.

Edmund fainted.

Chapter Twelve

Edmund smelled something he couldn't quite place. It was like a chicken barbecued in an outhouse with lantern oil. His stomach rumbled. Then the rest of his body reminded him how much pain he was in. He tried to open his eyes but found the left one was swollen shut.

"Hey!" a vaguely familiar voice called out happily. "There he is!"

Pond Scum?

Three people huddled in the center of the pit, roasting something over a crackling torch. Another person danced in the corner, gnawing on a bone.

Pit?

One of the three men limped to his area, his right foot dragging across the dirt as he approached.

The human called Vomit came within five feet of Edmund.

"May I enter?" he asked.

Holding his throbbing head, Edmund peered at him, unable to respond.

"Forgive me." Vomit entered Edmund's space. "Part of my duties as Pit Leader is to dole out food. Usually, you wouldn't get anything, given you didn't work today. But, seeing you're new and have some connection to the additional meal, a couple of us thought you might need this."

He held out a fistful of small ribs. Partly cooked meat clung to the bones.

Edmund recoiled.

"Go ahead," Vomit said. "It's dog. It's very good. It tastes like rat."

"Best we've had in months," Pond Scum called to Edmund. He bit into the canine's leg. "It's incredible."

"Did you succeed, Mr. Gurding?" Kravel had said.

"Well enough, I suspect," Gurding replied. *"Solid thigh strike. She won't go far. We can track her after we finish here if you wish. Or we can let her die on her own in an hour or so."*

Edmund began hyperventilating. Did they find Thorax? He couldn't remember. He recalled being dragged down the hidden stairs and waiting as the goblins explored the secret way Edmund discovered. There was a trail of blood. Did they ever reach its end? Kravel and Gurding seemed more interested in finding something else. What was it? What were they looking for?

An image of a cavern wall below Tol Helen coalesced in Edmund's mind. The wall had writing carved into its damp stone. What did it say? Kravel and Gurding wanted to know. They held Edmund's head in the cold underground lake until they were satisfied he'd told them the truth.

"Here," Vomit repeated.

Edmund didn't move.

"I understand. I'll leave it." He set the ribs on the bag Edmund was supposed to defecate in. "Perhaps saving them for later is the smartest thing."

Vomit tottered to the middle of the pit where Pond Scum and Turd roasted pieces of Thorax over the crackling flames. Pond Scum licked his black fingers, savoring every morsel. Turd stared intently at the meat dangling over the torch, contentment creeping over his face.

When they'd finished, they each placed the bones into their bags. Pond Scum and Vomit sat against the wall in their areas, put their hands on their sunken stomachs, and sighed.

Turd stood up. In the dimness of the dying torch, he looked like a monster rising out of a grave. Walking across the pit, he entered Edmund's area without permission.

"I want your boots," he said.

Scrambling to their feet, Vomit and Pond Scum got in front of Turd. They barely came up to his chest.

"Now, Turd," Vomit began.

Throwing a forearm, Turd sent Vomit flying across the pit. Vomit bounced against the wall and crumbled to the ground. Pond Scum retreated, his hands raised.

Turd seized Edmund's calf. "I want your boots."

The huge man jerked Edmund's leg.

Edmund flipped over and found himself dangling upside down.

"Let go," he begged, kicking wildly. "L-l-let . . . let go of me. Pl-pl-please!"

"Turd," Vomit said from the safety of the far wall. "This is against the rules. He came in with those. They belong to him."

"I don't care." Turd knocked away Edmund's feeble kicks. "I need them."

Edmund cried out in pain as Turd twisted his foot. The boot came off, and Edmund crashed to the ground.

"And I want his shirt," Turd said. "I'm tired of my hands hurting."

Pond Scum reached for Turd's sizable arm, then hesitated. "If you hurt him, he won't be able to help in the mines. Then we won't make our quota. And you know what that means."

"Look at him!" Turd said. "Do you actually think he's going help? He'll eat our food. He'll drink our water. That's what he'll do. We might as well kill him now, the fat pig." He grabbed Edmund's bloody wool shirt. It started to tear.

"Get off me," Edmund said with increasing anger.

He could barely see. Pain flashed between his ribs whenever he breathed.

"Get off!" Edmund hit Turd's forearm as hard as he could. It felt like he'd punched stone.

"If he doesn't perform," Vomit told Turd, "he doesn't eat, just like the rest of us. He'll only get his fair share. I'll see to that."

The front half of Edmund's shirt tore away. Edmund sprang to his feet. Vomit and Pond Scum stepped in between them again.

"You can have it when he dies," Vomit said. "You know the rules. I'll give you first pick of his things."

Turd shredded the fabric into strips and wrapped them around his callused right hand. He flexed his fingers with satisfaction.

"I'm tired of being hurt," he said. "I need his clothes and his boots."

"Think of it this way," Pond Scum said. "He'll be dead in a week or so. Ten days tops. All you have to do is wait!"

"No." Turd stepped toward Edmund. "I do most of the work here. I deserve them." He reached over Vomit and Pond Scum.

To everybody's surprise, Edmund didn't back away.

"Leave me alone." He slapped Turd's bandaged hand aside.

Furious, Turd tossed Pond Scum and Vomit out of his way and came straight for Edmund. Stepping forward, Edmund knocked Turd's hands away a second time. They were toe-to-toe, Edmund looking up as if examining the top of a tree.

"Get away from me," he said, the pain coursing throughout his body was overcome by fury. "I'm warning you. Get the hell away from me!"

Half snarling, half laughing, Turd lunged at Edmund. His bandaged hand reached for Edmund's throat. Edmund grabbed the big man's thick wrist.

There was a sudden burst of blue light.

Turd wrenched the makeshift bandages from his hand and threw them onto the floor. They were on fire. Everybody stared at the flames.

"Magic," Crazy Bastard muttered from the other side of the pit. "Magic!" he yelled.

Now you've done it! Now they know. They'll kill you for sure!

But how . . .? How did I . . .?

Pond Scum and Vomit hushed Crazy Bastard. But Crazy Bastard screamed, "Magic! Magic! Magic!"

A guard bellowed for silence.

Tackling Crazy Bastard, Pond Scum pressed his hands over the old man's mouth while Vomit whispered into his ear. Crazy Bastard's writhing and muffled screams subsided. Turd stood staring at the burning fabric. Then they all turned toward Edmund, fear and hope in their eyes.

"You're a . . . a witch?" Pond Scum said under his breath. "A real . . . live . . . witch?"

They're going to kill me.

No! You have them where you need them. Don't blow this. Don't show fear. Convince them you know what just happened.

Edmund flicked his chin at the smoking remains of what used to be the front of his shirt. Stepping toward Turd, he jabbed a finger into the mountain's stomach. "Don't ever touch me again. Or else!"

His body weakening, Edmund pulled on his boot. Going to his area, he lay down and faced the wall so they couldn't see him cry. "Everybody leave me the hell alone!"

Chapter Thirteen

Edmund woke from a dreamless void. Vomit and Pond Scum hissed at him from their areas of the pit.

"What is it?" Edmund demanded, trying in vain to get comfortable on the dirt floor. "What do you want?"

Unnerved, Vomit and Pond Scum exchanged glances.

"They'll be here soon," Pond Scum said. "The guards, I mean. They'll drop a ladder down. We'll climb up as fast as we can. And then they'll take us to wherever they want us to work for the day."

Edmund yawned as he pushed himself into a sitting position. He felt much better than he had the night before. His left eye was still swollen shut, two walnut-sized knots protruded from his forehead, and his bottom lip was several times its normal size. But most of the sharp stabbing pains were now more tolerable throbbing aches.

Thank goodness for mother's healing spell.

Don't you wish you'd learned more as a child? Shame you wasted so much of your life.

He spit, trying to get the dirt out of his mouth. But it wouldn't go away.

The sound of clanking metal approached. Pond Scum, Vomit, Crazy Bastard, and even Turd rushed to the center of the pit, forming a straight line. Pond Scum and Vomit watched Edmund. They exhaled in relief when he got up and stood behind Crazy Bastard.

"Your bag." Pond Scum pointed to Edmund's leather bag. Vomit had placed the partially cooked ribs on it the evening before. But both they and the bag had been trampled during the altercation with Turd.

Edmund grabbed his bag and flicked it, sending broken dog ribs across the pit. Crazy Bastard dove for them. "Fair game! Fair game!"

Two heavily armed goblins in chain mail glowered down at them. One lowered a narrow wooden ladder.

"Get in line," a guard hollered at Crazy Bastard. "Or there'll be hell to pay!"

Shoving the dirt-covered ribs into his mouth like a carnivorous chipmunk, Crazy Bastard scampered to the rear of the line.

Vomit, Turd, and Pond Scum shimmied up the ladder. Slowly, Edmund followed. Imitating everybody else's example, he reached the top of the pit and stood with his head bowed, his functioning eye riveted on the ground.

"Nice to see you still alive, Filth," one of the guards said. "Think you can manage to last another three days?"

The other guard poked Edmund's stomach with an iron club. "Look at this. Why, I'm surprised they didn't eat you. You would've fed your pit mates for a month."

Don't react. Don't antagonize them. Just stare at the ground!

"Don't give them any ideas," the first guard said. "I have a day's pay on this one. They can eat him at the end of the week."

Grabbing Edmund's midsection, the second guard jiggled the roll of fat hanging over the straining waistband of his britches. "By then, most of this will be gone." The goblin shook his head. "Pathetic. Absolutely pathetic."

Don't upset them. Stare at the ground. Don't make eye contact.

"All right. Enough of this fun," the first guard said. "Let's get them moving. There's a lot to be done today, and the work guards are waiting."

Edmund stole a glimpse around.

They were in a huge cavern, at least a hundred yards wide and even longer in the other direction. Edmund counted thirteen other pits by which haggard men stood in lines, staring lifelessly at their feet. Two goblins guarded each group of slaves. Each guard wore chain mail. Several had shields and various styles of helms. They also had swords, clubs, and whips. Along the cavern walls, another thirty goblins paced, all armed with bows.

There are too many of them. I'll never get out of here. Never.

Don't think about it. Don't think. Do what they tell you, and don't think.

The lead goblin marched them out of the cavern and into an adjacent passage. Crackling torches were mounted to the otherwise unadorned walls. Oily smoke lingered in black clouds. Edmund returned his attention to the ground.

For the better part of an hour, they marched through passageways populated sporadically by goblins going about their own business. For a time, these passages were like underground roads—flat floors, smooth walls, and room enough for several people to walk abreast. Then they entered meandering tunnels that appeared cruder and more cave-like.

The steady plunking of cold water dripping from the ceiling echoed around them. The guards' torches hissed and wavered.

Often, the tunnels became so narrow that they had to walk sideways. More than once, Turd got on his knees and crawled through low points.

They're marching us in circles. That's what they're doing. We've passed this spot twice before. I wonder why.

Shut up. Don't think about it. Don't think about any of this madness.

The goblins brought them to an underground quarry where five empty ore carts sat on tracks leading into darkness. In the middle of the chamber, rusty picks and bent shovels lay in a pile. On scaffolding made of thick wooden beams, a guard paced, a bow in his hand, arrow at the ready. Another guard stood by the main entrance, stroking a black whip. He grinned at Edmund.

"And good mornin' to ya, Filth. Glad you joined our little party?" He cracked the whip inches away from Edmund's right ear.

Flinching, Edmund followed Pond Scum and Turd to the tools. From the corner of his functioning eye, he watched as Vomit approached the guard by the exit.

"Don't stare," Pond Scum whispered to him. "When the time comes, grab a pick and follow me."

Edmund peered at the ground.

Vomit shuffled to the waiting slaves.

"They want us to excavate two tunnels, at least six feet high, four feet wide, heading straight that way and that way." He showed them the directions the guard had indicated.

Without waiting for additional explanation, the slaves silently split up—Turd, Vomit, and Crazy Bastard heading to one side of the cavern, Pond Scum heading to the other. Edmund followed Pond Scum.

Far off, the faint ringing of metal on stone echoed.

Standing before the designated wall, Edmund examined his pick. It was heavy. But its use as a weapon, or even as a mining tool, was questionable. Its tip was dull and dented. Further, its metal head wobbled on the splintered wooden handle.

Better get this over with.

Hefting the pick on his shoulder, Edmund stepped toward the rockface and swung hard.

The point of the pick struck the grey stone with a sharp clang and kicked back, wrenching itself from Edmund's grasp and landing on his big toe. He shouted and hopped around on one foot.

The guards laughed, joined seconds later by the rest of the slaves. Crazy Bastard hit the wall with an imaginary pick and then danced around in a circle, screaming obscenities.

Even Pond Scum chuckled.

"No, no." He made sure the guards weren't coming in their direction. "Take the pick with your hands wide apart, like this. See? Swing it up, like so. And then let the pick's weight hit the wall. Try not to use your muscles. We'll be here a long time, so conserve your energy. Let the pick's momentum do the work. Watch me."

Pond Scum's pick struck the wall. Flakes of stone fell to the ground.

"See? You try."

Edmund repositioned his hands along the handle. He raised the pick's wobbly head and let it fall on the rock. It bounced off with no discernible damage.

"Good." Pond Scum patted him on the shoulder. "You're getting the hang of it."

Edmund did it again.

"How, how long?" Sweat trickled down Edmund's temple. "How long do we have to do this?"

Pond Scum hoisted his pick and let it fall onto the stone. More debris slid to the ground. He smiled at Edmund, a calculating smile that hid some unpleasantness.

"Don't think about it," he said. "The time will go faster."

Edmund struck the rockface again. "H-h-how, how long?"

Pond Scum inclined his head at the five empty ore carts waiting in the middle of the cavern. "See those?"

Edmund nodded.

Pond Scum swung again. "We need to fill them—ten times."

Edmund examined the chips of stone gathering at his feet and then the carts. "About how, how long . . . how long does that take?"

Pond Scum hit the wall again.

"You'd better keep working," he said. "You don't want the guards coming over here. Trust me."

Edmund brought his pick above his head and let it fall on the stone. A little more dust fell. "How long?"

"See those?" Pond Scum thrust his chin toward the torches burning by the quarry's entrance. "When those are out . . ." He swung. "Then we should be done. If we get done early, we get to bring the torches to the pit. But there's a catch, you see. There's always a catch."

He swung again.

"If we get done too early, they make us work more next time. You know what I'm saying? Do you get it? It's all about getting the most out of us as possible."

Edmund struck the wall. A piece of stone the size of his thumb struck his swollen eye. He rubbed it, smearing dirt into the wound. His eye burned and watered. He swore.

"How long?" he asked. "In . . . in hours, I mean."

"About twelve, maybe thirteen."

Twelve, maybe thirteen . . . hours?

I'll never survive that long.

"Breaks?" More sweat matted his grimy hair. His breaths came in short bursts.

Pond Scum shook his head. He swung his pick. His blow opened a small hole in the wall. "To piss and crap. That's it. And get something to drink. But . . ." He swung again. "If you do that more than two or three times, Vomit will levy a fine. He'll withhold some of your food." He swung again.

Edmund heaved his pick.

This is what you get for being such a fool. You should've stayed in Rood. You should've left well enough alone.

For many moments, he and Pond Scum alternated ringing blows.

"So," Pond Scum said when the debris was ankle-deep. "How did they get you?"

Edmund balanced the mining pick on his shoulder and examined his hands. Around his palms, flaps of soft skin hung loose, revealing tender pink tissue beneath. "I'd, I'd rather not talk about it." He winced as he tried to wipe the grit from his palms.

"I understand." Pond Scum hit the wall. "But it helps, you know. Talking, I mean. It helps keep away the pain. And it helps pass the time." His pick created another fist-sized hole in the wall. "Vomit, Turd, Bastard, and me have been together for a while. We know everything about each other. Hearing some new stories would be like a breath of fresh air in this place."

Fresh air! What I wouldn't do to breathe fresh air.

Another chunk of rock fell to the growing pile.

Pond Scum nudged Edmund with his elbow. "Not to be an ass or anything, but you need to start swinging that pick. Or there'll be hell to pay. Either from the guards or from us. Nothing personal, you understand. You can't stand around like that."

Turd glared at them from across the cavern. He and Vomit had already amassed a pile of stone up to their knees. Crazy Bastard brought shovelfuls of it to the ore carts. Edmund tore off one of his sleeves and wrapped the wool around his hands as Turd had done in the pit. He raised his pick and let it fall on the wall. The constant clanging was giving him a headache.

Pond Scum's pick rang against the stone. "If you could say something interesting, I'd greatly appreciate it."

Edmund thought of his conversation with Norb when they debated the merits of the stories scholars and stable hands could tell.

That seems like a lifetime ago.

Edmund's pick hit the wall.

"Suit yourself," Pond Scum said, disappointed. "But you'll have to deal with me talking to hear my own voice. Otherwise, you can go work with the others."

"N-no." Edmund's pick rose and fell. "Go ahead. I'd, I'd prefer to kind of, to kind of listen, if you don't mind."

"I understand. Still getting adjusted," Pond Scum said. "You're doing surprisingly well. The last newcomer we had curled in a ball the morning afterward. Turd had to compel him to get up before the guards came down the ladder to get him. Fortunately, Turd is an effective motivator—at least to most people." He looked sidelong at Edmund. "You sure made him think twice last night."

Edmund struck the stone, the sharp impact jolting his bones. He brushed the sweat from his brow. He noticed his companion wasn't even breathing hard.

"That fellow," Pond Scum said, "the one before you. He only lasted two days. But I've seen others not make even that."

"What happened?" Edmund let his pick come down. "To the one before me, I mean."

Pond Scum swung again. "Sure you want to hear about it? Like I said last night, I want you to have an easy go of it at first."

This is an easy go?

A thin sheet of stone slid down the now concave wall.

"I'll hear it eventually," Edmund said. "G-g-go . . . go on. Say what you have to say."

"All right," Pond Scum said. "Anyway, the last one was named Excrement. He was a soldier from the south, from the war and everything. He was brought in in pretty bad shape. They beat him something fierce before he stopped saying his real name." Pond swung his pick. "There are some people who take a long time to die here, some people who die very quickly, and some people who are dead but don't realize it. Excrement, well, he wanted out. So, he found a way."

Edmund coughed on the dust. "Go on. You're right. Talking is helping. Wh-what . . . what happened?"

"On his first day—" Pond Scum kicked away debris that had fallen onto his bare feet. "—he went at a guard with your pick."

Edmund examined the red splotches staining the wooden hand. "But you, but you said he was killed on his second day."

"I also said there are things worse than being beaten."

Edmund wheezed. He wondered if it was too early to get a drink. Looking at the cask of water, he found one of the guards urinating in it. His heart sank even more.

"G-go . . . go ahead. Tell me what happened. I need to know the worst."

"Oh, this isn't the worst. Not by a long shot. But I'll tell you anyhow." Pond Scum swung. "He approached a guard. That was his first mistake. Like I told you last night, only Vomit can approach them. Always keep that in mind. Don't go near them. Don't look at them. Don't speak to them unless they tell you to."

Edmund grunted again. "All right."

"Also, he had a pick in his hands. That was his second mistake." Pond swung. "You don't get three mistakes here."

Edmund let his pick fall. A segment of stone the size of a man's head broke free and toppled to the ground.

"If you want my advice." Pond Scum struck the wall. "Take pleasure in small things. That'll help get you through the day. But don't let the guards see you happy—ever. Save your happiness for when we're alone in our pit."

Happiness? How can anybody be happy here?

"It's like developing a separate identity," Pond said. "Show one to the guards so they leave you alone. Cherish the other when you are in the darkness. Do you know what I mean?"

"I . . . I, I think so," Edmund lied.

"Good. Do as I do, and you'll be fine."

Perspiration dripped from Edmund's brow as he swung.

"And another thing," Pond Scum said. "Don't look around so much. Frankly, I'm surprised at how gently they've been treating you. They must have some sort of wager going or something."

Gently? I can barely open my eye.

His arms trembling, Edmund raised his pick. It seemed even heavier than when he first lifted it. He swung, producing yet another dull clang.

"Finish," Edmund said after a while, "finish your, finish your story. What happened to Excrement? What was worse than being beaten to death?"

Pond Scum pounded the wall. More fragments of stone slid down.

"The guard on the platform shot him in the leg."

More stones toppled from the wall.

"They hung him by his wrists and let him dangle above us while we worked. Twelve hours of him begging to be put to death. It wasn't pleasant for any of us—most of all him, I'd guess. The next day, he was dead. Rats had gnawed off his nose, ears, and eyes."

Edmund sensed there was more to the story. He struck the wall again. "And?"

"You sure you want to hear this?"

Sucking in air, Edmund nodded. "Yeah. Yeah, go . . . go on."

"That next day, we came in, and he was hanging there, dead white, the blood completely out of him. Most of his face was gone, like I said. Then the guard asked us which we'd prefer: working with his stinking, rotting corpse above us until the rats finished it off or eating him ourselves."

Edmund stopped. He didn't want to ask, but found himself doing so anyway. "What, what did, what did you say? What happened?"

Pond Scum hit the wall again. "We ate well for three days."

They labored away, their picks hitting the wall. Sweat coursed down Edmund's face and spine. When the flakes of stone reached their knees, Crazy Bastard appeared beside them like an insane rabbit, bobbing side to side. He tapped his forehead and giggled.

"Magic." He giggled some more and put his filthy finger to his old lips. "Magic." He hopped off to the ore carts with some of their stone.

"Is he, is he going to . . .?" Edmund said when Crazy Bastard was out of earshot.

"Tell the guards?" Pond Scum asked. "He's always saying things like that. Once, Turd told a story about a man from his village who talked to birds. For a long time after that, Crazy Bastard ran around trying to fly, chirping away. If the guards ever ask, we'll say we told him a story about a magician."

"What about Turd?" Edmund asked, huffing. He glanced over his shoulder. The big man hit the wall, grimacing with every blow. "Where's, where's he from? I can't place his accent."

Pond Scum stopped swinging, allowing Crazy Bastard to get another shovelful of stone. "He's Hillman. He was supposed to be the chief of his tribe. Then, one day, he was hunting alone in the forests, and he fell in a hole the Hiisi use to trap boars, bears, and—"

"Hiisi?" Edmund repeated.

"You know." Pond Scum inclined his head toward the guards. "That's what they call themselves. Don't ever use the g-word, ever. They hate that. They absolutely detest the name. The last Pit Dweller who used it . . ." Pond Scum shuttered. "Let's not talk about it. Try not to refer to them at all. If you say 'them,' we all know who you mean."

"There's so much to learn."

"Consider it a game. Keep your ears open, eyes down, and mouth shut. Maintain a positive mind. Work smart. And don't get hurt. That's all you can really do."

Crazy Bastard returned for another shovelful of stone. He placed his rank-smelling mouth near Edmund's ear and whispered, "Magic." He snickered, then brought more rubble to the ore carts.

"What about Vomit?" When Crazy Bastard was out of his way, Edmund swung his pick. "Why does he walk like that? What happened to his leg?"

"He tried to escape," Pond Scum said. "So they cut him behind his ankle. Sliced to the bone, cutting all the muscles and such."

"Why didn't they . . . why didn't they kill him? I mean, isn't trying to escape the worst offense to commit around here?"

"It is. That and insulting one of them. Using the g-word, in particular." Pond Scum wiped the sweat from his dirty face. "The Hiisi prefer to keep you alive. If you're alive, you're working—and suffering.

If you're dead, you're beyond their reach. They don't like that. So, for the first escape attempt, they cripple you. The second time . . ." He swung again. "The second time they make you play the Games."

"Games? I heard . . . I heard them talking about that b-b-before. What are they?"

"The Hiisi like to gamble. They bet on everything. I'm sure they have several wagers on how long you'll live and how you'll eventually die, whether one of us kills you, and if so, who. They're obsessed with such things."

Edmund's pick arced listlessly over his head.

"Anyhow," Pond Scum said, "they have this huge arena where various games are played. Pit Dwellers are selected or volunteer to join in on the fun, as it were. The Hiisi go wild betting and watching what happens. It's like a holiday for them."

"V-v-volunteer? Why, why in heaven would anybody volunteer?"

They stepped aside so Crazy Bastard could get to the pile of stones. Edmund leaned against the cavern wall for a few seconds to catch his breath.

"Some volunteer as a way of ending it all," Pond Scum said. "Others believe they can win."

"Win? What happens if they win?"

They resumed chipping away at the wall.

"Depends upon the game," Pond Scum said. "Fungus, a Pit Dweller who was around when I first arrived, played in the Games and won. He got a side of deer meat and a pelt. I tell you, when I saw them bringing him his reward, I nearly volunteered right then and there."

"What did he have to do? What . . . what game did he play?"

"He fought another Pit Dweller to the death." Pond Scum added, "But don't worry. The other slave wasn't from our pit."

They struck the wall several more times. They'd created an opening several feet wide and a couple of feet deep. Crazy Bastard filled about a quarter of one cart.

Edmund shook his head, sending droplets of sweat in all directions. He brushed his hair out of his eyes. "I, I still don't understand people's motivation. Why would people participate when the gob . . ." He stopped himself. "When . . . they, when they could easily not uphold the arrangement, you know? It isn't as if they have any honor."

"That's what I thought when I got here." Pond Scum struck the wall. "But you'll learn that, as ruthless as they are, they always keep their wagers. As fanatical as they are about betting, they're even more so about paying up." He swung again. "There's one sure way for a Hiisi to end up as a Pit Dweller, and that's to renege on a bet."

"There're gob . . . them . . . in the, in the mines . . . as slaves?"

"A few. But they don't last long. They either kill themselves, try to escape, or are killed by us. It's the only time we can go after one of them without fear of punishment. That, and when we're pitted against one of them in a game."

Breathing hard, Edmund set his pick down and put his hands on his knees. He was drenched with perspiration. His pungent body odor made his eyes water.

"Let, let me, let me ask you." He took several deep, gulping breaths and lifted his pick again. He heaved it over his head and let it fall. It struck the wall with the same dull clank as his previous hundred blows. "Has anybody, has anybody ever . . . ever escaped from here?"

"Oh, sure."

Edmund looked at Pond Scum, surprised.

"People escape all the time. At least, they run away all the time. I mean, look at it this way. There are five of us and two guards. They're more than a match for us if we try to fight. Even if Turd had a weapon, they'd cut us down like wheat. But if we all ran in different directions, they'd only get three, maybe four of us."

Four out of five. How can I improve those odds?

Don't even think about it. Keep swinging. Keep your head down. Concentrate on breathing.

"Of course," Pond Scum went on, "getting away is one thing. Living to tell somebody is another animal altogether. Most people probably die in a couple of days, lost in the mines without food and all. The rats eventually get them. Big mean things. You have to grab them behind their ears so they can't bite you. Then snap their heads to one side real quick like."

Edmund tried to push the image of Pond Scum snapping a rat's neck out of his mind. "Has anybody escaped completely? Gotten, gotten out of here and . . . and gone home?"

Pond Scum struck the wall.

"That's hard to say now, isn't it? I mean, it isn't like they'll send us a letter telling us they got to such and such a place. But the guards often tell us that so and so got out and is now home, drinking and having sex with every woman he can find, and so on."

Home . . .

"That's another thing about them." Pond swung his pick. "They like playing with your head. Their most effective torture doesn't involve any physical pain. You might want to remember that."

Gasping for air, Edmund glanced at the water barrel again. Turd bared his teeth at him, then continued pounding the wall. He and Vomit had formed the beginnings of a crude tunnel.

This is insane. Nobody could keep this up for twelve hours. Nobody.

Don't think about it. Hit the rocks some more. Raise the pick and let it fall. Let gravity do the work.

I can't keep doing this. I can't.

Say something. Keep the conversation going. It helps.

Edmund forced his quavering arms over his head. The pick bounced pathetically off the grey stone.

"Were you . . . were you kidding about, about eating that pit mate of yours?"

Pond Scum's pick came down again.

"Maybe we should talk about something else," he said. "Let me tell you about Crazy Bastard. He's an interesting one. Then maybe you could tell me a little about yourself. Again, anything you can say will be of interest."

Chapter Fourteen

Edmund collapsed in his assigned area. The dirt stuck to his sweat-covered body like flour on a fish ready to be fried. His back ached. His legs quivered. He could barely move his arms. Actually, they were the only part of him that didn't hurt. They'd stopped hurting several hours before. Now they were numb. They dangled at his side as if they weren't attached to his body. When Vomit gave him his portion of the food, a thin slice of unidentifiable meat and a chunk of stale bread the size of his fist, Edmund couldn't lift it to his mouth. He had to have Pond Scum feed him like he was an invalid. Unfortunately, he knew he'd feel much worse in the morning.

I can't do this. It's impossible!

They did it.

Edmund twisted his head so that he could see his pit mates. They were all exhausted. Even Turd, who did more work than anybody and received more food as a result, oozed sweat. His sunken eyes stared blankly at the ground, a flicker of desperation growing in them. He rubbed his right shoulder, then his neck, then his hands—wincing each time he moved.

They do it day after day for the gods only know how long.

I can't. I simply can't. I won't make it through tomorrow. Cast the healing spell again.

No. It doesn't help with the exhaustion. Besides, you should save your strength to cast the other spell once everybody falls asleep.

Sleep. Oh, blessed sleep. I hope I'll never wake up.

"Not bad for your first day," Pond Scum said to Edmund, the joy returning to his voice as soon as the guards withdrew from the top of their pit. "You surprised even me." He turned to Turd. "And you thought he'd only consume our food and water."

Turd didn't respond.

"So," Pond Scum said to nobody in particular. "What do you all want to talk about? Any topics of conversation anybody wants to bring up? Anything at all? Anything?"

No one said a word.

"Filth," Pond Scum said. It took Edmund a few seconds to realize he was being addressed. "Why don't you tell us about yourself?"

Edmund let his head fall in Pond Scum's direction. "How . . . how can you have the energy to talk?"

"Magic!" Crazy Bastard cried. He rammed his head into the pit wall. Shaken, the old man sat.

"He never shuts up," Turd said.

"Next," Vomit said, "he'll tell you to 'be positive.'"

"Well, it's important," Pond Scum said. "We can't stop our bodies from feeling the pain. But we can stop them from getting to us in here." He tapped his temple. "The trick is making them think they've crushed our spirit."

They have.

"Plus," Pond Scum went on, "talking helps pass the time. Didn't the day fly by once we started talking, Filth? Much better than wallowing in self-pity. So how about if you tell us a story? I'd love to hear something new."

Turd lay his mammoth body gingerly on the ground. "There's nothing he could say that'd interest me."

"Let me ask you this," Norb's voice said in Edmund's head. *"How exciting would it be to be married to a librarian or a stable hand? What new stories could we tell them each night as they served us our dinner?"*

"Ah," Edmund recalled replying, *"but, but, but that's where you, you are wrong. You see, I have a world of st-st-stories. Stories that are far better than this im-imposter can ever tell."*

"I . . . I could probably tell a brief tale." Edmund tried to sit up but couldn't get the momentum to roll over. "Maybe something from your culture, Turd?"

"What do you know about my people?" Turd scoffed.

"Not much, admittedly. But I remember a story m-m-my, my grandfather used to tell me. I always enjoyed it. It was from your people, I believe. It was about a fisherman named Ico."

Turd's tired eyes lifted.

"Have you heard it?" Edmund asked.

"My people tell many stories about Ico," Turd said.

"Go ahead," Pond Scum said.

"Yes," Vomit said wearily. "Please. Anything new will be welcome. Tell away."

"Okay," Edmund said, pleased to have something occupying his mind other than his present situation.

Gazing up out of the pit, Edmund imagined he was on Tower Hill, studying the bright stars. He cleared his throat.

"S-s-so there was this man named Ico, and he was a fisherman," he began. "One day, he was fishing alone along a river deep in the mountains. The sun was setting, and he wanted to go home. So, he pulled in his net and found a s-s-single . . . a single speckled fish flopping around in it. The fish was small and wouldn't make much of a meal. But Ico thought he could use it as bait. However, as he reached for the fish, it spoke to him.

"She said—the fish was a she—she said, 'Oh, please, great fisherman, please don't kill me. Spare me, and I'll bring you three fish tomorrow. They'll be far bigger and tastier than I.'

"Well, I-I-Ico, having no real need for such a small fish, agreed and cast her into the water. Sure enough, when he pulled in his net the next day, there were three monstrous fish bigger than any he'd ever seen. They were giant lake trout that were rare in the mountains. S-s-so, so Ico went home, happy that he and his family would eat such a fine meal.

"The following day, Ico went fishing again and returned to the very spot where he'd caught the three colossal lake trout. B-b-but when he pulled in his net, there was just the little speckled fish he'd caught before.

"'Oh please, oh wonderful and kind fisherman,' the fish said to Ico. 'Please don't eat me. Spare my life, and tomorrow I shall bring you three fish even bigger and tastier than the lake trout I brought you yesterday.'

"W-w-well, this pleased Ico because the lake trout were indeed extremely large and very tasty. He couldn't imagine anything better. So, he released the speckled fish and went home.

"The next day, Ico returned to the same spot and set his net. When he drew it in, he found three monstrous coastal catfish. And they were larger than anything anybody had ever caught in those mountains. They put up a tremendous fight, and it took him many hours to haul them to land. When he finally got them home, everybody in his village praised him and called him the b-b-best fisherman of his people.

"The next day, Ico borrowed as many nets as he could and returned to the mountain stream. Sure enough, when he hauled them in, the little speckled fish was the only one there.

"'Oh, little speckled fish,' Ico said. 'I will spare your life once again. But I want you to bring me three fish that are even bigger and tastier than you gave me before.'

"The little fish tried to explain that she had no more friends to bring to the mountains. But Ico demanded she do so, or he'd eat her. He, he, he even dangled her over his mouth, lowering her closer to his waiting jaws until she agreed to give him three even bigger and tastier fish. So, he let her go."

Edmund looked at his audience. Even Crazy Bastard was sitting and listening to him. Pond Scum waved for him to go on. Turd grunted a disgusted laugh but didn't turn away.

"So, Ico went to the river the next day and cast his net into the water. Immediately, something seized it. It pulled so hard that he flew off his feet and landed in the river's cold water. As he bobbed to the surface, the last thing he saw were the fins of three very large sharks swimming right for him."

Pond Scum and Vomit applauded as much as their fatigue would allow. Crazy Bastard jumped up and danced, hitting himself repeatedly in the chest. Turd shook his head.

"You can't tell a story to save your life," he said. "You ruined it with all that stammering. Do you even know what the moral of the story is?"

"Don't listen to talking fish?" Pond Scum suggested.

Turd shook his head again. "No. Don't trust women, for they're easy to catch but treacherous to possess."

"Not bad," Vomit said. "But Turd is right. You need to work on your delivery. But I appreciate the effort."

Above them, the clinking of armor approached. They all fell silent. A guard frowned at them and then continued his patrol.

"Okay," Pond Scum whispered when the guard had gone. "Let's get down to brass tacks. What do you think? Can you do it?"

Staring up into the darkness, Edmund pictured the stars twinkling in the night sky. He smiled. Then he realized Pond Scum, Vomit, and Turd were all watching him. "I'm, I'm sorry. What?"

"Can you get us out of here?" Vomit whispered.

"N-n-now?"

"Not necessarily right this second."

"Though, if you could, that'd be much appreciated," Pond Scum said. "What do you think? Can you?"

With an effort, Edmund rolled onto his side. His rubbery arms pushed him into a sitting position. Vomit and Pond Scum drew closer. Turd listened from where he sat. Crazy Bastard picked at the pit's wall.

"W-w-w-well . . ." Edmund said slowly.

Make them believe. Make them think you have value.

"It, it, it's like what you said before," he said. "Escaping is easy. It's surviving that's problematic."

Vomit raised an eyebrow at Pond Scum. "Escaping is easy?"

"What I meant was getting away was easy," Pond Scum said. "Fleeing into the mines and all. That's easy. But getting out and home is another animal, so to speak."

Don't blow this. Make them think you can get them out of here.

That's not going to happen.

If you don't make them believe, they'll have no use for you. They'll probably eat you like they ate Excrement and poor Thorax.

"Pond Scum indicated that if we all ran at the same time," Edmund said in his best business-like tone, "they might get three or four of us. But one or two might make it deeper into the mines. Is that, is that a fair approximation? One or two out of five?"

"That's about right." Turd flexed his injured right hand. "If we get away from the guards, could you get us outside?"

You know what he wants to hear. Just say it.

"Maybe," Edmund said. "But if we're going to do this, we must do it right. I don't want to get caught and have them slice open—" He suddenly remembered who he was speaking to.

Vomit motioned for him to go on. "No. Don't be embarrassed. You're absolutely right. We'll have only one chance. We need to plan carefully. My mistake was that I panicked and ran when I thought the guards weren't watching."

"What do you need from us?" Pond Scum asked Edmund. "What do you need to make a plan?"

They all leaned closer. Their desperate eyes fixed upon Edmund.

Don't blow this. Convince them you can get them out of here, and they'll leave you alone!

For a little while.

Edmund selected his words carefully. "The first thing I need is time." His pit mates exhaled, disappointed. "It would . . . it would seem to me the gob . . . they, it seems to me they will be expecting me to try to escape sometime soon, being new and all. They'll be watching and waiting. Is that a fair assumption?"

Vomit nodded. "They'll be watching until they think you've been broken."

"Right," Pond Scum said. "So, stop glancing around like you're sizing up the place. Keep your eyes on the ground."

"And act pathetic," Vomit said.

"That won't be difficult," Edmund told them. "But tell me. What do people usually act like when they're broken? Wh-what should I do?"

"Cry," Turd said from his area of the pit. "Cry like a woman."

"Yes," Vomit said. "Sob uncontrollably for a few days and then stop."

"At that point," Pond Scum said, "stare into oblivion. Do whatever the guards say. Do it without thinking. Don't flinch or hesitate. Let your face and body go numb. And do whatever you're told."

"Again," Edmund said. "That shouldn't be difficult."

"Okay," Pond Scum said. "What else? What else do you need?"

Edmund thought. "I need information. For instance, suppose we were to get away from the guards. How, how, how long could we hide in the mines? I mean, that is to say, how big are they? How long would it take them to find us?"

"They'd never find us," Pond Scum said.

"Never is a long time," Vomit said. "But they are vast. I've been here longer than anybody, except for Crazy."

Crazy Bastard yelped like a dog stuck with a pin. He put his knuckles in his mouth and bit them.

"In all the time I've been here," Vomit said, "I don't think I've worked in the same place more than twice. They do that so we can't get a feel for where we are and find our way around."

"The mines are extensive," Turd said. "If we get away and are smart, they won't find us. But we need to get out of them all together. We need to get home."

Home . . . What a wonderful word.

"But we'd have to survive in the mines," Pond Scum said. "Without food, we'd die in a week. Maybe ten days."

"We'll also need water," Edmund said, wondering how long he could keep his charade going.

"There's plenty of water in the mines," Turd said in a tone implying that Edmund was an idiot.

"Yes, yes," Edmund said. "Yes, of course. There always is, I suppose. But we need something to carry it in, you know? Otherwise, we'd be confined to hiding only where water is available . . . which is what the gob . . . they, it is what they'll be thinking. But, if we could get something to store water in, we could hide where they wouldn't be looking for us. Away from water, I mean. See my logic?"

Turd appeared to agree. "We could grab the water barrel as we run. But that'll slow one of us down."

"Perhaps. Or we can find another way to carry water."

"Great!" Pond Scum said. "That'll give us something to think about. What else do you need?"

"Well, again, the water and food are critical." Edmund thought. His stomach grumbled.

End this conversation so they'll go to sleep. Then cast your spell.

"Of course," Edmund said, "weapons would be handy. After all, we'll need to fight our way out of the mines, as Turd said. It'll take some time for us to—"

Pond Scum pulled two curved white sticks with sharpened ends from the loose dirt. He handed them to Edmund.

"What are these?" Edmund asked.

"Ribs," Pond Scum said. "Courtesy of Excrement."

Edmund shuddered and pushed them at Pond Scum.

"We would've made more," Pond Scum said. "But the guards examined the body every day. We didn't think they'd miss a couple of ribs. Which they didn't."

"Nice work," Edmund found himself saying. He wiped his filthy hands on his filthy chest. "Those, those are a start at any rate."

"What else do you need?" Vomit asked.

Buy time. Think!

"I need . . . I need to get a feel for how the gob . . . they . . . how they react and everything. I need to see the pattern of their behaviors, which guards do what, and so forth. For instance, perhaps some guards are more relaxed or distractible than others. Or slower."

"D'arco," Pond Scum and Vomit said in unison.

"He's older than most of the guards," Vomit said. "He's slow on his feet."

"Don't underestimate D'arco." Turd massaged his hands. "Don't underestimate any of them."

"True." Edmund tried to sound knowledgeable. "Also, I don't like the idea of only one or two of us making it out alive. I'd like to make sure we can all survive." They looked at him, doubtful. "Or, or at, at least reduce the number of casualties."

Everyone but Turd nodded.

"Look," Edmund said. "I think we need to wait and watch until they don't suspect anything. B-but, but right now . . . I need to sleep." His stomach rumbled again.

"I think that's a good idea." Vomit hobbled to his area. "We probably only have six hours before they come and get us."

"Six?" Edmund said. "We . . . we worked for, for maybe twelve, thirteen hours. We've only been talking for an hour, maybe two. We should have at least nine hours."

"Didn't I tell you?" Pond Scum said. "They keep us on a twenty-hour schedule. Sometimes shorter. Sometimes longer. It's another way they mess with our minds."

"Six hours before we start again?" Edmund muttered.

"More like five now," Vomit said. "So get some rest. We'll talk about this tomorrow."

Everyone returned to their areas. Even Crazy Bastard curled on the ground like a kitten. He giggled. "Magic!"

Edmund stared into the darkness, listening to his pit mates breathe.

They'll kill you once they realize you're a fake. They'll kill you, eat your fat carcass, and then use your bones for weapons. It's only a matter of time.

Maybe. But if I'm going to die, it's going to be while trying to escape. I'm not going to get injured like Turd or go insane like Crazy Bastard. And I'm sure as hell not going to let those goblin bastards slice my leg open and make me a cripple.

Do you really think you can get out of here?

I don't know.

Edmund listened. The clink of armor passed by their pit and then faded.

You might as well try now. They can't see you in this darkness anyway.

Rolling over onto its side, Edmund faced the wall. He concentrated on the spell his father taught him long ago. He'd rarely cast it. In fact, since his father was poisoned to death, he'd probably cast it no more than three times. He'd never had the need—until now.

He whispered the words.

"Mat av nå."

It appeared briefly in his tired mind and then slipped into a fog. He tried again.

"Mat av nå."

His head grew light. Pinpricks of cold sweat stabbed his face. A dark, swirling sensation filled his consciousness. His breath faltered. He was falling into blackness. Then his fingers twitched, and he felt it. With an effort, his trembling arms brought the biscuit to his mouth. He bit into it.

I don't remember these tasting this good.

Make sure you don't leave any crumbs. If they knew you could create food, they'd demand you make some for them. And you can't make enough for everybody.

Chapter Fifteen

"Still alive, Filth?" one of the guards said in mock disappointment. "A lot of people will be mighty upset to hear you're not dead yet. I suspect a few may pay you a little visit while you're sleeping tonight. But don't worry. As long as you make it past midnight, I'll be happy."

Edmund, his head down, hobbled into line. Like a corpse, his body had stiffened during the night. He couldn't turn his head without feeling pain. He couldn't raise his arms above his waist. Even breathing made him wince.

I can't lift a pick, let alone swing it for twelve hours. This is it. I won't be able to do a thing today. The guards are going to kill me. Cast the healing spell. Cast it now!

Calm down. You can't cast anything with everybody watching. And you'll need to save your strength. I don't expect you'll be earning much food today. You'll have to make it yourself.

"Ready?" a goblin with a torch called to the other guard. "All right. Move the vermin out. Double time. Let's go. There's work to be done."

A whip cracked above Edmund's head, but he was too exhausted to flinch. Following the guard with the torch, the line of slaves jogged out of the cavern and into a dark side passage. For an indeterminable length of time, they ran through countless tunnels winding steadily downward to the mountains' roots.

Puffing and wheezing, Edmund compelled his rubbery legs to keep moving.

I can't . . . I can't do this. I can't keep up. I have to . . . I have to stop.

You stop, and you'll feel more than wind from that whip. Keep going!

I can't! I can't . . . go on.

Pain flashed through his body with every forced breath. He started to cry.

"Shut your sniveling," one of the guards told him. "We're here. And you better thank me for it."

Doubled over, his hands on his knees, Edmund panted.

The guard brought his whip back. "What did I tell you?"

"Thank . . . thank you." Edmund coughed. "Thank you v-v-very, very much."

"Know how many other vermin would kill to have this job? Get to work, or I'll find something less pleasant for you to do."

The guard shoved Edmund into a cavern. He fell headlong onto a thick carpet of smooth pebbles covering the wet ground. For a moment, he lay there, catching his breath and sobbing, his body refusing to move. A hand appeared.

"You should get up," Pond Scum said. "Things will go poorly for you if you don't."

Edmund clasped Pond Scum's hand and willed himself to his feet. Knocking away the pebbles clinging to him like leeches, he peered around.

They were at the bottom of a gorge far beneath the mountains. A swift-moving stream, a couple of feet deep, flowed out from the shadows to their right and hurried into a tunnel to their left. Above them, cliffs extended into the impenetrable blackness.

Standing in line behind Pond Scum, Edmund eyed the water.

That's the most beautiful stream I've ever seen.

I just want to sleep.

Don't rivers flow out of mountains?

Rivers do. Streams like this might not. It might end in some underground lake or abyss.

Still . . .

"All right." Vomit limped to them. "They want us to take these rocks—" He indicated the three mountains of stone piled next to the water. "—and dam the stream where it exits over there." He waved a hand to the opening through which the stream left the gorge. "We need to take the larger slabs and boulders and place them down first. Then we can shovel the rest of the stones in front of it. We keep going until everything is gone. Got it?"

There was a listless murmur as everybody shambled to the mounds of quarried stone. Pond Scum lifted the end of a slab and told Edmund to grab the other side. Edmund nodded and bent over to pick it up.

"Use your legs," Pond Scum said. "Keep your spine straight."

Edmund lifted his end. "I can't move my spine."

"Stiff?"

Edmund groaned. "M-m-more than stiff. I feel like I'm about to snap in two."

"Don't worry. You'll loosen up soon enough."

Step by step, he and Pond Scum inched sideways toward the stream.

"Are we allowed to, you know, drink the water?" Edmund asked, the stone growing heavier in his blistered hands. "Or wash?"

"After we're finished," Pond Scum said. "But you might not want to do that even then."

"Why?"

They waded into the stream. Immediately, pain shot up Edmund's legs. It felt as though they were on fire. He cried out.

"Because the water here is damn cold," Pond Scum said. "They say if you fall in, you'll freeze to death within a minute."

Pond Scum gently set his end of the slab into the stream. When he withdrew his hands, they were a pinkish shade of blue. Edmund followed suit and then lumbered to dry land.

"At least you have boots," Pond Scum said. "Then again, my feet are so callused I probably could stand on flaming nails and not feel it."

"They don't keep the water out." Then, seeing Pond Scum's bruised and swollen feet, he added, "B-b-but I suppose they're better than nothing."

"Don't worry. Pretty soon, you'll be completely numb. You won't feel a thing below your knees."

That'd be a pleasant change. Shame it isn't everything below my hair.

As he staggered to one of the piles of stone, Edmund passed Turd, Vomit, and Crazy Bastard struggling with an eight-foot-long block of granite. Turd's face twisted in agony.

"H-hold," Edmund said to Pond Scum. "Hold on." Bending over with several fitful groans, he undid the seam at the bottom of one of his pant legs. He ripped it to his thigh and then tore the pant leg off. He did the same with the other side.

"What are you doing?" Pond Scum asked.

The guards watched him. One readied his crossbow.

Tearing the two pant legs lengthwise, Edmund produced four long strips of fabric. "Here." He handed a strip to Vomit and Turd. "Wrap . . . wrap each end around your hands. Then, slip the loop underneath the stone. It'll be easier to carry them."

"Wonderful idea," Vomit said, with no hint of emotion. "I'll keep this in mind when I allocate food."

"Get to work," the guard with the loaded crossbow shouted. "Or you'll not like what happens!"

The other guard cracked his whip.

Turd wrapped the ends of the strip around his bloated hands. He flexed his fingers.

"Thanks," he muttered and returned to work.

Pond Scum slid his cloth loop underneath a slab of stone and waited for Edmund to do the same. "That was good of you." He lifted his end off the ground. "And you're right. This is much easier. Hopefully, the guards won't increase our quota for the day. They hate it when we do something smart."

Like two crabs tied together, Pond Scum and Edmund carried their slab into the burning cold water and let it drop next to the rest of the rubble. The splash sent water leaping at them, biting their chest and face. Edmund hastened to land.

I'll be frozen soon.

At least you'll be clean. You haven't had a bath in weeks. You stink to high heaven.

"Tell me about yourself," Pond Scum said. "Last time, I did all the talking. Which is fine, but I'd like to listen for a while. Gets my mind off the work and all."

"I'm sorry," Edmund said. "In, in . . . in all honesty, I'm not in the mood to talk."

Pond Scum selected another stone from one of the piles. He lifted an end. Edmund lifted the other. They trudged toward the surging stream, the stone suspended on the straps of cloth dangling from their fatigued arms.

"Do you think you'll ever be in the mood?" Pond Scum asked. "I mean, take it from somebody who's been here a while . . ." They lurched into the water and lowered the stone next to the previous one. "Nothing about this place instills the desire to communicate."

There's nothing about this place that instills a desire to live.

"I'm . . . I'm dead tired," Edmund said. "And I hurt . . . everywhere."

"Hey, get used to it. You won't have many days as easy as this."

Easy?

"You should be positive," Pond Scum said.

Positive?

"If you want to know what pain is," Pond Scum said. "Wait until you work in the forges where they smelt the ore. It's so hot your eyes sizzle. And that's not an exaggeration. Your skin actually cooks. I worked there once, and I have to say, it makes me thankful for days like these."

He tapped the stone he wanted next.

"That's how I got these burn marks. Working in the forges, I mean." They lifted the stone. "At the very least, you won't go thirsty here. And, pretty soon, your legs won't feel a thing. That's nicer than it sounds, believe me."

They waded into the stream and set the slab into place.

"And, like I said before," Pond Scum went on, "talking helps. It gets you out of your head. That's where all the real pain is. A man can will himself to death with too many dark thoughts."

If only that were true.

With his good eye, Edmund studied the piles of stone towering above them. Even if they were all as strong as Turd, it'd take them several days to move it all.

We'll never get to all of this. Never. I don't know why we're even pretending this is possible.

Pond Scum sighed. "Okay. Suit yourself. But trust me, you don't know what it's really like yet. And you'd do well to listen to our advice."

Edmund pointed to a stone that looked light enough to carry. "You're right. You, you, you got me through yesterday. If you can get me through today, I'd appreciate it. What do you want to know?"

"Anything, actually," Pond Scum said. "What was your profession? You don't appear to be a soldier, or have things gone poorly for your people?"

Your people?

"Where are you from?" Edmund asked.

They deposited another block along the growing wall. Edmund slapped his bare calves, trying to get the feeling back into his blue skin.

"I'm from Mogador," Pond Scum said. "Ever hear of it?"

"The island? Yes. Yes, I have. I've read—"

"Calm down," Pond Scum whispered. He shot a glance at the guards. "Perhaps we should talk about something else. Something less enjoyable." He tilted a boulder so Edmund could slip his strap under it. "Are you married?"

"N-n-no," Edmund said regretfully. "No, I'm not."

Straightening their legs in unison, they lifted the large rock.

"But there's a woman," Pond said. "Am I right?"

Edmund fumbled over a few intelligible words.

"Molly?" Pond Scum suggested.

Looking at him, Edmund nearly let go of the stone.

"You talk in your sleep," Pond Scum said.

They dropped the boulder in the stream and rolled it into position.

"Tell me about her. Is she pretty?"

Edmund smiled for the first time since being captured. "I think so."

"Well, she's probably perfectly happy with some other guy. She probably doesn't ever think about you."

Edmund stopped, mortified. "Wh-wh-why, why would you say—?"

"To get that grin off your face. You can't smile like that, or the guards will knock it off with their clubs. Trust me. Be happy. But don't let it show."

Edmund nodded. Certainly, picturing Molly with another man took away any happiness he had left. It also made him forget about the freezing water as they strained to carry rock after rock to the dam site.

"So," Pond Scum said, "how did they catch you? Like I said, you don't look like a soldier. No offense. You look more like a cook, if you ask me. Do your armies have cooks? If not, I'm guessing you were a traveling merchant."

Edmund didn't particularly feel like talking anymore. Images of Molly with strange young men—stroking their broad shoulders and playing with their clean, neatly combed hair—wouldn't leave his mind.

"Filth?" Pond Scum said.

Edmund pulled himself out of his dark thoughts. "I wasn't a soldier or a traveling merchant. I was, I was . . . traveling."

"Seeing relatives? Friends?"

Edmund shook his head as he strained to carry his end of the stone.

"Okay," Pond said. "You were away from home, but you weren't a merchant or a soldier. And you weren't on holiday visiting anybody. You don't look like a tax collector. Are you some other sort of government official?"

The stone banged into Edmund's knee, leaving a bloody gash. He swore. "No."

"Well then, I'm stumped. You're a mystery to me, Filth."

They dropped the stone in the water. Breathing hard, Edmund bent over, not even caring about his bitterly cold feet.

"I," he began. Then he realized he didn't know what to say. "I was . . . I was walking."

"Walking?" Pond Scum left the stream. "I don't understand. Are you from around these mountains? I didn't think anybody lived this far north except them."

Edmund followed him to the closest stone pile. Crazy Bastard was on top of it, sending slabs sliding down, smashing at their feet. Pond Scum selected one of the bigger pieces. Struggling to straighten his legs, Edmund fought with the stone's weight for a moment and then let it fall onto the other rocks.

"I, I can't," he said. "I can't . . . I can't budge this one. Maybe . . . maybe, the others can."

Pond Scum chose a smaller block. "Go on. What do you mean you were walking?"

Yes, tell him about your brilliant idea to give your life meaning!

Sliding his strap under the block, Edmund put his feet hip-width apart and lifted.

"I . . . left. I just started walking."

They shuffled to the stream, waded into the icy water, and dropped their burden.

"I don't understand," Pond Scum said. "Did they banish you or something? You don't look like you were homeless."

"I wasn't," Edmund said. "Homeless, that is. I, I . . . I needed a change."

"So, you started walking?"

Gasping for air, Edmund nodded. "Something like that."

Go ahead. Tell him how you were going to become a famous adventurer!

"Why?" Pond asked. "What was so bad about where you lived? Was there famine or something? Was it dangerous? Were highwaymen robbing everybody? Corrupt government?"

Edmund arched his spine and twisted his torso. He grimaced.

"No. Nothing like any of that." He pictured Rood—the bakery, the park in the middle of town, the Wandering Rogue. He was surprised by the fondness blooming inside of him. "You know . . . I . . . I really can't say. It seemed so clear then. Why I left, I mean. Now . . . I don't know."

Something loomed behind them. Turning fast, Edmund threw up his hands to protect his swollen eye.

"Scum," Turd said, "go help Vomit and Crazy." Turd inclined his head at Edmund. "I'll work with him."

Oh, great! What does he want?

Who cares? Don't make him angry.

Surprised but not daring to disagree, Pond Scum went to help Vomit and Crazy Bastard. When he'd gone, Turd pointed to a slab bigger than anything Edmund had attempted before. It was as large as his dining table and two feet thick. With a fierce snarl, Turd wrestled it onto its side.

"I . . . I can't." Edmund shook his head. "I can't lift—"

"We'll push it." Turd set his shoulder to the slab.

Unsure what to do, Edmund got on the other side and put his shoulder below Turd's. With a great heave, Turd slid the stone toward the stream, plowing aside the pebbles covering the ground.

"Thanks for the cloth for my hands," Turd said, driving the stone forward.

Heaving as hard as he could, Edmund grunted.

"I want you to know," Turd whispered, "I think we can get out of here—the two of us."

Stunned, Edmund stopped pushing, although the megalith kept sliding at the same pace.

What's he up to?

Shut up and listen.

"There's no reason why we can't be the two out of five who escape into the mines," Turd said. "You and me. If you can figure out how to get food and carry water, like you said, I can take care of the fighting. And I can get us out of the mines."

Edmund resumed pushing.

"All right," he found himself saying.

He'd kill me as soon as I'd served his purpose.

Shut up. And don't look skeptical! Make him think you're willing to do what he wants.

Turd's expression toughened. "It isn't like Vomit or Crazy would be of much help. Vomit knows that. He can't run. But he wants to at least try. He wouldn't mind us thinking about ourselves. We can make sure he dies quickly."

The massive block slid into the water.

"What about Pond Scum?" Edmund asked.

"Scum's an idiot. If he survives, fine. If not, I don't care. We can't all make it. You and me have the best chance. If you can get us into the mines, I can get us into the mountains. I know how to survive in the mountains. They'll never find us."

He let the slab fall. It hit the stones already heaped in the stream and shattered with a terrific splash.

Turd leaned closer. "What do you say?"

Agree and get away from him. Make him believe you will—

An eerie silence settled about them.

Edmund straightened.

"Where are the guards?" he whispered.

Turd twitched. "What?"

"Where are they?" Edmund looked around.

The guards were nowhere to be seen.

Lowering their load, Pond Scum and Vomit glanced into a nearby passageway.

"They're not here," Vomit said.

"Quick," Turd said. "This is it. Grab one of the mining picks, and let's get out of here!"

They all raced to the pile of tools.

Giggling, Crazy Bastard shoved pebbles into his mouth.

There's something wrong.

"Wait," Edmund said.

Everybody stood motionless.

"Why?" Turd said. "We need to run while we have time!"

"There's something wrong. This isn't right. They wouldn't simply leave." Edmund scanned the darkness. "This is a trap or something."

"Who cares?" Turd hissed. "We have a running start. This'll increase our chances!"

Clutching their picks, Vomit and Pond Scum wavered.

"No," Edmund said.

"I don't care what you say. I'm going. I can't wait any longer!" The big man took a step toward one of the tunnels.

"Stop!" Edmund said. "I think I heard somebody cock a crossbow."

Everybody held their breath.

Turd's body tensed. "I didn't hear anything."

"I only hear the water rushing over the rocks," Vomit whispered.

Pond listened a moment longer and shook his head. "I don't hear anything either."

"It's a trap. Trust me." Edmund swung his pick at a stone, his eyes flitting from shadow to shadow. Pond Scum followed his example, then Vomit. Reluctantly, Turd turned and swung his pick.

Standing by the stream, Crazy Bastard shrieked, his voice reverberating in the chasm.

"Death!" he cackled.

He fell to the ground, his hands sending a spray of pebbles in every direction as he frantically dug.

"Death!"

He shoved his head into the hole he created.

"Death!"

Cowering from the unknown, Edmund collapsed to his knees. Vomit and Pond Scum cast aside their picks. Turd stood above them, unsure what to do.

Then, a familiar voice broke the stillness.

"What did I tell you, Mr. Gurding? There's more to our new friend here than meets the eye. Wouldn't you say?"

A deeper voice replied. "Perhaps, Mr. Kravel. However, I'm more interested in seeing how long he lasts. Don't forget, I still have three and a half more days in our new wager."

Kravel and Gurding stepped out of the darkness, followed by the two missing guards.

"Patience, Mr. Gurding," Kravel said. "First things, as they say, are first. Master Filth," Kravel called to Edmund, "would you do us the pleasure of joining us?"

What do I do now?

Vomit pushed him to his feet. "Don't keep them waiting. Go!"

"Do whatever they say," Pond Scum whispered.

Edmund hurried to the waiting goblins, his hands unconsciously smoothing his unkempt hair and straightening what was left of his clothing.

Gurding produced a small coil of rope from his pocket and formed a noose.

"I don't believe that will be called for, Mr. Gurding," Kravel said. "Wouldn't you agree, Filth?"

Staring at the ground, Edmund touched one of the purple bumps on his dirt-smeared forehead. He nodded.

"It's certainly wonderful to see you again," Kravel said to him. "You look splendid, I must say."

"He's lost weight," Gurding said. "But he's still fat."

"Ah! That's just like you, Mr. Gurding. Always seeing both sides of the matter." Kravel turned to Edmund. "I hadn't anticipated such a reunion so soon; however, as you'll soon learn, events have produced an outcome different than I had originally expected."

Edmund stared at the ground.

"As a result, you'll be spending some time with us." Bowing, Kravel motioned to a passage. "If you please, Master Filth."

Edmund looked at the two guards.

"Not to worry. Not to worry," Kravel told him. "Your guardians here understand your presence is required elsewhere. We will be responsible for your well-being. Come. Come. Being late would be detrimental to your present good health."

Chapter Sixteen

"He's certainly quiet this time," Gurding said as they strolled along a well-lit passageway. "Much better than before." He looked at Edmund following close behind. "Honestly, if we had to be around you for another day, I would've snapped your neck, orders or no."

Keep your mouth shut! Don't say a word.

"The Questioners do work wonders," Kravel said. "Still, I miss our witty banter, don't you? Not to mention Filth's endless crying. There's something about a sobbing fat man, would you agree, Mr. Gurding?"

"It depends upon how they are cooked, I suppose."

"Ah! Indeed. There's that wit of yours. You're a treasure, Mr. Gurding. A treasure." Kravel turned around. "But Mr. Gurding is correct. You certainly are a quiet one, Filth. Or have they cut out your tongue?"

"That'd make this afternoon rather difficult, to say the least," Gurding said.

Concerned, Kravel gestured for Edmund to open his mouth. Edmund's tongue twitched in the torchlight.

"Well," Kravel said, relieved. "That gave me quite the start! Could you imagine what would've happened if we brought him to the tower only to learn that he had no tongue?"

Tower?

Gurding shuddered. "It wouldn't have been pleasant. Not in the least bit."

They entered a chamber with a wooden platform connected to four thick chains extending upward into darkness. Two haggard and bloody slaves stood like plow horses at a wheel, ready to grind corn at a millstone.

Maybe I can escape. They aren't paying any attention to me.

Don't be stupid. They'd run you down before you took three steps. Do what they say. And keep your wits about you!

Edmund followed his captors onto the platform.

"To the top, if you would be so kind," Kravel said to the guard.

The guard flicked his whip.

Running in a circle, the slaves turned the giant wheel. Gears whirled. Chains creaked. The platform heaved unsteadily off the ground.

"I suppose you're wondering where we're headed, my dear Filth," Kravel said as they rose higher through a vertical shaft.

Below them, the whip cracked again. Somebody cried out as the platform rose even faster.

"I'm not sure I like him like this," Gurding said. "Not that I enjoyed all the stuttering. It drove me crazy. It took until now to get his squawking out of my head. But at least he had personality."

"Well said, Mr. Gurding. However, perhaps it's best Master Filth rests his spastic tongue while he can."

Edmund watched the shaft's grey walls slide by. Periodically, they passed openings where he caught glimpses of more goblins going about their business. There seemed to be hundreds of them.

"You see, Master Filth," Kravel said, "we've found some . . . shall we say, irregularities in the information you provided us earlier."

"You lied," Gurding said.

Uh oh! What did I tell them?

"That's a succinct way of phrasing matters, I'm afraid," Kravel said.

"We aren't particularly fond of liars."

"No, indeed. You are quite correct, Mr. Gurding. And I have to say, in one respect, I am disappointed you hid the complete and utter truth from us, my dear Filth. I thought we were friends, you and I. Then again, it seems you have helped promote our standing considerably. Mr. Gurding's and mine, that is. So, I'm inclined to overlook your little indiscretion for the time being. However, given that you have foiled the astute questioning of both ourselves and the Questioner you met when we arrived home, somebody else wishes to have a word with you."

"A very important somebody."

"Now you are understating things, Mr. Gurding. That's unlike you."

Trying to remember to breathe, Edmund stared at the wall while the platform rose through the mountain.

"You see, Filth," Kravel went on, "you will have a remarkable pleasure very few Hiisi have ever had, and perhaps none of your kind."

"At least none of your kind who've survived the experience."

"Quite possibly. However, Mr. Gurding is merely speculating. Such knowledge is not available to us, you understand. You see, Filth, you will be meeting somebody who has taken a personal interest in you."

Personal . . . interest?

That doesn't sound good.

Gurding's yellow teeth appeared in a kind of grin. "And he'll make sure you tell us everything you know. He may even cure your stutter."

"One can only hope, Mr. Gurding," Kravel said. "But let us not make any promises on His Majesty's behalf."

His Majesty?

Edmund's head lifted.

What have you gotten yourself into now, Edmund, you fool?

"Yes, indeed, my dear Filth," Kravel said in response to Edmund's horrified expression. "You will soon be honored to meet our magnificent and benevolent King! I trust you have brought something appropriate to wear. No? Never mind. I am sure he'll like you for who you are, as we do. Isn't that right, Mr. Gurding?"

"I never said I liked him," Gurding said. "In fact, I'm still mystified about this whole affair. Why His Majesty would want to meet the likes of him is beyond me. Personally, I hope His Highness kills the fat fellow—or allows us to do so."

"Interesting possibilities, no doubt. I suppose such events will depend largely upon how well Master Filth answers His Majesty's questions." Kravel shook Edmund's shoulder playfully. Edmund blanched, pain coursing through his stiff body. "What do you think, Master Filth? Will you be in a talkative mood this evening?"

"I bet you he'll be screaming more than talking."

Kravel thought about this. "I'll take that bet, Mr. Gurding. I believe Master Filth will do splendidly. I'm sure he will tell all he knows."

"If he doesn't," Gurding said, "we'll finally get to measure the length of his intestines."

Chapter Seventeen

"I'm terribly sorry for not greeting you sooner," a kind voice said from the impenetrable shadows surrounding Edmund. "But I wasn't aware you had joined us until earlier this morning. It is an oversight that has been severely reprimanded, I can assure you."

Rotating his head slightly, Edmund attempted to detect where in the ring of darkness the voice was coming from. All he could determine was that he was in some sort of room. Further, given the mortared stone walls and the fragrant pine-scented air, he guessed he was in an above-ground structure, maybe a fortress or castle.

A man was strapped to an iron table directly in front of him. Bound with heavy chains, the man's feet dangled over a small but growing fire—the only light source in the chamber. He'd been beaten. One of his eyes appeared dead, staring lifelessly in a completely different direction than his other eye. Blood seeped out of his broken nose and clenched lips. But, like a seasoned soldier, the man's demeanor remained defiant.

Even as he strained to keep his feet above the leaping flames, he glared at the ceiling above him.

Edmund shifted uneasily in his chair.

"Are you comfortable?" the voice asked.

What's this all about? What am I doing here?

It won't be pleasant, that's for sure. Keep your wits about you. Or you'll be on that table soon.

Something struck Edmund across his head, knocking him to the blood-splattered floor.

"Answer His Majesty," a guard demanded.

"Now, now," the voice said. "That isn't called for. Not yet. Our guest is merely acclimating himself. I can imagine all of this is exceedingly disorienting for him. We have all the time in the world to have our conversation."

Conversation?

"I'm, I'm s-s-sorry, sir." Edmund felt the growing lump above his right ear as he climbed into his chair. "I'm . . . I'm sorry. Wh-wh-what, what was the, the question?"

"I asked if you were comfortable," the voice said. "Would you prefer a different chair? A cushion, perhaps? You will be sitting for a while, I'm afraid. And I don't want you to feel any discomfort."

Comfortable? If you want me to be comfortable, let me go home!

"N-n-no. No, s-sir. Master? Sir? No. No, I'm . . . I'm fine. Th-thank you. Thank you, sir."

"They said you had difficulty speaking. I once had a sister with a similar affliction. She's dead now." The voice paused as if recalling a pleasant memory. "What's your name, by the way?"

"F-F-Filth. Filth," Edmund said. "It's . . . it's Filth, sir."

The voice laughed. "No, no. You misunderstand me. I mean your real name. For the moment, consider yourself human again."

"My, my . . . my real, real name?" Thinking this was a trick, Edmund's body tensed, ready for another blow. "M-my, my real name is . . . is Ed-Ed-Edmund, sir, master."

Another chuckle bubbled out of the darkness. "No need to use either 'sir' or 'master.' Imagine we are two old friends talking in your kitchen, chatting the autumn evening away."

"Yes, yes, sir." Realizing he'd said sir again, Edmund slapped his hands over his mouth.

More chuckling floated around him.

"Now, Edmund," the voice said as if getting down to business. "Would you care for some tea?"

"What? Tea?" Edmund said, wondering if he'd heard correctly. "Yes, yes sir . . . I, I mean. Yes. Yes, that'd be lovely. Thank you. Thank you very much."

"Splendid."

Why am I here? What do they want from me?

Stay alert and, for the love of the gods, don't upset him!

From the darkness to Edmund's right, a goblin guard appeared. He attached a copper kettle to the soldier's legs. The added weight dragged his feet into the rising flames. His face contorting, the man fought to keep them out of the fire.

"If you lift it too high," the guard told the soldier, "it won't boil. Now, will it? So lower your legs, or I'll pop your kneecaps off with this." He held up a knife.

The man strapped to the table glared at Edmund, curses in his remaining eye.

Edmund mouthed a silent apology. But the tormented soldier turned away, biting his bloody lip as he strained to keep the kettle close to the crackling fire without burning himself.

"It should be ready momentarily," the voice said. "Perhaps we should begin. You're of the northern human race, or am I mistaken?"

"What?" Edmund said. "Oh, y-yes. Yes, I'm, I'm of northern stock, as they say. Yes. Yes, sir."

"Excellent. Now, where are you from?"

"R-R-Rood. Rood, sir. I mean . . ."

What are you doing? Don't tell him that!

Why? What could it possibly matter? Tell him anything he wants to know!

"Rood?" the voice repeated thoughtfully. "Rood. I don't believe I am familiar with it. Where is it from here?"

Edmund shrank in his chair. "I-I-I don't know . . . sir. I mean, I mean, that is to say, I, I . . . I don't know where here is, if you understand me. So, I don't know. I'm . . . I'm sorry."

"Very good. And quite correct of you, I am sure. Let me restate the question. In what direction is your home from the tower where you were found? Tol Helen, your people used to call it, though it has other, more appealing, names."

"East." Edmund jolted. "No! No, west! West. It's west. I'm terribly sorry. I'm sorry. I'm, I'm, I'm a bit flustered. I'm sorry."

"No need to apologize. Slips of the tongue and all. I understand. You're doing fine. So, this Rood is west of the tower. Good. Due west?"

Why does he care about Rood?

He's trying to make you lower your guard. Answer whatever questions he has, or you'll end up with your legs in the fire.

"W-west and a little south. More west than south, if you get me."

"I do, indeed, get you. Thank you."

The kettle's lid jingled. Glancing at it, Edmund expected the water to be near boiling, but found the soldier's struggling legs were causing the noise. Scarlet flames climbed higher, licking the kettle and the man's calves. There was a sizzling sound and the scent of scorched hair and burnt skin.

"Rood," the voice said again to himself. "No, I can't seem to place it. Does it have another name? Perhaps something out of the distant pages of history?"

"P-people used to, used to call it Rut, as, as, as in 'Rut in the Road.' It's a very small town, you understand. Village, really. Insignificant to, to you, to anybody, I'm sure. Two hundred and forty-three years ago it, it became officially known as, as, as Rood. But, but that, that wouldn't interest you."

"Actually, it does. I am fascinated by such things, particularly how languages change over time. In fact, I once studied to be a philologist. Let's see. 'Rut in the Road' would be *Skutilsbraut*, in the older dialects of your original tongue. Maybe *Raufbraut*, 'hole in the road.' However, neither is striking a chord in my memory."

A growing fountain of grey steam arose from the kettle's spout and billowed around the man's blistering ankles. A soft whistle grew into an unnerving, high-pitched scream. A guard unhooked the kettle from the chains binding the man's feet. Exhaling with relief, the man lifted his legs higher above the fire.

"Is Rood by any geological landmarks?" the voice asked. "Bodies of water? Or perhaps old ruins?"

Don't tell him!

"It's . . . ." Edmund watched as the guard set an exquisite gold-trimmed teacup and saucer on the man's bloody chest. It heaved up and down as the man labored to breathe.

"If you make me spill," the guard told the soldier, "I'll become very angry."

He carefully poured the hot water into the teacup.

This is insane!

"Edmund?" the voice prodded.

"Wh-what? What?" Edmund jerked his attention from the man strapped to the table. "I'm . . . I'm sorry. What, what were you saying, sir?"

"I am trying to place this Rood of yours. I was well-traveled in my youth. I particularly enjoyed the lands where you come from, and I cannot recall any such settlement. Is it by any geological landmarks, such as bodies of water? Is it by any ruins from the Elder Days?"

Don't tell him! Be vague. He doesn't need to know where Rood is.

"It's, it's by Tower Hill. Does that help, sir?"

"No. No, I'm afraid not. But it's not of any importance. I was merely curious. Why don't you try your tea? It's batwing. Perhaps you are familiar with it. If not, don't let the name deter you. It doesn't contain bat wings or any other portions of bats."

"I know. It's . . . it's made from the black leaves of the Manglorn Vine, which look . . . which look like little bat wings."

"Very true. How did you know that?"

Edmund lifted the delicate teacup from the man's chest. The man glared at him again. Edmund winced another apology.

"M-m-my, my mother owned an apothecary shop. She taught me about such things, herbs and the like."

Shut up! Don't reveal anything else. He's learning too much about you.

How would that possibly matter? Mother is dead. And we'll be dead soon, too, if we don't cooperate.

Edmund sniffed the wisps of steam wafting from his teacup. It smelled like batwing tea. He tasted it. It tasted like batwing tea. Perhaps it seemed sweeter than he remembered, but it was good. Then again, anything tasted better than the dirty water the goblins gave them.

"Your mother was an apothecary?" The voice mulled over this information. "Interesting. Oh, I'm sorry. Would you like some cream?"

"What? Oh . . . oh, no. No, thank you."

"Honey or sugar?"

"N-n . . . no, no, sir." Edmund tried to sip the tea again without spilling it all over himself. "I'm . . . I'm f-fine. Thank you."

"Splendid. Then, let us move to other, more important matters, shall we?" A sliver of annoyance crept into the voice. "It would seem you misled your captors, Mr. Kravel and Mr. Gurding, when they questioned you at your first meeting."

The fragile teacup and saucer rattled in Edmund's shaking hands.

What did I tell them?

You were mainly babbling in between sobs.

Reappearing from Edmund's right, a guard set something across the bound man's bloody torso. The man moaned a protest. In retaliation, the guard seized his feet and shoved them deeper into the flames. The man stifled a cry and then screamed. The smell of cooking flesh found Edmund's nostrils. He became very hungry.

Averting his eyes from the soldier's blackened feet, Edmund realized his father's short sword was on the man's chest, its smoky steel glinting within arm's reach.

Edmund leaned closer.

Maybe I could —

Don't even think about it! They'd be on you before you could swing your first blow.

"Where did you get this, Edmund?" the voice asked flatly, its musical quality gone.

"I-I . . ."

What did you tell them before?

I don't remember.

Tell them the truth. It doesn't matter anyway.

Two guards appeared. One forced a wire cage over the soldier's head.

The soldier yelled. "No! Don't! Don't!"

As he thrashed his head from side to side, the other guard dropped in two half-starved rats.

"No!" the soldier screamed again.

"Where did you get this, Edmund?" the voice asked.

The rats grabbed hold of the man's face and scalp. He tried to shake them off, but their curved claws dug deeper into his flesh. One rat looked at Edmund, its pink eyes shining in the growing firelight. Sharp teeth appeared and then bit into the man's cheek. He screeched.

"Where did you get this, Edmund?"

A goblin stepped out of the darkness. He held another cage.

Edmund cried out. "M-m-my, my father! My, my, my father bought it . . . traded for it! Years! Years ago! Traded for it!"

As if digging a tunnel, one of the rats shredded the screaming man's cheek, tearing aside skin until it hit white bone.

"Who did he trade with?" the voice asked.

The other rat tore away a clump of the man's hair. Blood spurted from his scalp. More screams filled the chamber.

Oh god! Oh god!

"Who did he trade with, Edmund?"

"Tom . . . Tom . . . Thomas!"

"Who is Thomas?"

Edmund choked, unable to turn away as one of the rats bit off the shrieking man's earlobe.

"Who is Thomas?"

The rats tore strips of flesh from the man's head. More blood flowed to the floor. The man screamed louder, his body flailing. His legs snapped wildly in the air as if he were having a seizure.

The voice got louder. "Who . . . is . . . Thomas, Edmund?"

Edmund's breath came in short, panicked gasps. "Rood!" he forced out. "He, he, he . . . he lives, he lives in Rood. He sells them!"

"He sells swords like this?" the voice said doubtfully. "If you are lying to me, Edmund . . ."

The guard with the empty wire cage stepped closer.

"Oh god!" Edmund cried.

A rat found the soldier's swollen bottom lip. Wailing, he tried to arch his back, but the straps held him to the iron table.

"I'm, I'm, I'm . . . I'm not! Dear god, I'm not. I'm not lying," Edmund sobbed. "Please!"

The rat tore away part of the man's bottom lip, revealing teeth awash in blood.

"And this Thomas has more weapons like this one?" the voice asked.

The other rat, its fangs and fur now stained red, lifted one of the man's eyelids, revealing a blue eye twitching in all directions. The rat bit down. The man's shrieks hit an even higher note, his feet kicking above the dancing flames.

Edmund stood, his teacup and saucer shattering across the floor. Several hands gripped his shoulders. They forced him into his chair. He covered his eyes.

"Oh, god! Oh, god! Oh, god!"

"Thomas has more weapons like this one, Edmund?" the voice asked again.

"Yes!" Edmund cried out. "No! I-I-I-I . . ."

"Which is it? Yes or no?"

His face nearly gone, the bound man screamed until he had no breath, inhaled, and screamed some more. Goblins hooted and cheered.

"He, he, he sells antiques!" Edmund said. "Armor . . . armor and weapons. He has a lot, a lot of different things. Very old things. Oh god! Make it stop! Make it stop! For the love of god, make it stop. Mercy! Mercy!"

"Does he have more weapons like this one, Edmund?"

Edmund peered through his fingers, aghast. A rat clung to the wire cage, the man's eyelid in its mouth.

"Does he have more—?"

"I don't know!" Edmund shouted. "I . . . I haven't seen any! He has a barrel . . . a barrel! He has a barrel of swords. In his front room. Oh, dear god! Mercy. Mercy, please. Give him mercy!"

"Where is Rood, Edmund?"

"South of Azagra. South of the old ruins. Three days' walk from Lake Nuvelle. By the crossroads of the old north-south and east-west roads. Please! Give him mercy!"

"You give him mercy," the voice from the shadows replied, calmer. "Take the sword and end his suffering."

"What?"

"End his suffering."

"I, I, I can't. I can't. Oh, god. Give him mercy!"

Another shriek stabbed at Edmund. One of the rats found the man's eyeball.

"Thank you, Edmund," the voice said gently. "Your assistance is greatly appreciated. I'll have the guards bring you some food. You have certainly earned it. We'll meet again soon."

Retrieving the short sword, a guard wrapped it in a clean, white cloth.

"You really are a heartless bastard, aren't you?" the goblin said to Edmund as he watched the man convulse. A rat was snout-deep in his eye socket. "I would've killed him. But that's just me."

A door opened. Red torchlight streamed in.

Edmund leapt toward it. But a guard blocked his path.

"Have a seat." He shoved Edmund to the overturned chair. "We'll bring you something to eat in a little while. In the meanwhile—" He nodded to the wailing soldier. "—enjoy the show."

The door closed. A ring of darkness returned to the room.

Falling to his knees, Edmund bawled while the soldier begged him to end his life.

Chapter Eighteen

Edmund scratched his beard. He'd always wanted one. He thought it would make him appear more attractive and scholarly. But he could never tolerate the itchy stage when it first started coming in. Now that he had one several inches long, he wanted nothing more than a pair of scissors and a razor. He picked a louse from his chin. Its pallid body twisted between his dirty fingernails. He ate it.

"I'm not going to take this anymore," Turd said. "You haven't spoken since they brought you back. I don't know what happened, and I don't care. But either you'll help us get out of here or you won't, which is it?"

"Turd," Pond Scum said. "Give him time. He was covered in blood."

"It wasn't his blood!" Turd said.

"I'm inclined to agree with Turd," Vomit said. "I can't keep doing this, day after day, year after year. I want to go home or die trying. I say we begin making plans."

Crazy Bastard hopped in a circle.

Pond Scum tossed a small stone into the middle of the pit. "But three guards are watching us now."

"And why's that? I wonder. When they brought him back, everything changed. They're suddenly watching us more closely." Turd jabbed a finger at Edmund. "I want to know what he told them!"

Edmund didn't respond. He didn't know what to say anymore, so he said nothing. How many days had it been since he watched rats devour a screaming man's face? He couldn't tell. Time slipped away like smoke in the breeze. He got up when told, did what the goblins said, and then returned to the pit—where he lay in the dirt, staring up into the darkness. For the days he performed a full day's work, Vomit gave him some food. But it was never enough. Not that it mattered. As the others slept, he made his own. The magically created biscuits were dry and tasteless. But they cured his hunger pains and gave him the strength to go on for another day.

"Look, Filth." Vomit crawled closer to Edmund's area. "They've questioned all of us from time to time. We understand what they must've done to you. But you have to decide whether to give up or go on. We want to go on. We want to get out of here and go home. But we need your help. We need your—abilities."

"Magic!" Crazy Bastard chuckled, spinning around like a top.

"Can we count on you when the time comes?" Vomit asked.

Edmund let his head fall in their direction. He was exhausted to his soul. And there were images that wouldn't leave his mind. They plagued him even when he found fitful sleep. He stared at his pit mates' drawn faces. They were as bad off as he was—worse even.

"Filth!" a guard's voice bellowed into their hole.

The Pit Dwellers went rigid. They hadn't heard the goblin approach. How long had he been listening? Had he overheard anything?

A ladder slid into the pit.

"Get your worthless ass up here," the guard shouted.

Edmund forced himself to his feet, then tightened the makeshift belt he used to keep his pants from falling. He climbed the ladder.

"Move that slow tomorrow," the guard said, "and you'll feel the kiss of my whip. But for now, you're in the hands of these gentlemen."

Edmund lifted his unblinking eyes and found Kravel grinning at him.

"There he is, Mr. Gurding!" Kravel said, radiating with pleasure. "Looking splendid as always."

"I'm not sure I like the beard," Gurding said. "But at least he's not fat anymore."

"There's nothing like good hard work to whittle away both the body and the mind, wouldn't you say, Mr. Gurding?"

"I prefer the use of knives."

"Ah! So true. But we'll converse more about such things later. For now, His Majesty would like another word with you, my good Filth. This way, if you please."

Edmund followed Kravel and Gurding through a myriad of passages and climbed flight after flight of stairs. The walls around them changed from hewn rock to mortared stone as they entered the bottom cellars of some fortress or castle.

They kept ascending.

Fresh air, tinged with the fragrance of damp pine needles, brushed Edmund's face. Only a three-foot stone wall separated him from the outside. The torment was so great, he wanted to cry. But he didn't have the energy or the tears left.

Memorize the layout of this place.

Why bother?

Climbing a circular stair, Edmund saw above them a set of gilded double doors blocked by two guards in polished breastplates.

His captors halted.

"Here we go," Kravel said merrily. "As much as we'd love to join you, we've been instructed to wait here. So—" He bowed. "—good luck to you."

"Yes," Gurding said. "Don't do anything stupid."

Edmund examined the double doors. They were big enough for a troll.

"Come! Come!" Kravel propelled Edmund forward. "You don't want to keep His Majesty waiting."

Edmund trudged to the landing, his tired feet dragging on each exquisitely crafted marble step.

"He's going to do something stupid," Gurding told Kravel. "I know it."

"Quite possibly," Kravel said. "That's the fun of humans. You never know how they'll get themselves killed."

When Edmund reached the landing, a guard opened one of the doors. The aroma of roasted meat rolled out to greet him. His stomach rumbled like an approaching thunderstorm. He inhaled deeply.

He peeked cautiously into the room.

He stared into what appeared to be a formal dining hall. Along the far wall were seven slit-like windows, open and looking out into the black night. Through them, a breeze blew, chilled and damp. To his left, an inviting fire crackled and popped on the hearth. But the long table laden with lit candles and covered serving trays drew his immediate consideration.

I don't know which is better, the fresh air or the food.

You can't eat fresh air.

Edmund shuffled forward, drawn in by the exquisite smell. Behind him, the door closed with a decisive thump. He surveyed the table again.

There are probably severed heads underneath those covers. Or bloody rats. Whatever it is, let's hope it's dead and well-seasoned.

A familiar voice called gaily, "Edmund!"

Edmund shivered, but not from the cool air. For a moment, he forgot about the food.

"Please," the voice said as if in mid-song. "Please, come in. Have a seat and enjoy! Consider this meal a small part of your reward."

Reward?

"Where are you?" Edmund found himself muttering as he scanned the chamber. Two doors trimmed with gold stood shut on either side of the hall. Yet the voice seemed to be coming from nearby.

"Ah. Always the inquisitive one!" the voice said. "I can't tell you how happy I am that you've survived this long. Happy doesn't even come close to what I'm feeling, I can assure you. Please, have a seat and eat. You must be hungry. Or, if you wish, feel free to peer out the windows. It's a splendid view, especially this time of year. I love seeing the colorful leaves in the foothills."

Stumbling to the table, Edmund sat, more to rest his exhausted body than from the desire to eat whatever was under the silver covers. He was hungry, painfully hungry. But he'd cure that once his pit mates fell asleep.

"Tell me, Edmund, do you believe in what your kind calls magic?"

Edmund went rigid.

"M-m-magic? Magic?" His hand instinctively reached for the bottle of wine, almost knocking it over in the process. "No. No, I don't. Sir." He tried to laugh as if the idea of magic was ridiculous. But the sound came out forced and cackling. "Who, who believes in magic anymore?" He laughed again.

"Interesting," the voice said. "I would have anticipated a different answer altogether. However, that merely shows you are full of surprises, as Mr. Kravel and Mr. Gurding have learned. At any rate, to answer your question then, I'll say I'm close by and leave it at that. I hope you don't mind eating by yourself. Please, try the wine. It's a very old vintage. Exceptional for its flavor and body. After you finish, we'll have coffee if you are so inclined."

Expecting the worst, Edmund lifted a lid from one of the serving trays and found sautéed mushrooms with wild onions and sage. His stomach murmured again.

Oh, that looks so good.

Remember where you are.

He lifted another lid. Steam swirled around baked apples dusted with cinnamon. His mouth watered.

Remember where you are. Remember what he did last time. You can always make your own food.

Under the third lid, he found a golden-brown chicken glazed with honey. His stomach jumped over itself.

"Do you approve?" the voice asked.

Edmund nodded. Then, realizing the voice might not be able to see him, he said, "I'm, I'm sure it's splendid."

Edmund sniffed again and moaned in delight.

"Don't worry," the voice said. "I haven't poisoned or tampered with it in any way. Believe me, I want you to enjoy yourself this evening. I think we'll become good friends, you and I."

Edmund sipped the wine, his palate rejoicing. "Friends?"

Don't drink too much. That's probably his ploy. He wants to get you drunk and extract information from you.

What information? Besides, being drunk would be wonderful right now.

"Yes, friends," the voice said. "Indeed, I might even flatter myself to consider you a student or a mentee at some point. We, after all, have a great deal in common."

Edmund lifted the cover of the final serving tray and found warm bread.

"Common?" he repeated doubtfully. He stuffed a buttery roll in his mouth.

"You're an antiquarian, I'm told. And I have a particular fondness for books, though . . . I must say, probably for different reasons. Tell me, what's your favorite subject of inquiry?"

Edmund's soiled fingers wrenched off one of the chicken legs. He bit into it.

"History."

"Ah, yes. That's one of mine as well. Tell me, who's your favorite historical figure?"

Edmund added a couple of mushrooms to what he was chewing, gulped the wine, and swallowed what he could.

"Iliandor."

He bit into the chicken leg again, tearing the tender meat from the bone.

"Iliandor?" A tenseness materialized in the voice as he pronounced each syllable. "Yes, well. Being a child of the North, that would be logical. It's interesting you selected him out of all the fallen leaders from your culture. Extraordinarily interesting. Tell me, Edmund, do you believe in fate?"

Shrugging, Edmund pushed a piece of bread and then another mushroom into his mouth.

"I certainly believe in fate," the voice said. "And I believe you were brought to me for a purpose. A purpose that will serve us both well—very well, if you permit me to be dramatic."

What's he talking about?

Who cares? Eat as much as you can before he takes it away.

Edmund drank some wine and swallowed hard. He reached for the hot mashed apples.

"I have a question for you, Edmund. If you lie, well . . . I'm sure you can imagine the consequences."

Rats in a cage.

Don't lie. Tell him whatever he wants to know!

Tilting the bowl, Edmund spooned the apples directly into his waiting mouth.

"Why were you in Tol Helen?"

Edmund drank an entire glass of wine in one long swallow. Then he wiped his mouth with a formerly white linen napkin now covered with food and dirt.

"I, I . . . I wanted to be something I wasn't," he said, having thought about the same question many times over the past month. "I wanted . . . . I don't know. To be well thought of. I wanted to be a hero, I suppose."

He took another bite from a buttery roll.

"Fascinating," the voice said. "You realize, don't you, heroes rarely die of old age in the comfort of their beds."

At least they do something with their lives.

He's going to kill you. Or worse. Don't you understand? Sooner or later, he'll put a rat cage over your head. You're going to die here.

Edmund ripped a hunk of meat from the chicken's side and shoved it into his mouth. He refilled his goblet.

"You wanted more power among your people," the voice said. "More influence. I understand completely. But why go to Tol Helen, of all places? Were you searching for something? Something in particular?"

He knows. You might as well tell him.

Draining his wine glass again, Edmund leaned back in his chair with a contented sigh.

"Our . . . our new king, King Lionel, he . . . he issued an edict. Whoever finds the Star of Iliandor will be given lordship over his former fiefdom."

"And you thought the Star was in Tol Helen? Why?"

"I have Iliandor's d-diary. Or I did. It's in my library."

Edmund pulled off one of the chicken's wings. He wondered if he could somehow hide it in the remains of his tattered clothing.

"The diary hinted that the Star, his sword 'Druil,' and some . . . and some of his other belongings were hidden there," Edmund went on as he ate. "I got as far as the tower, but Kravel and Gurding captured me before I could search it."

"You want to be a lord?" the voice asked, amused. "To govern over others?"

Edmund nibbled along the chicken wing's bone, his teeth extracting every piece of meat they could.

"I don't know," he said. "I w-wanted something I didn't have, I suppose."

He bit into a roll, hoping that having his mouth full would decrease the amount of talking he'd have to do.

"Understandable," the voice said. "I believe we're all like that to some degree. However, let me ask you this. Did you find anything when you were in the cavern under Tol Helen?"

Edmund blinked slowly. The wine made his vision go out of focus.

"Anything at all?" the voice prodded.

There was something on the wall. What was it?

"You seem to remember something," the voice said.

Chewing, Edmund pushed himself straighter in the chair.

"There, there was something on the wall," he said.

"What was it? Do you recall?"

"Some writing."

"Yes, yes. Could you read it? It was written in Dunael. Your people spoke it once upon a time. I understand you can read many languages."

You might as well tell him. If you keep him happy, maybe he'll give you more meals like this.

"It said: 'The salvation of humanity can be found in buildings of wise men, doubly so in optimism of the learned, and in knowledge that is written on a daily basis.'"

Excitement flared in the voice. "Correct! Now, Edmund, do you have any idea what that means? It's a riddle of some sort, perhaps referencing something from your people I'm not aware of. Do you know the answer?"

Edmund tried to stifle a yawn but failed. Partly chewed food fell from his open mouth. He looked at the half-empty bottle of wine and wondered again if it had been drugged. Then he realized he didn't care. He'd sleep well either way.

"Edmund, this is important. Do you know what those words mean?"

Don't tell him. Play stupid!

But I don't have the slightest idea what it means. I couldn't tell him if I wanted to.

"They're simply words," he said through another yawn. "Poorly written, at that. The capitalization and grammar were all off."

The voice exhaled, frustrated.

"Very well, Edmund," it said. "I can see you're fatigued. We'll continue this later. But I want you to understand that if you ascertain what those lines mean, I'll reward you with more than a good meal. If you solve the riddle—you can go free."

Chapter Nineteen

"All right, vermin!" a guard called into the pit.

He was several hours early if the Pit Dwellers could judge time in the all-consuming darkness. Stretching in the dirt, Edmund groaned, the sensations of a pleasant dream fading in his mind. The other Pit Dwellers sprang to their feet and formed a line.

"Because of the benevolent love of His Majesty," the guard said, "I have a surprise for you worthless maggots."

Realizing where he was, Edmund slowly got in line behind Crazy Bastard.

"Naughty, naughty," Crazy Bastard whispered, his pungent breath punching Edmund's nose.

Edmund shoved Crazy Bastard's face away. Crazy Bastard shoved back.

"Filth," the guard bellowed, "stand at attention or I'll—" Then the goblin seemed to remember something. He stifled his anger. "Actually," he said in an overly kind tone, "it's because of Master Filth you'll not be working today."

Everybody looked at Edmund.

Edmund yawned.

"What did you do?" Turd snarled.

"But," Vomit called to the guard, "what about food? We're willing to work for our meal, sir. We'll work hard. Whatever Filth did, he should pay. Not us! Punish him!"

"Oh," the guard replied, "I think your lots are all cast together. As goes Filth, so go you all."

Their heads turned toward Edmund again. Only Pond Scum didn't have loathing in his eyes.

"I'm going to snap your damn neck," Turd whispered. "I don't care if you are a mag—"

"As for food—" The guard lowered a large basket into the pit. "Enjoy the generosity of your King and Savior."

Vomit limped to the basket and peered inside. Unhooking it from the attached rope, he dragged the basket carefully to the others. But the smell already told them what it contained.

"It's chicken," Vomit said in disbelief. "Cooked and, and seasoned and . . . everything!"

Turd, Pond Scum, and Crazy Bastard pushed around the basket, trying to get a glimpse of what was inside.

"There're three chickens!" Pond Scum said. "What's that?"

Vomit stuck his finger into a bowl and tasted it. "Baked apples! With cinnamon."

There was shoving as three sets of hands reached in at once.

"Hold on! Hold on!" Vomit shouted. "I'll parcel it out. Give me some room, or some of it might get wasted. Give me some room!"

Turd grabbed Crazy Bastard and Pond Scum by their ears and hauled them back.

"Oh, look at this," Vomit said. "I can't believe it!"

"What?" Pond Scum asked.

"Plates," Vomit said in awe. "They gave us plates. Actual plates! And there's a jug of clean water. And napkins!"

They all fell silent, marveling at the basket's glorious contents.

"Magic," Crazy Bastard muttered. "Magic!"

Chapter Twenty

"It's quite simple," the voice said as Edmund dried his wrinkled body with a white cotton towel. He hadn't been clean since he bathed in the River Celerin before the troll chased him to Tol Helen. So, when the guards led him to a small chamber with a copper tub full of steaming water, he didn't think twice about casting aside his rags and getting in. He lounged there until his calluses softened and tore from his prune-like hands.

"I'll give you and your colleagues certain liberties for ten days or so," the disembodied voice said. "During which time I want you to consider the lines written in the cavern under Tol Helen."

Edmund dried his long, clean hair. He wondered whether he could find something to tie it back, so it wouldn't keep falling into his face. But then he remembered where he was and why he'd been so filthy.

"But, sir," Edmund said. "They're only words. They're meaningless."

There was an oppressive silence.

"Edmund," the voice said with a hint of irritation. "No lover of books would call any passage 'only words.' Especially something scratched into rock where few individuals have ever tread. Those words mean something. And I need to know what."

Edmund dried his ears again merely to enjoy the mundane tasks he once took for granted.

"S-s-s-supp-supposing you're correct. Suppose those lines are a riddle, and I can bring meaning to them. What then? What do I get? I, I mean . . . sir. I'm sorry, that came out wrong."

"No. I want you to speak freely. You want to know why you should do as I ask. It's a fair question. As I told you, if you arrive at the riddle's answer, I'll give you what you want."

"You'll let me go?"

"You have my oath."

He's lying. Why would he let you go? Once you give him what he wants, he won't need you anymore. There'd be no more food. No more baths. No more special treatment. You'll be thrown into the pits and left there until you die.

Edmund picked up the soiled remains of his pants and tattered shirt, reluctant to have them touch his pristine body.

"I can imagine what you are feeling," the voice said. "The doubt. The torment. After all, why would I let you go? What would stop me from reneging on my word?"

"The thought had crossed m-m-my, my mind, sir."

"Perhaps you should consider the other side of the equation. What do you think will happen if you don't solve the riddle?"

Edmund felt his face, imagining the pain of rats ripping it apart, burrowing into his eye socket as he screamed helplessly. He struggled to inhale.

"Give me the answer to the riddle, and you'll fare much better than if you don't. I think that's something you can believe. Does that simplify matters for you?"

"Wh-wh-what, what if I try and I fail?" Edmund asked. "Or if I . . . I come up with the wrong answer?"

"Then you'll work for me until your life ends."

Air exited Edmund's lungs in fitful spurts. "Sir . . . why, why me?"

"Because something tells me you're the one I've been waiting for. You have certain knowledge—a certain perspective—that all my other servants lack. You know the language and the culture from which the riddle sprang. And I'm sure you know who wrote it and under what circumstances."

"Oh?" Edmund replied, feeling compelled to say something.

"Yes, Edmund. You've read Iliandor's diary. I have as well."

"You? You've read his diary?"

He's lying. He couldn't possibly have—

"Indeed. My spies obtained it for me years ago, or at least a copy. As a text, it isn't very interesting, as I'm sure you'll agree. But the last pages reveal a hint as to the whereabouts of something I've been seeking for many ages. You followed that same hint and found what I did not. That makes you valuable to me. Knowledge is always more valuable than gold or swords, wouldn't you agree?"

I'd rather have a sword right now.

Remember what he said. You're valuable to him. He won't hurt you if you have value.

"What?" Edmund realized the voice was waiting for a response. "Yes. Yes, it is. B-b-but . . . but tell me, what are you looking for? Perhaps you can tell me that, and we could start there."

"No, my dear Edmund, I think you and I will have some secrets. After all, if you ever learned too much, I would not allow you to live long enough to tell my enemies, nor would I let you return to your precious Rood. So, for now, concern yourself with solving the riddle. You have ten days. After that, I'll get angry. Do you understand?"

Edmund shivered. "Y-y-yes, yes, sir. I understand. I won't let you down, sir."

Chapter Twenty-One

"Okay," Pond Scum said. "Say it again. How did it go exactly?"

Somebody moaned.

"It doesn't matter," Turd grumbled. "It's pointless."

"I agree with Turd." Vomit rolled onto his back. His stomach was distended from all the meals the guard kept bringing. "Whether we solve it or not, it isn't as if they'd let you or anybody else go. They're trying to torment us by giving us false hope like they always do."

"The salvation of humanity can be found in the buildings of wise men," Pond Scum said to himself. "What's found in the buildings of wise men?"

"Chicken!" Crazy Bastard clucked from his area of the pit.

"Shut up, Scum," Turd said.

"Chicken," Crazy Bastard repeated softer.

In another pit, somebody screamed that he couldn't take it anymore and he wanted to go home. It wouldn't last long. It never did. Either the guards took care of it, or the Pit Dwellers did. A goblin cursed. A whip snapped. The cries became muffled and then ended abruptly. An unnerving silence filled the cavern.

"I think . . ." Edmund trailed off.

You think what? You don't have a clue what the riddle's answer is.

I have to do something. I don't want to get that voice angry.

"What?" Vomit asked. "Do you have a solution?"

"No." Edmund scratched his beard. He'd given up pondering the words days before. "But I think it's time to plan our escape. Turd, how are you feeling?"

"Stronger than I have since I got here." The big man sat up. "What do we do? What's your plan?"

What are you doing?

"I don't know," Edmund said. "But I think now's the time. We've had ten days of rest. We've been well fed. Things won't get any better for us, answer or not. If we don't act now, we'll slowly deteriorate to what we were before, half-starved and weak."

"Exactly!" Turd said. "Let's make a go of it the next time they take us to a worksite!"

"What about food and water?" Pond Scum asked. "What about having something to carry water in so we can hide where they won't look for us?"

Are you really going to do this?

If not now, when?

"Let's take the weapons you made," Edmund said. "I can take one, I think. I still have enough clothing left to hide it."

In the blackness, somebody crawled across the pit.

"Maybe put another in one of your boots," Vomit said.

"How will we do this?" Turd whispered. "Should we have some sort of signal?"

Somebody tapped Edmund's forehead.

"Think! Think! Think!" Crazy Bastard giggled and then scurried to his area.

"I think," Edmund said, ignoring Crazy Bastard, "I think we need to do it before we get to the worksite. I'd much rather fight the two guards conveying us than the three who supervise our work. The guards at the site have their bows ready. The guards who escort us tend to have only clubs and whips, occasionally a sword. We can reduce their effectiveness in the narrower tunnels. Maybe we could overpower them."

"Yes!" Turd said. "That's exactly what I was thinking. Good! So, what do we do?"

"Will you set them on fire?" Vomit asked. "Can you shoot fireballs? That'd make them think twice about recapturing us!"

Are you sure you want to go through with this? Is this how you want it all to end?

I don't want a cage of rats over my head. I'd rather kill myself than have that happen.

"Pond," Edmund said to the darkness. "Are you with us?"

There was no answer.

"Pond?"

Reluctantly, Pond Scum spoke. "I'm with you. But—"

"But nothing," Turd said. "Go on, Filth. What's the plan?"

Edmund sat up. He inhaled through his nose and then let his lungs slowly deflate.

"Okay," he said with a degree of finality. "This is what I want to do. The next time they're transporting us to a worksite, let's line up like this: Vomit in front, then me, then Crazy, then Turd, then Pond. When I cough twice in a row like this—"

The clinking of armor cut him off. It grew louder.

"Oh no," Pond Scum said.

"Shut up, Scum," Turd said. "Hurry. What then?"

A dim redness grew above their pit.

"What then?" Turd repeated louder.

It's too late now. They've come for their answer.

The clinking stopped. A guard with a torch looked at them. Then, the heads of Kravel and Gurding appeared. Kravel smiled and gave a slight bow.

"Filth!" he called. "Wonderful to see you and your charming friends again. Plotting your escape, no doubt. However, I'm afraid it'll have to wait. His Majesty requests your splendid presence. Please come with us if you'll be so kind."

A ladder slid into the pit.

Edmund exchanged glances with his pit mates.

"Filth," Kravel said, "if you please."

Edmund lifted himself to his feet.

"Good luck," Pond Scum whispered.

"Yes." Kravel laughed. "Good luck, indeed! Good luck to all of us. But, come, come. Let's not dally. It's an important day for you, I'm told. I trust you've thought long and hard about the riddle we found."

What are you going to do?

I don't know.

Edmund stepped onto the bottom rung and slid his hands upward along the ladder.

"Chicken!" Crazy Bastard screamed. Like a dog, he started digging where the sharpened ribs were buried.

Springing to his feet, Turd kicked him in the stomach. "Get to your area!"

Breathless and on his back, Crazy Bastard stared up at the giant. He pointed a frail finger at Turd. "Chicken," he whimpered.

"Charming." Kravel clapped his hands and rubbed them together. "All right, then! Off we go, Filth. His Highness is very eager to see you. Very eager, indeed! Say farewell to your friends."

Reluctantly, Edmund climbed out of the pit.

Chapter Twenty-Two

"I must say," the voice said. "I'm disappointed."

"I'm, I'm . . . s-s-sor-sorry, sorry, sir," Edmund said for the third time.

"I'm sure you are."

"What would you like us to do with him, Your Highness?" Gurding asked. "May we check the length of his intestines?"

"No, Mr. Gurding," the voice replied. "You may have an opportunity to do that later. And, if you do, allow me first to place a wager. But for now, I'd like to try a different tack."

He's going to kill me! This is it! I'm dead!

"You know, Edmund," the voice said. "There's an old saying among my people — 'If you want a dog to eat, take away its water.'"

What the hell does that mean?

It can't be good.

Edmund opened his mouth, closed it, and swallowed.

"Mr. Kravel," the voice said. "I think it is time to have another series of Games, wouldn't you agree?"

"I would indeed, Your Majesty," Kravel said. "It's been a few weeks. Shall we enter Filth in them? And if so, what should the game be?"

"No. No. You misunderstand me. I want Edmund to select one of his colleagues to play. After all, if he is to fill Iliandor's station someday, he'll have to get used to making difficult decisions."

What's he talking about?

He's going to kill one of your pit mates. You'll choose which one.

I can't—

"Edmund will keep putting his friends in the Games, one by one," the voice continued. "When they've all expired, it'll be his turn. Hopefully, he'll have the riddle's answer by then."

My turn?

"What do you say, Edmund?" the voice said. "Who shall go first?"

You have to figure out the riddle, or they'll all die. Think!

"Edmund?" the voice said.

Edmund dragged his moist palms across his bare chest. "I'm . . . I'm sor—"

"Yes," the voice replied, its tone growing frigid. "You've said that more than once. Frankly, I'm growing weary of hearing it. Which of your colleagues do you wish to play in the Games?"

I can't.

Edmund looked wild-eyed at Kravel and then at Gurding.

"I'd go for the tall fellow," Gurding whispered. "He's your biggest threat."

"Mr. Gurding . . ." the voice said sternly.

Bowing, Gurding retreated a pace.

Turd?

You may need him in the future.

This is ridiculous! I can't kill anybody.

You're not killing them.

I might as well be.

Edmund looked at Kravel again.

"Edmund?" the voice prodded louder.

"I'm . . . I'm s-sor—" He stopped, not wanting to irritate the disembodied voice more than he already had.

Kravel stepped forward. "Perhaps, Your Eminence, it would help Master Filth if he knew the game."

There was a grumble of frustration.

"Very well," the voice said. "We'll have armed combat between one of Edmund's friends and Gra' Runda."

Kravel waved a hand as if Gra' Runda was nothing to worry about.

"Who will it be, Edmund?" the voice asked. "I won't accept anything but an answer—unless you want to fight Gra' Runda yourself."

What should I do?

"Edmund? I am getting angry."

Edmund opened his mouth. Then he heard a name pop out. "Crazy Bastard!"

Kravel and Gurding whistled, impressed.

"It's not going to be much of a battle," Gurding said.

"Crazy Bastard?" the voice said. "Is he still alive? Interesting. However, I believe you two are missing Edmund's intentions. It's quite fascinating. On one hand, he's hoping to put the elderly fool out of his misery, which makes him feel noble and righteous. On the other hand, he retains anybody who might assist him later on. Further, those individuals will owe him a great deal of gratitude for not selecting them."

"He is a crafty one," Kravel said. "As I have indicated before."

"Crafty indeed," the voice said. "Mr. Kravel, set up the Games. And escort Edmund to one of the upper cells. He won't be returning to the pits."

Chapter Twenty-Three

Edmund lay awake on a double bed, the lambskin blankets under him rather than covering his mostly naked body, despite the icy draft rattling the windowpanes. The cell Kravel escorted him to was actually a small bedroom, pleasantly furnished with a three-drawer oak dresser, a sapphire-blue porcelain basin for washing his hands and face, an elegant rug, and a formidable door that locked from the outside. Along the door's edge were many deep claw marks, as if a dog had tried to dig through the wood. Some of the trim was stained red.

Edmund stared out the narrow window, his breath appearing ghostly white. Wisps of milky clouds obscured the bright moon and shivering stars.

He was in a lofty tower, standing isolated among the many peaks and crevices of what he guessed was the northernmost part of the Haegthorn Mountains. Below him were the tops of pine trees stretching down until they disappeared into the bluish night. Three inches of snow covered his windowsill.

He found Panis, the Guiding Star. Shimmering yellow, it was much lower in the night sky than he'd expected.

It must be mid-winter.

Time is meaningless here.

Depressed, he studied a painting on the wall depicting a flower-speckled field of gently rolling green hills. It reminded him of the farms around Rood.

I wonder if I'll ever see them again.

The lock clattered. Then, the door swung open, its hinges screaming like somebody being eaten by rats.

"Filth!" Kravel entered the cell. "Wonderful! You're still here."

"Where would he go?" Gurding asked, perplexed.

"Have you answered the riddle to His Majesty's satisfaction?"

"No," Edmund muttered.

"Well then—" Kravel motioned to the hallway. "Shall we proceed?"

Proceed where?

They're not letting you go, that's for sure.

Edmund followed the goblins down a wide circular staircase. Every couple of hundred feet, they passed landings where guards usually stood, blocking iron-reinforced doors with their polearms and stern expressions. Now, the landings were empty.

They descended below the tower into a labyrinth of squalid subterranean chambers, gathering halls, and dimly lit meandering passageways. A few goblins ran here and there as if they were late for an urgent appointment.

This would be the ideal time to escape. Nobody's around.

Edmund slid his eyes to his left. Next to him, Gurding spun a knife on his finger, his lips moving in rhythm to some internal dialogue.

Edmund slid his eyes to the right. Kravel grinned at him, winking as if he were in on some secret.

There's no hope. I'll never get out of here.

Then solve the damn riddle! What's in the buildings of wise men?

Somewhere in front of them, a deep rumbling grew, like the pounding hooves from hundreds of racehorses.

Rapids? A waterfall?

Whatever it is, it won't be pleasant. Brace yourself for the worst.

The roar grew louder as they approached a grand archway. Edmund took two steps through it and stopped.

They were in an immense oval arena, ringed with countless blazing torches and scores of magnificent chandeliers hanging from the domed ceiling. Tens of thousands of goblins sat along the elevated sides of the chamber—cheering, screaming, and stomping their feet. Their stench was overpowering.

There . . . there must be thirty thousand of them!

The goblins in these mountains were eradicated. How could there be so—?

Kravel beckoned Edmund forward. "Mustn't be late."

"Yes," Gurding said. "I don't want to miss this. I have wagers on the outcome."

"Wagers?" Kravel replied.

"If the old guy stays alive for two minutes, I double my money. If he draws blood, I triple it."

"His own blood?"

"We never specified."

"Ah!"

Kravel guided Edmund around the uppermost lip of the cavern. He pointed to an unoccupied bench. As Edmund sat, a tremendous clamor erupted around him. Everyone stood. Edmund and his captors did as well.

Far below, Crazy Bastard flew into the arena as if physically thrown. He skidded face-first onto the sand-covered floor as a portcullis slammed behind him. Running to the gate, Crazy Bastard shook its iron bars, looking in every direction at once. Letting go, he slumped to the ground, knees drawn to his chin.

Goblins threw refuse at him—rotten pieces of food, balls of excrement, dead rats. Whenever something struck him, the crowd jeered wildly. Through the ordeal, Crazy Bastard sat motionless, like a child unable to leave his bed for fear of the monster in the shadows.

From high overhead, a series of ropes lowered a wooden table arrayed with various weapons, shields, and armor. Crazy Bastard bounded onto the table and attempted to shimmy up the ropes. When he fell sprawling on the sand, the crowd laughed en masse. Crazy Bastard scurried under the table and rocked, his arms wrapped around his legs. One by one, the goblins took their seats.

Edmund started to cry.

Oh, Crazy! I'm so sorry! Please forgive me!

Gurding shook his head. "I'm going to lose a lot of money on this."

"I don't know," Kravel said cheerfully. "He might surprise you. Look at our friend Filth here. He's still alive."

Gurding glowered at Edmund. "Yes. And he's cost me a great deal of money as well."

A restless murmur rustled through the stands. Off to their right, an elderly female goblin with a missing arm stood and shouted, "Gra . . . Run . . . da! Gra . . . Run . . . da!" Others around her took up the chant. Soon, the entire chamber shook with each syllable.

"Gra . . . Run . . . da! Gra . . . Run . . . da! Gra . . . Run . . . da!"

Leaning closer to Kravel, Edmund hollered, "What are they saying?"

But Kravel couldn't hear him.

"Gra . . . Run . . . da! Gra . . . Run . . . da! Gra . . . Run . . . da!" The chanting quickened as thirty thousand goblins stomped and clapped in unison.

At the far end of the oval arena, massive gates opened. Through the shadows strode a gruesome figure, several times the height of even the tallest human and much broader. He had an enormous bald head, a pushed-up nose like a boar, and short tusks that swept out from his bottom jaw.

"Gra . . . Run . . . da! Gra . . . Run . . . da! Gra . . . Run . . . da!"

Edmund shook his head in disbelief. "An ogre? He's expected to fight an ogre?"

"Don't feel guilty," Kravel shouted, clapping with the rest of the multitudes. "At least the old fella will die quickly."

"But hopefully not too quickly," Gurding yelled.

This is your fault. His blood is on your hands. Turd would've at least had a fighting chance.

The ogre stepped into the pulsating stadium. He raised his massive arms to the crowd, a spiked club in one hand, a net in the other. He flexed his bulging muscles, tattoos rippling. Everybody but Edmund screamed, "Gra . . . Run . . . da! Gra . . . Run . . . da! Gra . . . Run . . . da!"

"I can't watch this." Edmund sat.

"Suit yourself," Gurding said. "But it won't change the outcome, you know. You might as well watch the show. You might learn something useful."

This is horrible. Poor Crazy Bastard.

"Gra . . . Run . . . da! Gra . . . Run . . . da! Gra . . . Run . . . da!"

Kravel nudged Edmund's shoulder. Wiping his tears away, Edmund looked at him.

"It's always interesting to see how far Gra' Runda can knock somebody's head from their shoulders." Kravel pointed to the opposite end of the cavern. "Once, he got an entire skull to reach the last row!"

"Gra . . . Run . . . da! Gra . . . Run . . . da! Gra . . . Run . . . da!"

Edmund put his face in his hands, tears streaming down his cheeks.

The poor old guy. He managed to survive in the mines for years, maybe even decades, only to be butchered for their wicked amusement.

"Gra . . . Run . . . da! Gra . . . Run . . . da! Gra . . . Run . . . da!"

He's getting butchered because you picked him.

What was I to do? I had to pick somebody.

"Gra . . . Run . . . da! Gra . . . Run . . . da! Gra . . . Run . . . da!"

Turd could've fought back. With those weapons, he might've even won.

Against an ogre?

The ogre bellowed at the crowd.

The crowd bellowed back.

"Gra . . . Run . . . da! Gra . . . Run . . . da! Gra . . . Run . . . da!"

I can't believe this!

Like Kravel said, at least he'll die quickly.

That's no consolation.

The ogre howled again, the net whirling over his head.

Pretty soon, you'll have to send Vomit and Pond Scum.

Thinking about Pond Scum's death intensified his torment.

What am I going to do?

Solve the damned riddle!

The crowd roared. "Gra . . . Run . . . da! Gra . . . Run—"

And then, to a goblin, everybody fell silent. A throaty gurgling sound filled the stadium, followed by a heavy thud. Thirty thousand goblins inhaled. Edmund leaped to his feet.

At the far end of the arena lay the ogre, sprawled on the sand, club and net beside him. Crazy Bastard jumped up and down on the ogre's chest, kicking like a convulsive monkey. The ogre didn't move.

"What the . . ." Edmund said. "What . . . what the hell happened?"

"You should've been watching," Gurding said.

"What the . . .?"

The goblins hollering and cursing. A blizzard of debris rained down into the arena as goblins threw whatever they could get their hands on. A deep horn blew three times. The portcullis withdrew into the ceiling. Crazy Bastard bolted into the open tunnel.

"What the . . .?"

"We'd better leave before this turns ugly." Kravel ushered Edmund out of the cavern.

"Wh-wh-what happened?" Edmund tried to glimpse the prostrate ogre through the furious crowd.

"Life happened, Master Filth." Kravel led him toward the exit. The shouts behind them grew even louder. "And life is full of surprises, wouldn't you say, Mr. Gurding?"

"Surprises?" Gurding said. "I believe you are understating things again, Mr. Kravel."

Chapter Twenty-Four

"I am a man of my word, Edmund," the voice said. "I want you to understand that."

Edmund fiddled with the telescope's knobs. As instructed, he trained it on a path winding from the tower's gate and into the pine forest filling the white valley below. Something came in and out of focus. He twisted more knobs. He saw it again. Crazy Bastard darted down the path, his arms waving above his head as if his hair were on fire. His bare feet kicked up snow as he ran.

"He's free. As per the rules of the Game," the voice said. "Although, technically, he attacked poor Gra' Runda before the match started. Still, as I indicated, I always keep my word."

Edmund watched his pit mate dash erratically down the rocky foothills until he disappeared amongst the snow-laden spruce and cypress trees.

"Won't, won't you simply re-recapture him?" Edmund surveyed the view from the open window. The frosty wind whipped into the tower, biting his exposed skin. He wrapped his arms around himself but didn't move away or close the shutters.

"Oh, make no mistake," the voice said. "There will be a hunt. Thirteen young warriors who've yet to come of age have been selected for the event. It'll be a good experience for them. But I can assure you, your friend will have a sizable lead—until dusk, in fact."

Edmund peered at the sliver of sun rising above the frozen mountain peaks.

He has a good ten hours, maybe more. Perhaps he'll get away.

It isn't as if he can get any help. You're hundreds of miles from civilization. And even if he met somebody, who'd understand him? He'll probably starve or fall in some hole.

Maybe it would've been better for him to die in the arena.

It would've been better if he were still alive in the pits.

Would it?

"How did he do it?" Edmund asked. "What happened? With, with the ogre, I mean."

"Weren't you at the match?" the voice asked. "I specifically instructed Mr. Kravel to bring you to the arena."

"He did," Edmund said. "But I . . . I had my eyes closed."

"Perhaps you should keep them open from now on. Live and learn, Edmund. Or die in ignorance. The choice is yours."

Edmund turned to the telescope. He scanned the valley for Crazy Bastard. But a green and white wall of snow-covered spruces blocked his view. He examined the nearby mountain peaks.

That mountain might be Rogorth.

"Let's bring our attention to the riddle, shall we?" the voice said. "Have you made any progress in deciphering it?"

Edmund noted a river stretching southwestward from the mountains.

Which would make that the River Laudrum. If so, I could follow it to the Celerin, and then—

And then what? You'd have to get out of here first.

"Edmund?"

"I'm, I'm sorry. N-no . . . no, sir. I haven't."

The voice exhaled in frustration.

"Edmund," the voice said. "You don't seem to be putting forth much effort. And that disappoints me far more than you can ever imagine. I'm afraid I will have to try other methods of motivating you."

The frigid room grew even colder. Edmund's breath appeared in hazy puffs, fogging the window's frosty glass. Withdrawing from the telescope, he stepped toward the fireplace and stopped short. Kravel knelt by its hearth, jabbing a glowing poker into the sizzling fire. He winked at Edmund.

"I . . . I." Edmund swallowed. "I, I can . . . I can, I can assure—"

"Yes, yes," the voice interrupted, its tone hard. "You can assure me you've given it a great deal of thought and reflection. But you see, Edmund, what I have failed to do is convince you how important this matter is to me. It is extremely important, I can assure you. Extremely— important."

Smiling, Gurding took a step in Edmund's direction. He held a tattered canvas bag.

Edmund retreated, even though he knew there was no place to run. "I-I-I-I . . . I-I und-understand—"

"No," the voice said, his anger now readily apparent. "No, you do not . . . understand. You . . . could not possibly . . . understand!"

Gurding closed the distance between him and Edmund with three quick strides. Edmund put an upholstered footstool between him and his pursuer. Kravel withdrew the poker from the blazing coals and blew on its tip. It changed from deep scarlet to a creamy white.

"I have been searching for something since before your miserable kind appeared in these lands," the voice shouted. "Something . . . extremely . . . important. You could help me, Edmund . . . but you don't!"

Edmund backed into the far wall. There was no escape.

Gurding stepped over the footstool.

Kravel, glowing poker in hand, followed close behind.

"You have wasted my time," the voice said. "And that makes me angry."

From the corner of his vision, Edmund saw the tasseled fringes on one of the silk tapestries move slightly as if an unseen figure had brushed against it.

He's invisible. He's a magic user!

Seeing his distraction, Gurding lunged forward and throttled Edmund's throat, slamming him against the wall. "You've cost me a great deal of money," he whispered in Edmund's ear.

Edmund squeaked, "Sorry!"

"Now, Edmund," the voice said, regaining some of its composure. "I'm fond of you. I mean that sincerely. I honestly appreciate having you with us. I could even consider you a pupil, as I've indicated before. But I'm afraid I need to try something else to increase your motivation in this matter."

Kravel stopped right behind Gurding. He blew on the poker again. Tiny red sparks fell from its glowing point like shooting stars.

"Mr. Gurding," the voice commanded. "The bag."

Gurding lifted the canvas bag.

Tensing every muscle in his body, Edmund squeezed his eyes closed. When a couple of seconds passed, he cracked one open.

Gurding growled, "Take it." He thrust the bag into Edmund's hands.

Still pinned against the wall, Edmund took the bag and stared at Gurding.

"Open it," Gurding said.

His hands fumbling, Edmund opened the bag.

"Idiot." Gurding punched Edmund's ear. Edmund's head snapped to one side. "Reach inside."

Gasping for air, Edmund slid his trembling hand into the bag and felt around. It seemed empty. Frightened and puzzled, he was about to withdraw his hand. But then his fingers grazed against something thin and cold—something metal. He pulled it out.

His mouth went dry.

I can't believe it!

It . . . it can't be.

It is. I'd know it anywhere. It's exactly like in his portraits.

In his sweaty palm, he held the Star of Iliandor.

"It's yours," the voice said. "Solve the riddle, and I'll let you go free. We will blindfold and escort you to Tol Helen. And our paths will never cross again."

Edmund gazed at the blue star-shaped gem, twinkling in the firelight. He studied the worn silver threads that once bound it to his hero's brow.

Is that one of Iliandor's hairs? His actual hair?

I can't believe it. It's magnificent!

It's more than magnificent. It's, it's—

"And if you become lord of Iliandor's fiefdom," the voice said, "I will relinquish my claims to the portions of Iliandor's lands that belong to us. None of my servants will ever step foot in your realm. Rood will be safe. I give you my solemn oath. All you must do is solve the riddle."

Edmund caressed the gem with his thumb.

"Now," the voice said, "burn out his eye."

Edmund looked up.

Chapter Twenty-Five

My eye! My eye!

Edmund tumbled through the air, his head smacking against something hard and damp. His body landed on a slime-covered metal grate that smelled like an overused outhouse. Still screaming, he pressed his hands against the burning hole where his left eye used to be.

"Why did you do that?" Kravel asked Gurding.

"That's what His Highness said to do," Gurding replied. "'Throw him in a wet cell,' he said. So that's what I did."

"I don't believe he meant it literally."

"Maybe. But he's angry. And I'm not going to make it any worse. If he says 'throw,' I throw."

"Perhaps you have a point. Always better to be safe than cut open, as they say. Excellent judgment, my friend."

"I'm going to kill you." Edmund rocked back and forth, holding the left side of his face.

"What did he say?" Gurding asked.

"I believe," Kravel said, "he informed us that he's going to end our lives, Mr. Gurding. Interesting turn, don't you think?"

"I'm going to kill you," Edmund screamed louder. "Do you hear me? I'm going to kill you!"

"I wonder which one of us he means." Gurding stuck his head into the small, cave-like cell. "Hey, Filth. Which one of us do you mean?"

Curled into a fetal position, Edmund rolled around the slimy metal grate forming the cell's floor, crying in agony. "I'm going to kill you! Do you hear me?"

"You said that part. But who exactly are you going to kill?"

Kravel tapped his chin. "Notice how he isn't stuttering? Remarkable improvement, don't you think? Simply remarkable."

"Perhaps we should have a wager on who he plans on killing," Gurding said. "I'll give you three to five odds he means you."

"Me?"

"You burnt out his eye."

"Good point." Kravel leaned into the cell. "You aren't cross about that, are you? It was only business, you understand. Orders and all. We're still friends, aren't we, Master Filth?"

Edmund stopped rolling and glared at the goblin. "You bastard!"

He lunged at Kravel. But the goblin's fist sent him reeling back. He crumbled to the metal grate, blood pouring from his broken nose.

"I don't think he likes you anymore, Mr. Kravel."

"Quite possibly, Mr. Gurding. It's a shame when friendships die. However, maybe his disposition toward me will improve when we return."

"You're joking, aren't you? I mean, about him enjoying our little surprise."

"I don't know. It's so difficult to tell with humans."

"They're not very appreciative," Gurding agreed.

"I'm going to kill you!" Edmund held his blistered left eye socket, his nose bleeding. "I'm going to kill both of you!"

"Well, that certainly clears things up." Kravel clapped his hands and rubbed them together. "At any rate, Master Filth, we must be off. Errands to run, and all that. You won't see us for a few weeks, I suspect. Perhaps longer. But I am quite certain you'll appreciate us more when we return. Enjoy your new surroundings. They aren't as pleasant as the high cells. But at least you'll have plenty of time to think about your task. Take excellent care of yourself!"

The cell door closed with a heavy clang.

"You really like the fat bastard, don't you?" Gurding asked.

"Filth? Of course! He makes me laugh. Besides, he's no longer fat. In fact, he's gotten quite muscular. Hard work in the mines and all. Why, for a moment there, his charging nearly unnerved me. He can be a ferocious one, that Filth."

"I believe you're pulling my leg again, Mr. Kravel."

"Quite possibly, Mr. Gurding. But time will tell."

Another metal door closed with a sharp clank. Other than a faint trickle of water and a soft sloshing sound far below him, all was quiet and utterly dark. Edmund, gasping through the pain, wiped away the blood pooling under his nose. He pressed both hands over his empty eye socket.

I'm going to kill them, the bastards. Them and that damned voice. Whoever it is. I'll make them pay!

Cursing and crying in the echoing blackness, he cast his healing spell. Then he cast it again and again and again.

Chapter Twenty-Six

Edmund whimpered, sniffed, and then threw up.

Rolling over, he gagged again. "Ugh!"

"You'll get used to it," an almost feminine voice said from somewhere in the impenetrable blackness.

Edmund stiffened. "Wh-what?"

"The odor." The voice cracked as if it hadn't been used for many days. "You'll get used to it."

Edmund covered his mouth. But the reek of feces, urine, and rotting corpses was as thick as paste. He could taste it in his throat. He crawled in random directions, hoping to get away from the assault. But every few feet, he hit a slimy wall.

"You're in a cell in the deepest levels of Thorgorim," the voice said. "Directly above the sewers, if that helps you become orientated."

Edmund felt around. He was on a slippery grate of thick interwoven metal strips. Between each strip was an opening the size of his fist. To his right, he touched an algae-covered, roughly hewn wall.

Oily water trickled over his searching fingers. To his left, he found the same thing.

"Thorgorim?" Edmund discovered the metal door to his cell. He threw himself against it, but it didn't budge.

"The fortress of His Royal Majesty Kar-Nazar." The disdain in the voice was nearly as palpable as the malodorous air.

Edmund's remaining eye watered. His stomach retched.

"What's that stench?" he asked. "It's horrid."

The contents of his stomach surged upward. He vomited all over himself.

"As I indicated," the voice said, "we're directly above the sewers. However, you might be referring to Morgan in the cell directly across from you. He died several weeks ago."

Edmund's stomach churned.

"This is horrible!"

He gagged again.

"You'll get used to it," the voice said.

"I don't believe you." Edmund opened his mouth. His throat expanded. His stomach heaved, but only a choking sound came out.

"It'll take time, but your sense of smell will eventually cease. Be thankful you aren't in the high cells. That's where Kar-Nazar pays closer attention to his captives."

Edmund raced his hands over the dripping walls, praying he might have missed something.

"You're human, are you not?" the voice asked. "Northern race? Would you prefer I speak in Dunael? When they brought you here, you cursed at the guards in the common tongue. I interpreted that as your native language. But perhaps you were speaking it so they could understand you."

"What? No. Nobody speaks Dunael anymore."

"Really?" The voice seemed to ponder this.

Grimacing, Edmund touched the puffy blisters where his left eye used to be. Pus seeped out of his eye socket. Then he felt something cold hanging around his neck. It was the Star of Iliandor. Kravel had tied it there like a necklace.

Strangely, as he clutched the Star, the overpowering stench seemed to subside a bit, though it might've been his imagination.

I have to get out of here.

Then solve the riddle.

Edmund untied the Star of Iliandor.

Maybe this can help somehow. Maybe it has powers like the legends say.

Maybe. But unless it can open cell doors and kill every damn goblin in the place, it's a worthless piece of jewelry.

Edmund fastened the Star around his head, the gem flat against his brow. He didn't feel any different.

He vomited a third time.

"You . . . you said something about somebody." Edmund spit. The reek was so putrid he couldn't taste what he'd thrown up. "Whose fortress is this?"

"We are in Thorgorim, the fortress of Kar-Nazar."

Edmund coughed on the pungent air.

"Kar-Nazar? That, that sounds like one of the elven names in the old faerie tales."

The voice laughed. The rolling echoes made him sound like a specter.

"You're clearly educated," the voice said. "But I'd already surmised that. Incidentally, you shouldn't invoke that healing spell so frequently. Your mind isn't strong enough to cast it more than three or four times without rest."

Edmund froze.

He knows!

"I . . . I, I don't know what you're talking about," he said too quickly to be convincing.

"Yes, you do. You're a Maûa. But don't worry. If it is a secret, nobody will learn it from me."

"A . . . a . . . Maûa?"

"Users of what your kind calls magic."

My kind?

"I am one, of sorts. But that's no secret to anyone here. It's the reason why I'm imprisoned."

Edmund coughed and retched again. But his stomach had nothing left to purge.

"And you?" the voice said. "The guards mentioned something about a task you're supposed to perform."

"You're, you're a magic user?" Edmund asked, lowering his voice.

"Indeed, though not a purebred. I was an alchemist in my youth. Consequently, I understand well what happens if you invoke an incantation more often than your mind can handle. But perhaps losing consciousness was what you'd intended."

You shouldn't talk to him. He could be a goblin or a spy!

"What's your discipline?" the voice from the neighboring cell asked.

"Discipline?"

Don't tell him a thing. This is a trap!

"The Maûan path you undertook. I assumed you were a healer. But given how easily such a minor incantation overcame you, perhaps I was in error."

Never mind this. Find a way out of here.

Edmund reached above his head. He couldn't feel the cell's ceiling. He jumped. He still couldn't feel a ceiling.

Ask him questions. Get him off the topic of magic. Find out who he is!

"You, you mentioned a . . . a name, Kar-Nazar." Edmund paced the five feet that separated each wall. "Who is he? Have you heard his voice?"

There was a disgusted grunt. "Yes, I've heard his voice. I hear it whenever I let sleep take me. He has other names you might have heard. Your people call him *Konge Spøkelse* in Dunael—the Undead King in the common tongue."

Edmund choked, but not on the stench around him.

The Undead King?

That's impossible!

"You're," Edmund managed to say. "You're joking. Iliandor vanquished him. He killed him!"

"Vanquish means to subdue in battle," the voice said, "which is inaccurate. In the most generous analysis, they fought to a draw. However, victors of battles are rarely revealed until well after the histories are written. As for killing him, that's obviously incorrect. Did Iliandor say he killed Kar-Nazar? That's a bold statement even for him."

Edmund opened his mouth but couldn't find the words.

He's lying. All of this is a lie. He's testing you. Trying to confuse you.

"What's your name?" the voice asked. "Or what would you prefer I call you? Hopefully, we'll be together for a while. I enjoy the company, though it never lasts as long as I'd like."

"N-n-never, never mind that," Edmund said. "What makes you think the Undead King is alive?"

"What makes you believe he's dead?"

"I, I have read hundreds of first-hand accounts of the Battle of the Ice Fields!"

"Read? That's promising."

"And how could this Kar-Nazar person still be alive if he were the Undead King? The final battle with Iliandor and his knights was nearly five hundred years ago."

"Indeed? Interesting."

"He can't be alive," Edmund said. Yet, part of him considered the horrific possibility. "He can't be!"

"First of all, many things under the sun and stars live well beyond five hundred years. Trees for one. The great sea turtles are another. In fact, many Hiisi live well over six hundred years. Especially the women, though they're few in number. To many, a century is merely a blink of the eye, as is the case with Kar-Nazar."

"Impossible!"

"Then why do your people call him the Undead King if not due to the length of his existence?"

He can't be alive. He can't be the same one.

Then how did he have Iliandor's Star?

Edmund touched the Star.

None of this makes any sense.

The voice went on, "I envy your predilection for reading. It is a feat I'll never undertake again, I am afraid. It's one of the many things I miss about my previous life. Perhaps you can share with me some of what you have read. Boredom, as you will learn, is our host's most effective torture."

"It's impossible," Edmund repeated, more to himself than whoever was in the darkness. "He can't be the Undead King."

"Impossible is a word of a closed mind."

Iliandor slew the Undead King. He knocked him to the ground, then drove his dagger, Narcrist, into the Undead King's throat. He chopped off his head and left it on a pike, just like the Undead King did to Iliandor's father —

"Am I correct in assuming you've only read accounts from your countrymen?" the voice asked. "Or have you read authors with other perspectives?"

"Other perspectives?"

"Yes, the Hiisi, for example. They have a lengthy literary tradition. Before your people came to this continent, they had extensive libraries and institutions of learning. Scribes were prized more highly than warriors."

Edmund snorted. "The goblins? Impossible."

"I would appreciate it," the voice said with some pain, "if you wouldn't use that word. And it's becoming increasingly evident that you are not as educated as I'd hoped."

A faint burbling sound echoed above them.

None of this makes any sense. Iliandor killed the Undead King. How else would the war have ended? Iliandor returned—

Iliandor returned dead. And whoever this Kar-Nazar is, he had Iliandor's Star.

Edmund touched the gem on his brow. Its smooth surface seemed slightly warmer than before.

"If you do not wish to entertain what I say," the voice said, "that is your prerogative. I'd hoped for an enlightening discussion. It has been a long time since I had one."

The burbling grew louder.

"However, if you wish to find value in my knowledge, I suggest you position yourself as flat against your cell wall as possible. And do not peer upward."

"What? Why?"

Edmund looked up. A wave of sewage knocked him down, pinning him to the metal grate. For many moments, he couldn't move. Then the assault was over.

"You peered upward, didn't you?" the voice asked.

Getting to his knees, Edmund spit repeatedly. He wiped his mouth, only to realize his hand—indeed, every part of him—was covered with feces, urine, and heaven only knew what else. He kept spitting.

"I've met many of your people over my lifetime," the voice said. "Their reputation for stubbornness is well earned. If you wish to survive here, I advise you to acquire what others have already learned rather than attempting to discover everything by yourself."

Edmund spit some more.

"Are you harmed?" the voice asked.

"How—" Edmund said. "How often does that happen?"

"Every three days or so."

He shook himself like a miserable dog. "Ugh!"

"It will get a lot worse. Whatever reason they have you here, they mean to make you suffer. Would you accept another piece of advice?"

"Yes . . . yes, by all means. Please."

"Don't lean against the walls for extended periods. Vihrea's Gift grows on it. It's an alga that is noxious to humans. Moreover, the water will eventually rot your skin away."

Edmund crawled to the center of his cramped cell. "What else can you teach me?"

Chapter Twenty-Seven

"They'll come for you soon, Edmund," Vorn, the voice in the darkness, said.

How many days had passed in the lightless bowels of the mountains? Edmund couldn't say. Vorn claimed it had been twenty-seven. Edmund had to trust his judgment. Time didn't seem to penetrate the putrid blackness around him.

"What are you going to do?" Vorn asked.

"I don't know," Edmund said.

You have to escape.

Yes, but how? I need time to think.

All you've had is time to think.

"You don't seem overly interested in solving the riddle you found," Vorn said.

"I try not to think about it," Edmund said. "It makes no sense to me."

"I'm relieved. Unfortunately, they'll make your last days beyond miserable if you don't arrive at a satisfactory answer. They haven't even begun to torture you."

He doesn't know what he's talking about. Things can't get any worse.

They could burn out your other eye. Then you'd never get out of here. They wouldn't even need to keep you in a cell. They could have you crawl around, feeling your way like a blind dog.

Edmund thought about this. Then something Vorn had said struck him. "Wait. Wh-why, why are you relieved? About the riddle, I mean."

"I don't want Kar-Nazar to have the answer."

"Why? Do you know what this is all about? Do you know what's going on?"

Vorn hesitated. "I don't know the answer to your riddle. But I understand Kar-Nazar all too well. No good will come from him having what he seeks."

"I don't understand," Edmund said with increased urgency. "What does he want?"

There was a silence, broken only by dripping water and sewage sloshing in the tunnels below them.

"Edmund," Vorn said. "How much do you know about Iliandor and his military victories over Kar-Nazar during their last war?"

"A great deal. That is, I've read extensively about all aspects of Iliandor's life. He's a hero of mine. I even have his diary."

"You have Iliandor's diary? Fascinating. I'm sure Kar-Nazar would covet such a prize. You might not wish to reveal that fact to him."

"Actually, he has a copy I made years ago. He said his spies acquired it, though I'm not sure how. But get back to what you were saying about Iliandor and the riddle. What does all this mean?"

"Kar-Nazar has a copy of a manuscript you transcribed? It seems to me your life has been intertwined with Kar-Nazar's for some time.

It's as if many threads of history are meeting at one point. I'm afraid you are very near its center."

He knows something.

"Please," Edmund said. "What's going on? Why's he doing this to me?"

"Are you familiar with the Battle of Tor' Age?" Vorn asked.

"No. What does that have to do with me, the diary, and the riddle?"

"Perhaps your people call it something else. I'm sure you know the battle. It's where Kar-Nazar's fortunes began to turn, and his attempts to reclaim the lands you inhabit began to slip through his fingers."

"Are you talking about the Battle of Endris Haflen? Where Iliandor and his thirty-two knights arrived as the town was being overrun?"

"Perhaps. But Iliandor had more than thirty-two knights at the battle I'm referring to. Let me pose this question to you. Why was Iliandor able to tactically defeat Kar-Nazar? Kar-Nazar's forces were several times larger and better trained. They were experienced, battle-hardened warriors. Yet, Iliandor defeated them with a relatively small army of peasants from the countryside. How?"

"It was because of Iliandor's leadership, his military genius—"

"Iliandor was a fool. His military genius consisted of becoming surrounded and fighting for as long as possible."

"He wasn't a—"

"Iliandor and his knights fared so well," Vorn said, "because of his armor and weaponry. Somehow, through magic or design, he produced an alloy far superior to anything Kar-Nazar had ever constructed. His shields couldn't be broken. His swords would slice through the armor of the Hiisi as if it were straw. The only way any of Iliandor's knights could be defeated was if they became too exhausted to fight or if somebody shot them through their visor."

"How do you know this?" Edmund asked. "I haven't heard of any of this."

"Why would you?" Vorn said. "Imagine if word got out that Iliandor's legendary victories weren't due to his leadership or genius but because of the quality of his weaponry. Imagine how his friends and enemies would attempt to acquire his secret, even at the point of a blade. What would a human king or lord give to have an entire army clad in Iliandor's metal? Who could defy them?"

Father's sword! Remember how it cut through those bushes? It passed through them like nothing!

"You're an alchemist," Edmund said, remembering aloud. "That's why you're here. The Undead King wanted you to figure out how Iliandor did it—how he created his weapons and armor. But you couldn't."

"You're very insightful. Now you understand my thread in this web."

"Tell me, this alloy you're talking about, did it have a d-distinctive color?"

"Indeed. It had a bluish-grey marble hue. Why?"

He asked if Thomas had any more weapons like that.

And you told him where Rood was.

Edmund's heart sank.

Oh no.

"Edmund?"

"I, I had a short sword made of some strange material. It was very light and exceedingly sharp. That's why Kar-Nazar took such an interest in me at first. He wanted to know where I got it."

"You had such a weapon, and they still managed to take you prisoner?"

You should've fought them.

Edmund put his head in his hands. "I don't want to talk about it."

None of this makes any sense. Iliandor defeated the Undead King. He drove him into the Ice Fields and defeated him in hand-to-hand combat.

And all princesses are pretty.

Edmund shook his head again, unable to do anything else.

And remember the troll's den? Remember all those shields? They shouldn't have been there. None of those knights died in this region, at least not according to the histories you've read.

I wonder how much of what I know is actually true.

Father always said histories and faerie tales were the same thing.

"What does this have to do with the riddle?" Edmund asked the darkness.

"I do not know," Vorn said. "But it seems Kar-Nazar believes the riddle is somehow connected to Iliandor and the method by which he created his alloy. Nothing else matters to him. Once he learns how to produce such armor, he'll sweep down from these mountains and drive humans completely off the continent. He'll exterminate all of you."

Isa. The Tower. They weren't trying to hide the Star of Iliandor. They were trying to hide the alloy's formula!

"The salvation of humanity can be found in buildings of wise men, doubly so in optimism of the learned, and in knowledge that is written on a daily basis," Edmund said to himself.

A sharp clink sliced through the darkness as the outer door to the wet cells unlocked.

"Oh no!" Edmund said, panicking.

"Good luck to you, Edmund," Vorn said. "May the gods guide your soul."

Footsteps echoed toward them.

Hurriedly, Edmund unclasped the Star of Iliandor from around his head. With shaking fingers, he pushed the thin strands of silver into the tiny gap between the cell door and the jamb.

The footfalls grew louder.

Edmund closed his eye and tried to recall the proper cadence.

"*Forstørre nå,*" he said.

Nothing seemed to happen.

The footsteps stopped directly outside his cell. Torchlight spilled underneath the door.

"*Forstørre nå,*"

The chain stayed the same size.

"Well, Master Filth!" Kravel said from the other side of the cell door. "Still alive, I hope."

Kravel!

When he opens the door, go for his throat.

There are two of them.

There are always two of them. I won't let them burn out my other eye.

"It stinks down here," Gurding's muffled voice said. "I hate it."

"I believe that's part of the charm," Kravel said. "Very motivating, I would think."

Edmund touched the chain and muttered under his breath, "*Forstørre nå,*"

He grew lightheaded. Black spots floated in and out of his vision.

Forget about it. You'll have to fight them.

The narrow window in the cell door slid open. Blinding light flooded the cramped quarters. Crying out, Edmund fled to the far corner, both hands covering his remaining eye.

"Ah! There he is, Mr. Gurding. Looking as well as ever."

"Give him his present, and let's leave."

"Patience, Mr. Gurding. Some things should be savored. Much like this lovely meal we had specially prepared for you, Master Filth." A tin bowl slid underneath the door. "I hope you appreciate the extra nourishment. I'm sure they aren't feeding you as well as His Majesty did. Oh well, something to aspire to, I suppose."

Cowering in the corner, Edmund shielded his eye from the excruciatingly bright light.

"Let's leave him to his food," Gurding said. "He'll get to it eventually."

"Perhaps, Mr. Gurding. Perhaps. Still, I feel some sadness at our friend's silence. Makes me want to comfort him in some small, meaningless way."

"It makes me want to slit his stomach open. Let's go."

"Very well. Take care of yourself, Master Filth. Enjoy your meal. And think of us. I'm quite certain we'll see you shortly."

The window at the top of the door slid shut, cutting off much of the light from the other side.

"Couldn't we have one of the guards fetch him next time?" Gurding said. "I hate this place."

"As you wish, my friend," Kravel said. "However, I do enjoy the peaceful atmosphere. It reminds me of the catacombs."

The outer door closed with a decisive metallic clang, plunging Edmund's cell into utter blackness. He uncovered his eye.

"What did they bring you?" Vorn asked.

Edmund found a tin bowl and brought it to his nose. Then he remembered he could no longer smell anything.

"It feels like the same stew they always bring," he said.

He dumped the bowl's contents through the holes in the floor. Something metal hit the grate with a muted clink.

What was that? A coin?

Why'd they put a coin in your food?

Maybe a key?

Feeling around, Edmund's hand grazed over a soft lump, perhaps three inches long, with a metal band around it.

What's this?

He squeezed it.

It's a . . .

A what?

Then it hit him.

It's a finger with a ring!

Chapter Twenty-Eight

"A finger?" Vorn repeated. "Whose?"

Edmund felt the finger again, surprised he wasn't repulsed by touching it. The bone was cleanly cut, and the flesh was still squishy.

"I haven't a clue," he said. "I probably couldn't tell even if I had light to see by. Who notices people's fingers?"

"People who do not have any."

Good point.

Edmund considered igniting a strip of cloth from what remained of his pants. But dry sewage caked every inch of him and his clothes. Even with his fire spell, he'd never get it to ignite.

Why would they put a finger in my stew?

Maybe Vomit was right. Maybe all of this is a big game to them. Maybe they're betting on what you'll do next or how you'll react.

Edmund took the ring off the finger.

"It's unadorned," he said. "And light. It's probably made from copper or cheap brass."

"I used to be able to determine the difference by taste alone," Vorn said. "But that was ages ago."

"The finger has a jagged nail."

What does it matter? Get rid of it.

"Could it be from one of your friends in the pit?"

"I have no friends in the pit." An image of a smiling Pond Scum appeared in Edmund's mind. "Well, maybe one. But he didn't have a ring. The guards took everything of value we had. They even took my boots and belt."

He slid the ring onto his pinkie.

It's small.

Who cares?

"Then I'm at a loss," Vorn said. "Perhaps the finger was merely a way to disgust you."

"I'm already disgusted." Edmund tossed the finger through the grate. It landed in the sewer with a muffled kerplop. "If this is the w-w-worst they can do, I'll be fine."

"It is not the worst. Believe me. They haven't even begun to torment you."

Edmund felt the puffy hole where his left eye had been. Pus had finally stopped seeping out of it.

They won't have an opportunity to burn the other one out. Next time they come, I'll—

"What spell were you trying to cast when the Hiisi arrived?" Vorn asked. "It didn't sound as if it progressed particularly well."

"It didn't. It was a spell I once used long ago. I thought it might help, but I can't remember how it goes."

"What were you trying to accomplish?"

"I put something between the cell door and the metal jamb and tried to enlarge it so the d-d-door wouldn't open. It was stupid."

"Not at all. It was rather ingenious. Keep trying. All you have here is your wits and time. Optimize both."

"I only know four spells," Edmund said regretfully. "And none of them are very powerful."

You should've trained harder.

I should've done a lot of things.

"It's said that the least of a person's abilities grants them what they need to succeed."

"You sound like my father," Edmund said.

"Perhaps if you'd listened to him, things would be different for you now. Just as if you listen to me, perhaps things will be different in your future."

Iliandor said something very similar once: *"From today's learning grows tomorrow's success."* Or at least, that's what the plaque at the bottom of one of his statues said. Edmund wasn't sure who the real Iliandor was anymore.

"Are you going to practice?" Vorn asked.

"All right. But it won't work. I've already tried."

"Then try until it does work."

It couldn't hurt. At the very least, you'll lose consciousness and be spared a few hours from this festering hell.

Leaning forward, Edmund felt for the Star of Iliandor. Its finely wrought silver chain was still wedged in the door crack. Touching it, he closed his remaining eye and attempted to recall his father's exact words.

"*Forstørre nå,*" he said.

Nothing happened.

This will never work.

"Try again," Vorn said.

Taking a deep breath, Edmund waited for the dizziness to dissipate.

"*Forstørre nå,*" he said, changing his inflections.

There was a sound like cracking ice.

"Did you succeed?" Vorn asked.

Edmund felt the chain. "I, I . . . I think so. It's thicker, but not by much. If I cast it again, I wonder if the chain would get even wider."

He chuckled despite his situation.

"Why are you laughing?" Vorn asked.

"I asked my father the same question many years ago," Edmund said. "He'd given me a piece of candy for doing my chores well. I asked him if I kept casting this spell, would the candy grow bigger than our house? He said it would, but my head would explode."

"Odd thing to say to a child. And not accurate in the slightest."

"I know." Edmund's smile faded as he remembered his father dying. "He had a strange sense of humor."

Shame you didn't spend more time with him while you could.

Who would've thought he'd died like that? Anyway, he hated being around me.

"Try it again," Vorn said.

Taking a deep breath, Edmund touched the chain and tried again. The sound of metal expanding echoed in the darkness.

"Hey!" Edmund exclaimed. "Twice in a row."

"Congratulations," Vorn said. "Keep practicing all your abilities. You never know when the least of your skills will turn failure into success."

Success . . .

Success is getting out of here, not finally mastering some spell you should've learned when you were five.

Edmund ran his fingers along the chain. It was much thicker than it had been. He tugged on it. It didn't come free.

Maybe if I enlarged something else, I could make a weapon or something to pry open the door.

He took the ring off his little finger.

Maybe I could use this to—

Down the passageway, the door to the cell block burst open. Blinding light shot underneath the cell door, sending shadows and Edmund scurrying to the corner, covering his eye.

"Filth!" a guard bellowed, his voice amplifying as it reverberated through the dank tunnel. "You're coming with me. His Majesty wants to look at your other eye!" His heavy footfalls strode closer.

"May the gods protect you," Vorn whispered.

If the gods don't, I will.

Get ready!

Edmund positioned himself in the back of his cell as if he were cowering, his bare feet pressed against the far wall for leverage.

As soon as the door opens, knock him down and go for his throat.

A key slid into the lock.

Edmund's legs tensed.

This is it. Kill him!

The tumbler turned.

Edmund raised his shoulder to where he thought the goblin's chest would be. He imagined the guard fumbling with the cell's keys in one hand and the blazing torch in the other. Edmund planned to be on him before he could draw his weapon.

The guard pulled on the door.

Like a cobra, Edmund launched himself across the tiny cell.

Kill him! Kill the—

The top of his head smacked into the metal door. Shaken, he fell to the grate.

"What the hell are you doing?" The visor slid open. The guard peered in. "What're you up to in there?"

Ugh! My head! My head!

The guard pulled on the door again.

"What did you do?" The guard pushed and then yanked the handle as hard as he could. Still, the door refused to budge. "Get back, or I'll stick you through this hole. You understand? Get back!"

Holding his throbbing head, Edmund crawled to a far corner of his cell while the guard jerked on the door's handle.

"Blast it!" The guard kicked the door. "I'll get the damned thing open."

He stomped up the tunnel, cursing.

Edmund felt the top of his head. A tender bump erupted underneath his hair.

You blew it! Next time, he'll be ready for you. Idiot! Who runs into a door? I can't believe this!

"Edmund," Vorn whispered. "What's the duration of your enlargement spell?"

Edmund groaned. "I don't know. A few minutes. M-m-maybe a little less. But I can disengage it at any time with the counterspell." He rubbed the growing bump, but that only caused him more pain.

"Cast the counterspell."

"I can't right now. I hurt my head running into the damn door."

Idiot! You—

There was a snap in the darkness, followed by a creaking sound.

What was that?

It sounded like . . .

He extended a hand in the blackness but couldn't feel anything.

"The guard never relocked your cell," Vorn whispered.

Edmund inched forward, both of his hands outstretched. The door to his cell was wide open.

"Listen to me," Vorn said urgently. "In the guardroom, up the passage is a tunnel on the right. Take it. Hide in the mines. Stay hidden for as long as you can. Weeks, if you are able. Hide and wait until they've given up looking for you!"

Stumbling, Edmund got to his feet.

He felt for his cell door.

"What are you doing?" Vorn said. "Go! Flee!"

Edmund shot his hand over the outside of his cell door. "I'm trying to find the keys!"

"Go!"

Run! Get out of here!

Edmund brushed against a ring of keys, still dangling from the lock. He wrenched them out. They bobbled and fell somewhere to the unseen floor with an echoing clatter.

Run!

"Go!" Vorn said.

Panicking, Edmund fell to his knees, his hands sweeping in the darkness in ever-widening arcs. "We can both get out."

What are you doing? Run before the guard returns!

"Forget about the keys. Run to the mines. Run!"

Edmund's fingers felt something cold. Instinctively, he swept it up.

It's not the key. It's—

He'd picked up the Star of Iliandor.

Run!

"Run!"

"We both can—" Edmund began.

"Don't worry about me. Run!"

Edmund got to his knees. "I'm, I'm sorry," he said. "I'm so sorry."

"Run!" Vorn shouted.

But Edmund was already halfway up the passage, sprinting as fast as he could in the blackness.

Chapter Twenty-Nine

A dim reddish light seeped around the edges of the door at the end of the corridor. Edmund listened, but all he could hear was himself panting. He held his breath and peered into the guardroom. It was unoccupied. He opened the door wider.

Don't panic. Remain calm and think.

To his left, an expiring torch sent ribbons of thick black smoke wavering above a small table and chair. Directly before him, a narrow flight of stone stairs rose out of view. To his right stood a dilapidated wooden door, boarded over and blocked with a crate.

Edmund crept into the room and pushed aside the crate as quietly as possible. Cautiously, he tugged on one of the planks that barred his way.

Next to him, the torch hissed. He jumped, ready to run.

Idiot. Hurry up! Rip the boards down. They're half-rotten anyway. What are you waiting for?

Edmund yanked harder. The worm-eaten wood snapped in his hand.

Hurry!

Forgoing stealth, he grabbed boards and pulled with all his might. Soon, a terrific clatter arose, rotting wood crashing to the floor around him. When they'd all been torn away, he put his shoulder to the door and pushed it in. Its hinges tore from the wooden frame.

He cast the door aside.

Beyond it was a tunnel crisscrossed with tufts of silver cobwebs wafting toward him like ghostly hands. The torch crackled to life, burning the dust in the air.

"Did he do something?" a goblin said from the stairwell.

They're coming! Go!

"Naw," another goblin replied. "It's the dampness. It makes the doors stick."

What are you doing? Run! Run!

I need supplies!

"This should pry it open," the first voice said. "Or we can take the pins from the hinges. Pop the door right off."

Come *on!*

Edmund wrenched the sputtering torch from its holder.

That won't last more than ten minutes. Hurry!

He kicked the crate's top off. Inside was a stack of torches. He grabbed an armload and then pushed through the cobwebs. He ran up the tunnel, his bare feet slapping on the stone.

Chapter Thirty

Edmund peered down into the cavern he'd found a quarter mile or so from the boarded-over door. He shivered uncontrollably. His chattering teeth echoed in the tight crawlway in which he was hiding.

Below him, fifty goblins with ropes and nets dashed this way and that, their rushing feet splashing through the shallow pools covering the cavern's floor. Others examined a small waterfall where Edmund had scrubbed the sewage from his body moments earlier. Their torches hissed and popped as water from countless stalactites dripped on them. Sinister shadows danced along walls pocked with tunnels and fissures.

Stay calm. They won't find you up here. Stay calm.

Two figures strolled into the cavern like an old married couple admiring a colorful garden. They halted beneath Edmund.

"What makes you think he's still here?" Gurding asked. "If I were him, I'd be long gone by now."

Kravel watched the guards darting from passageway to passageway, hunting for clues. "Because, my friend, I know Master

Filth. He is a wily one, as I have said before. Exceedingly intelligent and resourceful, as I have also previously mentioned. He won't go far."

"Why?"

"Because, Mr. Gurding, this cavern has three things he needs. First, it has water. We've already seen evidence of him using this pool to bathe himself. Undoubtedly, so we couldn't track him by his smell. However, he'll also need water to drink."

"But there're other streams in the mines," Gurding said. "Lakes and rivers, too."

"Yes, but he doesn't know where they are. Which leads me to my second point. He knows how he got into this cavern and how to get out. All he has to do is return the way he came, and he'll be by the cells. From there, he could find the city and steal food and supplies. But if he strays too far—"

"He'll get lost and starve."

"As always, Mr. Gurding, you cut right through to the heart of the matter."

Gurding grumbled, "I'd like to cut right through to his heart."

"Yes, yes. I can appreciate your frustration. But be thankful he didn't escape while we were with him."

"He wouldn't have escaped if we were with him."

"Possibly. Possibly. But don't underestimate our good friend. Who knows what he is capable of?"

"You said this cavern has three things Filth needs," Gurding said.

"Good of you to keep count," Kravel said. "The third is that this cavern has many places in which he can hide. Look around. There are scores of passages, tunnels, crawlways, nooks, and assorted places where he could conceal himself. He knows we can't search them all. In fact, I bet you anything he's within earshot as we speak."

Gurding glanced at the cavern walls behind him. Nearly a hundred feet above them, Edmund pulled back to the deep shadows, praying they couldn't hear his shivering.

"All right." Kravel clapped his hands. "Could you all stop what you are doing for the moment?"

The goblin searchers crawled out of the various holes they'd been investigating.

"Splendid." Kravel strolled to the middle of the cavern. "Edmund!" he called. "Edmund, let me first say how extraordinarily impressed I am with your escape. Truly impressed indeed, as is Mr. Gurding here."

"Impressed?" Gurding said. "I'd like to hang him by his spleen."

"However, my dear friend," Kravel went on, shouting to the shadows, "you have simply traded one cell for another, I'm afraid. Look around you. Do you honestly believe you will find your way out of here? Even our most experienced miners get lost in these tunnels, dying slowly of starvation, their bodies gnawed on by rats and other delightful creatures you will soon encounter."

I'll get out. Or I'll die trying.

I believe you saw an opportunity and took it without contemplating your next move," Kravel said. "Even now, as hunger stabs at your stomach, I bet you are reevaluating your actions. Perhaps you even wish you were where you knew you'd get regular meals."

Edmund gritted his chattering teeth, trying to stop his body from trembling. After untold weeks coated with rancid filth, he was finally clean. But his wet skin was numb, and lying on the cold stone of the crawlway didn't help matters any.

Talk all you want, Kravel. You'll never take me prisoner again. You'll have to kill me.

"I suspect this logic will not persuade you to return with us," Kravel said. "But I believe we have somebody who will."

Edmund wanted to laugh.

The echoes of Kravel's voice gradually faded.

"Did you find our little present in your stew?" Kravel ambled around the cavern, inspecting its numerous rock formations. "Did you discern whose it was?"

I don't care in the slightest.

Edmund exhaled into his hands, trying to warm them.

Then Kravel said, "Your wife is very pretty, Edmund."

Wife?

"I think she's rather fat," Gurding said.

"Eye of the beholder, Mr. Gurding," Kravel said. "Eye of the beholder."

"It wasn't my eye that was complaining," Gurding said. "It was my back. I had a devil of a time getting her fat carcass over that wall."

What the hell are they talking about?

Ignore them. They're trying to rattle you. They probably assume you're married and are trying to get you to reveal yourself.

Married?

Edmund's thoughts drifted to Molly. If he ever saw her again, he'd walk right up to her and ask her to marry him. He wouldn't hesitate any longer. He wouldn't care if the moment wasn't perfect. He'd finally reveal his heart.

No more regrets.

"We have your wife with us, Edmund," Kravel said.

Well, I'd love to meet her! Ha!

Drawn by curiosity, Edmund crept toward the opening, wondering who the hell they were talking about.

What are you doing? Lay still. Don't fall for their stupid games.

"She's up in the tower," Kravel yelled.

See! They're making things up. They don't have anybody, let alone your 'wife.'

"She's in the same room you were in," Kravel said. "You could be with her. You could be with her right now if you like, sleeping together in a warm bed, eating His Majesty's excellent food. If you solve the riddle, you both could go free. Every lord needs his fat whore by his side. Am I correct, Edmund?"

Edmund closed his eye, wishing the goblins would go away. He was cold and tired. He wanted to light one of the torches he stole and huddle over it until his skin baked.

"Of course, Edmund," Kravel said, "if you wish to remain here, we honestly have no need for your pretty female."

Gurding laughed. "But I'm sure we could think of something to do with her."

"Why, Mr. Gurding, what are you implying?" Kravel asked. "We'll take excellent care of your wife, Edmund. Eventually, she may not even wish to leave."

There was a long silence. The dripping of the stalactites mingled with the restless movements of the waiting searchers. Lying in the darkness, Edmund breathed into his shivering hands again.

"Very well, Master Edmund," Kravel shouted. "I suspect you need time to consider your predicament. In the meantime, we have some company for you."

Something was dragged into the cavern. Several goblins cursed as if pulling a great weight. Whatever it was, it fought back but was losing the struggle. A wailing screech ricocheted around the rock formations. Edmund couldn't help himself. He had to look.

The goblins erected a tall spear. It stood upright, its point high above the damp floor. On it was the guard who left the key in Edmund's cell door. The spear's gory point glistened in the wavering torchlight as the screaming guard slid down its shaft. The pools of water beneath him turned bright red with his blood.

"We'll leave you with your accomplice," Kravel yelled above the guard's wails. "I'm afraid he won't be of much assistance to you. He'll probably only live for a few more hours."

The searchers filed out of the cavern. Kravel and Gurding were the last to leave.

"I hope we have the pleasure of your company again, Master Filth," Kravel called out. "We have a great deal to discuss. Rood is an exceptional village. Very quaint."

"We're thinking about relocating there," Gurding said.

"Yes, indeed. It would seem your library will be for sale soon. What do you think, Mr. Gurding?" Kravel asked as they strolled out of the cavern. "Can you picture me as a business owner? A librarian like our friend Filth?"

"Would you get to kill people?" Gurding asked.

"Quite possibly. If they didn't return a book, I suppose. Or if they bent the pages or some such offense."

"Then I can see it," Gurding said. "As for me, I'd like to own that tavern. What was it called?"

The guard slid farther down the widening spear shaft. His screams obliterated Kravel's answer.

Get out of here.

No! That guard has clothes and boots. I need to get warm.

Are you stupid? That's what they want you to do. There are probably a dozen goblins hidden in the shadows. Go before they start searching again!

Edmund tucked his knees under his chin and turned around. Facing the other direction, he crawled deeper into the tunnel, dragging the bundle of torches behind him.

Let's see where this goes.

Chapter Thirty-One

Edmund stepped closer to his unsuspecting prey.

Cast the spell again. It needs to be bigger. You can't afford to miss.

"Forstørre nå."

The brass ring he found on the severed finger grew to the size of a fat man's belt. After weeks of practicing in the cold darkness of the abandoned mines, he could now cast his spells at will.

That should do nicely.

Is this really necessary?

Yes! At some point, you'll have to fight your way out of here. You need that sword and lantern.

He stalked within twenty feet of the lantern light.

"That's good," the adult goblin said. "But you still need to follow through. Remember, they're taller than you. So, swing high. Go for their head. Force them backward, and then use your momentum to lung forward with the second strike. Here. Watch me."

This was the third time Edmund had encountered this father teaching his young son how to fight with a wooden sword. Why they were in the mines, he couldn't guess—perhaps for privacy, perhaps so the young goblin child wouldn't be distracted. Edmund didn't care. Now, he was ready for them.

Closer . . .

"Good," the father said. "But remember, you must be prepared to block as well. Don't overexpose yourself. Stand like this."

Take your time . . . Don't rush . . .

Holding his breath, Edmund inched through the shadows.

Stick to the plan. You can do this.

The father parried his son's wild blows and countered with a soft jab to the boy's midsection. The boy doubled over, the air knocked out of him.

"See," the father said. "You aren't listening. You left yourself open. Pay attention, or you'll lose the next tournament as well. Is that what you want? Do you want to be a loser? Or do you want to be a warrior?"

"A warrior," the child managed to say as he rubbed his stomach.

"That's right! Now, don't forget the enemy has many more weapons than what he's holding in his hand. He can kick, bite, hit— throw dirt in your face. They're animals. You must protect yourself from all possible actions. Understand?"

The boy nodded and resumed his fighting stance.

Stones crunched beneath Edmund's bare feet.

You're close enough. Rush him!

No. Get closer. You're no match for him if he reaches that sword first.

Edmund waited for them to start swinging again, the reverberating clash of wood against wood and the grunts from the boy concealing the sounds of his footfall. He stalked closer.

Patience . . .

The father's wooden sword connected with the boy's left ear. The boy dropped his mock weapon, tears flowing as he clutched the side of his head.

"All right," the father said. "None of that! Warriors don't cry. If you want to cry, I can arrange it. Is that what you want? Is that what you want me to do? Do you want me to make you cry?"

Sniffling, the boy shook his head.

"Okay then," the father said. "Let's get to work. Pick up your weapon."

Edmund edged within ten feet behind the father. He raised the enlarged ring.

Glancing in Edmund's direction, the boy's watery eyes went wide.

"What?" the father asked.

Now!

Dashing from the darkness, Edmund leaped onto the father's back.

The father fell forward, tumbling face-first to the ground. He cried out and then twisted, throwing his elbows and kicking wildly.

"Get off me!" he shouted.

Edmund plunged the enlarged ring over the goblin's head and pulled.

The father choked, clawing at the shining brass around his throat.

Straddling the goblin's shoulders like he was riding a bucking horse, Edmund recited the counterspell. *"Abnormitet nå!"*

Suddenly, the ring returned to its original size.

The father's head rolled to his son's feet, completely severed from his body. Its eyes moved as its mouth strove to speak. The boy stared at it.

Hurry!

Breathing hard, Edmund snatched the scimitar propped against a rock outcropping. He pointed it at the boy.

Now what?

His heart pounding, he stared at the goblin child.

"Pl-pl-please," the boy whimpered. "Pl-please!"

Kill him.

He's a child!

He's a filthy goblin. They all deserve to die. Think about what they did to your eye. Think about what they did to Thorax. Think about all the atrocities they've committed over the ages!

Edmund and the boy looked at the decapitated body lying in a growing pool of thick dark blood, then at each other.

"Please," the boy repeated.

Do it quickly and get it over with. Don't think!

The curved blade of the scimitar approached the boy's neck. Edmund's knuckles whitened.

"Get out of here," Edmund heard himself saying. "Go on. Go!"

The boy retreated a step, tears tumbling down his cheeks.

"Go!"

The boy beheld his father again. The head was still—its mouth open, its unfocused eyes staring at where his son had been standing.

"Go!" Edmund shouted, his voice echoing through the passage.

The boy fled into the darkness, crying.

As Edmund searched the body, the boy screamed at him. "I'm going to k, k, kill you!" The sound of running resumed.

You should've killed him.

I won't murder a child.

But you'll murder his parents?

Edmund stripped the blood-soaked clothes from the corpse.

Take everything and get out of here.

The boots won't fit.

Take them anyway. You never know when you can kill somebody with a giant boot.

What should I do with the body? Hide him?

No! They'll find him anyway. Take his stuff and run.

Edmund ran deeper into the mines—lantern in one hand, sword, boots, and bloody clothes in the other.

Watch the blood. They'll follow the trail.

Let them. They'll never suspect where I'm hiding. They couldn't follow me even if they tried.

Turning a sharp corner, Edmund hurried into an intersecting tunnel.

Passing several other openings, he entered a chamber with a crumbling aqueduct and a paddlewheel lying partly on its side. He plunged the bloody clothes into the aqueduct. The water turned pink.

Far off, a horn blew. Its echoing blasts rolled through the mines like an avalanche.

Edmund spun the goblin's clothes over his head. Bloody water sprayed in all directions. Dashing around the chamber, he flicked them into the nearby passages.

You don't have much time!

I need to confuse my trail.

Edmund slid the scimitar into its sheath and buckled the weapon belt around his waist. Knotting the laces together, he draped the boots over the sword's hilt. Tying his newly acquired clothes around his battered knees, he gripped the lantern's handle in his teeth and scrambled up the side of the rusty paddlewheel.

Icy water poured onto the paddlewheel from a vertical mine shaft in the ceiling. Standing on top of the wheel's uppermost rim, Edmund shivered. He gauged the distance to the narrow opening above him.

You can do this. You've done it a hundred times before. Concentrate.

Edmund crouched and then sprang upward, his hands finding the familiar holds in the wet stone. He pulled himself into the shaft. His legs and back pushing against opposite walls, he shimmied higher above the chamber below. Water cascaded over him, numbing his skin. The lantern sizzled.

Another horn blared, this time closer.

Reaching over his head, Edmund set the lantern in a fissure. Unbuckling his weapon belt, he slid the scimitar and boots next to it. He then flung himself into the opening, pulling the rest of his body inside.

Shoving the lantern, boots, and sword before him, Edmund slithered along the tight passage, thankful for the goblin's clothes cushioning his knees. When the crawlspace widened, he turned and wedged a large rock behind him, blocking the way he came. Sitting up, he pulled himself through a break in the low ceiling and into a small cavity. Reaching down through the hole, he retrieved his new possessions.

Muffled voices echoed from the way he came.

Let them shout. They'll never find me here.

Using an old board he'd found weeks earlier, Edmund covered the hole in the floor and rolled a sizable boulder on top of it. He listened over the stones plugging his other escape routes. All was quiet.

Edmund tossed the goblin's clothes and boots next to a dented helmet full of clear water, three unused torches, thirteen burnt-out torch stubs, a pile of rotting wood, and a broken handle from a mining pick. Then, the enormity of what he'd done hit him. He put his head in his hands and wept.

I killed somebody.

You killed a goblin. You're a hero, like that storyteller at the Rogue.

I don't feel like a hero. I feel like an animal.

In the cavern below, a goblin hollered.

Edmund drew the scimitar from its sheath.

At least now I can defend myself.

You've never swung a sword in your life. You don't have a clue how to use it effectively.

I know how to use it on myself.

Another horn blew. It shook the stone beneath Edmund's tired feet. There was more shouting.

I need to find a way out of here.

How? Going to the tower is too dangerous. There are thousands of goblins. Even with a sword, you can't fight them all.

There has to be another way out. All these tunnels have to go somewhere. They have to exit the mountains.

Maybe . . .

As Edmund pushed his wet hair out of his eye, his fingers grazed the Star of Iliandor on his brow. He unclasped its chain and examined it. The damp stone shimmered blue in the lantern light. The silver chains were worn with age, but the intricate runes carved on them were still easy to see. He traced them with his fingertips.

So much for my first adventure.

More shouting came from the cavern below. Somebody hollered for Kravel.

Edmund yawned as he set the Star of Iliandor next to the lantern.

Get some sleep.

Sleep? I can't remember the last time I slept.

Then practice your spells until you lose consciousness.

No. I'm tired of practicing. I've already mastered the four spells I know. I can't get any better at them.

Solve the riddle. What's in the buildings of wise men?

I don't care anymore. I just don't care . . .

Chapter Thirty-Two

Edmund sat up with a lurch, his breath coming in sharp bursts. This was the fourth night in a row he'd had a nightmare about a horde of rats devouring him. He felt for the lantern he'd taken from the goblin father, then cast his fire spell. A tiny flame appeared. Shaking, he huddled in the wavering scarlet glow.

Ghostly voices, dismembered by endless echoing, seeped through the surrounding stone. They shouted his name.

Damn that Kravel. He'll never give me a moment's peace.

Then find a spot deeper in the mines so you can't hear the bastard.

I'm tired of running. I'm tired of all of this.

Edmund dipped his hands into the rusty helmet full of water and washed his face. He knew he'd be caked in mud and silt as soon as he crawled around. But the ritual made him feel more human.

He bit into one of the biscuits he created the evening before and forced himself to swallow.

I can't eat these anymore. I want real food: a steak, an apple—anything.

Then you'll need to get out of here.

He let the uneaten portion of the biscuit drop to the ground. Unable to stand in his snug confines, he arched his spine and stretched. Dark shadows flitted around him like ghouls.

He examined his sword. It was an ugly thing with wicked images etched along its curved blade. Whenever he tried to climb, it got in his way. But having a weapon within arm's reach gave Edmund a sense of security. At the very least, he knew the goblins wouldn't take him alive.

Maybe if I searched by that wide tunnel, I could find an exit.

The goblins are always there.

Edmund stared at the rough grey stone forming the cavern's walls and then at the remains of the magically created biscuit he'd let fall to the ground.

I can't keep sitting here. I can't!

Then do something.

"All right." He summoned the strength to move. "Now is as good a time as any to die."

Sliding aside the stone blocking one of the exits, Edmund crawled into the exposed tunnel. He pushed the nearly empty lantern in front of him as he went.

Chapter Thirty-Three

Edmund crept through a series of twisting tunnels and caverns. Eventually, he found the slender stone ledge where he often sat and thought. He let his callused feet dangle over its edge.

Below him was a passage unlike any other he'd come across in the mines. It had a smooth road wide enough for three wagons to traverse side by side. Further, every three hundred feet, magnificent white columns rose to sculpted arches like the bleached ribs of a giant snake. Torches used to be mounted on every other column, lighting the way. But Edmund stole them. Now, the passageway was utterly dark.

Edmund occasionally saw lines of haggard Pit Dwellers marching to some worksite or another, their gaunt faces showing their exhaustion and despair. He'd considered trying to rescue them. The more bodies he had, the greater his chances of fighting his way into the tower and out the front gate. However, as soon as he acquired a sword, the number of guards doubled. All he could do now was watch the slaves stumble off to their doom.

In the blackness, alone and tired, he wept.

Far to his left, a tiny red light appeared, bobbing and weaving as it drew closer.

Brushing the tears from his eye, Edmund pulled his legs up from the ledge and withdrew into a deep notch in the wall. Voices echoed toward him. Soon, two goblins came into view, talking in whatever language the Hiisi spoke to themselves. They walked at a leisurely pace, huge packs hoisted high on their shoulders.

Grinding his teeth, Edmund watched them pass below him.

Damn it! If I were in position, I could've had everything in those packs—food, clothes, maybe even blankets! Damn it!

Packs . . .

There are only two of them. And in those coats, they could barely move their arms. I could've killed them before they drew their swords. Damn my luck!

Edmund stepped out of the shadows.

The goblins continued walking, the light from their lantern dwindling to a swaying speck in the darkness.

Coats. Long . . . thick . . . warm . . . coats . . .

Why would they have packs and—?

His heart skipped several beats and then pounded the inside of his chest.

There's an exit nearby!

Hurry! Catch up to them!

Clambering from his hiding spot, Edmund grabbed the ledge and threw himself over. Extending his arms, he let go. Springing up from the ground, he drew his sword and raced after the goblins.

Chapter Thirty-Four

For what seemed like a lifetime, Edmund followed the two goblins, keeping within sight of their lantern but not so close that they could hear his footsteps. Then, abruptly, their light disappeared. He stopped.

The passage probably turned.

Probably.

He listened but couldn't hear anything.

He stalked forward, the point of his scimitar leading the way.

The passage bent to his left.

Up ahead, another light appeared, red like the goblins' lantern but much brighter.

Edmund crept closer.

The air grew warmer. It drifted past him in gentle waves. The taste of wood ash wafted over his tongue.

There was talking.

Somebody laughed.

More talking.

Suddenly, a puff of cold wind stormed along the passage. It enveloped him and then was gone.

Two or three goblin voices periodically broke the silence.

Minutes limped by in the blackness.

Edmund inched toward the light.

There was movement ahead.

He flattened himself behind one of the granite columns lining the tunnel.

He waited.

Nothing happened.

Gripping the hilt of his sword with both hands, Edmund took a deep breath and slunk along the wall. The light got brighter. The air grew warmer. Wisps of smoke burned his eye and dried his throat. He fought the urge to cough.

An archway appeared. Beyond it, portions of a room came into view. He could see two booted feet propped on a table and the rim of a fire pit where red flames danced.

Edmund halted.

What are you waiting for? This is it. Didn't you smell that air? It was from outside! There's an exit!

Edmund drew his moist palms across the remains of his pants. Licking his dry lips, he tightened his grip on the scimitar until his fingers hurt. Slowly, he stepped closer.

There are guards.

It doesn't matter. Run in there and go for their knees. Cripple them. Then finish them off when you can.

The legs on the table shifted. Edmund stopped again.

Rush in there and start swinging! Hit anything that moves. Chop them in two. Think about what they did to Thorax. Think about the rats in the cage. Think about Kravel grinning as he came at you with the poker!

Edmund gritted his teeth.

This is it! Freedom or death. Kill them. Kill them and go home. Make them pay. Make them pay!

He took a step toward the archway, then two more. He started running.

Edmund burst into the room, his sword held high. He swung down on the legs. Bones splintered. Blood spurted. Somebody screamed.

He turned to his left. A shocked goblin held a tin cup to his gaping mouth.

Edmund brought his weapon around as the goblin with the cup tried to dive out of the way. The blade connected with the guard's left shoulder and skimmed across his arm. Clothing and flesh split apart, then turned a purplish red. More screaming filled the room.

Edmund hoisted his scimitar again. Trying to shield himself, the goblin raised his good arm over his head. He shouted.

Something struck Edmund from behind. He stumbled forward, nearly falling on top of the guard with the partially severed shoulder. Two arms wrapped around his chest. Edmund regained his balance and turned sharply. The goblin on his back held on, his hold tightening.

Edmund drove backward, smashing into the corner of the archway. The goblin behind him cursed. But his grip continued to drive the air out of Edmund's lungs. He threw himself against the corner a second time. The goblin's hold weakened.

Edmund spun. The goblin tumbled across the floor. He bounded to his feet and reached for a spear leaning against the wall. But Edmund was right behind him. Leaping at the goblin, he swung. The goblin's severed hand fell to the bloody floor with a wet thud.

A horn blared, shaking the small room.

Flinching, Edmund wheeled and found his first target on the ground, one leg missing below the knee. He held a horn to his lips and blew a second time, panic in his eyes. Edmund's scimitar swept through the smoky air, slicing the horn blower's head open. The gore-covered horn fell to the floor and rolled next to the overturned table. Edmund hit him again.

In the corner, the goblin with the wounded shoulder and arm struggled to his feet. He shouted something, perhaps pleading for his life. Edmund couldn't hear through the screams. He lunged at the goblin, the tip of his scimitar punching into his chest. White ribs appeared, snapped, and then were awash in blood.

Edmund swung again. A gash erupted across the goblin's forehead. The goblin crumpled in the corner.

Edmund swung again and again.

The ceiling dripped red.

There was shuffling movement behind him. The goblin with the missing hand staggered through the archway, shrieking. Edmund chased him into the passage and planted the point of his sword in the goblin's kidney. The goblin gasped, then fell face down. Edmund jumped on him, swinging his sword until it chipped the stone beneath the bloody corpse.

More screams.

Edmund sprang into the room, sword upraised. Thick blood coursed along its blade and hilt. He wheeled around, searching for his next target. Then, he realized he was the one screaming.

With an effort, he made himself lower the scimitar. His chest pounded. His muscles shook. His gaze darted from body to body to body. They were all beyond dead. Each was hacked to pieces. Blood was everywhere. It even streamed down the walls. Somebody's head rolled in the fire pit, its skin turning brown as the hissing flames licked its cheek.

Across the room stood an iron door, frost glittering around its edges. Edmund hurried to it and then stopped.

Calm down. And take everything you can.

They blew a horn! Guards will be here any moment.

It'll take them a few minutes to realize what happened. You need supplies.

Sheathing his sword, Edmund threw open the chests lining the walls. There were piles of kindling wood, extra weapons, and stores of food. Edmund shoved strips of jerky in his mouth and containers of dried fruit under his arms.

We need something to carry all of this.

There were no backpacks, no tapestries on the walls, no blankets or rugs. And the goblins' clothes had been slashed to pieces.

No matter. Search them. Take anything of use.

His hands skimmed over the guards' bloody bodies. He found coins of unknown denomination, two knives, a set of keys, and several betting slips. He took a knife and threw everything else onto the ground.

Standing in the middle of the battlefield, he scanned the room for anything else he could use.

Forget it. Get out of here. Run!

Clutching as much food as he could carry, Edmund shot to the door and turned the handle.

Freedom—

A blast of icy wind drove him back. Fierce snow bit Edmund's exposed body. He raised his hands to fight off the blinding onslaught. Jars of preserves fell from underneath his arms and shattered on the ground. He struggled to inhale.

Before him, shards of bright snow swirled about a shallow dell. The cutting wind consumed a line of footprints heading into a forest of fir and cedar trees, their green branches bent under blankets of thick ice.

Running into the hip-high drifts, Edmund waded toward the snow-covered trees. His numbing feet faltered.

It's too cold! It's too cold!

But you're free!

I'll freeze. It's too cold!

He fled to the guards' chamber, the cold burning his body. His feet and legs felt dead and heavy, his face frozen into place. He couldn't move his lips. Standing by the fire pit, he slapped his bluish-pink skin and hopped up and down.

Damn it! This isn't going to work.

But . . . I'm, I'm . . . free! I'm finally free!

He examined what the goblins were wearing. Their boots were too small for him. His enlargement spell would help, but only for a few minutes at a time. Thanks to his sword work, their clothing was useless. But it didn't matter. He needed more than a few wool shirts and pants to survive the winter in the Far North.

Sticking his head outside, he studied the overcast sky.

Maybe February?

More like late January, judging by the arc of the sun.

He stepped into the dell, but another frigid gale drove him back.

He gazed mournfully outside a moment longer, his skin hardening in the bitter cold. He wanted to cry, but he'd used all his tears.

Damn it! Damn it! Damn it!

Chapter Thirty-Five

At least three weeks had passed since Edmund stole armloads of dried fruit and jerky from the guards' chamber. However, those supplies were now gone. And he was as hungry and desperate as before.

Since his near escape, an unnerving quiet had settled over the mines. He rarely saw guards patrolling the major passageways anymore. When he did, they didn't appear particularly alert. They chatted to each other, weapons sheathed at their sides or leaning against their shoulders. He hadn't even heard the rhythmic ringing of metal on stone as Pit Dwellers labored for their paltry rations. Day after day, everything was completely silent—except for the constant dripping of distant water and the squeaking of the rats fighting over the remains of Edmund's biscuits.

He tried catching one once, hoping to have something new to eat. But when he grabbed it behind its head like Pond Scum had said, the rat spun like a viper and bit deep into his hand. Its black, scythe-like claws dug into his skin, shredding his flesh. Edmund had to beat it against a stone to kill it. And even in death, the rat didn't let go. He had to pry its jaws from his thumb. Now, the rats kept their distance, watching him with their pink, untrusting eyes.

Edmund's stomach rumbled.

If I eat another damn biscuit, I'll—

He sniffed, then sat up.

Venison?

It's your imagination.

No, it isn't! It's real. I can smell it!

Who'd be cooking venison in the mines?

Maybe there's another guard's chamber around here. Maybe there's another way out!

He sniffed each tunnel around him.

His stomach rumbled again.

He slid sideways into a fissure and sniffed. The smell grew stronger.

The fissure narrowed into a crawlway. Wriggling forward on his elbows and knees, Edmund followed the wonderful scent.

The passage turned sharply to the left.

A faint red light wavered on the wall in front of him.

He could hear at least one person gorging themselves.

He stopped.

There was definitely more than one person eating.

Kravel? Gurding?

He hadn't heard either of his captors since shortly after the massacre in the guard chamber when they and a hundred other goblins swarmed down the column-lined passageway. Kravel cursed the dead guards and shouted for his hunters to search the forest. Since then, all had been quiet.

Why would Kravel and Gurding be eating in the mines?

Why would anybody?

Edmund approached the red light and the unmistakable smell of roasting meat. Someone smacked their lips. Edmund's stomach grumbled again.

I can't stand this any longer!

With excruciating slowness, he peeked around the turn in the crawlway and stifled a gasp. In the middle of a vast cavern sat two distant figures huddling around a pile of blazing torches, devouring a slab of meat the size of a moose's hind leg. Through the deep shadows, Edmund could see the back of a hulking figure silhouetted by the bright crimson glow.

Turd?

He escaped? But how?

Edmund squinted. It was undeniably Turd. He kept clenching and unclenching his massive hands.

Somebody else was with him. Directly across from the fire, a smaller figure with a black beard peered wildly around as he shoved partially cooked food into his mouth.

Pond Scum?

Edmund retreated.

They both escaped? I wonder what happened to Vomit.

He couldn't run with that leg. You can guess what happened to him.

Edmund's stomach rumbled louder.

He rubbed his sunken belly.

This doesn't make any sense. How did they get the meat?

Hurry before they eat it all!

Edmund propped himself on his elbows, listening. He could hear his former pit mates scarfing down food as fast as they could, the crackling of the torches, and the periodic dripping from stalactites echoing in the cavern—but nothing else.

He rubbed his temples, hoping his headache would go away. His stomach churned as he peered around the corner again, careful not to expose himself.

He whispered through the opening. "Psssst! Turd. Pond Scum."

They didn't respond. Staring intently at the meat as they dangled it over the smoky flames, they licked their fingers.

What are you waiting for? It's Turd and Pond Scum. They have meat!

Something isn't right about this. Where would they get that?

Maybe from a storage room. The goblins made jerky, didn't they? They must have smokehouses somewhere. Or maybe Turd killed some hunters bringing in a deer carcass from the forest.

Maybe . . .

Edmund rolled a small stone between his dirty fingers as he watched Turd consume another hunk of venison.

Think how much easier it'd be having two other people. You could actually get some sleep while they kept watch and prevented the rats from biting you. You wouldn't have to jump at every noise. Get another couple of swords, and you could start killing goblins at will. You could free more slaves. Maybe start an armed uprising in the mines. You can make them pay for your eye. You can make them pay for everything!

Edmund weighed the stone in his hand and then flicked it to the ground. He touched the Star of Iliandor on his brow. The gem was cold.

Crawling closer to the opening, he stuck his head into the cavern and glanced about. Other than Turd and Pond Scum, the cavern seemed empty. But the shadows were black, and hiding spots were many.

He pulled his knees to his chin, rotated, and slipped his legs out of the tunnel. The rest of his body followed.

"Turd," he whispered. "Pond Scum."

Again, there was no response.

He stalked closer through the smoke and meat-scented darkness. His mouth watered. His stomach jumped over itself.

"Turd," he said louder. "Pond Scum."

There was a rustle.

Grabbing fistfuls of meat, Turd hunched over the torches.

Pond Scum's head snapped up. Springing to his feet, he yelled. "Filth! It's a trap! Run!"

From the surrounding shadows, countless figures flew at Edmund.

"There he is!" Turd inched toward the cavern's main exit, his retreat quickening with every jab of his finger. "Get him! Get him!"

As soon as Pond Scum had screamed "trap," Edmund realized what was happening. Spinning, he bolted to the crawlway. But goblins blocked his path. Lowering his shoulders, he plowed between them, their fingers sliding off his grimy skin as they grabbed at him. Somebody threw a net, but it fell short.

"Remember," Kravel announced from somewhere in the cavern, "don't kill him."

"And take the other one to the wet cells," Gurding said. "The miserable screamer. We'll deal with him later."

Edmund dove into the crawlway.

Somebody seized his ankle and pulled.

Edmund slid backward. Kicking and twisting, he broke free. He propelled himself forward, bloodying his knees as they thrust against the jagged stone. Somebody shot into the crawlway after him.

"Come here, you dung rat," a goblin said.

He grabbed at Edmund's left calf. Edmund's heel connected with the goblin's jaw. The goblin swore.

Edmund pulled himself around the corner.

Stay and fight? Only one can come in here at a time.

No! Get out of here, now!

Hands clawed at Edmund's right foot.

Edmund scrambled deeper into the crawlway.

The goblin cursed again. "Damn you!"

Up ahead, the end of the passage came into view. If Edmund could reach it, he'd dive out, turn, and kill the goblin as he emerged from the opening.

A rope snagged his leg. It tightened around his ankle. The goblin yanked.

"Gotcha!"

Edmund drove forward, but the rope suddenly jerked taut. With his free leg, he pushed in vain against the floor. His fingernails tore at the walls. He slid backward toward the cavern.

"I'll drag you out of here piece by piece if I have to," the goblin said.

"I don't think so," Edmund said.

Grabbing a rock, he turned and shoved it beneath the goblin's head. *"Forstørre nå!"*

In a flash, the stone filled the crawlway. There was a crushing sound, like an elephant stepping on a coconut. The bloody rope went slack. Slipping his ankle free, Edmund scrambled farther into the darkness, the shouts of Kravel and the goblin hunters fading behind him as he fled.

Well, that was certainly close!

Too close. Had it not been for Pond Scum —

Edmund stopped crawling.

What are you doing? Don't!

He backtracked to a different passage.

You're making a big mistake!

Maybe. But the goblins won't be expecting it.

You're falling out of the pan and into the fire.

Either way, I'm cooked. Better to die trying to help somebody.

You're going to get captured.

But Edmund stopped listening. He crawled out of a crevice, dropped to the floor below, and trotted up a wide passageway. Deeper in the mines, turmoil raged. But it moved away from him, and he from it. He increased his speed, knowing the passage as well in the darkness as he did in the light.

Chapter Thirty-Six

Edmund came to the boarded-over door he'd ripped from its hinges countless weeks earlier. A red glow appeared through its cracks. In the guardroom on the other side, somebody screamed in pain. Goblins shouted.

There was the sound of a body hitting stone.

The screaming stopped.

Edmund flattened himself next to the doorway.

"He'll be punished all right," a goblin said.

"The Games?" another goblin asked.

"Something far more painful, I'd think, after what he's done."

"Don't let this one get away," a third goblin said. "The Torturers will want to tickle him from the inside out, if you get me. Nice and slow like."

"He's not going anywhere," the second goblin said.

"If he does," the third said, "you best kill yourself. We'll fetch him after we go report."

Footsteps faded away.

A chair screeched as if pushed against a floor.

Somebody coughed.

In the darkness outside the guardroom, Edmund gripped his scimitar with both hands.

Make it quick. No screaming this time.

He nodded to himself.

Taking a deep breath, he threw open the door and bounded into the guardroom, his sword held high. The chain mail-clad goblin sitting in the chair vaulted to his feet, drawing his own scimitar. He raised his sword to parry Edmund's blow.

But Edmund swung low, clipping the goblin's knee. The guard collapsed.

Edmund thrust the tip of his sword into the guard's neck. Gurgling, the guard choked on blood. Edmund hit him across the side of the head. The guard stopped moving.

Take everything! Take his mail and clothing!

No time! Get Vorn and Pond Scum. Then get the hell out of here.

Grabbing a ring of keys from the nearby table, Edmund ran down the damp corridor to the wet cells.

"Pond Scum!" He covered his nose. "Vorn!"

"Edmund?" Vorn said from somewhere in the darkness. "What are you—?"

"No time to explain! Where did they put the new prisoner?"

"In one of the first cells. On your right, judging from the sound. But—"

"Pond Scum?" Edmund called. He opened a visor and peered into a cell. But it was too dark to see.

I should've taken the torch.

Too late now. Hurry!

Fumbling with the keys, he slid each into the lock. One fit. He turned it and tugged the cell door open.

It was empty.

He tried the next cell.

"You shouldn't have returned," Vorn said.

"We're getting out of here," Edmund said. "All of us. I should've gotten you out before. I'm sorry."

He wrenched open the next door and found a shriveled body huddled in the corner. White rats shot from the corpse and stampeded out of the cell.

"You shouldn't have come here," Vorn said. "They'll be anticipating that. They'll be waiting."

"They think I'm somewhere else."

He heaved open another door. There, slumped on the grated floor, was Pond Scum, his head bloody, his hands bound behind his back. Edmund shook him. "Pond Scum."

He didn't answer.

"Edmund," Vorn pleaded. "Don't waste time. Leave here. Take the other prisoner and go!"

Sheathing his sword, Edmund pulled Pond Scum over his shoulder.

"We're all getting out of here," he said. "I found a way out. But it's guarded. I have weapons, b-b-but I need your help. Together, we can fight our way out."

"That won't be possible."

Edmund made his way along the dim corridor, attempting to discern which cell was Vorn's.

He retched. "I forgot how badly this place stinks."

"Go!" Vorn said. "I can't help you. Go now, before they return. Please, I'm begging you!"

"Keep talking."

"Edmund . . ."

Here he is! Hurry. Get the door open.

He tried several keys. Finally, one glided in.

"We're all getting out," Edmund said.

Balancing Pond Scum on his shoulder, he pulled open the metal door and froze.

"Y-y-you, you, you're an . . ." Edmund stammered in disbelief. "You're an . . . elf!"

Elves exist? I . . . I must be dreaming.

Vorn lifted his head, revealing the deep holes where his eyes used to be. "We prefer the term Huldran. But yes, I'm an elf. As is Kar-Nazar. Or at least he was before the Dark Magic made him a Vaettir, and he began ruling the Hiisi. However, we can't talk about this now. You've got to go. Flee while you can."

Edmund's knees buckled. He repositioned Pond Scum over his shoulder. "We all can escape."

You can't carry both of them.

"As you can no doubt see." Vorn gestured with fingerless hands to his missing eyes and the stumps at the end of his shriveled legs. "I can't help you."

Edmund's gaze darted to the guardroom.

"But, but I . . . I can't leave you here!"

"I cannot help you." Vorn dragged himself closer across the metal grate. Edmund retreated a step. "But you can help me."

"How?"

"End my misery. Kill me."

Edmund shook his head.

It'd be the most humane thing to do.

"Kill me, Edmund."

"I, I, I . . . I can't!"

"You must. Please."

Edmund repositioned Pond Scum again and glanced up the passageway. "I, I, I can't." He drew the knife from his belt and held it out to the blind elf. "You can—"

"I can't. Or I would've done so a millennium ago. My soul won't ascend if I take my own life. But you can end it for me. End my misery, Edmund. Please, end it."

Pond Scum groaned. His warm blood trickled along Edmund's sweaty shoulder. Edmund stammered, his legs weakening under Pond Scum's weight.

"Promise me you'll never give Kar-Nazar what he craves," Vorn said. "Don't answer the riddle. His heart is black. I should've seen that sooner. I shouldn't have helped him for as long as I did."

He's an alchemist! Remember the stories he told?

"You're Kar-Vorn . . . the, the Elven blacksmith from the old faerie tales!"

"It's time you connected what you've read to what's happening around you," Vorn said. "You need to understand what those books of yours truly mean. There's more inside their covers than you realize. But I cannot help you anymore. Please, help me."

Edmund lowered his knife. "Please, tell me what this is all about."

"Kill me."

"I can't!"

"You must."

Kill him. Put him out of his misery. This could've been you. It still could be if you don't get out of here.

A burbling sound resonated far above them.

"Please," Vorn said. "This is no way to live for eternity."

"What do I need to do to stop Kar-Nazar?"

"Get Iliandor's diary and destroy it. Burn it. Make sure he never gets the original."

"But why? He has already read an identical copy."

The burbling grew louder.

"Do as I say. End my life and destroy the diary."

Edmund stared at the blade in his hand.

"Please," Vorn pleaded.

From up the passageway, goblin voices echoed.

Sewage plunged into the cells.

Chapter Thirty-Seven

Pond Scum groaned. "Where am I?"

He coughed. Chunks of blood spewed across the grey stone slab on which he was lying.

Brushing the tears away from his eye, Edmund said, "You're with me—Filth. You're safe." He turned up the lantern's flame.

Pond Scum surveyed their cramped surroundings through blackened eyes. Tiny crystals in the stone glittered green and yellow like constellations. He coughed again.

"Nice place. Very pretty." He sat up with an effort. "Thanks, Filth." He gave a bloody smile. "I appreciate you saving me. How did you manage it?"

Edmund grumbled something.

"What?" Pond Scum asked.

"We're not saved yet," Edmund said louder. "We're right around the corner from the wet cells. Guards are swarming all over the place."

He stared at the lantern. Its flame flickered. "Thanks for telling me about the trap . . . and everything in the pit. I'm in your debt."

"Cook me breakfast, and we'll call it square." Pond Scum laughed. He winced and held his right side.

A biscuit the color of dry sawdust fell into his lap.

Pond sniffed it. "What's this?"

"Breakfast," Edmund said. "And lunch, and dinner . . . for the rest of our lives."

Pond Scum took a bite.

"Not bad." He finished it off. "Splendid, actually. Where did you get it? I didn't realize the Hiisi were bakers."

Edmund put his hands together. *"Mat av nå."* When he opened them, he held a small, round biscuit. He tossed it to the startled Pond Scum.

"You can make these?" he asked. "Magically?"

"It's easier now than before. B-b-before, when I was in the pit, I couldn't make enough for everybody. Now I can feed an army of rats."

"Oh," Pond Scum said, his mouth full. "I'm not accusing you. I understand completely. I'm just impressed." He swallowed. "Can you make anything else? Red wine, perhaps? Or honey? Honey would be great on these. It'd give them a little more flavor."

"Unfortunately, I can only create this and water. Would you like another?"

"Absolutely."

Edmund handed him another biscuit. Pond Scum savored each mouthful with exaggerated moans. He gestured to Edmund's face. "Sorry about your eye. Do you want to talk about it?"

Touching the indentation where his left eye used to be, Edmund turned away. "No."

"All right then. Let's sing songs!"

Edmund laughed despite himself.

"There you go!" Pond Scum grinned, blood and brown crumbs streaking his beard. "Things aren't that black, are they?"

"Wait until the oil in the lantern burns out."

"But we're alive. We have wonderful food. Water. And we're free! What more could we hope for?"

Edmund's expression turned bitter. "Free? We're merely in a bigger cage, that's all."

"The world's a cage if you let it be. The same with your mind. The trick is to make your cage what you want it to be."

"Keep saying things like that, and I'll send you back to the pits."

"All right, all right. I won't lecture. Still, brooding doesn't help, does it? Be happy we're finally free, different cage or not."

"We're not free," Edmund said angrily. His voice reverberated in the small cavity in which they were camped. He rubbed his head. "I'm sorry. But we're not. In many respects, things are much worse. The sooner you realize that, the better."

"But we're alive," Pond Scum said. "And that's something to celebrate. They didn't tell us anything about you. They only hinted at the agony you were in. Then they took Crazy away. We never saw him again, the poor guy."

Crazy Bastard . . .

"Actually—" Edmund picked at the pommel of his scimitar. "Crazy . . . he . . . he got away."

Pond Scum stopped eating. "You're kidding me."

"At least," Edmund said, "that's what it looked like. It's a long story."

"Hey," Pond Scum said. "We have nothing but time, right? Is he in the mines somewhere? Maybe we can find him."

Edmund shifted, unsure of what to reveal. "You see, I . . . I was told . . . I was told to select one of you for the Games. If I didn't . . ."

"And you picked Crazy. That's perfectly understandable. I would've done the same."

Edmund lifted his head. "You would've?"

"Sure. Look, being happy and optimistic is one thing. Being practical and keeping yourself alive is another. Go on. What happened?"

"They put him in this big arena where tens of thousands of goblins were all shouting and clapping."

At "goblin," Pond Scum recoiled, then laughed. "There were tens of thousands of them . . . of goblins, you say? I never dreamt there were so many."

"My thoughts exactly. I wonder how they've gone unnoticed."

"We're a long way from no place," Pond Scum said. "I don't know about you, but it took them three weeks to drag me here after they waylaid my caravan. Who knows how many secret holds they have up and down these mountains? But go on. What about Crazy?"

"At any rate, they threw him into this arena with hordes of goblins all stomping and screaming. Then an ogre came out."

"An ogre? Great gods!"

The shadows around them deepened as the lantern's flame dimmed.

"He came in hollering and waving his spear and net around," Edmund said, "getting the crowd whipped into a frenzy."

"What did Crazy do? He must've been scared out of his wits, poor guy. Did he shit himself?"

"He was terrified. He hid underneath a table that had weapons on it."

"What happened then?"

Yes, Master Storyteller, what happened then?

Edmund shrugged. "I don't know. I looked away. I didn't want to see what was about to happen. So, I covered my face. And then . . . and then the ogre was dead. He was on the ground with Crazy Bastard jumping on his chest like a drunken rabbit."

"The ogre was dead?" Pond said in disbelief. "What the hell happened? How could Crazy kill an ogre? I mean . . . an ogre?"

"I don't know. I've played it over and over in my mind, and I still don't have the slightest idea."

"What happened next?"

"Then a horn blew, and they let him leave the arena. I was brought to the top of the tower—"

"Tower?"

"Yeah, there's a t-t-tower above us, hidden away in a deep fold in the mountains. It isn't of human construction; at least, none I have studied. It seems far older than anything else in this region."

"Okay, go on. What happened to Crazy?"

"They gave me this telescope and told me to look at the path leading from the front gate. And, sure enough, Crazy Bastard was running away, screaming like he always did."

"Were they—the goblins—were they running after him?"

"No. They said they would. But they were giving him a head start as part of his prize for winning the fight. I don't know." Edmund tossed his hands. "They could've killed him as soon as I left the window. But at least he got a good way away when I last saw him. A couple of miles, I should think. He might've been able to hide. The forest in the valley is pretty dense. Finding food would've been his biggest problem."

He's probably dead in some hole somewhere, frozen solid by now.

Pond Scum rested against the cave wall. "An ogre? Huh." He munched on his biscuit. "Do you think maybe Crazy Bastard wasn't all that crazy? Could it have been an act?"

"I don't know. M-m-maybe I'm the crazy one."

"Don't be so negative. You got out. You're free. Maybe not 'free,' but you're one step closer, now aren't you?"

Edmund threw a small stone at the wall.

You should've rescued Vorn, too.

I couldn't carry both of them.

"Have you solved the riddle?" Pond Scum asked.

"No," Edmund said, not liking the reminder.

"Do you want to talk about it?"

"No!" Edmund rubbed his temples. "I'm . . . I'm sorry. Just, just forget about the damn riddle. Let's worry about getting out of here." He pushed his matted hair out of his eye.

Pond Scum pointed at the Star of Iliandor on Edmund's brow. "What's that?"

Edmund let his hair cover the gem. "It's nothing. It's something I found."

"Looks expensive. Perhaps you can sell it when we get out of here. Can I see it?" Reaching forward, Pond Scum flinched, his face contorted in pain.

"I'm, I'm sorry," Edmund said. "I should've done this sooner. Hold still."

He put his hands on Pond Scum's ribs.

"Smerte av reise."

The swelling subsided. The purple hue turned a dull brown.

Pond Scum exhaled more easily.

"Well, you're full of surprises, aren't you?"

Edmund put his hands on Pond Scum's bloody face.

"I can't make eyes grow back," he said. "B-b-but I can heal some things. Minor cuts and bruises, simple broken bones. That's about it."

He cleared his mind.

"Smerte av reise."

The bleeding from Pond's nose slowed and then stopped.

"Sorry, I wasn't much help in the pits. I couldn't—"

"No need to explain." Pond Scum wiggled his jaw and pursed his lips. "Oh! This is much better. It's still tender, but . . ." He twisted his torso. "But the pain is almost completely gone. Thanks! Now, if you can sprout wings and fly us out of here, I'd be much obliged."

"It won't be that easy, I'm afraid."

"It can't be that difficult. What's the problem? I see you have a couple of swords and some other gear. What do you say we start freeing some more Pit Dwellers? We could raise a small army. Like you said, you can feed them now."

Don't take any more risks. Hide and wait for spring.

"I think it'd be better to lie low for a bit."

"But you have a plan, am I right? I mean to get us out of this cage and into the bigger one we call the world."

"It's not much of a plan, I'm afraid."

"But at least you have one, so there you go. Let's hear it."

A thin ribbon of blue flame skated across the lantern's wick. Black smoke floated to the cave's ceiling. The lantern's oil was nearly spent.

Edmund lay down and stared at the glittering stone a few feet above his head. "There's . . . there's a way out. There's this passage leading to the west side of the mountains—"

"Terrific! So, what's the problem?"

"The first is that it's the middle of winter. Everything is frozen solid. There must be four feet of snow outside. We'd die within ten minutes if we left now, even if we had decent clothing."

"All right," Pond Scum said. "We'll bide our time. We can hide and sing songs. We'll have fun. You can tell me more stories from those books you keep talking about."

Books . . .

They got me into this mess. I should've been a carpenter.

"The second problem," Edmund said, "is they know I'm still here, and that I know where the exit is. It'll be guarded. You can only surprise the goblins so often before they start looking for it. They'll be armored in plate mail and have bows ready. They'll cut us down before we set foot outside."

"Don't be so pessimistic."

Edmund raised an eyebrow. "How good are you with a sword?"

"Me? I've swatted flies before. It's basically the same concept, right?"

Edmund rolled his eye.

"Well then, if that way is no good," Pond Scum said, "how about finding another exit? Maybe the River Gate."

"River Gate?"

"Yeah. It's only a legend. Something some of the Pit Dwellers mentioned, you understand. Vomit claims one of our predecessors saw it once—"

"What happened to Vomit, by the way?" Edmund asked. "Why wasn't he with you and Turd?"

"Ah, that! Your friend, Mr. Kravel, didn't think you'd believe all three of us escaped. So he only had the two of us sit there."

Makes sense.

"G-g-go, go on." Edmund waved for Pond Scum to continue. "What about this River Gate? What did Vomit say about it?"

"From what he told me—and this was years ago when I first got here, mind you. He said this big river runs underneath the mountains and goes outside. It's gated with bars or something, so nobody can get in or out that way. But maybe we can open the gate or knock it down. At least it's another option."

A big river . . .

Maybe the Hawthorn?

I think we're farther north than the Hawthorn. Perhaps a river heading east to the Sea?

"And we have time to look for it, you know?" Pond Scum said. "That or, when spring comes, we can make a mad rush for the exit you found, swords swinging."

Maybe with both of you, you can fight your way out. If you hide for a month or two, they might think you're dead. There'll be fewer guards.

"What do you say?" Pond Scum asked. "Shall we go looking for the River Gate?"

"Let me think about it."

From time to time, Edmund had heard rushing water as he explored the mines. Occasionally, he found small streams here and there. However, whenever he followed them, they either plunged into a chasm or disappeared into a crack too small for him to crawl through. A river, on the other hand, would almost certainly flow out of the mountains and into the lowlands. The trick would be finding it.

The darkness deepened around them. Edmund could barely see Pond Scum an arm's length away, humming to himself. Pretty soon, if they wanted to see, they'd have to burn the scraps of wood he'd collected or light a torch. Pond Scum yawned.

River gate . . .

Maybe it's nearby.

Maybe.

"I can't wait to get home," Edmund muttered to the growing shadows.

"Me—" Pond Scum yawned again. "I'm just happy to be out of the damn pit."

"You don't want to go home?" Edmund asked. "Don't you have family?"

"Sure. I was married before I was brought here."

"You were?"

"Yeah, we had two terrific kids . . . and one I really didn't care for."

Pond Scum appeared to be serious.

"Why haven't you mentioned them before?" Edmund asked. "Don't you miss them?"

"Of course. But I have my memories of all the good times we had. That's all I need."

"It doesn't sound like you're too anxious to see them."

"You might find that you can't go back. I mean, what you remember, what your home means to you, may only exist in the past, or in your mind. That's why I don't have any real desire to return. I want to live the rest of my life as well as I can, wherever I can."

Pond Scum strained to stifle a yawn.

"Besides," he said, "my wife has probably remarried. The kids have all grown and gone on with their lives. I wouldn't want to complicate things. They're over me by now. I want them to be happy and cherish what we had and to nurture what they have now, whatever that is."

Pond Scum rolled over onto his back.

"If you don't mind." He stretched out. "I'm a bit bushed. I'm going to sleep the sleep of the dead. Wake me when breakfast is ready." He yawned louder. "Thanks again, Filth."

"Call me Edmund," Edmund said. "And yeah, I'm exhausted, too. It's been a day I'd rather put behind us."

"Edmund, eh? I thought you'd be a Henry or maybe an Arthur. But Edmund suits you." Pond Scum put his hands behind his head. "Call me Pond. It's better than my real name. Besides, it's who I am now. Good night, Edmund."

"Good night, Pond."

Chapter Thirty-Eight

"Are you sure you don't want to talk about your eye?" Pond asked again.

"Yes!" Edmund said in a harsh whisper.

"It'll make you feel better."

"Shhh! Your voice carries. They'll hear you in every passage for a quarter mile around."

"Sorry."

"And stop b-b-banging your sword into everything. You might as well ring a gong and announce where we are."

"Sorry. I'm kind of new at this adventuring stuff. I'm a merchant by training, you understand. Textiles and the like—"

"Shhh!"

They were in a series of abandoned mine shafts far from any of the passages Edmund had previously searched. He was so far from the main tunnels that he doubted he could find them again.

He examined a pile of stone blocking their way.

There's no way you can get through that.

No. But maybe I should climb up and explore the hole in the ceiling. It seems to connect with another fissure.

Don't be stupid. Follow the mines. They have an exit. Natural caves usually dead-end.

Edmund touched a beam supporting the mine's ceiling. The wood crumbled and toppled to the ground. The echoing clatter rolled through the passages around them.

"Hopefully, nobody heard that," Pond said.

"Even if they did," Edmund said, "they wouldn't pay much attention. There are cave-ins all the time around here. That's why I'm reluctant to take any of these tunnels."

He swept his torch across a wall of cobwebs blocking another opening. The webs sizzled and disappeared in a great puff of grey smoke, revealing a steep passage heading into darkness.

I don't like the looks of that decline. Coming up will be difficult, if not impossible.

Rivers are likely to be lower than higher.

Maybe.

Edmund listened again. Flowing water was somewhere nearby. But the constant echoes made it challenging to pinpoint exactly where it was.

The smoke from his torch wafted into Edmund's face, making him cough.

He hated torches. They gave off too much light, and their oily smoke left a scent trail a blind man could follow for hours. Further, he couldn't simply turn off a torch like a lantern. However, they were out of oil, and they needed to see.

Edmund took a few steps into a passage to their left and reconsidered his options.

"Why did you stop?" Pond whispered.

"I'm trying to determine which way to go," Edmund said, annoyed.

"The water sounds like it's coming from up ahead."

"It isn't about sound," Edmund said with forced patience. "The echoes are coming from all directions. I'm trying to ascertain if any of these passages were created by water."

"Why?"

"Please, just . . . just stop talking for a moment. I need to think."

The echoing of their voices settled into the surrounding stone. Edmund pondered his options. Pond tapped on his shoulder.

"I hear it again," Pond whispered. "It's closer this time."

"As I said before," Edmund said, "they're only echoes. Rocks fall. Passages collapse. Dripping water sounds like a hammer or people running. You'll get used to it. Now, please, give me a moment to think."

He listened at each dark passage. The sound of rushing water continued unabated in all three.

"I think you may be right," Edmund said.

"I am?" Pond said, surprised.

"Maybe. At any rate, let's try the way you suggested. We can always double back again if it doesn't go anywhere."

Hunched over so their heads wouldn't hit the low ceiling, they stalked along a passage angling to the left.

"What's this?" Pond pointed to discoloration in the crumbling stone.

Edmund glanced at it. "It's gold."

"Gold? Why would they close these mines if there is still gold here?"

That's a good question.

"It's like throwing money—"

"Pond," Edmund said sternly, "please . . . hush."

Putting his finger over his lips, Pond winked.

They continued along the passage in silence for several minutes. Then, it opened on a ledge overlooking a colossal square cavern that appeared to be an abandoned quarry. Water falling from countless waterfalls poured into a clear lake that glistened in the red light of their crackling torch.

"It isn't a river," Edmund said. "But maybe there's a tributary leading away from here that we can follow. Hold this while I climb down." Edmund handed Pond the torch.

"You're going down there?" Pond looked over the edge, aghast. "It's a thirty-foot drop!"

"It's only twenty, if that."

"Are you sure?"

"You can do it. Just watch me."

Edmund swung himself over the ledge, lowered himself, and then let go. He landed in waist-high water. The splash resounded throughout the cavern.

"All right," Edmund called up. "Now you try."

Pond looked doubtful.

"Trust me," Edmund said. "If you can survive the pits, you can do this. But toss me the torch first."

Pond still didn't seem convinced. But he did as he was told.

"Okay." Pond grimaced as he lowered himself. "Here I go!"

He didn't move.

Edmund watched him hanging there, clinging to the ledge.

"Come on!" he called up. "It's a ten-foot drop, if that."

"You said it was twenty!"

"Twenty, ten—same thing. You'll be landing in water either way."

"Are you sure I won't kill myself?"

"No," Edmund said. "But you can't hang there forever. You might as well drop and take your chances."

"Okay." Pond muttered something that might have been a prayer. "Here I come."

He let go and plummeted like a stone, landing beside Edmund with a splash.

"I can't believe it." He looked at the ledge, water dripping from his nose. "I did it! I jumped forty feet into a pool of water!"

"Forty feet?" Edmund said. "I'm sure it was at least fifty."

"Really?"

"No. Stick with forty. People will believe that." Edmund waved for Pond to follow him. "Come on. Let's get to dry land. The gods only know what lives in subterranean pools like this."

They waded toward a rock embankment.

Pond pointed to the waterfalls. "Do you think those come from outside?"

"Probably not."

"Why?"

"N-n-notice the temperature of the water?" Edmund scrambled on top of a pile of rocks lining the lake. "It isn't freezing. Water coming into the mountains would be—"

An immense splash erupted where they'd dropped into the lake. Weapons ready, Edmund and Pond whirled around as an enormous figure stood in the water behind them.

"Turd!" Edmund said.

"I told you somebody was following us," Pond said. "I knew I wasn't crazy!"

Turd's massive form strode toward them. He was thinner than before, but his shoulders and arms were still round with muscles. "My name is Barnatol," he said in a commanding voice. "Prince of the Hildorim."

Edmund sneered at him. "You'll always be Turd to me."

Turd snarled. Then he noticed their swords. He hesitated, water lapping at his thighs. "You've got weapons? Give me one. We can fight our way out of here. I know the way to the city!"

"Give you a weapon?" Edmund said in disbelief. "After what you did to me?"

"I've done nothing to you."

"'There he is!'" Edmund mimicked. "'Get him!'"

"I did what I had to do," Turd shouted, his voice thundering throughout the quarry. "Anybody would've done the same."

"He didn't!" Edmund jabbed a thumb at Pond.

"That's true," Pond said.

"What did it matter? They already knew you were there." Turd took a step forward.

Edmund pointed his sword at him.

Turd halted.

"I needed to get away," he said. "I needed to distract them. I was taking advantage of the commotion!"

"Then why didn't you simply run?" Edmund asked. "Why draw attention to yourself? Why get me caught?"

"Give me one of the weapons," Turd said. "We can fight our way out. I can wield a blade better than Scum can. You know that."

"Not a chance," Edmund said. "I can't trust you."

"You can trust I want to get out," Turd said. "And I have a better chance with you than without you. Together we—"

"No!"

He's right. With him, we'd have a better chance.

He'd turn me in in exchange for his freedom. He's probably working for Kravel.

They stared at each other—Edmund high on the rocky bank, Turd below, still in the crystal-clear water.

"Damn it, Filth!" Turd said. "I'll leave if you don't want my help. But give me a weapon."

"You can leave and get your own weapon."

Turd's fists tightened. The veins in his thick neck reddened. "Then give me food. You aren't starving. That's plain. Give me something to eat, and I'll leave you be."

Edmund laughed. "There's food all around you. You're just too stupid to realize it."

Turd opened his mouth, eyes narrowing. Then, they suddenly widened. Screaming, he jerked his leg out of the water. Blood flowed from his calf. Dozens of crimson lights pulsated in the lake around him. He screamed again.

"They're called Carnlokë," Edmund said. "You might know them as Red Jaws."

Diving for the shore, Turd heaved himself on the rocks. Three translucent fish a foot long clung to him like leeches, burrowing deeper into his flesh. An organ above their jaws flashed scarlet with each bite. He ripped them from his legs and cast them into the water.

"You threw away your dinner," Edmund said, his sword still pointed at Turd. "You must not be very hungry."

Turd pressed on the gashes. "You miserable—"

There was running.

Two young goblins with fishing poles were fleeing into a nearby passage. Then Pond cried out. One of Turd's big hands had thrown him to the ground. The other snatched his sword away. Turd put the curved blade against Pond Scum's throat as he lay on the rocks. In the water, red lights swarmed.

"Give me food!" Turd said.

"Does it look like we have food?" Edmund gestured to the rags around his waist. "Where would we keep it?"

Turd trembled with fury and frustration.

"We have to get out of here," Edmund told him. "They're going to raise the alarm."

Turd studied the passage where the goblins had run.

"If you want food," Edmund said, "you'll have to steal it from the guards. Or fish. There are also rats. But I'm not going to help you. Not after what you did. Now, let Pond go."

Turd heaved himself to his feet, his sword pointing at Edmund, Edmund's sword pointing at him. "You're a fool, magic user or not. You're a fool, and you'll die here. You need me."

"No, I don't."

"You'd rather have this?" He kicked Pond in the head. Pond shouted.

"Absolutely." Edmund drew closer. "And if you kick him again, you'll die here as well."

For several moments, they stared at each other. Then they heard goblins yelling for help. Turd hobbled to one of the side tunnels.

"You're a fool, Filth," he said. "I hope they cut out your other eye and leave you to wander around down here until you starve."

With that, he disappeared into the darkness.

This isn't the last you've seen of him.

Who cares? Without food, he's done for.

Edmund helped Pond to his feet.

Pond rubbed his head. "He always was a pleasant fellow."

"Come on. The guards will be here in a minute." Edmund led Pond to the cavern walls. He pointed high above them. "Climb up there. To that opening. See it?"

"You're joking! Jumping into water is one thing. Climbing above a bunch of rocks is another. If I fell, I'll break my back!"

"Then you won't have to worry about the guards."

Studying the wall, Pond shook his head. "I can't."

"Please, trust me," Edmund said. "We have no choice."

Pond sized up the wall again. "All right. What do I do?"

With Edmund instructing him where to put his hands and feet, Pond slowly scaled the side of the quarry. Breathing hard, he hauled himself onto a narrow shelf fifty feet above the lake.

"Great!" Edmund tossed his torch into the tunnel down which Turd fled. "Move over."

He scurried up the wall like a spider. "Lay flat. No talking."

Seconds later, the clanking of armor raced toward the cavern.

"There!" a goblin shouted below them. "Follow the blood!"

Shouts and footfalls echoed. Then, only the sounds of the waterfalls remained.

"That was close," Pond said.

"It's always close." Edmund shimmed along the shelf to a narrow crawlspace. "Let's get out of here before Kravel and Gurding show up."

Chapter Thirty-Nine

This one seems to be flowing fairly quickly. Maybe it heads to the River Gate.

Or maybe it flows into another giant chasm like the last dozen streams you've followed.

"Hold this." Edmund shoved the last of their torches into Pond's free hand. Kneeling in the calf-deep water, he peered into the crevice the stream raced into.

You aren't going to crawl in there, are you?

Why not? It clearly goes somewhere. Look how fast it's moving.

You'd better hope there aren't any Red Jaws lurking about, or worse. Heaven only knows what beasts dwell this far below the mountains.

It's too shallow for Red Jaws.

You're taking a risk.

If we don't take risks, we'll never get home.

"Stay here," Edmund said.

"Right," Pond said. The sizzling torch cast an orange glow across his round face. "What if something happens?"

"Like what?" A drop of cold water from the ceiling struck Edmund's already damp head. He shivered.

Pond shrugged. "Goblins? Turd?"

"Use the knife I gave you."

"Right!" Pond said. "How about if I scream for help instead?"

"By all means. I'll return and lay pretty flowers on your corpse."

"Okay then. Off you go!"

Edmund lowered himself into the cold water. His hands and knees sank into the gritty red clay at the stream's bottom. He couldn't stop his body from shaking.

Damn, this is cold!

He peered into the narrow crevice again, the swift current swishing around him. The opening seemed large enough, but he couldn't see more than a few feet.

You'll get stuck one of these days. You'll get stuck, and then you'll die a slow death, trapped forever under these accursed mountains.

Pond would—

Edmund considered his companion.

Pond stopped humming. "What?"

"What would you do if I got stuck in here?" Edmund asked.

Pond's shoulders lifted. "Call for help?"

"If I ever get stuck and can't get free or if I'm about to get captured or something," Edmund said, "I want you to kill me. Slit my throat or stab me in the heart. Do you understand?"

"Absolutely."

"So, you'll kill me if the time comes?"

"Oh no! Not a chance."

Edmund threw up his hands. "Then what would you do if I got stuck? Leave me?"

"No. I wouldn't leave you. I'd probably pull on your legs or push or . . . something."

"And if that didn't help?"

"I'm sure things would work out." Pond grinned. "They always do."

He's kidding.

Maybe.

"Give me the knife." Pond handed it to him. "I'll kill myself, thank you very much. I'll be b-b-b-back in a few minutes."

Pond waved. "I'll be here."

Trembling with cold, Edmund scrutinized the opening a third time. It was definitely big enough. He just hoped it led somewhere.

If I don't get out of here soon, I'll —

What? Jump into one of the gorges?

It'd be a quick and relatively painless end.

Let's hope it doesn't come to that.

He crawled into the hole. Almost immediately, darkness enveloped him. Frigid water lapped at his chin. His toes and elbows dug into the silt-covered ground, propelling him forward.

The walls of the tunnel narrowed. His shoulders skimmed the wet stone. The top of his head grazed against the low ceiling. He flattened himself more. As he slithered along on his stomach, the water rose to his shivering bottom lip.

I wish we had extra wood for a fire. I'll need to thaw out after this.

You've felt worse. Keep going forward.

The stream turned slightly. Edmund followed, his head bumping into the unseen ceiling a second time.

That drew blood.

You're fine. Whatever you do, don't panic.

The water inched higher. He tilted his head and exhaled out the corner of his mouth. As he pulled his numbing body through the blackness, his splashing echoed endlessly around him.

The water rose even higher. He lifted his pursed lips closer to the ceiling. He was practically kissing the rock. He squirmed onward, his chest and stomach sliding along the bottom of the stream.

The passage dipped abruptly. Edmund's face plunged into the icy water. He retreated, spitting out water that had infiltrated his mouth. He coughed, long hacking coughs that bounced his body against the surrounding stone.

This is stupid. If you don't get stuck here, you'll freeze to death or drown.

That's better than dying here of old age.

With searching hands, he felt the sides of the passage before him.

It's wide enough.

Yes, but the water goes all the way to the top. Better turn back while you can.

Edmund took three deep breaths, then lunged forward. His feet slipped on the gritty clay. He floundered. Instinctively, he yanked his head up. It cracked against the ceiling. This time, he knew he drew blood. He could taste it in the water.

Reaching before him, his fingers found cracks in the walls. He pulled. His body raked across the streambed. His shoulders grated against the walls as they closed in. Then he stopped, unable to go forward or back.

Trapped!

Completely submerged, Edmund thrashed and turned. His nose hit stone. More blood mixed with the cold water. His lungs burned as they attempted to retain their air. His legs kicked. His arms pulled. Slowly, he scraped through the bottleneck, rocks gouging into his sides and stomach.

Forward or back?

Forward! Hurry!

Edmund inched forward, panic washing over him like the stream's frigid current. Desperate for air, he lifted his head. He cracked it against the ceiling a third time.

He felt air.

Angling his head, he lifted his lips above the waterline and gasped, his chest heaving.

Relax. Everything is fine. Just relax . . .

Relax? I almost died.

You still might die if you don't relax.

When his pulse calmed somewhat, he resumed crawling in the blackness.

The passage widened. Soon, he was on his hands and knees again, his head completely free from the water. Frosty air stung his face. His body convulsed with uncontrollable shivering.

Across the bottom of the stream, Edmund's fingertips found more cracks. But something about them was strange. They were straight and seemed to form rectangles.

Bricks?

His hands swept over the walls.

More bricks?

Maybe this is an aqueduct of some sort.

Searching above his head, he couldn't find the ceiling. Gingerly, he stood, his arms outstretched. Sounds of his quaking echoed in the darkness around him.

Is that a breeze?

Don't let your imagination run wild. Find something to burn. You need light and heat. What about Pond? He'll never get through that crawlway. Never in a million years.

First, figure out where 'here' is.

Shivering, Edmund felt the wall to his left. It was smooth, like polished metal. Dripping, he stepped out of the stream.

Almost immediately, his legs bumped into something lying on the floor. It collapsed with a clatter. Edmund bent down, his fingers tracing a rib cage picked clean by rats.

Human?

Maybe. Maybe a large goblin.

Maybe it's another Pit Dweller who escaped and died in these damn mines.

Searching the floor, Edmund found scraps of rotting fabric. Casting his spell, he lit it on fire. His eye adjusted to the light.

A crumpled skeleton grinned at him.

That'll be you and Pond soon.

Not if I can help it.

He glanced around, holding the burning fabric as close to his shivering body as possible without dripping water onto the tiny flame.

He was in a room. Not a cavern or a natural passageway or even a mineshaft, but a beautiful triangular room constructed of three smooth walls of white marble. The stream at his feet flowed into the basin at the room's center and then flowed out through seven brick-lined troughs resembling a starburst. The remnants of what appeared to be a statue of a child reaching to the heavens lay in pieces about the dust-covered floor. Overhead, a crystal chandelier glinted under a thick blanket of cobwebs.

The flames scorched Edmund's trembling fingers. He draped the cloth over one of the skeleton's thigh bones, then added more scraps of clothing he found nearby. The flames leaped and crackled. Puffs of black smoke whirled to the domed ceiling.

What is this place?

Goblins didn't make it, that's for sure.

Stepping through one of the three doorways, Edmund found himself dripping water in a wide corridor crisscrossed with thick cobwebs, swaying slightly in a faint breeze. Strewn about the floor were more bones and debris.

He found a skeleton wearing a mail shirt. The bones and armor were wrenched apart. A few feet away, a shield lay cloven in two.

Edmund poked the webs with the flaming thighbone. They disappeared in great sheets, leaving behind grey wisps. He stalked along the corridor, knife in one hand, the flaming leg bone in the other.

Don't go too far. You don't want to get lost.

Something crunched under his bare feet.

Stooping, he felt a black substance covering the floor.

Dirt?

Why would there be a pile of dirt here?

He squeezed it in his hand. The smell of rancid ammonia made his eye water.

No! It's not dirt. It's —

His heart leaped.

It's bat guano!

And where there are bats, there's an exit!

Chapter Forty

Pond emerged from the stream, hacking and sputtering. He cast himself onto the tiled floor beside the crumpled skeleton, gasping for air. "I thought . . . I thought you said . . . that . . . that it was an . . . an easy . . . crawl!"

"Did I?" Edmund brushed the cold water from his body. His skin, though now clean, had a bluish tint to it. His fingers were wrinkled and without sensation. But he didn't care. There was an exit somewhere nearby, and he was going to find it—or die trying.

"You did." Pond coughed some more. "Mother's milk, you called it. Keep your head down, you said. Easy as walking, you said. You didn't say anything about that part in the middle."

"Imagine that. Anyway, here you are."

"Like a drowned rat crawling onto the deck of a freezing ship!"

"You'll live. We'll feel warmer as soon as we dry off."

"Maybe. But I can't feel my fingers. They're completely n-n-numb." Pond looked around as he sat shivering. "Wh-wh-where, where's here, by the way?"

"I don't know. It seems to be a deserted fortification or city."

Maybe it's Álfheim.

Don't be absurd! That's only in children's faerie tales.

How can you say that after everything you've seen since leaving Rood? Elves exist. You met one! This could be their ancestral home.

It could be hell for all I care, as long as it has a way out.

"Wherever we are—" Pond wrapped his wet arms around his dripping chest. "—it's cold!"

"Yes, and the, the, the air is moving. Can you feel it? We need to find where it's coming from."

"All right. Sounds easy enough. But what about the winter? We'll need clothes and supplies."

"The winter might be over for all we know. But for now, our primary problem is that we have very little fuel for a fire. Soon, we'll be completely in the dark. And I don't want to stumble blindly into some trap."

"Right." Pond got to his feet. "Then you lead on. I'll guard our rear."

Holding the thighbone with a small scrap of burning fabric, Edmund led Pond into a wide hallway.

"Grab anything you find that will burn," he said. "Clothing, wood, hair—anything."

"Will do!" Pond picked up the rotting remains of what might have been a wall tapestry or rug. "Do you really think there's an exit nearby?"

"Absolutely!"

If there isn't, I'll kill myself.

They took another hallway. Alabaster statues standing in gilded recesses greeted them, their hands lifted in tokens of welcome and goodwill.

"These aren't goblins." Pond inspected the statues. "They don't look like humans either."

Edmund walked slowly through the gallery, shielding his tiny flame from the wafting air. "They're elves."

"Elves?" Pond laughed.

Edmund gestured to the statues' pointed ears and angular facial features. "See."

The chuckles died in Pond's throat. "You mean, the children's tales about them and magic are true?"

Edmund raised an eyebrow.

"Oh." Pond scratched his dripping beard. "Right! I keep forgetting what you can do. Sorry. It's just that, ever since I got captured, everything seems like a dream, you know?"

"More like a nightmare. And it's time we both woke up."

They reached a gathering hall lined with columns of clear crystal. They glittered in the light from their small flame, sending rainbows dancing throughout the room. Mouth open, Pond gazed at the domed ceiling and the faded murals of elven children running naked over fields dotted with yellow wildflowers.

"I still can't believe this," he said. "Elves! Who would've thought? I wonder what happened to them, or what else from the old legends is real. Wights? Dragons? Demons! It's enough to make your head spin."

Edmund beamed. "We're almost out of here. I can feel it!"

He peered into one passageway and then another. Both went off into darkness.

"What do you want to do when you get home?" Pond gave Edmund a handful of threads from the tapestry he found. Edmund added them to his small fire. "I mean, are you going to sell books and all that? Or will you continue adventuring?"

Taking care not to drop the burning cloth at the end of the leg bone, Edmund resumed walking through the chamber. "I haven't thought about it."

"Well," Pond said, as if raising a delicate issue. "If you're interested, maybe we could go into business together or something. Books, textiles . . . I can sell anything!"

Edmund grinned at him. "I bet you can!" He laughed. "I'll tell you what. When we get out of here, I'll buy you the best shop in Rood. It'll be right in the town square. And you can sell anything you like! We'll be partners."

"Partners." Pond mulled that over. "All right. It's a deal. What should we call it? The store, I mean?"

Protecting the flame with his hand, Edmund moved slowly to the next doorway. "I don't know. How about 'Things You Can't Get In A Pit'?" He laughed.

"That'll do."

Edmund inclined his head toward a doorway to their right. "The breeze seems to be coming from over here."

He blew lightly on the smoldering embers. They glowed dark red and then erupted into orange flames as he added another precious few threads of rotting fabric. He looked up, the fire reflecting in his unblinking eyes. His mouth moved silently. The flaming fabric slid off the femur and fluttered to the floor, singeing the thick dust at their feet. The fire went out.

"There!" Edmund said in awe.

Cutting through the blackness like a beacon, a golden light illuminated a distant archway.

"There!" Edmund repeated louder.

Freedom!

Edmund ran toward the light. Pond followed, crying out and jumping. Shielding their eyes from the brilliance, they reached the archway. Cold, fresh air gushed down upon them.

Finally! Freedom!

He wanted to shout for joy.

Free—!

They entered a circular chamber. Around them, light reflected off walls of polished silver. A sarcophagus trimmed in glittering gold and flashing sapphires sat on a raised dais in the middle of the room. On the beautifully tiled floor, snow melted into small holes. But it was to the ceiling where Edmund's gaze drifted. His smile crumbled.

No!

Dazzling sunlight streamed from a shaft directly above them.

Edmund squinted at the blue morning sky. "No!"

"Maybe we can climb up there somehow," Pond said. "It's probably only a hundred feet or so."

More like two hundred feet straight up. Then you'd have to get past the bars.

Edmund collapsed to the floor, his tears of joy turning bitter.

I can't believe this!

"Hey." Pond patted Edmund's damp shoulder. "It isn't all bad. There must be an exit somewhere around here. It isn't like they built this place and didn't have a front door. Right? We simply have to find it. That's all. Meanwhile, we have light and fresh air. Everything is good! You'll see."

"Oh, shut up!" Edmund shouted. "Shut up and leave me alone, will you? We're going to die in here." He sobbed.

He stared at the shaft, the sunlight illuminating his tears.

End this. Take your knife and end all of this.

"Edmund," Pond said. "You—"

"I don't want to hear it. I'm tired of staying positive!"

Pond peered out of an archway across from where they'd entered the chamber. "I really think you should see this."

Scowling, Edmund pulled himself to his feet and staggered to where Pond stood.

They were high up in a magnificent cavern bigger than anything Edmund had ever seen. Its stone ceiling was fashioned into a perfectly rounded dome the color of indigo. On it, flecks of white and violet twinkled like stars in the gloaming.

Below the dome, built on a series of ledges, appeared to be a small city. At the bottommost level was a kind of town square with the remains of fountains and benches, sculptures of fruit trees, fronts of what might have been shops, and an avenue bisecting the ruins. Leading away from them, the avenue disappeared into a gaping tunnel. From the tunnel, bright sunlight shimmered.

Chapter Forty-One

Edmund and Pond sprinted toward the dazzling sunlight.

Reaching the tunnel's entrance, they found it blocked by three towering portcullises. Through the bars, they could see sheets of ice slipping from the bent boughs of spruce trees. Streams of melting snow trickled along an overgrown road leading away from the gate. Far off to the horizon, white hills receded. As they rolled west, they turned greener in anticipation of the approaching spring.

They sucked in the scent of damp pine needles.

"This is merely a challenge to be overcome," Pond said.

We're so close! I can practically touch those trees.

"We have to find a way to lift these gates," Edmund said.

"Maybe we can use that spell of yours. You know, the one that makes things bigger? Maybe we could find a boulder or something and put it between the bars. You can enlarge it, bending the bars wide enough for us to crawl through."

That's a good idea.

No, it's not.

Edmund examined the bars. They were made from smoke-colored steel.

"This doesn't make any sense," he said to himself.

"What? That they have three gates when one would've done just as well?"

Edmund pulled on the bars. Then he heaved his weight against them. They didn't even rattle. "Your people are travelers. Have you ever seen or heard of anything like this metal?"

Pond inspected the portcullis. "No. We're a seafaring people. We specialize in wood. It isn't like you can build boats out of metal. Ask me about different varieties of wood or carving or boats, and I can tell you something. This is pretty, but I don't know a thing about it. What does it mean?"

"It means we can't bend them with or without my spell." Edmund pulled on the bars again. "And Iliandor didn't invent his secret alloy."

"Secret alloy?"

"The Undead King, this, this . . . Kar-Nazar I told you about, believes Iliandor created a kind of magic metal that can't be broken. Warriors armed with it are almost like gods, unable to be killed by blade or arrow. Weapons made from the stuff slice through ordinary steel like wire through cheese."

"Incredible! I'm surprised I've never heard of it."

"If you had, it wouldn't be a 'secret' alloy."

"Good point."

Edmund scanned the upper interior walls of the tunnel leading outside.

"Is that what the riddle was about?" Pond asked. "This magical metal?"

"I don't know."

And I don't care. If I can open these gates, I won't ever have to think about that damn riddle again.

Pond followed his gaze. "What are you looking for?"

"In every book I've ever read, there was always a guardroom that controlled gates like these. And there are always windows guards can look through to see when to open and close them." He pointed to three narrow slits in the tunnel's ceiling. "Like that!"

"So," Pond said, "all we have to do is get to the guardroom and raise the gates, right?"

"Right!" Edmund raced to the city square.

Pond scrambled after him. "How do we find the guardroom?"

"The, the, the first rule of defense is to place all of your critical areas as far from the enemy as possible."

"I'm not sure I follow you."

"It's simple. If you were defending this place and invaders snuck in, you wouldn't want them to gain control of the guardroom controlling the gate. Otherwise, they could let their friends in."

"Makes sense."

"The guardroom must be above the gate. That's a given. They have to look down and see the situation, whether friends or foes are approaching, and so forth." Standing in the center of the town square, Edmund turned in a circle, scanning the uppermost tiers of the cavern. "But access to the guardroom needs to be difficult. It has to be defensible so a small group of guards can hold it against a superior force."

Pond shook his head in amazement. "How do you know all of this?"

"I read. Though, apparently, you can't always trust what books say." Edmund peered at the far reaches of the cavern, high above the town. "What does that look like to you?"

Pond squinted. "It looks like a kind of bridge and an opening. I don't know, maybe a . . . Where're you going?"

Chapter Forty-Two

"Don't look down," Edmund said as he inched across a narrow stone bridge. They were hundreds of feet above the abandoned city. Light shone through the tunnel leading to the outside. "We're almost there."

He glanced back.

Pond lay on his stomach, his eyes firmly shut, his arms wrapped tightly around the walkway. "Are you sure we need to go here?"

"No," Edmund said. "But it seems logical. It's heading to where the guard chamber should be and is defensible. Imagine one person with a spear defending this bridge. He could hold off an entire army, pushing them off one by one to their death."

"Did you have to say that last part?"

Edmund laughed, a sense of joy and anticipation he hadn't felt since entering Tol Helen swelling inside of him. "You could've stayed behind on the balcony, you know."

"And do what? I want to be an adventurer, too. Thank you very much!"

Edmund laughed again, then stopped.

Pond opened an eye. "What's wrong?"

Edmund stood on a landing, looking inside a doorway. Dusty bones and ancient armor littered the floor.

"This is it," Edmund said to himself. Then he added louder, "It's the guardroom. We're going to get out of here!"

Getting to his knees, Pond crawled faster. He found Edmund in a long rectangular room, inspecting three levers, each the size of a tall man. Mammoth chains as thick as tree trunks rose from gigantic gears and disappeared into shafts in the ceiling.

Edmund smiled at Pond. "We're getting out of here!"

He pulled the closest lever. It moved, but nothing happened.

Edmund stared through narrow slits in the wall. Far below, the gates were still closed. He inspected the gears and chains. He pushed the lever in the other direction. Still, nothing happened.

They should be moving.

"Maybe you should try the next one," Pond said.

Edmund tried the middle lever. He pushed. He pulled. Nothing happened.

I can't believe this.

"No," Edmund muttered. "No!"

We're never getting out of here! Never!

He pulled the last lever.

Ringing bells erupted throughout the cavern, shattering the silence and shaking the room. Gears and chains whirled. Pond held onto the doorway. Edmund braced himself against the wall and peered out the window slits. "The first one's opening!"

"What?" Pond shouted, covering his ears.

Hugging Pond, Edmund lifted his feet off the ground. He shook him by the shoulders. "The first gate . . . it's opening!"

The gears and chains stopped. Edmund pulled the middle lever. Again, the bells rang throughout the cavern. Gears churned. The enormous chains rattled. Somewhere, a massive counterweight landed with a ground-shaking thud.

Edmund beamed at Pond. "One more." He pulled the remaining lever. The room shook a third time. "It's opening! We're free. We're free! We're finally free!"

Chapter Forty-Three

Edmund and Pond dashed toward the tunnel once barred by the three portcullises. Outside, green grass peeked out of melting snow.

Edmund ran faster, leaving Pond several strides behind.

A voice boomed throughout the cavern. "Master Filth!"

As he looked behind him, Edmund tripped. He fell to the floor, skidding to a stop a hundred yards from freedom. Goblins poured into the uppermost regions of the subterranean ruins. Before the growing horde stood two familiar figures. One waved at him.

"I really must commend you," Kravel called from a distant balcony. Scores of guards clad in plate mail streamed onto the balconies from adjacent tunnels. "How you snuck past our warriors is a mystery to me. You must tell me your secret."

Edmund shook his raised fist. "Not this time, Kravel!"

"What the hell does that mean?" Gurding shouted. "Not what?"

Clutching Edmund by the arm, Pond lifted him to his feet. "Come on!"

Edmund ran with Pond toward the gate.

They were about to enter the tunnel to the outside world when Kravel shouted again.

"Edmund," he called.

The first barbed portcullis dangled high above their heads. Goblins sprinted down the stairs to the next tier of the city. They had seven more tiers to traverse before they reached the town square and the road to the gate.

Edmund kept running—seventy-five yards to freedom.

"You're going to die in the cold wilderness if you leave," Kravel shouted. "Then neither of us will be happy. Besides, we—"

A horn blast echoed throughout the cavern.

Chapter Forty-Four

Edmund glanced behind him. Goblins thundered down the stairs leading from the uppermost reaches of the cavern. But Kravel and Gurding were no longer in view.

Faster!

Edmund and Pond kept running, sweat pricking their chilled skin.

Twenty-five yards to freedom.

The shock of burning cold shot through Edmund's legs as his toes touched snow.

We're out! Finally, out!

Before them, steep forested slopes plunged into a broad river valley. To their left, an overgrown path wove its way along the mountainside. To their right, another path headed farther up into the mountains.

Which way?

"What now?" Pond panted. "Where, where do we go?"

Come on, think!

Edmund glanced through the tunnel. Goblins were almost to the lowest level of the city.

We need to buy time.

If only we could close the portcullises.

Poking out of the melting snow, bones and rusting weapons lay scattered about the ledge.

"Ed!" Pond shouted. "Which way?"

"Grab one of those shields," Edmund said. "No! Not that one. The pavisse! The big one!"

It's too steep! You'll kill yourself.

It's faster than the road. Besides, it's better to die this way than in a pit with my leg sliced open.

Pond snatched one of the bent shields and cast aside the skeletal arm clinging to it. "What are we going to do? Fight?"

Edmund threw himself on another shield and teetered on the cliff's edge. "Did you ever sled as a kid?"

"I have no idea what you're talking about."

Goblins reached the town square.

"Grab ahold of the straps," Edmund said. "Shift yourself to the right or left to steer."

"Mine doesn't have straps! They're gone!"

But Edmund had already pushed off. Skimming over the snow, he shot down the slope, trees swishing by in green blurs.

Chapter Forty-Five

"What did you call that again?" Pond put a fistful of snow on a jagged gash across his forehead. The snow turned pink and then dark red. Blood dribbled between his eyes.

Holding his black and purple ribs, Edmund winced in pain. "Sledding."

"And children do that for fun?"

"Usually, there aren't trees and boulders in the way."

Far up the mountain, goblins swarmed through the gates. Some were running down the slope after them. Others were taking the winding road heading into the valley.

Edmund helped Pond to his feet.

"Hurry." He hobbled along the churning river.

"What about the shields?"

"Leave them. They'll slow us down."

"Do you think they'll follow us for long?" Pond asked, trying to keep up.

They'll never let you go. They'll follow you to the ends of the continent.

"Can't you go any quicker?" Edmund said.

Limping badly, Pond waved Edmund onward. "You go ahead. I'll . . . I'll catch up."

"We're not splitting up."

Actually, that might help one of us get away. They might—

We're not splitting up.

"Hold on." Edmund touched Pond's swelling knee. "*Smerte av reise.*"

Then he cast the spell on his ribs.

The tenderness faded. He could breathe without stabbing pain.

That'll help.

"Thanks!" Pond said. "I can go much faster now. Lead on."

They ran southwest along the rocky bank of a distended river as the evening shadows deepened around them. Their gasping breath appeared as ghostly clouds.

Edmund glanced back.

Behind them, two goblins had reached the river's edge. They lay crumpled in the snow, dead from their fall. The other goblins sledding down the slopes weren't faring much better. Their shields, helms, and pieces of armor flew about the mountainside as they struck trees and smashed into exposed rocks.

A horn blew.

In the mountains to their left, the remainder of the goblin horde descended where the slope was less steep.

It'll be completely dark soon. Maybe we can hide from them.

They'll follow our tracks right to us. Besides, there isn't a cloud in the sky. The stars this far north are bright enough to read by. Running is our only option.

Edmund urged Pond forward.

They ran with renewed strength, putting even greater distance between them and the black dots descending the snowy slopes. But the cold numbed their skin. Their sweaty bodies shivered. Their feet grew heavier. Soon, their speed diminished to a quick jog, then to a brisk walk. After another mile, they plodded along the river. The half-moon rose above the towering pine trees, blocking the goblins from view. A cobalt hue reflected off the shimmering snow.

Somewhere in the surrounding hills, something howled.

"Wolves?" Pond asked.

Great! That's all we need!

You can't outrun wolves.

"Did you hear that?" Pond asked. "Do you think it was a wolf?"

"If it was, we're—"

A distant voice cut him short.

"Hey," it shouted. "Up here! Hey!"

Something familiar slapped Edmund's exhausted mind.

They spun around, scanning the tree-lined ridges above them. High overhead, a figure on a huge horse was silhouetted against the twinkling stars.

"Hey, you two," a voice from a different life hollered to them. "Have you seen anybody else around here? A woman?"

Not stopping at the ridge, a black and white dog bounded toward them, dragging a rear leg lifelessly behind her.

Edmund cried out. Pond started to run.

When it reached the bottom of the slope, the dog catapulted herself into Edmund's arms. Dropping his sword, he grabbed her and fell backward into the snow.

"Thorax! How—?" He hugged the dog as she licked his face.

"Get off him!" Pond kicked Thorax in the side. She squealed.

The rider urged his great horse forward.

"Get off of him, you damn beast!" Pond Scum brandished his knife.

"Stop it!" Edmund shielded Thorax. "Pond! It's Thorax! It's Thorax!"

"Thorax?" Pond repeated. "I thought you said she was dead."

Above them, the warhorse slid down the slope, plowing a pile of snow in front of its enormous hooves.

Pointing at the shouting rider, Pond inched away. "What about him? He doesn't look like a goblin. But it's said they employ human spies."

From the grey Percheron, the rider yelled, "Leave her alone, or I'll cleave you in two!" He raised his sword and shield as he charged.

"It's all right," Edmund called to the rider. He clutched Thorax tight to his chest, his cold face sticky with her saliva. "She belongs to—" He caught sight of the rider's face.

Norb?

"Norb!" Edmund cried.

Startled, the stable hand checked the horse, his sword and shield lowering slightly.

"Norb!" Overcome with joy, Edmund sputtered, "What the—? How? Where—? What are you doing here?"

But then, in between beats, his heart faltered.

Wait. "Have you seen a woman?"

A woman?

My 'wife' . . .

Molly!

Dropping Thorax into the snow, Edmund raced to Norb. "How's Molly? Is she okay? She's in Rood, right? Tell me she's fine!"

Norb backed his horse away.

"Ed?" he said in disbelief.

With the desperation of a drowning man, Edmund latched onto the stable hand's woolen coat. "M-M-Molly! Where is she? Do you know? Where is she?"

Grimacing, Norb stared at Edmund's gaunt face. "Ed? Is that really you?"

"Damn it, Norb, you know it is! Now tell me . . . where's Molly? She's in Rood, right? She's, she's, she's there, isn't she?"

"The goblins are coming," Pond said urgently.

Edmund shook Norb hard. "Where is she?"

Norb tore his gaze away from the hole where Edmund's left eye used to be. "Ed! My god, we looked for you. Honest."

"Norb! Where's Molly?"

Norb stammered. "She's gone. Molly's gone."

The cries of goblins floated on the night wind. The horse snorted and stamped.

"Wh-wh-what . . . what do you mean gone?" Edmund nearly pulled Norb out of his saddle. "She can't be!"

Glaring upriver, Thorax growled, the hair between her shoulder blades standing on end.

"Ed," Pond said.

Hundreds of black shapes swarmed into the ravine behind them.

"What do you mean—gone?" Edmund repeated.

"Things . . ." Norb tried to pull away but couldn't break Edmund's grip. "Things have happened. Back in Rood. Bad things."

The goblin voices were clear now. They waved their scimitars over their heads and shouted hoarse battle cries in anticipation of their impending victory.

"I don't believe it." Norb stared up the slopes. "Goblins . . . here . . . this far north?"

"Yes," Pond told him. "And there're thousands of them. Ed, talk later."

"What happened?" Edmund demanded, his breath appearing as puffs in the frosty air. "What happened? To Rood? To Molly? Where—?"

"We gotta get out of here," Pond said to Norb. "Can we all ride?" He looked doubtfully at the horse.

More shouts.

I can't believe she's gone.

Farther up the mountains, another horn blew.

"Quick," Pond said. "Give me your shield and rope."

"Shit!" Norb said. "You weren't kidding. There are hundreds of them!"

Pond seized Norb's shield and the coil of rope hanging from his saddlebag. He gave an end to Norb. "Tie this to your saddle horn! Hurry!"

Molly!

Thorax barked viciously.

Gone . . .

Molly's . . . gone.

Edmund's hands slipped lifelessly from Norb's coat.

Kravel . . .

Pond guided Edmund to the shield, now fastened to Norb's rope.

The Percheron reared and snorted.

Grabbing Thorax, Pond sat behind Edmund. He shouted to Norb, "Ride!"

Snow kicked up under the warhorse's hooves, showering Edmund and Pond as they clung to the shield.

Molly . . .

Chapter Forty-Six

Pond draped another blanket around Edmund's shivering shoulders as he stared at the campfire.

They'd ridden south for many hours. Dawn was approaching, and they hadn't seen any goblins since the volley of arrows fell around them as they sped away. Everyone hoped their pursuers had given up the chase, but Edmund knew they wouldn't—not while they needed the answer to the riddle, and he was still alive.

"My god, Ed," Norb said. "What the hell happened to you?" He held out a cup of hot coffee. "Where have you been? And what happened to your—?"

"Never mind all that." Edmund stared at the crackling flames. "What happened to Molly? Where is she, Norb?"

Brushing the snow off his bedroll, the stable hand sat on the other side of the fire. "I honestly don't know where to begin."

"At the damn beginning," Edmund said. Norb flinched. "Begin at the beginning. What happened after I left?"

"Ok," Norb said. "The beginning. All right. Well, I felt bad. You know - about what I said to you. You know, when we was behind the Rogue and all. I can't remember exactly what I said, but—"

"You said M-M-Molly wouldn't be interested in a guy like me. And that I wasn't a hero like the storyteller."

"Yeah . . . that. I'm, I'm sorry. Honest."

Edmund glowered at the fire.

"Well—" Norb took a tentative sip of the coffee he'd offered Edmund. "I-I felt real bad afterwards. I did. Then I heard what you'd done, giving all your things to Mol and all, and how you up and left."

Red sparks floated above the fire and dissolved into the blackness. Edmund didn't move.

Throwing a pinecone on the snapping flames, Norb went on. "When you hadn't returned in a couple days . . . well, we was all worried. Me, Molly . . . everybody."

At the mention of Molly worrying about him, Edmund lifted his head.

"Anyways." Norb examined the rim of his cup. "We searched for you for a bit, you know. Went as far as some of the eastern ranches and to the Barrens. But you were nowhere to be found. Nobody had seen hide nor hair of you. Then . . ." He took another sip of coffee.

"And then?" Edmund said. "And then what? What happened to Molly?"

The wind whistled between the fir trees on the surrounding hills. Cold stars shimmered blue and green.

Norb hunched closer to the fire, orange light flickering across his uneasy face.

"Molly?" he repeated. "Well, you know, we . . . we all thought you were good and gone. Happy for a change and all that. Doing what you always said you'd do, you know. Traveling and such. Honest. That's what we figured."

Appearing like a man needing to be absolved of some evil treachery, Norb looked at Edmund. But Edmund glared at the hissing flames as they fought their way around the damp wood.

"Go on," he said.

Swallowing hard, Norb gave a tired shrug. "So . . . so Mol went on with her life. She sold a few of your books to poor ol' Tom and toasted your health at every meal."

Edmund's cheeks flushed as he imagined Molly toasting him. For a moment, his body finally felt warm.

She loves me.

But she's gone. Kravel has her. He thought she was your wife.

She should be my wife. I'll ask her the moment I see her again.

Edmund's scowl turned to confusion.

"Wait a second," he said. "Poor ol' Tom?"

Norb fingered the cup's handle.

"You, you, you hated Thomas," Edmund said. "What's changed?"

"Who's Thomas?" Pond asked, his mouth full of bread.

Edmund waved him to be quiet. "He sells antiques. My father bought a short sword from him years ago. I'll explain later. Go on, Norb."

"Tom is dead," Norb said. "A lot of people are."

"Dead! How?" He stammered. "Wh-wh-what, what happened?"

"We don't rightly know," Norb said. "But some are talking about wights coming down from the hills like in the old tales, you know? Everybody's beside themselves. I've never seen anything like it."

Dead?

"Anyway, Thomas was the first to go missing. Then a few others disappeared. William the glassmaker, for one. Henry and Bryce, the night watchmen, were two others."

"Wait," Edmund said. "Are they missing? Or dead?"

Norb threw another pinecone into the fire.

"Well, both. They were gone. And then we found them in the woods outside of town. Thomas was hanging from a tree with this big hook under his jaw like he was a caught fish or something." Unnerved, Norb exhaled, his breath appearing in the cold. "His lower half was clean gone, like it was eaten by wolves. Bait for wolves—that's what he was like. It was horrible."

A hook?

Damned goblins.

Edmund's body sank as if deflated.

You shouldn't have said where Rood was.

I caused this. I caused all of this.

"Do you know what's going on, Ed?" Norb asked. "'Cause nobody back home has a clue. Not even these Highmen, these knights that appeared in Rood right after you left. After Mol vanished, they took over the town. They're running things now. Organizing watches and everything."

"Knights? In Rood?"

One of the hissing branches in the fire popped loudly, sending a spark shooting into the snow.

"Where's Rood from here?" Pond asked. "Can we walk there?"

Edmund motioned for his pit mate to wait a moment. "Why are knights in Rood? Are they from Eryn Mas?"

"Yeah, King Lionel sent them." Norb scanned the dark hills around them. "He wants Rood back in the Kingdom. So, he sent a company of these knights storming into town to help with what they call 'the readjustment.' Nobody was none too happy about it. The knights bully everybody something terrible. And this King Lionel wants us to start paying outrageous taxes and worse."

"Worse?"

"He wants us to send two hundred young lads to Eryn Mas to join his army. Everybody told the knights that there weren't two hundred young men in Rood and all the surrounding farms put together. But they won't listen. Anyway, these knights took over everything. They even kicked Harris out of office. They say they're running the town until a new lord of the Highlands is named. I thought there was going to be bloodshed over the whole thing. There still might be, I don't know."

Behind him, the grey Percheron snorted and tossed its mane.

"Is that where you got the horse?" Edmund asked, trying to piece everything together.

Norb turned as white as the snow.

"I had to! Molly disappeared and . . . and these highfalutin knights and their nasty squires weren't going to do anything! So, I . . . I . . . borrowed one of their horses and some of their gear. I had to! How else was I going to find Mol?"

Edmund shook his head in disbelief.

Knights in Rood . . . Goblins in the mountains . . . It's like history is repeating itself.

Pretty soon, there'll be war.

And Rood will be caught in the middle again.

Edmund exhaled heavily. "You said you thought I was okay and, and, and Molly finally had money and was toasting my health. What happened next?"

"Like I was saying," Norb said. "She was happy you were happy. So, she . . . she went on living, you know."

"Then what happened?"

"Nothing for a few months." Norb gestured to Thorax, lying next to Edmund. She licked the calluses and cuts covering his shivering hands. "Then, this dog comes limping into town like she was looking for someone, all upset like. She was hurt. Somebody shot her in the leg or something."

Edmund stroked Thorax's head.

"Anyways, the dog's smart. I can't explain it, but it was as if she knew something. When Mol disappeared, I said to her, I said, 'Do you know where Molly is?' And she went wild. Barking and all. That's when I took the horse and rode out of town. I know it sounds crazy, but I've been following her ever since."

Good work, Thorax. We'd be dead without you.

Edmund patted Thorax's side. "And?"

"And . . . well, we found this ruined tower and some traces of an old campsite. But no signs of Molly. Then the dog here led me up this way, toward these mountains, like we were hot on Mol's trail." He threw another stick onto the fire. The flames spit and snapped as ice on the wood dissolved and fell into the glowing coals. "There isn't much left to tell."

Thorax rolled onto her side. Edmund petted her.

"What about Tom and everybody? You said a lot of people are dead."

"Tom is the guy who sells the swords, right?" Pond asked.

Edmund hushed him.

"It's hard to say," Norb said. "Thomas disappeared one night. That was a month or so after you left, maybe two months. I don't know. Anyways, days later, Steig and Mary's youngest kid, the one with the curly red hair, he found him strung up like I said."

Why would Kravel and Gurding go after Thomas?

Because you told them he sold the sword to your father. They wanted to see if he had more weapons like it.

Edmund rubbed his face.

You shouldn't have mentioned Rood, Thomas, or anything else.

I'd be dead if I hadn't told them—a rat cage over my head.

But Molly and everybody would still be safe.

Edmund wondered what the goblins did to female prisoners. He hadn't seen any in the pits. He didn't want to think about it.

"Then what?" Edmund asked. "After you found Thomas in the tree, wh-wh-what, what happened next?"

Thorax sighed as Edmund scratched her stomach.

"Nothing happened," Norb said. "Leastways, not for a while. And then, a couple of months or so later, the two night guards disappeared. We found their bodies in the woods, hacked to pieces. The next morning, I realized Mol was gone."

Edmund studied the fire.

"You found everybody's body," he said. "Everybody but, but . . . but Molly's? I mean, you haven't found her body?"

"We've searched everywhere," Norb said. "There wasn't a sign of her. It's like she up and disappeared."

For many chilly moments, no one said a thing.

Edmund watched the sputtering flames, his hands shaking from the cold and exhaustion. Dawn was a couple of hours off, and he hadn't slept in over a day and a half.

It was Pond who eventually broke the silence.

"Have you seen anybody else around here?" he asked. "Anybody out of the ordinary?"

For a moment, Norb didn't respond. Then he realized Pond was talking to him. "A few weeks ago, I came across a beggar dressed much like you two. Or not dressed, if you get me—"

"Did he say anything?" Pond asked, excited. "Did he say what his name was? What did he look like?"

Norb recoiled, startled by the intensity of Pond's questions.

"He was disturbed. He appeared out of nowhere, cackling like a witch." Norb stirred the fire's glowing coals with the tip of his knife. "He poked me in the forehead and called me a chicken. Then he grabbed one of my food bags and ran off, shouting something about magic."

"Crazy Bastard!" Pond said to Edmund.

"That's what I thought," Norb said. "But seeing him made me feel like we was on the right track somehow. The dog seemed to think so, at any rate. I've been following her ever since, making a beeline toward these mountains. I was about to turn back and get more supplies when we came across you two."

Another silence enveloped the small campsite. Above them, the stars grew old, and a faint pink light crowned the mountain peaks to the east. Tethered to a nearby tree, the giant horse swished its braided tail.

"I need to know something, Ed," Norb said. "And I need you to be straight with me. Okay?" He looked at Edmund, his lips dry and trembling. "Do you know where Molly is?"

Edmund felt where his left eye used to be.

"Yes," he said. "And we're going to rescue her."

Chapter Forty-Seven

Grunting, Edmund heaved a leg over the ornate saddle. Underneath him, the grey Percheron snorted, apparently not happy having Edmund on its barrel-like back. Pond lifted Thorax into Edmund's arms.

"What's the horse's name again?" Edmund asked.

Norb handed him the reins. "It's Blake. Stupid name for a horse. But that's what they called him. Seems to answer to it well enough. He's faster than all get out, so don't let the brute throw you."

Towering above his friends, Edmund adjusted himself in the saddle. "I'll meet you in six weeks. Are you sure you know where?"

"Where the East-West Road crosses the River Celerin," Pond said. "You said there's a ford there. And hills."

"Right. Bring the knights occupying Rood and everybody else you can get hold of. Tell them everything I've told you."

Norb didn't look too sure.

"Ed," he said, "if they catch me, they'll string me up. Them knights love their horses more than they like people. You know what I'm saying? And they know I stole him."

"Then have Pond go into town alone," Edmund said. "You can hide in the woods. Or better yet, g-g-go, go to the Jensen's farm. If I'm any judge, they'll be madder than hell about this rejoining the kingdom business. They'll hide you."

Norb's expression eased. "That'll work. The ranchers are as upset as anybody."

"Pond," Edmund said, "go with Norb to Rood and tell everybody what I told you. Tell them we know where Molly is. Tell them what I'm doing. They'll be more willing to help if they know I'm bringing an army from Eryn Mas."

Pond saluted. "Yes, Captain!"

"There's one more thing," Edmund said as Blake dug his huge hooves into the snow. "I need a book from my house. It's a very old diary with a black leather cover. It should be on the top left-hand shelf as you enter my library. It'll be the fourth book from the corner. Above all else, I need that diary. Do you understand?"

"Why?" Norb asked.

"It may help us save Molly."

"Then you'll get it if I have to sneak into town and get it for you," Norb said.

"Fourth book from the corner on the top left-hand shelf," Pond said. "Got it!"

"And don't forget the other gear. The candles, rope, chalk, oil flasks . . . everything. I'll see you at the River Celerin in six weeks."

Lifting his head, Blake trumpeted.

"Here." Norb handed Edmund his pack. "There's some extra clothes and money in there. Not much. But it'll buy you some food on your way."

"Oh," Pond said, "he won't need food—"

"Pond," Edmund interrupted with forced calmness. "It's essential you keep some things to yourself. No need telling people wh-wh-what we suffered through." His remaining eye narrowed at him. "Understand?"

Pond saluted again. "Gotcha! I understand. I understand completely!" He tapped his temple.

If he tells people you're a magic user, you're as good as dead.

Don't worry. I can trust him with my life. I wouldn't be here if it weren't for him.

"Make sure you get everything," Edmund said. "Get the diary and bring the knights and everybody to the river. Bring as many people as you can, anybody who can swing a sword or shoot a bow. Are you both clear as to what I need you to do?"

They said they were.

Edmund examined his companions in turn. Norb's face was intensely earnest, mixed with some unresolved guilt. He could barely look at Edmund. Pond was humming.

"Remember," Edmund said, "if anybody in Rood balks, remind them we're doing this for Molly. And don't take no for an answer. She needs us, and we don't have much time."

"I'll make them come," Norb said.

"Good," Edmund said. "I'll see you soon with an army of knights."

Turning Blake southward, Edmund raised himself higher in the stirrups, Thorax sprawled uneasily across the saddle in front of him.

"Ed," Norb said.

"What?"

"I'm sorry for what I said behind the Rogue. About how you and Molly and all. I didn't mean for any of this to happen."

"I know, Norb. There're no hard feelings." He nodded at his pit mate. "Take good care of Pond here. I owe him my life."

"I owe you mine," Pond said.

"Remember, six weeks. No later. Okay?" Edmund said. Blake shifted underneath him. "Gather everybody you can muster."

"I'll be here." Pond smiled. "You can count on me."

"I know I can."

Ready to charge off, Edmund rose in the stirrups again.

"Ed," Norb said again.

"What?" Edmund asked, annoyed. "We have to get moving. Molly needs us!"

"Are, are . . . are they going to do to Mol what they did to you?"

Lie.

"I don't think so, Norb. They need Molly to get to me. They'll keep her safe and sound, otherwise they won't get what they want."

"What do they want? What's this all about? Why did they take her?"

But Edmund put his heels to Blake's ribs and shot southward through the melting snow.

Chapter Forty-Eight

For two weeks, Edmund and Thorax raced along the river, bolting out of the northern Highlands and into the snowless lowlands, where King Lionel and his army of knights still held control. Vast plains flatter than the ocean stretched as far as Edmund could see. The tall grasses turned green in the early spring sunlight. Crocuses of yellow and blue dotted the river's rocky banks.

Ignoring the beauty around him, Edmund went over his plan until he was sick of thinking about it. Everything hinged on Pond mustering the people of Rood and King Lionel listening to what Edmund had to say. The townsfolk would come. They all loved Molly. It was the King who'd need convincing.

If he's half the warrior I've heard him to be, he'll want to fight. No king can walk away from a good battle. But he needs to send enough soldiers. That's the biggest issue. He needs to believe there are thousands of goblins and not some isolated band.

Up ahead, a road appeared. It crossed a stone bridge spanning the river.

"See those trees?" Edmund pointed to the line of ancient maples angling away from the bridge and extending to the horizon. "I bet they mark the Old North-South Road that leads up to Hillode, Rockdale, and eventually to Rood. Which means it leads south to Eryn Mas. That's where we'll find King Lionel and his knights."

Thorax sniffed the fragrant spring air. Her back stiffened.

"I know. I see them." Edmund scratched her ears. "But we need to follow the road southward. So we must cross that bridge."

He stroked the horse's neck. "How are you feeling, Blake? Ready for a race? We may n-n-need some of your speed in a few moments."

Blake reared and trumpeted, almost tossing Edmund and Thorax to the ground.

On the bridge, hidden figures leaped to their feet, weapons in hand.

"Well, they certainly know we're here now. Let's see if this is what I think it is."

Nudging Blake's ribs with his bare heels, they slowly approached the bridge.

Three men stood in front of it, blocking Edmund's way. One was a large, heavy-set man with a wooden quarterstaff. The other two were smaller and had makeshift clubs. All three were smiling as if greeting a long-lost friend.

Even goblins don't grin like that.

Don't worry. I can deal with them.

"Hail, traveler!" the man with a wooden quarterstaff said. "Fine morning, isn't it?"

Edmund reined Blake to a stop.

"It beats living in a pit," he said.

The man with the staff laughed as his colleagues flanked Blake. The hair between Thorax's shoulder blades rose, but she swallowed her growls when Edmund stroked her head.

The two men with clubs whistled as they circled.

"Mighty nice horse you've got here, mister," one of them said pleasantly enough. "Mighty nice."

"Don't see many like this," the other added.

Edmund didn't say anything.

"We're the official toll keepers for this here bridge," the man with the staff said, still blocking Edmund's path. "We're charged with taking tolls from any travelers that use it, such as yourself. King's orders and all."

"The King, eh?" Edmund said.

Snorting, Blake dug a hoof into the dirt.

"Don't believe me?" the man with the staff said with exaggerated surprise. "I'm not sure I like being called a liar by a thief. How about you, lads?"

He stepped toward Edmund, the wood staff thumping against his palm. His friends strolled closer. Thorax's teeth appeared. Blake's tail twitched.

"Thief?" Edmund repeated.

"You ain't got money for boots, let alone clothes that fit proper," the bearer of the staff said. Edmund examined the patched shirt and pants Norb had given him. They hung from his now svelte frame like robes. "No way this beautiful horse is yours. In fact, I think I'll have to confiscate him until we can find his owner."

Still smiling, he nodded at his companions.

The men on either side of Edmund took another step forward, clubs raised.

With a twist on the reins, Edmund turned Blake so one of the men was in front of him and the other directly behind.

"Up," Edmund told Blake.

Blake reared high above the man before him. His hooves came crashing down just as the highwayman dove out of the way.

From behind, the second man rushed forward.

"Kick," Edmund said.

Blake's rear hooves swept back, connecting with the second man's chest. There was a crunching sound as the man flew twenty feet. He was dead before he hit the ground.

Drawing his scimitar, Edmund pointed it at the man with the staff. "How f-f-far . . . how far to Eryn Mas?"

"It's—" The man with the quarterstaff pointed a shaking finger down the road. "It's five days. Maybe four if you press on into the night."

"Get out of my way."

"Absolutely." The man ran off the road.

"Let's go, Blake."

Whinnying, Blake pranced forward, his horseshoes clomping on the bridge's wooden timbers.

Chapter Forty-Nine

The capital city of Eryn Mas rose out of the southern plains like a bejeweled mountain. Edmund could see its golden domes and spires glinting in the sunlight a day's ride away. As he drew closer, its majesty overwhelmed him.

Its walls soared four hundred feet overhead. Flags and banners of every color fluttered from the parapets, many embroidered with the crests of royal families and heroes of old. Even the sparrows and swifts swooping about the cloudless sky seemed grander and more majestic than the birds Edmund had seen in the north.

It's incredible!

I can't believe how tall those walls are! No wonder Arnett the Black never took the city by force. No siege towers could ever reach that high.

If only Rood had walls like this.

As Edmund surveyed Eryn Mas, Blake clomped up the causeway leading to the northern drawbridge. Many people were entering the city—peasants, merchants, farmers, travelers from neighboring towns.

Some openly stared at Edmund, evidently surprised that a disheveled, one-eyed man would have such a horse. Taking little notice, Edmund rode Blake through the immense gates.

On the other side of the walls, a cobblestone avenue appeared. It forked in three directions. To the right and left, it skimmed the interior of the battlements, passing by guardhouses and narrow stone stairs weaving up to wall walks behind the parapets. The center road headed through a park of green grass.

Edmund looked around in amazement.

It's beautiful. Absolutely beautiful.

Scores of people pushed past him. Several swore when manure fell from Blake, splattering on the cobblestones under his swishing tail. A worker with a shovel appeared and quickly deposited Blake's waste into a small cart.

This is the cleanest city I've ever seen!

It's the only city you've ever seen.

Edmund gawked at the cathedrals and their stained-glass windows. Even Thorax seemed impressed. Blake snorted.

"It's incredible, isn't it, girl?" Edmund said to Thorax.

Somewhere in the park, people sang and played stringed instruments.

I wonder if there's a festival. The Spring Faire will start in Rood soon. I wish I could be—

Focus! Think of Molly! Heaven only knows what those blasted goblins are doing to her.

He imagined Kravel whipping Molly, her soft skin splitting open, blood oozing down her spine. He shuddered as her imaginary screams lingered in his mind.

She's probably dead by now.

No. The goblins need her to get to me.

Edmund watched the masses of people going this way and that.

What now? I can't ride to the castle and demand to see the King. What if he refuses to see me?

He won't refuse. Not since you have this.

He patted the Star of Iliandor in his pocket.

More people pushed past Blake as he stood idly in the road.

"All right, Blake," Edmund said. "Let's go see the K-King."

At that, Blake heaved forward, plowing his way through the crowd with deliberate strides. They passed lines of merchants standing by wagons full of goods, markets with dead chickens, geese, and piglets hanging in the window, and stately homes of the upper classes. As Edmund gazed at everything around them, Blake ascended the road to the fortress overlooking the city.

The fortress rose from the hill, ringed by three walls. Around each wall were seven towers of heights grander than anything Edmund had ever seen. Each one made the tower of the Undead King seem like a child's imitation built from sand. However, on the hill's crown was the real jewel of Eryn Mas—Tol Aden, the Castle of the Kings. With its gables and spires of white granite and mammoth statues of gargoyles and dragons, each level rose until it reached a dome covered in glittering rubies and sparkling sapphires.

As he stared at the magnificent citadel, Edmund suddenly realized Blake was approaching the main gate. Two guards in suits of polished plate mail and halberds stood in the middle of the road. Blake stopped before them.

"State your name and purpose," the guard on the left said without enthusiasm.

"Oh yes, m-m-my, my name. My name, yes indeed," Edmund said.

The guards blinked at him. One yawned.

"Well, m-m-my, my name is Edmund of Rood. And I'm here to meet with the King regarding an urgent matter. You see—"

"Let me guess," the guard on the right said. "You found something you want to give to him. Something priceless. A relic of some sort."

Surprised, Edmund's mouth opened, his hand falling to his right front pocket where the Star of Iliandor was hidden.

"Don't tell us," the guard on the left said. "You've found the Ring of Ingram the Cleric."

"Why'd you guess that?" the guard on the right asked.

"Because Rood is over in the swamplands of Anthica. Which makes it more likely he—"

"It's not in Anthica. It's along the coast by Eddenbury, in Ringold Province. And he hasn't gotten the Ring of Ingram the Cleric. That's already been turned in."

"Has it? I hadn't heard. But I don't think Rood is in Ringold. I'd wager a day's pay on that."

"You're on then. And I say he's found the Shield of Uzbad if he's found anything at all."

"Oh, that's a stupid guess. I mean, where'd he put it? Under his saddle?"

"Okay, fair enough. You got me there."

Lifting their visors, the guards inspected Edmund with increasing curiosity.

The guard on the right scratched his nose. "Maybe he's bringing His Highness that dog. The King loves dogs, after all."

"A dog? No. When we asked him what he brought, he touched his pocket. Whatever it is, it's something small, like a gem or a necklace."

Opening his mouth again, Edmund raised a finger to interject, but the guards waved him to be quiet.

"Something small," the guard on the right repeated thoughtfully.

"Honestly," Edmund said, "I haven't m-m-much time."

"Be quiet," the guard on the left said. "Or we'll throw you in the dungeon." He studied Edmund and his gear.

Edmund closed his mouth.

The guard on the left pointed at Blake as he pulled great heaps of grass from the roadside. "That there's one of those High Horses, that's plain. They're specially bred in Meadowshire. What're people looking for in Meadowshire?"

"A golden horse turd?" the guard on the right suggested.

The guard on the left shook his head in defeat. "Okay," he said to Edmund. "We give up. Where's Rood, and what do you think you've got?"

"Rood is in the Highlands up by—"

The guard on the right snapped his fingers as if he knew where Rood was all along. "That's right."

"The Highlands?" the guard on the left said. "I thought only sheep lived up there?"

"Evidently, people do as well." The guard on the right gestured to Edmund as if to prove his point. "Of what sort, however, I haven't a clue. They're poor by the looks of it." He returned his attention to Edmund. "Okay, what do you have for His Highness? It's jewelry of some sort, am I right?"

"I, I suppose," Edmund said, unsure if he was expected to produce what he'd brought. "I have the Star of Iliandor and wish to talk with the King about—"

"What's a Lilly and Door?" the guard on the right said to the one on the left.

The guard on the left lifted his palms. "Beats the hell out of me."

"Iliandor," Edmund said again. "The Overlord of the Highlands?"

They stared at him.

"Supreme General during the Northern Goblin Wars?" Edmund said.

"Northern Goblin Wars?" the guard on the left repeated doubtfully.

"Founder of the, the, the—"

The guard on the right waved for Edmund to stop. "We're mostly having fun with you. We don't care who he is. One lord is the same as another for all I know. Follow this road to the left and ask around for the Hall of Magistrates. If you see a bunch of old men who look constipated, you've found it."

Chapter Fifty

"Wait!" Edmund yanked on Blake's reins. "They said left. Left!"

The enormous horse plotted along the street to the right, ignoring his rider's protests. Eventually, he came to a stable. The heads of twenty other warhorses peered through open windows. Blake whinnied. The other horses whinnied in reply. A large black Percheron snorted and shook its braided mane.

A boy about to enter his teen years slid open the stable doors.

"Blake!" he cried.

Then he noticed Edmund riding him. "Who're you? Where's Sir Hanley?" He grabbed a pitchfork leaning against a wall. "And what're you doing on Blake?"

Uh oh! Think, quick!

"Let m-m-me . . . let me explain." Edmund clamored from the saddle.

Act like you belong here.

He set Thorax on the ground. She hobbled around, sniffing the various piles of manure. Riderless, Blake ambled inside the stable to another chorus of neighing.

Trying to buy time, Edmund massaged his rear end.

What name did he say? Sir Hanley?

The boy's eyes flitted to a building across the street. Raucous laughter and shouting shook its windows. It looked as if he was about to run for help.

"Let me ex-ex-explain," Edmund said again. "You see, Sir Hanley lent Blake to me."

"That's a lie! He'd never do such a thing." The boy inched toward the stable doors, pitchfork still pointed at Edmund's chest.

"Would I steal a knight's horse and then return him to where he belongs?" Edmund asked.

The boy straightened slightly. "I don't know. Maybe."

You need to come up with a better explanation.

"You see," Edmund said, praying his story was believable. "Sir Hanley is hurt."

More doubt crept into the boy's face.

"He's . . . he's badly hurt. There's been an attack. Bandits, you see. Thirty or forty of them. They attacked and, and Sir Hanley was badly hurt. I've . . . I've been sent to talk to the King about getting reinforcements."

The boy smirked, sarcastically. "Reinforcements for only thirty or forty bandits?"

"Yes, well . . . there were at least that many. Anyway, you're . . . you're missing the point. They sent me here to talk to the King. I'm on an urgent mission!"

The boy stepped to his right, pitchfork at the ready. Whether he was going to stab him or run, Edmund couldn't tell.

"Why send you?" the boy asked. "Why not Sir Maxwell or any of the others? Why not one of the squires?"

"I . . . I don't know anything about a Sir Maxwell," Edmund said, rightly guessing the boy made the name up. "Look, they can't abandon the town. They need reinforcements, or all the townsfolk will be slaughtered!"

The pitchfork lowered a tad.

Show him the Star of Iliandor.

"Plus, they sent me because I found this."

He produced the Star of Iliandor from his pocket. Its blue gem flashed in the light of the setting sun.

"Holy cow!" the boys cried. "What is it?"

"It's the Star of Iliandor. If I return it to King Lionel, I'll become Lord of the Highlands."

"Wow!" Something seemed to occur to the boy. "You'll become the new Lord of the Highlands?"

"Yes! Well, that is . . . if I can get to see King Lionel and everything." Then Edmund saw what the boy was thinking. "You see, that's why Sir Hanley gave me his horse. I'll be his lord. He was following my orders."

"Then tell me this," the boy said. "What's the name of the town they went to? In the Highlands, that is."

"Rood."

The boy's expression eased. "Well, nobody else would've known that!" He set his pitchfork against the stable. "Still, you must be on some important mission for Sir Hanley to do such a thing. He didn't even let me exercise Blake, let alone ride him. Then again, if you're the new lord and all . . ."

The boy wiped his hands on a grubby cloth hanging from his belt.

"I'm Toby, by the by. I tend the horses here while I study to be a farrier. I'm apprenticing with my cousin, Master Gorin."

He held out his hand.

Edmund shook it. "Pleased to meet you, Toby."

"Blake looks well. So that's one good for you. Are Sir Hanley and the others all right? I mean, they haven't been killed or anything, have they?"

Don't give too many details. You'll never remember them.

"Yes, he's . . . he's fine. Or at least he was fine when I left him a few weeks ago."

Be more confident. Nobody will believe you if you act guilty of something.

The boy seemed to consider this.

Ask him about the Hall of Magistrates!

"How did you lose your eye?" the boy asked. "Are you a veteran?"

"In a manner of speaking," Edmund said. "A goblin burned it out."

"My god, that's horrible! I'm sorry. My father fought in the Battle of Bloody Rock," the boy said proudly. "He killed twelve goblins all by himself."

"That's w-w-wonderful, Toby. Twelve fewer goblins to worry about. But I can't chat about such things right now. I n-n-need, need your help."

"Why do you talk like that? The stuttering, I mean."

"I was dr-dropped on my head as a child."

"Boy, you've had a rough life!"

"You m, might say that. But you can help it become a little better."

"Sure. What can I do?"

"I've been told to go to the Hall of Magistrates, b-b-but, but Blake brought me here. Can you tell me where to go? It's urgent."

"Sure! But what do you want with the magistrates? Forget to pay your taxes?"

"No. Nothing like that. Look, it's a matter of life and death. So, please, can you tell me where it is?"

"Absolutely. It won't even cost you nothing. Here. I'll show you where it is." Toby closed the stable doors. "Good night, everybody!" he called into a window. "See you bright and early tomorrow."

Several horses neighed in reply.

"It's this way," Toby said.

Suddenly, the door to the building across the street opened. Half a dozen drunk men fell out onto the street, laughing. They grappled each other as they rolled about the ground. One of them giggled as he held up a woman's brassiere.

"Don't mind them." Toby waved for Edmund to follow him. "They're just His Majesty's knights."

Chapter Fifty-One

"There it is." Toby pointed at an official-looking building with larger-than-life statues poised stoically in front of it.

Two elderly gentlemen dressed in expensive waistcoats and cloaks stood by the building's gold-trimmed doors. The gentleman on the left held a lantern. The one on the right leaned on an intricately carved ivory cane. They both had sour expressions.

"Perhaps I should stay," Toby said, "just in case you need anything. Then you can tell me more about your urgent mission and things in the Far North. Any tales are good ones, as the saying goes."

Edmund studied the two men, unsure of what to say.

"You should hurry," Toby prodded. "They're closing."

Edmund stepped toward the men, a limping Thorax by his side. They stopped speaking and glanced at Thorax, and then at Edmund.

"If you are a beggar," the gentleman with the brass lantern said, "I'll have the gate guards flogged."

"N-n-no, no, sir," Edmund said. "I've been t-t-told to come here. It's, it's about one of His Majesty's edicts."

"Can't you see we are closing?" the man with the cane said. "Return tomorrow."

"I'm really sorry," Edmund pleaded. "But it can't wait until then. It's important."

"Important?" the man with the cane said doubtfully.

"What silly trinket do you think you've found, pray tell?" the other asked.

Edmund produced the Star of Iliandor from his pocket.

The men looked at it, unimpressed.

"What is it?" the man with the lantern asked.

"This," Edmund said, straining not to stutter. "This is the Star of Iliandor!"

"What? Another one?" The man with a cane said to the man with the lantern, "How many of the blasted things are there?"

"A-a-another . . . another one?" Edmund repeated. It felt as if the bottom had dropped out of his soul.

"Well, if there is more than one, I'm sure His Royal Highness will know what to do," the lantern holder said. "Perhaps he'd have them thumb wrestle or some such feat of skill to decide the matter." He regarded Edmund, then shook his head. "All right, all right. Come in, and we'll get this cleared up."

"If you are going to take care of this . . ." His comrade jabbed the tip of his cane at Edmund and wrinkled his nose. ". . . this . . . gentleman, then I'll be off. Unless you'd prefer me to stay or call for a guard."

"No need on either account. He looks destitute, not dangerous. If he gives me any difficulties, I shall step on his toes."

"Don't get your shoes dirty." The man with the cane chuckled as he strolled along the darkening avenue. "Good evening to you."

"And to you and your family," the man with the lantern said.

He unlocked the building's door. With an exaggerated sigh, he walked inside. "Come this way," he said to Edmund. "But leave your mutt outside. I don't want the place reeking of hound."

"Stay here," Edmund said to Thorax as he followed the magistrate inside. But Thorax limped into the building behind Toby.

The man led them to a finely crafted desk made of polished black walnut. He set his lantern next to a neat stack of papers and fell into a chair with the heaviness of a man who'd worked a long day.

"I'm, I'm t-t-terribly . . . terribly sorry for the, for the inconvenience, sir." Edmund bowed, still clutching the alleged Star of Iliandor. "It's just that it's imperative that I—"

The man waved his hand at Edmund. "Yes, yes. I understand. You're sorry. I am William, son of Harrison, magistrate second class," he said as if required to say such things.

"Ed . . . Edmund s-s-son of Evert . . . librarian," Edmund replied, not sure what the proper response was. He motioned to Toby standing next to him. "This is—"

"Let me see it," William said impatiently.

Edmund gave the Star of Iliandor to the magistrate.

Examining the Star, the magistrate leaned closer to the lantern. Taking a magnifying glass from a drawer, he studied the Star even closer. He tapped the gem with a well-manicured fingernail. He inspected the runes surrounding the stone. Then, he looked at each link of the chain in turn. Eventually, he leaned back.

"I don't know," he said.

"You don't know?" Edmund said in disbelief. "Wh-wh-what . . . what do you mean, you don't know?"

Did you really believe the Undead King would give you the real Star of Iliandor? This is another of his games.

"I don't know," William repeated louder. "It's not my field of inquiry. I studied law, not antiquities. I'll need to send it to somebody to be sure."

"S-s-s-send, send it to somebody?"

"Of course, you don't want to part with it. Understandable," the magistrate said. "It's probably the only item of potential value you own. Let me do this."

He took a candle from his desk and lit it. Carefully, he dribbled the honey-colored wax over both sides of the Star. Once the wax hardened, he peeled it off and set the impression carefully in a large red envelope.

He handed the Star to Edmund. "You should hear something in a few weeks."

"Weeks!" Edmund exclaimed.

"That's okay." Toby stepped in front of Edmund. "As long as it isn't within the next couple of days. We've got things to do."

"Weeks!" Edmund said again, his anger growing.

I can't wait weeks!

"So, if you could be so kind as not to bother contacting us until then," Toby continued. "We'd much appreciate it."

William scowled at Toby. "I assure you, young man, things will proceed on our timetables, not yours. Now, sir." He turned to the fuming Edmund. "Where can I reach you?"

Weeks! Damn it! Curse my luck!

"As I said," Toby said. "Master Edmund here will be abroad for the next few days, but you can send any information to the Royal Stables. I'll make sure he gets it when he has time."

Now, it was William's turn to get angry. "When he has time? Young man, this is royal business." He faced Edmund, the veins in his neck turning scarlet. "Sir, you may certainly come and go as you please.

However, if you are not here when summoned, I'm afraid you'll forfeit any claims you may have!"

"As you say." Toby pulled Edmund to the door. "Remember to send the summons to the Royal Stables. But not before the end of the week, if you please. Then we'll see if he can come."

"See if he can come?" the magistrate shouted after them. "Sir, teach your son proper manners, or I'll be tempted to raise my hand to him myself!"

Pushing Edmund out of the building, Toby smirked at the magistrate. "Come on, puppy!" He patted his thigh for Thorax to follow them.

"And you brought your dog in here after I expressly—?"

Toby slammed the door to the Hall of Magistrates.

"I can't wait weeks," Edmund said, standing by the grand statues in front of the building. "There has to be another way to see the King."

Toby waved a hand as if his effort were nothing to be rewarded. "Oh, you won't wait that long. Don't worry. You'll hear from him tomorrow or the next day, guaranteed."

"What do you mean?"

"You have to know how these fellows work. If you want to meet with them sooner, you must make them think you're too busy. Then they'll call for you out of spite. Trust me. You'll hear much sooner now."

"Are you sure?"

"Of course," Toby said. "Say, do you have a place to stay? You look like you're down to your last copper piece."

Chapter Fifty-Two

Edmund spit the straw from his mouth.

Though the stables were more comfortable than any place he'd slept in for many months, he didn't get much sleep. The entire night, he kept worrying about whether he could see the King and when. Also, the constantly shifting horses made him jump.

The stable doors slid open. Horses whinnied as Toby came in, a sack of oats over each young shoulder.

"I hope you and Thorax slept well." He dropped the sacks on the ground. "I would've had you stay at our house. But my mom wouldn't hear of it—you being a scary stranger with one eye and all."

Covered in straw, Thorax stretched and yawned.

"Has anybody sent word from the magistrate's office?" Edmund sat up. "Have you heard anything?"

"No," Toby said. "And they wouldn't have. It's not even dawn."

"Damn."

"I'm sorry, but I got to kick you two out before someone finds you." He handed Edmund a bag. "Here."

"What's this?" Edmund opened it, his mind flashing to the last time somebody had given him a canvas bag.

"Something to eat during your day. Come here after dark, and I'll see if I can get you some decent supper. But you have to get going, or somebody will think you're a vagrant. You don't want that. They'll whip you and throw you out of the city. Then you'll never become Lord of the Highlands."

"I don't care about that. I just need to see the King." Then, taking Toby's bag, Edmund added, "Sir Hanley is counting on me."

"Why don't you go to one of the castle guards and tell them what happened up north?"

I might have to do that. I could tell the guard about the goblin army.

And if the guard doesn't believe you?

Edmund shook his head. "Would you believe me if you were a guard?"

Toby glanced at Edmund's threadbare clothes. "I suppose not."

"I think the only way to get an audience with the King is by using the Star. Then I can tell him everything."

"Well, I bet the magistrate will send word later today."

"I hope so." Getting up, Edmund brushed the straw from his lap. "And thank you, Toby. You're very k-k . . . kind. I wish there were some way I could repay you for all your help."

Toby cocked his head, a sly look creeping across his youthful face. "I could say any friend of Sir Hanley is a friend of mine," he said. "Which is true. But I'm hoping you'd do me a favor."

"I'd love to. I would. But I'm not in a position to grant many f-f-fav-favors at the moment. All I have in life is what you see me wearing."

"Ah, but you'll be able to do something—if that necklace is real."

"It's not a necklace. It is worn on the brow. But go on. What can I do to repay your wonderful hospitality and assistance?"

Toby grinned. "Make me a knight!"

Edmund laughed despite his growing anxiety. "I can't."

"You can once you're a lord."

"Unfortunately, that's not true," Edmund said, trying not to disappoint the boy. "You see, you need noble blood to become a knight. Then, there are the years of sacrifice and service to the common people. Not to mention the endless training. Becoming a knight is the p-p-pinnacle of achievement. Not everybody could reach such a high station."

Toby hooted. "Maybe in your day! Nowadays, knights can be appointed."

Edmund pretended to consider this.

"Trust me," Toby said. "Any lord can appoint his own knights. They do it all the time to curry favor with wealthy merchants and the like. Why, Lord Farnor knighted over forty people last year! He made a fortune. That is, until one of them slept with his wife."

Humor the boy. Let him have his dream while he can. What harm could it cause?

"I'll tell you what," Edmund said. "If I become Lord of the Highlands, you can be one of my knights. But you must do something for me first."

"Name it!"

"Let me know the second the magistrate sends word about the Star. All right? The very second it arrives, come get me."

"Deal!" Toby shot out his hand. Edmund shook it. "Now get out before somebody sees you here. You too, Thorax."

Thorax shook the straw from her fur.

"Where should we go?" Edmund asked.

"Anywhere but here." Toby led them to the stable door. "Go sit in the park or something. It feels like it'll be a nice day."

"All right. But keep an eye out for a messenger from the magistrates."

"I will! I will!" Toby pushed Edmund out into the pre-dawn street. "Remember, don't come here until after dark. And don't look like a vagrant, or they'll kick you out of the city."

"All right. Thanks, Tob—"

The stable doors slid closed behind Edmund. Faintly, he heard Toby giggle and say, "Sir Toby the knight!"

He'll be devastated when he learns knights can't be appointed.

It's all part of growing up, I suppose. Better to learn how things are now than when he's forty years old.

Leaving the stables, Edmund wandered the dark streets of Eryn Mas, trying not to think of how Molly might be faring. Soon, he found himself in the park surrounding the lower city. Sitting on a wooden bench under a budding crabapple, he inspected the contents of Toby's bag. There was a ham and onion sandwich on black bread and an apple.

I better save this.

Norb had given him some coins and a few tiny garnets that might fetch a handful of bronze pieces. However, the money wouldn't last long, especially if he had to stay several days. And he didn't want to eat any of his biscuits if he could help it.

Weeks! Damn it!

Maybe if I forged a letter from this Sir Hanley, I could get word to the King about the goblins in the mountains. I could say I'm a messenger from Rood, and none of the other knights or squires could be spared to make the trip.

You'd need Sir Hanley's official seal on the letter.

He shook his head in dismay, his apprehension growing. He felt like he would explode if he sat around much longer.

He exhaled loudly.

Thorax put a paw on Edmund's knee, her eyes drifting to the bag.

"Oh! Okay. You certainly deserve half of this. I owe you, girl. Here."

Edmund broke the sandwich in two and handed the bigger half to Thorax. She lay at his feet, picking out the pieces of ham.

What now?

Remember what Vorn said: Always use your time to your advantage.

Poor Vorn. That advice helped in the mines. But what can I do to my advantage here besides seeing the sights and trying not to get thrown out of the city?

A young man in his early twenties walked past, a blue robe traditionally worn by clerics billowing behind him in the wake of his quick strides. He held a small book.

"Excuse me!" Edmund hurried after him. "Sir?"

Turning, the young man flinched when he saw the hole where Edmund's left eye used to be.

"I'm t-t . . . terribly sorry." Edmund adjusted his eagerness a bit. "I didn't mean to startle you, sir. But I was w-wondering if you could help me."

The young man resumed walking. "I don't have any money for you." He said over his shoulder, "Learn a trade."

"Yes, I understand." Edmund followed him. "Actually, I'm interested in your b-b-book. I'm an antiquarian, you see."

The man stopped, his pinched expression showing considerable suspicion.

Edmund went on. "I was wondering if there's a library here access-access-accessible to the public, to the, the common people, that is."

"Library? You know how to read?"

"Yes, sir. In several languages." Edmund motioned to the book in the man's hand. "Shall I demonstrate?"

The man considered his book, then Edmund's dirt-encrusted fingers. A piece of straw fell from Edmund's unkempt hair.

"There're many rare book dealers in the city," he said.

Many?

I wonder what they have.

"But if you are looking for book lenders." He nodded to a nearby street. "Go three blocks up and two over to the left. It's a four-story building on your right." The man observed Edmund's bare feet. "But it isn't free. They'll charge you for looking."

"Thank you, sir. Thank you very much." Edmund rushed up the street. "Come on, Thorax!"

Grabbing what was left of the sandwich, Thorax hobbled after him.

"Thorax?" the man repeated.

"It's a long story!"

Chapter Fifty-Three

The sun rose over the city's towering walls, giving the elegant facades of the surrounding buildings a pink tinge. Immaculately dressed people from the upper classes strolled up the stone stairs leading to a pair of double doors. The words "Book Lender" were painted across them in yellow letters. Edmund stood outside, straightening his hair and baggy clothes to little effect. Opening one of the doors, he peered in.

Inside, he found a brightly lit chamber filled with rows of long wooden tables. Several dozen people sat throughout the room. Some were children training to become scribes. Others were elderly men poring over various scrolls, books, and unbound manuscripts. A few appeared to be merchants examining law texts.

An ancient man with a hunched shoulder smiled kindly at Edmund as he crossed the threshold.

"May I help you, young man?" he whispered, bowing as much as his bent spine would allow.

"Y-y-yes . . . yes, you may . . . I believe. This, this is the library, is it not?" Edmund smoothed his soiled clothes again.

"Indeed," the old man said pleasantly. "It is the Lower Library. I am Horic, its curator."

"Well . . . that is, I'd, I'd like to do some research. I understand there's a fee involved. May I ask how much?"

"A silver piece per day."

There goes a nice meal.

Fumbling, Edmund reached into his pocket. As he withdrew Norb's small coin pouch, the Star of Iliandor tumbled out and fell rattling onto the floor. Many people looked up from their work, annoyed. Horic hunched closer, his grey eyes growing brighter as he stared at the blue gem. Apologizing, Edmund snatched the Star, shoved it into his pocket, and held out a silver piece.

As if in thought, Horic was slow to take it. "This way."

He led Edmund to a counter behind which a frumpy woman in her late twenties sat, reading an age-worn book.

"This is Edith," Horic said. "She can assist you in finding whatever you are looking for."

The woman closed her book and put on an affable smile.

"I would request, however," Horic said, "that you leave your animal outside. There are rules, you understand."

"Oh, yes. Yes, absolutely." Edmund grimaced at Thorax. "I'm sorry, girl. But can you go entertain yourself for a while?"

Thorax got up and limped out the door.

"Remarkable," Horic muttered. Then, to Edmund, he said, "Please let me know if you require anything. I am at your service."

"Thank you. I'm at yours."

When Horic had gone, the young woman shifted uneasily as if waiting for a command she didn't particularly want to perform.

She noted Edmund's shabby attire and redirected her gaze to the counter. "What may I get for you?"

Now what?

"Yes, thank you. I, I . . . I need information on the northern Haegthorn Mountains," Edmund said. "Particularly the west side, if that's possible. I believe Sir Franklin of Overshire led an expedition to map the region in the year 235—"

"He returned in 235," she said, cutting him short.

"I beg your pardon?"

Edith winced. "I'm sorry. I didn't mean to interrupt."

"No, please, miss," Edmund said. "By all means. You were saying?"

"Sir Franklin returned to Eryn Mas in 235," she whispered. Edmund had to lean forward to hear her. "His expedition of the Haegthorn was from 229 to 234."

She's smart!

She should be surrounded by all these books.

Let's hope there's something here that can help us. Otherwise, you wasted a silver piece.

A silver piece . . . I remember when I wouldn't pick up a silver piece from the ground.

"Wonderful," Edmund said. "Do you have any copies of anything he might've written about his journey? A journal or a secondhand account, perhaps? Anything showing the topography of that region would be useful."

What are the chances Sir Franklin got within sight of the Undead King's tower? None. This is all a waste of time and money.

I need a map of the area or a description to help the knights plan their attack.

That's if you can speak with the King.

I will . . . one way or another.

"I understand," Edith said. "Please have a seat. I'll return momentarily." She disappeared through a doorway behind her.

Unsure of where to sit, Edmund examined his options. There were rows of tables, each flanked by long benches with plump green cushions. However, every table already had numerous people sitting at it, reading or copying manuscripts by the light of crystal lamps.

Who should I sit by?

Somebody who has a poor sense of smell. You haven't bathed in days. And sleeping with horses didn't help at all.

He selected a table toward the rear of the hall. It was occupied by a boy carefully transcribing a lengthy scroll and an older gentleman peering over a thick tome of faded brown parchment. Edmund sat across from the boy.

"The oratories of King Baris the Second," Edmund said, examining what the boy was working on. "Wonderful!"

The boy put a finger to his lips.

"Oh," Edmund whispered. "Sorry."

As he surveyed the room, something poked Edmund's leg. He looked underneath the table. Thorax winked. Edmund laughed. Several people glowered at him, including the boy.

Good girl!

He patted her head.

Moments later, Edith appeared with an armload of parcels, scrolls, and books. As she approached, her eyes slid to where Thorax lay by Edmund's grubby bare feet. Edith and Edmund exchanged glances. She smiled.

"This is what I found for you," she whispered as she set the materials before him.

One of the scrolls rolled off the table. As she went to retrieve it, she scratched Thorax behind the ears.

"Remember," she said. "These are originals. Not copies. Please take utmost care."

She handed Edmund a moist towel.

"Oh, I will." Edmund cleaned his hands. Then, nodding toward Thorax, he said, "And thank you for not saying anything. I'll make sure she doesn't bother anybody." He handed the towel to Edith. She took it, curtseyed, and returned behind the counter, holding the blackened towel as far from her as possible.

For many hours, Edmund studied the materials Edith had given him. Most were loose pages of notes written by Sir Franklin during his travels, papers that were the basis of a book Edmund had in his library. Some of the maps were interesting. But without points of reference, it was impossible to determine exactly what part of the mountains they depicted.

I'll never locate the River Gate this way.

Then try something else. Maybe you could find where the door to that guard's chamber is.

Perhaps. But it'll be guarded.

I'm sure the knights could force their way in.

First, I need to speak with the King.

Stretching, Edmund groaned.

The boy across the table frowned at him.

Think. What pieces of information am I missing? What do I need to get into the tower?

Besides a thousand heavily armed knights?

Carefully, Edmund gathered the materials together and brought them to Edith. She looked up from her book, surprised to find somebody standing over her.

"Thank you for all this," Edmund said.

"Not what you wanted?" she asked.

"No. I, I, I mean, it was fascinating. But it didn't contain anything new for me."

"Perhaps you'd like to examine something else? You still have a few hours before we close for the afternoon."

Edmund drummed his fingers on the counter, thinking.

"Do you have anything about Lord Iliandor of the Highlands? Specifically, about his interest in metallurgy?"

"I'll check. Half a moment."

She disappeared again through the doors behind her desk.

Trying not to disturb the boy or the old man, Edmund returned to his seat.

Do you honestly believe Iliandor published the formula for his secret alloy?

No. But I have to do something with my time.

Edmund imagined Molly in the wet cells, sobbing in the foul darkness. He could almost feel her tears.

Reappearing from the storage rooms, Edith placed five books before Edmund. Edmund was about to thank her for her troubles when he saw what was on the top of the stack. He sprang up with a cry, knocking over his bench and sending the cushion skidding across the floor. Underneath the table, Thorax leaped to her feet.

Many patrons hissed for him to be quiet.

"What's wrong?" Edith whispered. She withdrew a step as if Edmund might be delusional.

Perched on top of the pile, like a specter from his past, was Iliandor's diary.

"Wh-wh-what? What?" Edmund said, trembling. "Oh. I'm . . . I'm fine. Thank you. Thank you very much. There was a bee. That's all. A bee."

"A bee?"

"Yes," Edmund said, his heart still pounding. "But it's gone now. Everything is fine. Thank you."

Edith walked to her counter, turning and looking periodically at Edmund as she went. When she'd gone, and all eyes were off him, Edmund righted his bench and sat. With shaking hands, he lifted the diary.

What are you so spooked about? You asked for information on Iliandor, and she brought his diary. There's no meaning behind it. Calm down. You're making an ass out of yourself.

His chest pounding, Edmund opened the diary's cover. He perused several of the pages. There was no doubt about it. It was one of the two copies he made over twenty years earlier. Even with one eye, he could recognize his own work.

What are the chances?

You sent a copy to the Royal Library in Eryn Mas. Obviously, they didn't want it, and the book wound up here. Relax!

He set the diary aside and examined the other books Edith had brought him.

None of this is useful. This was such a waste of time.

I hope Pond is having better luck than I am.

Something gnawed at the recesses of Edmund's mind. From the corner of his eye, he kept peering at the diary as if to make sure it wasn't a figment of his imagination. He closed the book he was skimming.

It's your copy. There isn't a doubt in the world.

Edmund opened the diary again.

Something's wrong with it.

He flipped through its pages.

Everything is exactly like it—

He got to the last page.

This isn't right.

The last page of the diary wasn't the last page he'd copied all those years ago.

Edmund looked closer at the binding.

Somebody had meticulously cut out the pages describing the attack at Tol Helen.

Who would've—?

Then, the answer came to him.

Someone who didn't want anyone else looking for the Star.

No, not the Star—the riddle written in the cave!

Chapter Fifty-Four

The shopkeeper showed a pair of ruby earrings to an overweight noblewoman.

"Yes, my lady," he said with exaggerated grace. "I can assure you they are authentic. They came from the High Courts of the Longborough Providence. They once belonged to Lady Josephine. In fact, they were a birthday gift from Queen Isabel."

Edmund listened from the rear of the gallery, pretending to read one of the overpriced books lining the merchant's many shelves. After learning nothing of use at the Lower Library, he had been exploring the city's numerous antique shops, hoping to find a map of the northern mountains or maybe a weapon made from Iliandor's smoke-colored metal. Unfortunately, he couldn't find anything that would help him rescue Molly.

He doesn't know what he's talking about. Lady Josephine would've been only three years old when Queen Isabel died.

Stay out of it.

I hate fakes.

Edmund exhaled in disgust. Sitting beside him, Thorax tilted her head and raised her floppy black ears.

"I'll explain later," Edmund told her.

The noblewoman examined the earrings in the lantern light.

She doesn't have a clue what she's looking for.

Stay out of it.

But she's being taken advantage of! How can I stand here and do nothing?

It's none of your business.

The noblewoman opened her coin purse. "I will take them."

The amount of money she handed the salesperson made Edmund look twice.

This is worse than highway robbery!

Stay out of it.

But he's robbing her!

Stay out of it.

If he had a knife to her throat, I'd be expected to do something. Why shouldn't I do something now? She's being robbed just the same!

"Thank you so much for your business, Lady Annette." The shopkeeper bowed. "And if I come across anything else you might like, I will be sure to keep it in the back with the merchandise for my special customers."

"It is always a pleasure, Reginald." She put the fake ruby earrings on. "You are my favorite, you know that. So many of these other dealers are nothing more than poorly dressed charlatans."

He's nothing more than a nicely dressed charlatan.

The salesman chortled as he escorted her to the door. His chuckles became more genuine after she'd gone. Then, he noticed Edmund standing by the stacks of books.

"My dear sir!" Slipping the woman's coins into his pocket, he hurried to Edmund. "I'm dreadfully sorry. I didn't see you. Please excuse my horrid oversight. I—"

Taking in Edmund's ill-fitting attire and bare feet, the pleasantness drained from his face.

"Oh!" Edmund examined his baggy clothes. "These." He winked knowingly at the merchant. "Consider this a disguise. I'm actually n-n-nobility."

"Of course you are, sir," Reginald said. "How may I be of assistance? Beautiful animal, by the way. We usually don't have customers bringing them into the shop. This is a rare treat."

Thorax bared her teeth.

"That's a fine work you are examining." He motioned to the book in Edmund's hand. "It's an original dating from the early 400s, most likely written by Eol the Scribe."

The ink is barely dry. The pages are brown because they were placed by a fire. I can smell the smoke.

Edmund slipped on a smile. "You have such a beautiful shop. It's positively wonderful! I've been all over this city, and I must say, there is no other establishment its equal."

Reginald's face eased somewhat. "You honor me. How can I repay your kindness? Are you looking for anything specific or merely browsing? We don't sell shoes, in case you weren't aware."

Edmund ignored the sarcasm.

"I was hoping you might have something from the old n-n-northern lands, something from Iliandor's time? He's of great interest to me, you see."

"Iliandor?"

The fake doesn't know who Iliandor is.

"How about weapons?" Edmund asked, changing the topic. "Have you ever seen antique weapons made of a smoke-colored metal?"

"Smoke-colored metal?" Reginald repeated. "I'm sure I don't know what you mean, sir."

"It's of no great matter," Edmund assured him. "It's simply an inferior alloy that turns color as it ages. Very rare. I'd pay a great deal for such an item."

At this, Reginald's eyes regained their twinkle.

Edmund pretended to think. "Do, do, do you have any books or maps from the Highlands? Perhaps something you only let your exceptional customers see?"

"You know," Reginald said as if an idea had dawned on him. "I have just such the thing for you. And if I remember correctly, it came from Iliandor's personal library."

"You don't say?" Edmund said with mock amazement. "I'd love to see it."

Reginald considered Edmund's appearance again. "You understand, these items are quite rare and, although reasonably priced, not everybody can afford such treasures."

Edmund snorted a laugh. "Let me see what you have. I can assure you, I have m-m-more than enough money."

Still skeptical, the salesman went to a back room.

When he was out of view, Edmund withdrew the three tiny garnets Norb had in his coin pouch. Grinning at Thorax, he put his finger to his lips. Thorax lay back down.

"*Forstørre nå.*"

The stones doubled in size.

"*Forstørre nå.*"

They grew again. Edmund stole a glance around, making sure the salesman hadn't returned.

"Forstørre nå."

Now, the garnets were as large as walnuts. They were still flawed and crudely cut, but by size alone, they would fetch fifty gold pieces each from any reputable dealer.

Reginald returned with a towering stack of books. He beckoned to Edmund as he arranged them in a line across a table.

"I'm sure one of these will be of interest to somebody with such a fine eye for—" He stopped, his hand covering his mouth. "I, I . . . I am truly sorry. I meant . . ."

Touching where his eye used to be, Edmund waved a hand. "Oh, not to worry. Not to worry. Please, show me what you have. They look splendid."

"Thank you, sir. You're most kind." Bowing, Reginald finished arranging them across the table. "As I said, they came directly from Lord Iliandor's personal library in the northern city of Azagra. Did you know he had one of the most extensive libraries on the continent? It contained some of the oldest texts ever written, it is said. It's a shame it was burned down in the year 439."

He looked all of that up when he was in the back. He doesn't have a clue what he's talking about.

Edmund examined the books with forced eagerness.

These are all cheap forgeries.

You shouldn't be doing this. Leave now before you get yourself into trouble.

He stole money from that woman, and somebody should teach him a lesson. Don't!

I'm tired of running from fakes!

Picking up a small book of poetry with a faded green cover, Edmund read the title aloud. "Leaves of Spring." He sucked in air as if he'd found a Crown Jewel from the Gods.

"You have tremendous taste, sir," Reginald said. "Lord Iliandor read these poems to his beloved wife every night before she fell asleep."

I bet.

Don't do it. Just walk away.

Edmund clutched the book as if he couldn't stand to part with it. "How much?"

"For you, a new customer, I'll give it to you for one hundred and fifty silver—a bargain, as I'm sure you'll agree."

"I would indeed!" Then Edmund let a sad expression settle on his face. "B-b-but can you hold it for me? I don't have many coins. Horribly heavy things, you understand."

A look of validation appeared on Reginald's smug face.

"But I have an appointment with a jeweler tomorrow," Edmund continued. "He's going to give me ten gold pieces for each of these." He opened his hand, showing the three monstrous gems. They shone in the sunlight.

His fingers rising to his lips in astonishment, Reginald took a small step back, unable to breathe. "May, may I . . .?" He held out a hand.

Edmund gave him the garnets.

Reginald inspected them closely with an eyeglass, the pulse in his neck quickening.

"You know," the salesman said, his voice trembling ever so slightly. "I have a good friend who is looking for garnets this shade of blue. If you like, I could buy these from you for, say, twelve gold pieces each. That would save you the trip to the jeweler. I'd even throw in the book for free."

"Are you sure?" Edmund asked. "That's a lot of money."

"Of course. Anything for a valuable customer, such as yourself."

Reginald counted out the coins and pushed them at Edmund. "And, of course, your exquisite purchase." He handed Edmund the small green book.

Edmund returned the smile. "Thank you s-s-so much. Everybody is correct about you. You are a fair and honest businessman."

"You're too kind." Still clutching the three inflated gems, Reginald bowed. "But you'll pardon me. I must put these in a safe place."

"By all means. And thank you. I'll return whenever I need—"

But Reginald had already run to the back room.

Beaming, Edmund turned to leave. He nearly bumped into a woman standing behind him.

"Oh!" Edmund attempted to calculate how long the garnets would keep their present size. "Hello . . . Edith, is it? Yes. Hello. How, how are you doing this afternoon?"

"You shouldn't purchase anything here," the woman from the library said. She wiggled her fingers at Thorax. Thorax wagged her tail. "Most of these items aren't genuine."

Wanting to be as far away from the shop as possible when the stones reverted to their original size, Edmund strolled out of the boutique. Edith and Thorax trailed after him.

"Really?" he said with forced disbelief. He examined the book of poetry. "It's a fake?"

"You knew that already," Edith said.

Get out of here! Those gems will revert back in ten minutes, if not sooner.

Relax. It isn't like he'll stare at them for that long. He'll gloat for a few minutes and lock them in his safe. He won't notice anything wrong until morning.

Then what will happen?

"Wh-wh-what brings you here this evening?" Edmund asked, attempting to change the subject as he hurried along the street.

"I found something that might interest you."

"Oh?"

What could she have possibly found that would warrant her searching all over the city for me?

"You expressed a desire to see maps of the northern portions of the Haegthorn Mountains."

"Maps?" Edmund's stride faltered. "What did you find?"

"I think it'd be best if I showed you."

Chapter Fifty-Five

Edith brought Edmund and Thorax to the Lower Library. Being well past sunset, it was closed. But Edith had a key and let them in.

Inside, all was dark.

Lighting a small lamp, Edith led them through several storerooms.

They passed thousands of shelves overflowing with books. Crates, chests, and cabinets lined the walls. Countless yellowing scrolls sat in holders like priceless bottles of wine.

Edmund gaped around him as they walked.

There's more here than I could read in a lifetime. Who knows what lost pieces of literature are tucked away behind one of these boxes, forgotten by the world for centuries?

"You initially indicated you were interested in the Haegthorn Mountains," Edith said. "Particularly maps of the western side."

Except for the three-foot ring of light around her lamp, everything was completely black, like an endless void. Their footsteps echoed in the rafters high overhead. Edmund inhaled the familiar scent of ancient parchment with satisfaction.

"I thought you might be interested in a small collection we have," she said. "We don't let many people see it. But it may be what you're looking for."

Climbing a ladder to the top shelf, Edith pushed aside several dusty crates. Reaching as far as she could, she pulled a book the size of a tombstone from the shadows.

She carefully descended the ladder. "This is what I wanted to show you."

Edith set the book on a worktable. She studied Edmund's expression as he opened it and turned its thick pages.

On the left-hand page were notes written in High Ruduel, one of the ancient languages scholars once used when humans first voyaged to the continent. It was an arduous tongue, especially in its earliest derivations, but Edmund knew it fluently. Fascinated, he skimmed through the many records and sketches.

"This part seems to be a paleographer's translation tablet," he said. "Whomever it belonged to was attempting to decipher—" He beheld the right-hand page.

Those runes . . .

"You've seen these symbols before," Edith said.

They're the same as that book in the troll's cave. I wish I could've rescued it. I wonder what it said.

"What?" Edmund said. "Yes . . . yes, I have. Briefly."

He turned a page, examining the runes painstakingly printed on the right side of the book.

"The Royal Library has an entire room full of manuscripts like this," Edith said as Edmund scrutinized the pages. "But nobody can read them."

Maybe with a little time, I could.

You don't have time, remember?

He turned up the lamp's wick. Black smoke spiraled into the darkness above them.

"When a seller approached Master Horic with this text," Edith said, "he purchased it with his own money. He never cataloged it for fear somebody might wish to check it out."

Marveling at the quality of the sketches. Edmund turned another page. "I bet he paid a fortune for it."

"He did. He spent nearly his entire savings."

It's worth every penny. It's a shame nobody came to Rood with something like this.

"Every few days or so, he takes it down and tries deciphering the characters. He's been trying for decades but can't make heads or tails of what they say. As I said, nobody can."

Edmund examined the book's binding. It seemed to be bound by some strange silver thread.

What does this have to do with anything? Yes, it's remarkable. But why is she showing it to me?

Edmund looked at her, perplexed. "Why—?"

"Because I thought you might like to see these."

Carefully, she turned past several hundred pages of topographical charts and drawings of flora and fauna. She came to a series of simple maps. Faded arrows and notations adorned the margins.

"I believe this—" She pointed to a dark line angling off to the left. "—is the River Laudrum."

Edmund nodded in agreement as he studied the precision of the contour lines.

His heart jolted.

The River Laudrum!

That might've been the river I saw when Crazy Bastard ran away! If we followed it north, it'd lead the knights right to—

Scanning the upper right-hand portion of the map, he found a tiny cartographer's icon for a tower. A faded line connected it with a notation off to the side.

Page 1811.

His heart rising, he searched for page 1811. His trembling fingertips made it difficult for him to turn the pages.

"Be careful," Edith said. "You'll tear the vellum."

He found page 1811.

A wave of cold washed over Edmund's clammy skin.

"Are you okay?" Edith asked.

Edmund pointed at the book, his throat feeling as if it were being squeezed closed. He fought to breathe.

There, on page 1811, was a meticulous pencil and ink drawing of the Undead King's tower.

"Wh-wh-where . . . where did you get this?" He examined the drawing closer.

It was so clear and precise that he could make out the window from which he'd watched Crazy Bastard scamper into the valley below. It was as if he could see himself in the picture, gazing out longingly with the telescope. Even the trees in the foreground appeared identical to what he remembered.

"As I said," Edith said, "Horic bought it years ago, long before I came to work here. Before I was born, I'm sure. Would you like some water?"

Edmund shook his head as he read the annotations at the page's bottom.

It was abandoned when this was made—whenever that was.

He turned to a page number in the margin, then clutched Edith's arm like a stumbling blind man.

"What is it?" she asked.

It's the entire layout of the tower! Every . . . single . . . floor.

With this information, we could rout out every goblin from every hiding spot in the entire tower.

The goblins won't have a chance!

"Are you sure you're okay?" Edith asked again.

Edmund nodded. "Y-y-yes, yes I am. Wonderful, in fact. Thank you."

There were more illustrations detailing every foothill, every stream, and every mountain peak in the region. There were even indications of where caves were, as well as crude schematics of entire cavern systems—where they could be accessed and where they became impassible. One page even had a lifelike drawing of the three portcullises through which he and Pond had escaped.

Edmund read aloud the notations under the picture. ". . . unable to open . . . extraordinary alloy . . . unexplored ruins on the other side . . . skeletons of unknown origins . . ."

"How old is this book?" he asked Edith. "Best guess."

Edith's scrawny shoulders lifted. "A thousand years? But Horic believes it is a copy of a much older text. If you notice, the handwriting is all different, as if it were copied by a series of scribes and bound. It's far too precise to have been written in the field."

"I need to study this," Edmund said. "Can I—?"

Thorax sprang to her feet.

The echoes of a door closing rolled through the darkness toward them.

Edith went white. She closed the tome. "We have to put this back."

"But I need it," Edmund said.

Edith scrambled up the ladder, slid the book into the shadows, and repositioned the crates.

"Please, I need—" Edmund said.

Edith grabbed his hand. "Come on." She led him deeper into the storage room. "If he finds us, he'll fire me."

She pulled him through another door, closed it softly, and urged Edmund and Thorax behind a line of iron-bound chests. She blew out the lamp's flame and waved away the black smoke.

"I need—" Edmund began.

Edith's nails dug into his forearm. "Please, be quiet!"

A scarlet glow appeared underneath the door. There were slow, halting steps, then shuffling movements, as if crates were being repositioned.

An eternity passed. Edith clung to Edmund's arm, her sharp breaths rasping in the darkness. Then, slow steps walked away, the red light retreating with the echoes.

When they emerged from their hiding spot, the tome was gone.

Chapter Fifty-Six

The next day, Edmund, Thorax, and Toby exited a fashionable clothier in the upper levels of the city, their arms laden with packages wrapped neatly in paper. Edmund was eight gold pieces poorer. But his new boots and clothes were worth the expense. They were more elegant than anything he'd ever worn. In them, he actually felt like a lord.

"Are you sure they said this afternoon?" Edmund asked Toby again.

"Yes!" the boy said. "I even double-checked. Your audience with the King is at four bells. Not a second later."

Moments before, the bells in the Grand Tower rang two o'clock.

Thank the gods! If I had to sit around here any longer, I would've gone crazy!

They stood in the street outside the clothier's shop. Edmund felt his hairless chin.

I should shave.

You shaved this morning.

It wouldn't hurt to shave again. And maybe bathe again. I have a couple of hours.

You better not be late! This is the most important day of your life.

"Let's go to the bathhouse," Edmund told Toby. "I want to freshen up and get ready."

He headed up the street.

"I can't believe you're going to be a lord!" Toby said, loud enough for all to hear.

I just hope the King will listen to me.

He will. What King could pass up killing thirty thousand goblins?

Somebody seized Edmund's arm and spun him around, packages flying out of his hands.

"What the—?" he cried.

"What's your name?" a bearded man demanded, his sword drawn and pointed at Edmund's stomach.

"I-I-I . . . I beg your pardon?" Then Edmund noted the pendant the man wore on his grey cloak. It had a gold tower surrounded by red rays of the setting sun—the official symbol of Eryn Mas. "M-m-may I help you, sir?"

The bearded man's expression eased as if he'd found exactly what he thought he'd find. He observed Thorax squatting next to Edmund, leaving a smelly pile of excrement on the cobblestones.

"I'll clean it up." Edmund tried to pull free from the man's grasp. "Honest!"

The law enforcer's gaze shifted to the scimitar dangling from Edmund's belt. Grinning, he lifted the point of his sword to Edmund's neck and snatched the scimitar from its scabbard.

"Hey!" Edmund shouted. "That's mine. Give it back. What the hell are you doing?"

"Come with me." The man pushed Edmund up the street. "You're under arrest."

"Under arrest? For what?"

It's those gems you gave that merchant! Idiot! I told you they'd get you in trouble!

People stopped and stared at them.

Thorax growled as she hobbled after Edmund.

"What's this all about?" Toby asked. "You don't know who you're talking to. He's going to be a lord!"

"I don't care who he is." The law enforcer pushed Edmund. "He's under arrest for murder."

A murmur rustled through the crowd.

Murder?

"You've got the wrong m-m-man!" Edmund said as the man forced him up the street.

What's this all about?

It's a mistake. Go with him and clear everything up.

"Toby!" Edmund pointed to the packages scattered about the ground. "Grab those."

The law enforcer shoved Edmund another few steps, the muttering crowd around them growing.

"I don't . . . I don't have time for this," Edmund shouted. "I have a m-m-meeting with the King!"

The man laughed. "Sure, you do."

"He does!" Toby ran after them, packages in his arms. "Really!"

"He'll swing from the gallows by sundown if the witnesses identify you."

"W-w-witnesses?" Edmund sputtered. "This, this is all a, a, a mistake. Honest. I have an audience with the King in a couple of hours. I can't be late!"

"Oh, I have the right man, all right." He kicked Thorax out of his way. "How many stuttering, one-eyed men with a black and white dog and a goblin scimitar are there in Eryn Mas?" He pushed Edmund up the street. "You'll hang after what you did."

What's he talking—?

Then Edmund remembered the bandit from the bridge flying through the air, his chest caved in by Blake's rear hooves.

But he was a thug! He would've killed me.

If the other two men testify, they'll say—

The man shoved Edmund again.

"Come on and move it. Or I'll stick you with this." He shook his sword.

This can't be happening. Not now!

At least forty people gathered around them.

"Hang him!" somebody shouted.

Hang him?

No!

A grumble of agreement swept through the crowd.

Edmund looked around frantically. He saw Toby clutching the packages, his mouth hanging open.

"Toby!" Edmund said. "This is a mistake. Take the packages to Blake. I'll m-m-meet you there when I get this all cleared up. Okay?"

Toby blinked at him.

"Go!" Edmund shouted. "I'll be fine. It's all a mistake. But I need to go with him to prove it."

Nodding, Toby retreated into the angry mob.

The man stabbed his sword at Edmund's midsection. "Hurry up, or I'll—"

"Okay! Okay!" Edmund raised his hands in surrender. "Hold on, will you? Give me a minute. I need to get my d-d-dog."

Edmund bent down and picked Thorax up. As he stood, he threw his knee into the law enforcer's groin. The man snapped forward sharply, dropping both his sword and Edmund's scimitar. Edmund's fist collided with his jaw. The man's head cracked back as he collapsed to the cobblestones.

Sweeping up both swords, Edmund said, "I'm, I'm . . . s-s-sorry. I'm really sorry about this. But I can't be arrested now." He put his scimitar in his scabbard. Turning to the astonished crowd, he shouted, "I'm not a murderer! I was defending myself. Those men were bandits!"

The law enforcer groaned as he rolled about the ground, holding his groin.

Get out of here!

"I'm not a murderer," Edmund said. "Honest! N-n-now . . . now, leave me alone, and nobody will get hurt. Please!"

Edmund ran.

"Help!" somebody yelled. "Murderer! Murderer!"

"Get him!" someone else shouted.

The crowd converged around the law enforcer. Several children helped him to his feet, but nobody chased after Edmund.

Chapter Fifty-Seven

Edmund paced outside the Royal Audience Hall. Towering double doors gilded in gold blocked his way. Thorax sat nearby, watching her partner stride back and forth, wringing his hands together.

Down the hall, another door opened.

Edmund spun, fearing the law enforcer had come to arrest him. When the people who emerged into the hallway strolled in the opposite direction, he exhaled and swabbed a cloth over his sweating forehead. Two royal guards watched him with amusement.

It's a misunderstanding. That's all. Those men were bandits. The King will understand.

Don't tell the King anything about it. He needs to send his knights to the tower! That's the only thing that matters right now.

Right! Everything will be fine. It has to be—for Molly's sake.

Edmund tried to pay attention to the courtier lecturing him.

"Remember," the old man continued, "when the doors open, you wait, head bowed. When His Highness is ready for you, he'll command you to enter. At which time, you are to walk briskly to the center of the room, bow for at least three seconds, and then proceed to the dais. There, you will kneel and wait to be spoken to. Do not make eye contact until he tells you to rise. Do you understand?"

Nodding, Edmund exhaled again and resumed his pacing.

What am I going to say?

Tell him about the tower, the thousands of goblins, and how you escaped.

Thorax pawed his leg.

"Hey, girl." He scratched behind her ears. "You've g-g-g-got to stay out here, okay? I mean it. All the other times you've followed me were fine. But this is different. Do you understand?"

Thorax's ears drooped.

"Actually—" The old man picked dog hair from Edmund's new cloak. "His Highness adores animals, dogs in particular. You may do well to bring the beast in, if it can behave itself."

Thorax stared up at Edmund, a look of 'I told you so' in her brown eyes.

"But if it so much as piddles on the floor," the courtier said, "the King will execute both of you. The choice is yours."

Suddenly, the gilded doors swung open. The guards snapped to attention. Edmund bowed his head, staring at Thorax with increasing anxiety.

They stood motionless before the open doors, heads bowed, as numerous voices argued. One voice rose above all, a regal tone causing all the others to fall silent.

"I don't care who takes the blasted post," he shouted. "It could be a drunken monkey for all I care, as long as he can provide me with fresh men capable of killing those arrogant horse-breeding bastards!"

Cold sweat trickled along Edmund's armpits.

"They were allies," the voice said, emphasizing the past tense. "And what of it?"

Several people spoke at once.

"What is the use of being king during times of peace? I mean, honestly! What would be the point? I might as well go to rot."

Somebody tried to say something, but the regal voice shouted him down. "We have an army, don't we? Well then, let's use it!"

That's a good sign! He wants to fight.

Then tell him where he can find thirty thousand goblins to cleave to pieces.

More voices joined the fray.

"Armies are not good in witch hunts!" he shouted. "What fun is that?"

Good. Leave us magic users alone.

"Oh, shut up! All of you!" the King commanded. "I've made my decision, now silence."

The room fell quiet.

"Enter!" the King called to Edmund.

His head bowed, Edmund walked quickly into the Royal Audience Hall. Much to his annoyance, Thorax remained by his side.

"A dog?" the King said. "Why, I like this fellow already. See the benefits of our little games? Appointing some dreary lesser nobility to the post wouldn't have been nearly as much fun!"

Edmund and Thorax reached the center of the room. Had it not been for Thorax bowing first, Edmund would've forgotten to do so.

"Splendid!" the King called. "Absolutely splendid! The dog is actually bowing. Jeffrey, do you see that? See if we can teach our beasts that trick." He called across the hall to Edmund. "Come, come. Let's get this over with."

Edmund and Thorax straightened and, as if they'd rehearsed the routine hundreds of times before, walked to the dais and knelt before the King. The King applauded.

"Splendid! Talented mongrel—and human. Though I dare say I'd cut off that lame leg. The dog's, not the human's, you understand. Stand and entertain me!"

Edmund stood.

He was in an extraordinarily long ceremonial hall, hundreds of feet in length. Sunlight streamed through stained glass windows, sending rivers of red and blue light dancing across the sparkling white floors. Underneath the windows, scores of royal advisors sat on benches, mumbling to themselves in agitated voices. Above, beautiful images of child-like angels floating in a blue sky adorned the frescoed ceiling.

Before Edmund, twelve broad steps led to a dais. At the center of the dais sat a tall man with flowing yellow hair that Edmund guessed was dyed to match the golden throne.

The King's expression twisted. "Good god, man! What the devil happened to your eye? And your face—it's positively revolting!"

A dwarf in multicolored robes and a floppy hat sprang to the King's side. "Did somebody say, 'revolting'?" He banged a small gong.

"Oh!" The King laughed. "Good timing, Lester! And I supposed the last thing a king should say is . . . 'REVOLT-ing,' get it?"

Banging his gong repeatedly, the dwarf danced a jig as the royal advisors produced stilted laughter.

"Ah!" The King dabbed his eyes with an embroidered handkerchief. "That was too precious. Revolting!" He chuckled some more.

Edmund waited.

"All right then," the King said when he'd finally composed himself. "You're the poor, ugly fellow who found the Star of somebody or some such thing, correct?"

Edmund and Thorax exchanged glances.

He's crazy!

"He has to consult with the dog!" Rolling on the floor, Lester kicked his bell-covered slippers in the air.

"Well, it is the better-looking one of the two," the King replied, getting more forced laughter and gong-ringing. "It's probably more intelligent as well."

Not sure what to do, Edmund fought the urge to look at Thorax again.

"I'm sorry," the King said, turning to Edmund. "You were saying?"

Edmund bowed for no reason other than to hide his mounting irritation. "Your H, H, Highness . . ."

"Your H, H, Highness . . ." The dwarf mocked as he danced.

The King waved for Lester to stop. "You found the something of somebody or another. It must not have been too difficult to acquire if you managed the task."

"No, Sire," Edmund said, trying to keep his face emotionless.

"So, my ugly little fellow, what is it that you do? What is your profession? Have you run a fiefdom before?"

Tell him about the goblins,

I will as soon as I can get past these stupid questions!

"No, Sire. I haven't run a fiefdom before," Edmund said. "And I'm a . . . a librarian of sorts. However, what I—"

"Egad!" The King recoiled. "A librarian? How incredibly boring!"

"Yes . . . yes, sir. I suppose it is. But, but, but . . . what I'd like to talk to you about—"

"Then tell me about your eye, the one that is either really, really small or missing altogether. Not the normal one. I have no interest in it."

Good! Now tell him about the goblins.

"W-w-well . . . well, Sire, th-th-that, that's . . . that's why I wished to speak to—"

"Good god!" The King turned to those around him. "He's a stuttering imbecile! We can't have an imbecile become nobility!"

"Why not?" Lester, the jester, asked. "He'd fit right in."

The King considered this and then howled with laughter. Dancing in a circle, the dwarf banged his gong.

"Ah, Lester!" The King said, still laughing. "You are priceless. Fit right in!" He chuckled some more. "So true. So unbelievably true!"

Don't look at Thorax. Don't look at Thorax.

"Okay," the King said, his chuckles dying. "Master Lester is correct. You shall be like all the others. Stutter away, imbecile."

Gritting his teeth, Edmund shifted from one foot to another.

He's a moron! How did he ever become king?

Never mind that. Focus! Nice . . . smooth . . . speech!

"You see, Your Highness," Edmund said, "my, my eye was burnt out by goblins. They're—"

Leaning forward, the King nearly got to his feet.

"Those bastards! Good thing we made them pay, the vermin! Please forgive my jester for making light of your truly horrifying appearance. He had no idea you were a veteran. Now, I will be proud to make you a lord!"

The King searched around his throne. "Where is my lord-making sword?" he bellowed. "No, not that one! The pretty one with the sparkly diamonds all up and down the hilt."

Tell him!

"A-a-act-actually," Edmund said, wondering whether he should interrupt the ranting King. "I'm not a, a veteran. Strictly speaking, that is."

The King raised an eyebrow. "What are you? Strictly speaking."

"You see, my eye was b-burnt out by goblins in the northern Haegthorn Mountains. I was captured and held captive in a tower—"

"What?" The King huffed. "Nonsense! There hasn't been a goblin in the north for generations. And thanks to my sword arm and, to a lesser extent, the Providence of the Gods, they are now vanquished here as well!"

He's an arrogant horse's ass!

Keep your mouth shut. And don't show anger. Be humble and pleasant. Explain to him what happened.

"S-s-so, so it would seem, your Highness," Edmund said. "But, but there is an entire kingdom of goblins up north. Thirty thousand strong!"

The King sat back, his lips forming a wry smile.

"Oh, I see," he said, delighted. "This is a joke! And a very good one! Lester, bang away."

The dwarf banged his gong and danced in a circle.

"I'm not joking," Edmund said, irritation creeping into his tone. "Up in the Haegthorn, there is a tower, and tunnels, and a ruined city, and thousands of goblins! They're led by the Undead King. Iliandor didn't kill him after all. You must send your army to defeat them so I can rescue the woman I love!"

The King looked at Lester. The dwarf shrugged.

"Honestly," the King said to Edmund. "You need to work on this one. It's not terribly funny."

"I tell you," Edmund's voice rose to a shout. "It isn't a joke! There are over thirty thousand goblins hidden under the northern peaks of the Haegthorn Mountains. You need to send your army up there—"

"Now you're being insulting!" the King said. "And not a least bit entertaining. Goblins up north. Thirty thousand of them?" He guffawed. "That's lunacy!"

Lester stepped forward, his face strangely unnerved. "Actually, Your Highness, he may be telling the truth."

The King regarded his jester with surprise.

"You see," the dwarf went on, "many ages ago, scrolls were found written in a strange language that none could read. They took decades to decipher, but one of your predecessors eventually untangled the riddle."

"Go on, Lester," the King said. "You intrigue me. What did these scrolls say?"

"Master, they told of the future and how a mighty goblin horde with indestructible weapons and armor would one day sweep out of the northern lands and drive humans into the sea. And that we only have one hope for salvation."

The royal advisors ceased their murmurings.

The King leaned closer to the dwarf.

"Go on," the King said. "What is our one hope?"

"A middle-aged, one-eyed librarian who stutters."

The King looked at Edmund and then at his jester. "Are you serious?"

"No."

The room shook with laughter.

Chapter Fifty-Eight

Trying to appear as calm and normal as possible, Edmund hurried along the street leading to the royal stables. He glanced behind him again. People milled about, but nobody seemed to be following him. He scanned their faces. He didn't see the law enforcer. Trying to hide Thorax tucked under his left arm, he pulled his newly purchased cloak closer around him. He increased his pace.

I can't believe he kicked me out.

You're lucky he didn't throw you in the stockades . . . or worse! Never antagonize kings.

The ass thought I was making some sort of stupid joke.

Edmund shook his head in disgust and desperation.

Now what?

Maybe you should tell him you were only kidding and that there aren't any goblins in the northern mountains.

How would that help us rescue Molly?

I don't know.

"I suppose we should start thinking of another plan," he told Thorax.

Several people passing by gave him odd looks.

We could try rescuing Molly with a smaller group. We could force our way into the tower, grab her, and get out.

That wouldn't solve the goblin problem. They'd still be there, biding their time until they came out of the mountains and killed everybody.

But Molly would be safe. All we'd need is a hundred stout men and that book from the library.

A cart driver shouted for him to get out of the way. Edmund stepped aside as the cart clattered past.

"I suppose we should take one thing at a time," he said.

Hidden underneath his cloak, Thorax's head bobbed up and down.

"Let's see. There'd be me, Pond, Norb, and the knights occupying Rood . . ."

Not all the knights will come. They can't leave the town unguarded. Somebody will have to stay behind and care for the women and children.

"So maybe six or seven knights and their squires and maybe forty townsfolk. Maybe another twenty lads from the farms . . ."

Edmund thought about this.

He knew Norb and Pond would help. But they weren't warriors. Neither were any of the men from Rood or the farms.

Perhaps Borst the blacksmith will come. He could knock the heads off a few goblins, especially if he has a couple of drinks in him.

He'll come. But most of the dirty work will be done by the knights. Just me and the knights . . .

We need more seasoned warriors.

As he approached the stables, Edmund scanned the shadows for the law enforcer. Nobody seemed to be waiting for him.

How am I going to find skilled mercenaries?

Hoarse laughter burst from the building across the street. Startled, Edmund wheeled around. People gave him a wide berth.

Remembering the knight's tavern, he exhaled with relief.

Then, an idea shot to mind.

Running to the building, he cast open its door.

A bright fire burned in the fire pit, illuminating rows of wooden tables. Many lay on their sides or tipped over. Scantily clad women strutted around, serving drinks to burly men with muscles covering their mountainous bodies. There was shouting as steins of beer flew across the room. Several of the men had women sitting on their laps.

Are you sure this is wise?

We need men who can fight. And they can fight!

Setting Thorax down, Edmund climbed onto one of the tables and waved his arms.

Nobody paid him any mind.

"Excuse me," he said.

The uproar continued unabated.

"Ex-excuse me," he repeated louder.

Still, no one took notice of him.

Edmund screamed, "Hey!"

Everyone fell silent. A room full of enormous men and serving girls peered at him.

"I, I, I . . . I'm, I'm terribly sorry, sirs," Edmund began, not knowing what to say. "But I need your help. You see—"

One of the knights shouted, "A song!"

Everybody banged their fists on the tables.

"Yes, give us a song, master dwarf!"

"I'm not a dwarf," Edmund called out.

More cheering and thumping shook the room. Somebody started singing. Others joined in. Soon, the entire tavern bounced with an old drinking tune.

"Hey!" Edmund screamed even louder.

They quieted.

"Good sirs, please listen!" he said. "I need your help rescuing a w-w-woman!"

"Is she pretty?" someone shouted.

Several knights snickered.

"How big are her breasts?" somebody else asked to even greater laughter.

This is of no use. They're all drunken louts.

I have to try.

You'll never get their attention.

Maybe I can.

Reaching into his pocket, Edmund snatched the Star of Iliandor and held it aloft for all to see. Bewildered, the men around him stared at it.

"This," Edmund announced as awe-inspiring as possible, "this is the Star of Iliandor!"

"What the hell is that?"

"The, the . . . the King, King Lionel, has issued an edict," Edmund called out, pausing for dramatic effect. "Whoever brings him the Star of Iliandor will be granted lordship over Iliandor's former fiefdom!"

"So, why don't you give it to Old Yellowhair?"

More giggling.

"I'd like to give it to him," somebody grumbled. "Right between the eyes."

"Why? You wouldn't hit anything he uses."

The room reverberated with drunken laughter. Several of the knights rolled around on the beer-sodden floor.

"Good sirs!" Edmund shouted. "Good sirs! Please, it's a matter of honor!"

Most of the knights quieted again.

A knight with tattoos of snakes intertwining around his bulging biceps said, "Go on. What's this all about?"

"My love—" Edmund fought back the emotion rising in him. "Goblins are holding my love. I need your skill, your, your . . . swords. Whoever helps me can have this!" He shook the Star over his head. "And will become Lord of the Highlands!"

"Highlands?" somebody repeated. "Who the hell would want to be Lord of the Highlands?"

"Who'd want to be a lord, period?" another knight replied.

The knight with the tattoos seemed interested and relatively sober. "Goblins, you say? Where? We crushed them into pulp."

A great cheer went up as they lifted their steins. Calls for more drinks rang out.

Don't blow this.

"In the . . . in the northern mountains," Edmund hollered over the cheering. "There are still a few goblins to the far north. A few here and there, you see. They hide in deep caves."

Nobody paid any attention. Two knights in the far corner sang. Another knight grabbed a serving girl and hoisted her above his head. She squealed as her tray crashed to the floor.

"As, as, as I was saying!" Edmund shouted louder. "I need . . . I need skilled mercenaries to rescue her!"

More knights joined in the song. They passed the protesting serving girl from table to table.

"Who, who, who . . . whoever helps me . . . whoever helps me can have this!" Edmund shook the Star of Iliandor again.

The serving girl slipped through somebody's upraised hands and thudded on the floor, her face bouncing in a pool of beer. The knights around her fell off their chairs and benches, howling with laughter.

"I have a question for you," a drunk knight said to Edmund, his head wobbling on his thick neck. "What's stopping us from beating the crap out of you, taking that thingamabob, and turning it over to Old Yellowhair right now?"

Uh oh!

Edmund's mouth went dry.

Many of the blurry-eyed knights grinned at him. Several exchanged mischievous glances.

Do something!

Edmund drew his scimitar and said, "My sword! And my love for Molly. That's what would stop you!"

All motion in the tavern stopped.

Oh no. What have I done?

Fifty knights blinked at Edmund. The ones lying on the floor got to their knees. Benches creaked under the weight of their occupants as they leaned forward. For many heartbeats, they all stared at Edmund.

Then, one of the knights slowly got to his feet, pointed at Edmund, and shouted, "Get this man a drink!"

Suddenly, a shower of beer flew at Edmund from all directions.

Chapter Fifty-Nine

Edmund stepped out of the Knights' Tavern, dripping beer.

Another colossal failure.

It was worth a try.

Limping next to him, Thorax shook herself, spraying the people passing by.

Is there anybody in this damn city who isn't insane or a drunkard?

Toby opened the stable door.

"Master Edmund!" he said. "What happened with the enforcer? Did you get everything cleared up? Is everything okay?"

Then he noticed Edmund had created a sudsy puddle in the street.

"What the heck happened to you?" Then he said, "You were celebrating, weren't you?" He grew even more excited. "Tell me about the King! What happened? What's he like? Tell me everything! When can you make me a knight?"

"Hello, Toby." Edmund brushed the beer from his eye. "It's a . . . it's a long story." Pulling the sopping hood over his head to hide his face, he glanced around. "Listen, I need your help."

"Sure! Name it." The boy beamed. "By the way, I have your packages at home. I didn't want them to get dirty in the stables. If you need them, I can run and get them straight away. Just say the word!"

"What? No. You can have them," Edmund said. "Sell them if you can."

"Really? They cost you a fortune."

"They're all yours. As a matter of fact." Edmund pulled out the pouch of coins he'd conned from the charlatan shopkeeper. "Here."

Toby opened the pouch and gasped. "By the gods! Where did you get all of this?"

"Never mind about that. It's all yours. You've earned it."

Toby fingered the gold coins. "How?"

"By helping me when I needed help the most. I appreciate everything you've done."

Toby counted the gold coins, struggling once he got past thirteen.

"I need you to have Blake saddled and ready to go tonight," Edmund said. "By the middle of the night, if possible. Can you do that?"

Still clutching the pouch, Toby looked sidelong at Edmund. "You aren't in any trouble with the law, are you? I mean . . . you're a lord now, right? A real lord who can make people knights and everything."

Lie.

"Yes, I'm now Lord Edmund of the Highlands." He gave a flamboyant bow. "At your service."

Toby laughed.

A bearded man in a grey cloak fought through the crowd a couple of blocks away. His head twisted and turned as if looking for somebody. Edmund motioned for Toby to walk with him to a less busy side street.

"I'm a lord," Edmund repeated, getting out of view. "That's how I got the money. The King gave it to me. You know, to get things started up north and all."

That seemed to make sense to Toby.

"But I can't take office yet. I need to rescue the woman I told you about."

Edmund guided Toby to the grazing yard behind the stables.

"What about Sir Hanley and the bandits?" Toby asked.

What?

"Oh yes." Edmund checked to see if they'd been followed. "The, the King has sent reinforcements. Everything will be fine. I'll return Sir Hanley's horse so he can go off and fight them."

Starting over, Toby resumed counting the gold coins.

"But I need Blake ready and everything," Edmund said. "Can you do that for me?"

"Okay, but . . . why in the middle of the night?"

Yes, why?

"Because I need to leave as soon as possible, but I . . . I have a couple of errands to run first. I need supplies and all of that." Edmund's stomach grumbled. "And I'm famished. Not to mention, I need to bathe." He picked at the beer-soaked clothes clinging to his body. "I won't be ready to depart for several hours, but I'd rather leave earlier than later, if you get me."

A doubtful look seeped into Toby's face. "Will you still make me one of your personal knights?"

Poor kid. He's going to be devastated.

"Absolutely. But I want you to wait until you're sixteen. Finish your apprenticeship and then come see me in Rood."

Toby grinned. "Then Blake will be ready to go! He's been pining away for Sir Hanley anyway. He'll race all the way there like he's on the wind."

"Good," Edmund said. "Because I'll need all the speed I can get."

Chapter Sixty

Edmund scanned the dimly lit street. For the second time that night, he couldn't shake the feeling he was being followed. Thorax seemed to sense it as well. She kept turning around, ears perked. However, after waiting many still moments in a dark alley, he couldn't detect anybody else out and about.

Come on! The night guard will return any minute.

Approaching the Lower Library, he gave one last glance around. There was nobody in sight.

He touched one of the doors.

"Forstørre nå!"

The thick wood attempted to expand, but the masonry around it wouldn't budge. The door cracked and buckled inward, splitting the yellow "Book Lenders" sign in two. Shoving the fractured door open, Edmund slipped inside.

Feeling his way through the dimness, Edmund found the storage room and bumped into the ladder Edith had used to reach the top shelf.

He pushed it to where he guessed the book was hidden. The ladder's legs screeched as they vibrated across the unseen floor.

You're noisier than Pond!

I'm fine. There's nobody around.

Climbing to the top, he swept his hands about the shelf. They hit a square box made of flimsy wood.

Hopefully, this is it.

He pushed the crate aside. Extending his hands into the blackness, his fingertips felt the familiar sensation of worn leather. They latched onto the book's binding and dragged it from its hiding spot.

Now you're a thief! You're hardly turning into the heroes you always worshipped.

Better to put this to use than to let it rot on some cobweb-infested shelf.

"Edmund," a female voice said.

Edmund froze, the tome clutched to his chest.

Edith?

It sounded like the librarian's voice. Yet it had a sharpness Edith had never shown.

"Thorax?" Edmund said, still perched on the ladder.

"She's fine," the female voice said. "She's right here with me."

"Who . . . who are you?"

"First, answer this," she said. "Do you know how to read the runes in that book?"

Edmund's right boot found a lower rung. He stepped down, wondering if moving would place him or Thorax in greater peril.

"No. No, I can't. But I've seen them before. They were in a text I found in a troll's la-la-lair up north. They're quite exceptional."

"Indeed. Exceptional is an apt description."

There was a silence. Edmund strained his ears, but all he could hear was his heart pounding against the heavy book.

"Look," he said. "I've dealt with enough unseen voices to last a lifetime. If you don't mind, can we discuss this in the light? I can explain everything. There's n-no, no need to call for the authorities."

There was a blue flash and a puff of oily smoke. When Edmund's vision adjusted to the light, he saw Edith standing beside his ladder, stroking Thorax's stomach, a curved dagger in her hand.

How did she—?

The tome nearly slipped out of his startled grasp. "You're a magic user!"

"As are you," Edith said.

She's holding that knife like she's used it before.

If she wanted to kill you, she would've done it by now.

Don't be too sure.

Grasping the book as if it were his last possession, Edmund stepped off the ladder.

"I need this," he said. "I'm, I'm sorry . . . but I have to take it."

"Why?"

"It's a matter of life and death."

"Whose life?" she asked. "Whose death?"

You don't have time for this. Hit her and run like hell out of here.

Shall I burn her eye out as well?

"There's, there's this . . . this woman," Edmund said. "Molly. Goblins are holding her captive up north. I know that sounds crazy. But they still exist up in the mountains. There're thousands of them!"

Edith's expression grew grave. "And you plan on giving them the book in exchange for her freedom?"

"What? No. No, I need the maps and the layout of the tower where she's being held so I can rescue her."

"Tower?"

"It's a long story. Please, let me have the book. I promise to return it if I can."

Edith lowered her knife. "You're risking your life to rescue a woman?"

"I have to," Edmund said. "I love her."

"You'll probably die in the attempt," she said. "You know that, don't you?"

"Yes." Edmund's voice cracked with desperation. "But I must try. Please, help me."

Edith patted Thorax's belly and stood. Rolling over, Thorax shuffled to Edmund, smiling.

Traitor.

"Don't think too harshly of your friend," Edith said, as if reading Edmund's thoughts. "She is a noble breed, and there's more to her than you realize."

Thorax peered at Edmund, pink tongue lolling out of her mouth. She pawed his leg. Begrudgingly, Edmund scratched her ears.

"Had I listened to you," he said, "I'd still have my eye . . . and Molly would be safe."

Edith sheathed her dagger.

"Copy the pages you need and go save your love," she said. "If you survive, we'll meet again. Then we can discuss other, more pressing matters."

"Thank you. Thank you so much. Thank you."

"And we'll take care of the enforcer looking for you," Edith said.

We?

"But stop using your abilities so frivolously. Your trick on the shopkeeper drew far more attention than you can imagine, and not just from the authorities. As will what you did to the front door." Her expression grew cold. "There are far deadlier entities in this world than Kar-Nazar, Edmund of Rood."

Edmund faltered. "You . . . you know, you know about Kar-Nazar?"

"Anybody who truly understands the old tales knows what's happening in the north," she said. "But you and I don't have time to discuss them. Leave Eryn Mas immediately. Or you may not live long enough to save your beloved Molly."

Chapter Sixty-One

Edmund leaned against the trunk of a weeping willow growing along the banks of the River Celerin, studying the notes and sketches he'd frantically copied from the book lender's tome. Thorax sat by his side, picking apart the remains of a trout they'd caught earlier that afternoon. Above them, the budding branches swayed in the warm spring breeze, producing a sound like rain. Had circumstances been different, he would've been utterly content.

The book lender's tome described every room in the Undead King's tower, but it didn't indicate what they were used for or where guards might be stationed. Still, with a thorough understanding of where the central stairs were located and how to get to the upper stories, Edmund was much better off than before. Now he needed to figure out how to get into the tower and divert the attention of thirty thousand goblins.

The knights will know what to do.

They're late.

Only by a day. They're probably equipping everybody. Half the town will want to come. They might not have enough horses, so they'll need to walk here.

Even if half of the able-bodied men of Rood come, we should have enough to create a substantial diversion, allowing me and the knights to sneak into the tower.

At least that many will show. Everybody loves Molly.

Edmund smiled as he pictured Molly as a teenager, waving to the cheering crowd in Rood's town square as the mayor crowned her Queen of the Spring Faire. She looked so beautiful with her hair done up. He always regretted not asking her to dance that night.

So many regrets . . .

You'll take care of all of them once you rescue her.

His thoughts returned to how they'd get into the tower.

Don't forget about the men from the surrounding farms and ranches. A good many of them will help as well.

Edmund did a quick calculation.

That should be at least fifty, maybe seventy-five people.

An army of peasants, just like Iliandor led. It's curious how history is repeating itself.

Tethered to a birch tree, Blake thrashed his mane.

"Somebody's coming," Edmund told Thorax.

Finally!

Edmund scrambled up the hill. Shielding his eye from the bright afternoon sun, he peered westward. Far below, two, maybe three, figures headed toward him along the dirt track winding through the trees. They lead a pack animal.

What? Where is everybody?

Maybe they're only traveling merchants.

Edmund watched them plod closer.

It's Pond and Norb.

Maybe they're leading the way. Maybe the others are coming and are a little behind, out of view.

He scanned the distant green plains but didn't see anybody.

Leading a heavily laden donkey up the slope, Pond waved at him.

Edmund's heart sank.

I'm sure there's an explanation. Maybe the knights picked a different place to assemble, somewhere more secure and secretive. That's probably it.

"Where's everybody?" Edmund called when they got closer. "Where are the knights? Wh-where . . . where are all the others?"

But Norb's expression told him what his heart had already guessed. *This can't be it.*

By the river below, Blake whinnied.

"Where's everybody else?" Edmund called again.

Norb reached the hilltop. "Nobody's coming. Curse the miserable cowards!" He spat on the ground and glanced about the hills. "Where's the army from Eryn Mas?"

Edmund stared westward in disbelief.

Nobody's coming? Nobody?

Pond pat the large bundles piled on the donkey. "But we have everything you wanted, including some splendid weapons."

"I don't believe this!" Edmund tossed his hands. "Didn't you tell them everything I told you? Did you tell them we know where Molly is?"

"A lot of people said they wanted to help," Pond said. "But they're afraid."

Norb threw a rock at a tree. It ricocheted against its trunk and tumbled down the hill. "They're damn cowards. The whole lot of them! No luck with the King?"

Nobody came?

Edmund couldn't speak.

"Figures." Norb shook his head. "Nobility aren't worth a damn. The whole lot of them should be put to the sword. They'll take your money and call it taxes. But they're never around when you need them. Same with these knights."

"They don't know what to believe," Pond said. "They didn't exactly trust me. Besides, with people disappearing and all, their primary concern is protecting the town."

Edmund glared off into the distance.

I can't believe this!

They have an obligation to the town.

He stared toward Rood.

How could they forsake her?

"They're knights!" Edmund shouted to the hills. "Rescuing damsels trapped in towers is what they're trained to do. What . . . what about their honor? What about their oaths? Wh-what . . . what about—?"

They have to think of everybody else's safety. They can't jeopardize hundreds for one person.

"They're worthless." Norb threw another rock. "A waste of skin. All of them. Big Borst looked scared out of his wits when I told him about the goblins. So was Haverson. For all their talk and bluster, they're both cowards."

Gazing northeastward toward the grey mountain peaks, Edmund imagined Molly crying helplessly in some dark and rank pit, begging to go home.

It's up to me to save her.

Me . . .

Edmund exhaled. For once, everything seemed clear. The doubt in his mind faded like cooling embers.

I'll exchange my life for Molly's.

"Pond," he said with an effort. "I want you to go with Norb. He can help you find work and a place to live in Rood."

"You can't go alone," Pond said. "It's suicide."

"I have to rescue her." Edmund tightened his sword belt. "Go with Norb to Rood. Or maybe head south to Hillode or Rockdale. There should be some work for you there. Maybe you can start a new family."

"I'm going with you," Norb said.

Pond stepped forward. "As am I."

"Thank you," Edmund told them. "But—"

"But nothing," Norb said. "I'm going!"

Edmund considered the stable hand.

He'll get himself killed.

Everybody has the right to decide how they're going to die. Besides, he could cause a diversion in the mines while I sneak into the tower. If that doesn't work . . . I'll give myself up.

"Ed," Norb said. "I'm not the drunk shoveler of shit everybody thinks I am. I can help. Please!"

Edmund rubbed his face. He took a deep breath and nodded. "Okay."

"I'm going as well!" Pond said.

Edmund beheld Pond. He appeared different now that his hair was clean and trimmed. In his new clothes, he seemed every bit like the successful textile merchant Edmund imagined him to have been before being captured.

He's a good friend, despite how often I yell at him.

Without him, you'd never have survived your first day in the mines.

"Look, Pond," Edmund said. "You're very kind. But you don't even know Molly."

"It doesn't matter," Pond said.

"There's a good chance we won't make it," Edmund said. "And you know what the pits are like. Remember Vomit? They'll slice open your leg like they did to him. You'll never be free again." He put his hand on Pond's shoulder. "Take Blake and the donkey and ride home . . . and have a good life, okay?"

"Home?" Pond repeated. "Home? I don't have a home! My home is a thousand miles away and ten years in the past. My family has moved on. They might even be dead, for all I know." He gazed at the blue sky, tears teetering on his eyelids. "I don't know anybody in this world except you!"

He knows what he's getting into far more than Norb does.

Yes, but I don't want him to die.

"Pond—" Edmund stopped, not knowing what else to say.

Pond brushed away his tears. "You saved me. You risked your life coming for me in the wet cells."

"And you saved me in the pits," Edmund said. "You're the only friend I have. I don't want you to come because you think you owe me. You don't owe me a damn thing."

"Then consider it revenge. The goblins took ten years of my life. And I want them to pay!"

There's not a vengeful bone in his body.

"Please, Ed."

Defeated, Edmund stared at Thorax.

"I don't suppose you'd go to Rood if I told you to," he said to her.

She sat next to him.

You're wasting time.

Sighing, Edmund nodded. "All right. Let's go."

Chapter Sixty-Two

Edmund and Thorax crouched behind a moss-covered boulder halfway up one of the forested foothills in the northern Haegthorn Mountains. He drew his scimitar. Norb and Pond brought many weapons from Rood—bows, swords, knives. But, in the end, Edmund decided to keep his goblin blade.

It's served me well enough thus far.

From behind the boulder, he studied the dell a hundred yards beyond the trees. In it was the black iron door through which Edmund would've escaped had it not been for the bitter cold. All seemed still and quiet. Even the birds seemed watchful. The shadows deepened as the evening sky slowly turned a darker shade of indigo. Stars twinkled.

He hooted like a horned owl.

Norb ran up and threw himself beside Edmund, clutching the hefty battle ax he stole from one of the knights occupying Rood. It was an impractical weapon for the close confines of the mines. But Norb wouldn't listen to reason. He kept muttering how he would cleave every goblin he met in two.

Edmund hooted again.

Pond ran up the slope next, waving a gem-encrusted rapier that was more ceremonial than functional. The entire fortnight since leaving the River Celerin, he kept prattling on about how light and pretty it was.

As long as he doesn't get himself killed, he can fight with a pillow for all I care. It's all up to me, anyway.

Up to me . . .

"What do you think, girl?" Edmund asked Thorax. "Is anybody around?"

Thorax sniffed the air and growled.

Let's hope there are only a few guards.

And that they don't suspect anything. If they're waiting for you, all is lost.

Edmund inspected his companions through the growing darkness. Clutching his ax like he was throttling somebody, Norb appeared to need a stiff drink. Humming next to him, Pond polished the sapphires on his sword's hilt.

They're going to get killed. Both of them.

Then you won't die alone.

Edmund signaled for everybody to huddle together.

"Leave the packs here," Edmund whispered.

Nodding, they unslung their shoulder straps.

"Remember," he said. "Stick to the plan. I'll knock the first one down and push into the room. You two finish him quickly and come in for the rest."

"All right," Pond said.

Norb nodded.

"Above all," Edmund said, "make sure nobody escapes or blows a horn. Do you need me to draw a diagram of the guard's chamber again?"

They shook their heads.

"If you're scared," Edmund said. "If you don't want to do this—"

"Let's kill them," Norb muttered.

"Yes," Pond said. "Let's kill them all."

Surprised by the anger in his voice, Edmund looked at his pit mate.

"You saved my life," Pond said. "I'm with you on this, no matter what."

"Thanks, Pond," Edmund said. "That means the world to me. You too, Norb. Thanks. At the very least, we'll kill a few goblins before this is over."

Edmund scanned the hill above them.

It's dark enough. Come on, let's go!

Closing his eye, Edmund pictured the guardroom on the other side of the black iron door. He imagined three, maybe four, guards sitting around the wooden table, unprepared for the assault he was about to unleash. His fingers tightened around the hilt of his scimitar as he envisioned how he would burst in, cut off any chance of retreat, and kill every goblin he found.

He exhaled.

"Let's go save Molly."

Scrambling up the slope, they left the fragrant fir and cedar trees and darted into the shallow dell. The iron door stood black and imposing in the starlight.

Edmund pointed to where he wanted everybody to be. When they were in position, he pushed gently on the door's handle.

It was locked, but Edmund had anticipated that.

You'd better hope this works.

If it doesn't, I'll find another way in.

Touching the narrow visor through which the guards could view the outside, Edmund cast his enlargement spell. The visor swelled, its metal crinkling. At the same time, he pounded on the door with the pommel of his scimitar as he guessed an angry goblin would.

"Password," a goblin said from inside. Somebody tried to open the visor and cursed.

Edmund kept hammering as if he hadn't heard.

"All right! All right!" The goblin fumbled with the door.

Readying himself, Edmund looked at Thorax and then Norb and Pond. Holding their breath, they tensed, weapons held high.

The door opened.

"All right!" the goblin said. "No need to—"

Edmund seized the startled goblin by the throat and yanked him into the dell.

Norb's battle ax swung down, splitting the goblin's skull in two.

They bounded into the guard chamber.

Inside, three guards clad in full chain mail sat at a wooden table stained with dried blood. Shouting, they sprang to their feet and snatched their weapons. Jumping in front of the tunnel leading to the goblin city, Edmund cut off their escape.

One of the goblins reached for a horn hanging from a peg. But Thorax bit into his knee. Falling to the floor, the goblin screamed. Stomping on his chest, Pond stabbed him through his neck. Blood spurted as the goblin flailed and gagged. Pond stabbed him again and again.

A second guard charged Edmund with a spear. But Norb darted behind him and buried the blade of his ax in the goblin's back. The guard fell lifeless to the blood-splattered floor.

In a far corner, the third goblin dropped his scimitar and shrieked for mercy. Norb flew at him, his gore-covered ax raised.

"Wait!" Edmund shouted. "Norb! Hold it. Wait! We need a prisoner. Don't kill him!"

Norb skidded to a halt, barely able to control himself. Breathing hard, he reluctantly lowered his ax.

The goblin raised his hands above his head. "Spare me! Spare me!"

"Where's Molly?" Norb demanded.

The goblin shook. "I . . . I don't know what you're talking about."

"I'll take care of this," Edmund said. "He's a lesser guard. He wouldn't know anything about the important prisoners in the tower."

He nodded to the darkened passageway leading from the chamber. "Pond, you and Thorax go up the tunnel a couple of hundred feet and listen. Make sure nobody is coming. Be careful. Don't step in the blood. We can't leave tracks."

"Aye! Aye!" Pond said. "Come on, Thorax."

He and Thorax disappeared into the darkness.

Edmund returned his attention to the goblin cowering in the corner. Putting the point of his scimitar under the goblin's quivering chin, Edmund asked, "When were the last Games?"

The goblin trembled. "What?"

"You heard me." The tip of his sword dug into the goblin's throat. "When were the last Games?"

"Three . . . three weeks ago or so. Maybe four or five. I, I don't remember exactly. But we're having Games for the Ithil Mereth. Lots of Games! And, and a feast! Please, don't kill me!"

"The Ithil Mereth?" Edmund repeated. "The elven Lunar Festival?"

"Yes! Yes! Exactly. The elven Lunar Festival. We celebrate—"

"Who cares about damn games?" Norb said.

Edmund ignored the stable hand.

"When is it?" he asked the goblin. "When is the festival?"

"The, the first . . . first new moon after the equinox," the goblin said, his hands still raised.

That's tomorrow night.

We don't have much time.

"Please," the goblin begged. "Give me mercy."

"No." Edmund stepped away and nodded to Norb.

The guard screamed.

Norb swung his ax.

The goblin's head rolled at their feet, blood pouring over the floor, thick and red. Horror filled the stable hand's eyes as he watched the goblin's headless body twitch.

"I . . . I can't believe it," he said. "I just killed two—"

"Don't think about it," Edmund said. "Think about Molly instead."

His face pale, Norb gritted his teeth. "Right. Molly."

I should've had them bring some brandy. He'll need a drink before this is over.

I could use one myself.

"Take your boots and stockings off," Edmund told Norb. "Run through the blood and go get our packs."

Norb averted his gaze from the headless goblin. "Why?"

"Just do it. We don't have much time. Also, untie Blake and the donkey. Spook them westward. They shouldn't die because of us."

Taking off his boots, Norb ran out of the guardroom, leaving a trail of bloody footprints heading outside. Edmund opened the crates, stole an armload of provisions, and stripped one of the guards of his clothing and weapons.

"Pond," Edmund said in a hoarse whisper, "is anybody coming?"

Pond's jovial voice floated through the darkness. "All clear here!"

Well, this went better than expected. Who would've thought Norb could swing an ax like that? He may be useful after all.

Maybe.

Norb returned to the guard's chamber. He had their three bulging backpacks. "What now?"

"Walk around the blood," Edmund told him. "Go up the tunnel to where Pond and Thorax are and put your boots on. And hurry. They'll be ch-ch-changing guards soon."

Norb eyed the darkened passageway doubtfully. "Where does it lead?"

"To the goblin city. But first, let's find a defensible campsite. Tomorrow, we'll enter the tower."

Still clutching his ax, Norb took an uneasy breath. "Okay. Let's go!"

He ran up the passageway.

Edmund stayed a moment longer, surveying the battlefield.

Let's hope the goblins think an escaped prisoner did this.

If they don't, we're all dead.

Leaving the carnage, Edmund strode up the tunnel as if he'd come home.

Chapter Sixty-Three

Edmund, Norb, and Pond stared through the shadows into a dimly lit quarry not far from where they'd hidden their supplies. A hundred yards below, seven human slaves grunted and toiled as they broke stones with rusty picks. Their stench was overpowering.

A whip cracked.

Shrieking, one of the men arched his back. Blood trickled along his spine.

The guards jeered. "Get to work, you sniveling bag of shit. Or you'll feel the kiss of my whip again!"

Weeping, the wounded prisoner struggled to raise his pick. He let it fall on the rock with a lifeless thud.

Edmund was about to signal everybody to crawl back the way they'd come when another slave came into view. He was a gaunt man with a big man's frame. His ribs protruded as he labored to carry a small boulder. He dropped his load onto the pile, teetered for a moment, and flexed his hands. As he turned, Edmund saw his battered face.

Next to him, Pond nearly cried out.

Edmund put a finger to his lips.

They watched Turd get another rock, his left leg dragging behind him.

I should've saved him. I should've let him join us.

He wanted the goblins to capture you.

He did what he needed to do to escape. He was trying to cause a diversion.

He didn't give a damn about you.

I didn't give a damn about him, either. I would've done the same thing had our positions been reversed.

A whip cracked above Turd's head. His hobbling quickened.

He's lost a lot of weight.

He looks like death. He won't last much longer.

That's probably good. Death would be a relief for him.

Turd lurched to a rock pile, a look of desperation growing in his exhausted eyes.

Edmund shook his head.

I always thought I was a noble man, like the knights in the tales of old.

Perhaps the knights of old weren't any better.

I should've done something. I should've helped.

Too late now.

Motioning for Pond and Norb to follow, Edmund crawled to their campsite. The echoes of metal hitting stone and the grunting of men trailed after them.

"Shouldn't we do something?" Norb asked.

Tearing a piece of dried pork in half, Edmund handed some to Thorax. She wolfed it down without chewing.

"There are only two guards," Norb said. "We can kill them and free those men. Then we'd have eleven with us. That'd improve—"

"No."

"But Ed, we could—"

"No!"

"How can you let them suffer like that? We could free them!"

Thorax put her head on Edmund's lap. She was covered with dirt and stank. They all did. But Edmund didn't notice. He stroked her head.

"You knew one of them," Norb said, an accusation in his tone. "Didn't you? The tall one who looked like a skeleton."

Edmund and Pond didn't respond.

"How could you let him live like that?" Norb asked. "How could you?"

"Life is full of hard choices," Pond said. "Yes, we could rescue them. And they may or may not help us get into the tower. But what about the hundreds of other Pit Dwellers? We can't rescue them all."

"Maybe not," Norb said. "But we can rescue them!"

"And what about Molly?" Edmund shot back, his voice echoing in the surrounding passages. "If we start freeing people, don't you think that would ruin our chances of saving her? Don't you think the goblins would become more alert or increase the number of guards?"

The lives of Turd and seven strangers versus Molly's life . . .

It's not even close.

"Look." Edmund rubbed his temples. "Let's . . . let's stick to the plan. When the Games begin, we'll sneak up to the high cells. If we get Molly home safe and sound, then maybe we'll return and see what we could do."

Would you really come back to save Turd and those men?

I'm tired of feeling like a savage.

But would you come back?

I don't know.

"You're right," Norb said. "I'm sorry. It's just . . . it's just seeing them like that, it's-it's—inhumane, you know?"

I know.

"I wish we'd brought some wine," Norb said.

So do I.

They sat listening to metal ringing on stone. A whip cracked. A voice cried out. As the shouts died in the crawlways, Norb chuckled to himself.

"What?" Edmund asked, puzzled and angered by the stable hand's amusement.

"I was . . . I was thinking," he said. "Remember when Mol spilled soup all over Old Man Sveltsen's head?"

I remember. I paid Sveltsen a gold piece not to have her fired.

Norb chuckled again, his mirth mixed with nervous guilt. "I . . . I was the one who accidentally tripped her. I never had the guts to tell her it was my fault. I meant to, you know. But I never did. I never apologized. Never."

"You can tell her tomorrow," Edmund said.

Norb stared at Edmund through the deepening shadows.

"What?" Edmund asked.

"You've changed, Ed," Norb said. "You aren't the same guy who was chased screaming out of The Rogue by that storyteller."

Pond pulled the cork from his water skin. "Storyteller?" He took a drink.

"It's a long story," Edmund said. "And I wasn't screaming."

"Maybe. But you've changed," Norb said. "Nobody in Rood would deny it."

I have changed.

Yes, but the question is—have you changed for the better?

"Get some rest," Edmund said. "All of this will be over tomorrow night, one way or another."

Chapter Sixty-Four

Sitting in the cramped crawlway where they'd set camp, Edmund turned another page of Iliandor's diary. He knew it by heart. But this was the original that Pond had brought from Rood, and something told him it held the answer to the riddle written under Tol Helen. Somehow, it held the answer to everything.

It's a book. It can't help us.

Then why would Vorn make me promise to destroy it?

Vorn . . .

Pains of regret stabbed at him as he pictured the legless elf dragging himself out of his wet cell, begging Edmund to end his life.

Perhaps I missed something. Maybe there's a clue that wasn't necessarily in the words used but in how they're arranged on the page.

He turned to the final entry scrawled by Sir James of Windell. Hoping to find some code or pattern, Edmund examined the letters at the beginning of each line. Then he looked at the last letters. But there simply wasn't anything meaningful.

There's nothing here. It's just words.

Just words . . .

The salvation of humanity can be found in buildings of wise men, doubly so in optimism of the learned, and in knowledge that is written on a daily basis.

What's found in the buildings of wise men?

Forget about the riddle. It doesn't matter anymore. All of this will be over by tomorrow night.

If we can't rescue her with force or trickery, you'll need the answer to the riddle. It's what the Undead King really wants.

He wants the secret to Iliandor's metal.

Somehow, the riddle and Iliandor's secret metal are connected. Think! What is in the building of wise men?

The riddle is meaningless. If we can't rescue Molly, I'll exchange my life for hers. I'll rescue her one way or another. If she's still alive.

Edmund listened as yet another heavily armed company of goblins stormed through one of the nearby tunnels, shouting obscenities as they ran. The goblins had certainly been stirred up after finding the bodies in the guardroom. If the commotion didn't diminish, Edmund didn't think they'd be able to sneak into the tower.

At least Kravel and Gurding haven't been around taunting me.

Kravel . . .

What? Will you return to this hellhole to kill him and Gurding? Why stop there? Why not kill the Undead King as well? Evidently, Iliandor couldn't do that. What makes you think a stuttering librarian from an insignificant village can?

Edmund petted Thorax as she slept beside him. With her quick ears, no goblin would sneak up on them. But he worried about her mobility. She could hop quickly for brief periods. But with her lifeless hind leg, she couldn't run. He also had to carry her whenever they climbed into a crawlspace or mineshaft.

Remember what Edith said. There's more to Thorax than meets the eye.

Edith's a nut.

She's also a fellow magic user. Perhaps she could teach you some new spells after this is over.

After this is over? Chances are, I'll be dead in a few hours.

He studied his companions as they slept.

They'll be dead too soon.

More regret bloomed within him. It was nearly smothering.

I shouldn't have let them come.

Edmund stroked Thorax's stomach. Her three functioning paws twitched as if she were chasing something in her dreams. She snarled, her upper lip rising to reveal her long white canines.

He yawned.

Get some sleep.

I'll sleep later.

Edmund returned to the last pages of the diary.

This must have the answer. Why would they send Isa away with a book?

It was Iliandor's diary. It was destined to be a relic.

But what about the Star? Or his sword and armor? They were destined to be relics as well. Why send only the book away and not everything else? What makes this so precious? It doesn't even say anything interesting.

He took the Star out of his pocket and fingered the stone.

Was it worth it?

Caught in Edmund's discouraged exhalation, the candle on the ledge next to him fluttered. Dark shadows bobbed around the crawlway. Far off, metal rang on stone. Yawning again, Edmund rubbed his dirty forehead, wondering when he'd last slept.

All right, think about this logically. There must be an explanation for all of this. What exactly do I know?

They could've saved the Star but elected to save the diary instead.

Why? It doesn't say anything besides hinting about the cavern under Tol Helen.

So why is the cave under Tol Helen important?

It had the riddle.

So maybe the diary is nothing more than a way to find the riddle. Which brings me back to what's in the buildings of wise men?

He rested his head against the wall. He needed a different approach — a different way of thinking about the problem. But what that way was, he hadn't a clue.

Then, somewhere in the dim recesses of his mind, another phrase repeated itself like an annoying song he wanted to forget.

"Knowledge that is written on a daily basis," he muttered.

Diaries are written on a daily basis.

Edmund closed the diary and stared at it.

"What makes you so special?" Edmund whispered.

Bringing the candle closer, Edmund examined the diary's binding.

It was a bit loose. But other than that, there was nothing unusual about it.

He examined the cover.

It was made of leather that might once have been black but was now the color of dry dirt. There were a few places where the leather had worn thin. But that would be expected for such a well-traveled artifact.

His fingers found a small crack in the cover.

Maybe . . .

He picked at it.

The crack widened.

He slid a finger underneath the leather.

Nothing.

He probed deeper. The ancient leather split.

Now you've ruined it.

I couldn't care less what happens to it. I wish I'd never laid eyes on the damn thing.

He lifted the torn cover.

As he suspected, there was a second layer of leather beneath. Such double binding wasn't uncommon for books of great importance. A second layer protected the book from potential wear and damage from heat or water.

Edmund scratched the underlayment.

That's not leather.

It's . . .

He tore the cover off the book's spine. Into his hands slid several sheets of vellum.

Unfolding them, he began reading. The pulse in his neck quickened as he flipped the pages.

It's the formula for Iliandor's secret alloy!

Chapter Sixty-Five

Edmund crept through the dark passageway, his ears straining to detect any noises other than Pond and Norb's labored breathing behind him.

"What do you think?" he whispered to Thorax. "Is anybody around?"

Thorax sniffed, her black nose twitching. She looked at Edmund. Edmund stroked her head.

"What would I do without you?" he asked her.

She winked.

Hurry. Who knows when the patrols will return?

They were nearly out of the mines, stalking into the well-maintained tunnels directly beneath the tower. Thus far, they hadn't seen a single goblin.

This is like when Kravel tried to trap me with the smell of roasting venison. Keep alert!

Attempting to determine where they were, he examined the notes he'd copied from the book lender's tome.

The stairs Kravel and Gurding used are over this way. I'm sure of it.

They snuck along in a single file, bunched together in the red glow of their small candle.

"Where's everybody?" Norb whispered. "I thought you said this place was crawling with goblins."

"It is," Edmund said.

"Then where are they?"

"They're at the Games."

"How do you know?"

"The Pit Dwellers aren't working. The mines are completely quiet."

"So?"

"The only days we didn't work," Pond said, "were when the goblins had their little party."

"Plus, see those sconces?" Edmund inclined his head at the wall next to him. "Notice how the guards haven't replaced the burned-out torches? That's because they won't be around until after the festival."

Which will be very soon.

"Okay." Norb gripped his battle ax even tighter. "What do we do now?"

"Shut up and follow me."

And hope whoever is fighting in the arena lives long enough for us to save Molly.

They came to an intersection of three passages.

Peeking cautiously around the corner, they found the tunnel to their left had an alcove.

That's probably a guard's station.

They wouldn't post guards just anywhere. We must be getting closer.

Heading to the left, Edmund beckoned for everybody to follow him.

Up ahead, dim scarlet light flickered.

Blowing out his candle, Edmund flattened himself against the passage wall and waited.

"Why did we—?" Norb began.

Edmund put his hand over Norb's mouth and listened.

He didn't hear anything. "This way. And keep quiet."

They edged through the blackness toward the light. Soon, they saw two dying torches flanking an opening in the wall. Their smoke lingered in the still air.

I bet that's the way to the tower.

Edmund signaled for Pond and Norb to stay where they were.

"Come on, Thorax," he whispered.

They snuck to the opening and listened again. There was a faint rumble above them, like a distant avalanche.

The Games are already underway. We don't have much time!

Edmund stole a glance around the corner. Beyond the opening, a wide stairway spiraled upward in a tight corkscrew.

This is it.

"Do you smell anything?" he whispered to Thorax.

Thorax looked at him.

"Good. Lead us to fresh air. Okay?"

Thorax limped up the stairs.

Edmund waved for Norb and Pond to hurry. They scrambled out of the shadows.

"Where to?" Pond asked.

"To the very top," Edmund said.

They followed Thorax, the heavy tread of their boots echoing in the closeness around them. The noise above them was unmistakable. Tens of thousands of goblins were clapping and cheering. The walls shook with each syllable of their chanting.

"Ga . . . Ram . . . da! Ga . . . Ram . . . da!"

This might work! Everybody is at the Games.

Yes, but this place will be swarming with goblins as soon as the Games end. We don't have much time to get to the top, find Molly, and get out.

Edmund grabbed Thorax.

"Sorry, girl. But we need to go quicker." He readied his scimitar in the other hand. "Follow me and stay close," he said to Norb and Pond.

As they jogged up the stairs, the noise got louder and louder until it was nearly deafening.

Ahead and to their right, an archway appeared. Through it, they could see a wide hallway lit by blazing torches. Above them, the passage kept spiraling upward.

Edmund stopped.

"I know where we are," he shouted through the noise. "We're right across from the arena. These stairs will take us to where they held me."

"How do you know Mol is there?" Norb called back.

Good question. Pray Kravel wasn't lying about where they were keeping her.

"They w, w, wouldn't put her in the pits where she could get killed," Edmund said, hoping he was right. "The Undead King would want her close by."

Close by . . . And do what to her?

Gritting his teeth, Edmund forced the image of the Undead King molesting Molly out of his mind. He urged the others onward. Running, they passed the opening to the arena.

"Do you smell that?" Norb asked over the fading clamor of the cheering goblins. "It's fresh air."

As he ran, Edmund said, "Keep your voices—"

Something coming down the stairs plowed into him.

Dropping Thorax and his scimitar, Edmund flew backward. He toppled end over end. When he came to a stop, he lay sprawled on his back, eye to eye with a stunned goblin.

There was a mad rush of shouting voices. Pond attempted to kick the goblin, but kicked Edmund instead. Thorax growled and snapped. Norb raised his ax. The goblin screamed for help.

Seizing the goblin's neck, Edmund heaved him to one side.

There was a body-jolting crunch as the goblin shrieked in pain. Norb embedded his ax into the goblin's shoulder.

Blood coursed over Edmund. Norb yanked his ax free. The goblin continued screaming. Suddenly, the point of Pond's rapier appeared through the goblin's chest, nearly stabbing Edmund. The goblin gurgled and went limp.

Breathing hard, Edmund clambered out from underneath the dead goblin, warm blood covering both him and the stone floor.

"You . . . you two, you two could have killed me!" Edmund said. "You could have cut my head off!"

"Sorry." Norb panted. "I panicked."

Calm down! Everything is fine!

Pond helped him to his feet.

Edmund considered all the blood splattered about the stairwell.

Now they'll know we're here.

"We have to hurry." He grabbed Thorax and his scimitar.

"What about the body?" Norb asked. "Shouldn't we hide it or something?"

"No time. Follow me!"

Leaving a trail of bloody footprints, Edmund led Pond and Norb up the stairwell as it revolved through the heart of the Undead King's tower. Taking two at a time, they scaled the rutted steps, worn from centuries of climbing feet. Far below, the chants of goblins lessened.

The Games are ending!

With Thorax tucked under one arm, Edmund ran faster, Norb and Pond desperately trying to keep pace. They passed narrow windows looking out into the moonless night. They passed an unoccupied landing, then several more. They continued sprinting up the steps.

We're getting to the top.

Molly, here I come!

"Wait!" Norb called to Edmund. "I . . . I need a break. I have to rest!"

But Edmund didn't wait. Like a rampaging troll, he barreled around a corner.

Above him appeared the set of metal double doors Kravel and Gurding once led him to. A guard holding a polearm stood on the landing. Seeing Edmund, the guard smiled and readied his weapon. He took a step forward.

Then Pond and Norb lumbered around the corner, weapons drawn.

The guard's gaze went from Edmund's scimitar to Norb's ax to Pond's rapier, and back to Edmund again. His smile wilted.

Still carrying Thorax, Edmund charged up the remaining stairs.

The guard swung. Edmund ducked and launched himself into the goblin's chest, driving him against the double doors. He smashed the pommel of his scimitar into the guard's helmet.

"Where's Molly?" he demanded.

The guard swung his polearm again. But Edmund blocked the blow. He slammed his knee into the goblin's thigh. The guard crumpled to the ground. Edmund hit him again.

"Where is the female prisoner?"

Winded, Norb and Pond reached the landing.

I'll find her myself!

Lifting his scimitar, Edmund brought it down with all his fury. The goblin's helm split open. The guard stopped moving.

Hurry!

Leaping over the body, Edmund yanked on the door handles.

Locked!

"Search him," he said. "Get his keys!"

Pond and Norb riffled through the guard's belongings.

"He doesn't have any," Norb said. "What now?"

"Never mind."

Setting Thorax on the landing, Edmund placed a hand on either door.

"Forstørre nå."

The metal doors vibrated like a harp string stretched to its breaking point. The stone surrounding them cracked.

"Forstørre nå!" Edmund repeated louder.

The metal shuddered. The arch above the doors fractured. Chunks of marble crashed to the landing around them.

"How, how is he—?" Norb said. "Oh god, he's . . . he's a witch!"

"He's a magic user," Pond said. "But he's not going to hurt you. Let him do what he needs to do."

"Forstørre nå!"

The doors squealed as they strained to expand. They shuddered and buckled inward, crashing into the room as if battered by a herd of elephants.

Edmund staggered, cold sweat trickling over his ashen face. Pond caught him as he collapsed.

"It'll . . . it'll pass," Edmund said. "Find Molly."

Keeping a wary eye on Edmund, Norb climbed over the twisted doors.

"Thorax," Edmund said. "Go. Help him . . . go help him find her."

But Thorax wouldn't leave Edmund's side.

"Mol?" Norb shouted. "Molly?"

A voice answered him. Running, Norb disappeared around a corner. There was yelling and the sound of splintering wood.

Molly?

Pond helped Edmund stumble along the corridor. They found Norb cleaving a door with his ax. From the other side, a woman screamed.

Edmund lifted his reeling head.

"Do, do you hear that?" he said to Pond.

"I hear her," Pond said.

Molly!

A woman called Norb's name.

Oh, my Molly! Finally! Finally!

Edmund wept as he clung to Pond.

Norb swung again. The door broke in two. He cast it aside and raced into the room.

Molly!

Pond leaned Edmund against what was left of the doorframe.

A naked Molly flung herself into Norb's arms. She kissed him over and over again, saying his name in between sobs.

The ring finger on her left hand was gone.

Those bastards. I'll kill them for what they've done to her. I'll kill them all.

Edmund let go of Pond. He teetered into the room, his arms open wide. "Molly!"

But she didn't leave Norb.

She doesn't know who you are. You're missing an eye, and you're fifty pounds lighter. You're a stranger to her.

Norb and Molly hugged, each saying the other's name.

"Molly?" Edmund said weakly. "Norb?"

"Norb!" Pond shouted. "We have to leave."

Norb turned, Molly still in his arms. He looked at Edmund. His joy dimmed.

"Mol," he said. "Mol, this is Ed."

She stopped kissing him.

"Ed?" Molly said. "My god! What . . . what happened to your eye? And . . . and you're so thin! What happened to you?"

Taking off his cloak, Norb wrapped it around her.

"Here." He pulled a bundle out of his pack. "I brought you a few of your things."

He brought her clothes? And shoes?

I should've remembered to do that.

Quickly, she slipped on what Norb gave her. She kissed him again, her arms wrapped around his neck.

Why does she keep kissing him? What about me? Doesn't she know what I've been through? I rescued her!

Norb's voice resonated in the depths of his mind. *"Molly went on with her life, Ed. She sold a few of your books to poor ol' Tom and toasted your health at every meal."*

She went on with her life . . .

Edmund realized Molly was touching his forearm.

"Thank you!" Her tear-sodden face had more wrinkles than he'd remembered, but her green eyes still shone with the same spirit she always had. "Thank you, Ed!" She kissed him on the forehead and hugged him tight.

Edmund couldn't move.

She went on with her life.

"Don't thank us yet," Pond said. "We still have to get out of here. Ed, now what? Ed?"

She and Norb?

Thorax snarled.

"Ed!" Pond shook him. "What now?"

Edmund blinked. Then he recalled where they were.

"Hurry." He pulled himself out of his thoughts. "We have to find a way out."

The Games are over. The entire tower is filled with goblins. We can't go the way we came.

"We . . . we need to find the Undead King's private quarters," Edmund said. "He probably has a secret escape route."

Molly blenched. Then her expression hardened. "I know where they are."

Following Molly, they raced through the dining room where Edmund had eaten roasted chicken and potatoes, then through the parlor where Kravel burnt out his eye. She opened a door, revealing a bedroom fit for a king who'd lived many centuries. When she saw the grand canopied bed, Molly recoiled. Edmund stepped closer to comfort her, but Norb was quicker. She buried her head in the stable hand's chest and bawled.

Edmund stood and stared at them.

Pond hurried to the windows and looked out. "Maybe we could use the bed sheets to—"

"No." Edmund stared at Molly. "No," he repeated louder. "We're too high up."

He searched the room's interior wall, pushing on the mortared stone.

"What're you looking for?" Norb asked, his left arm still wrapped around Molly, his right hand clutching his bloody ax.

Edmund surveyed the wall. "In, in . . . in every, in every story I've ever read, places like these always have a secret exit. It's always in the King's chambers."

Sometimes, it's in an adjacent room.

Dashing across the bedroom, Edmund threw open another door. He gave a muted gasp.

In front of him, a labyrinth of bookshelves reached from the floor to the ceiling. They overflowed with books and scrolls and unbounded manuscripts of all shapes and sizes.

The others ran to him.

"Is it the way out?" Norb asked.

All these ancient books! Who knows what's—

Come on. They're only books! Find a way out!

Edmund pointed at the far wall. "Check behind those shelves. Look for anything that might hide a secret door. Spread out."

They cast the books into great heaps and peered behind the shelves.

The hair between Thorax's shoulder blades rose. She bared her teeth and emitted a guttural growl.

"Well, well," a wispy voice said.

Edmund spun.

Kravel and Gurding stood in the doorway. Behind them were thirty other goblins, all armed with nets and swords.

"It seems we've been hunting for Filth in all the wrong places, Mr. Gurding," Kravel said. "Just like that Sir Henry fellow and the trog."

"I never did like that tale." Gurding fingered his knife's blade. "I always felt sorry for the trog."

"And look. Filth has brought a new friend who happens to be holding his beloved!" Kravel tutted at Norb. "Hello again." He winked suggestively at Molly. "Have you told Edmund your little secret? Do you think he'd still be here if he knew it?"

Norb pushed Molly behind him. Hefting his ax, he took a step toward Kravel. Kravel retreated in mock terror.

Damn it! The Undead King is probably nearby as well.

If he comes, we're done for. We can't fight what we can't see.

"Norb!" Edmund shouted.

Norb hesitated.

"And look," Gurding said, "they have that mutt, the one from the tower."

"Ah! Right, you are, Mr. Gurding," Kravel said. "It would seem you didn't end its miserable existence after all. I believe you lost our little bet."

"Norb," Edmund shouted again, "remember what I told you to do? Do it now. Pond . . . you too."

Unslinging his backpack, Pond extracted an armload of brown flasks he'd brought from Rood. Reluctantly, with Molly cowering behind him, Norb followed Pond's example.

"Why, Mr. Gurding," Kravel said in exaggerated delight, "it appears they have some sort of plan."

"It'll be interesting to see what it is," Gurding said, "seeing there's no way out other than through us."

More goblins charged into the bedroom beyond Kravel and Gurding. They watched as Pond and Norb threw the flasks against the floor. The flasks shattered, sending a thick black fluid oozing across the stone.

From his vest pocket, Edmund pulled several sheets of vellum.

"Oh no." Gurding groaned. "He's written a speech."

"Now, now, Mr. Gurding," Kravel said. "At least he'll have his thoughts organized. Perhaps he'll start with a joke."

They grinned at Edmund, their yellow fangs glinting in the torchlight.

Edmund waved the pages over his head. "I know the answer to the riddle."

"Do you, now?" the Undead King said.

The goblins behind Gurding and Kravel stepped aside, forming a lane to the library door. Some of their cloaks moved as if caught in the wake of somebody moving briskly by.

Too late! He's here!

Remain calm and stay alert. You have what he needs. He'll do anything to learn the secret of Iliandor's steel. We should be fine as long as Pond and Norb don't do anything stupid. Don't panic.

"I knew you were the proper person for the task, Edmund," the Undead King said from somewhere in the room. "By all means, enlighten the rest of us."

Clinging to Norb, Molly whimpered.

Pond and Norb swung their weapons in the air as if they might hit something their eyes couldn't perceive.

"The salvation of humanity can be found in buildings of wise men," Edmund recited, "doubly so in optimism of the learned, and in knowledge that is written on a daily basis. What's found in b-b-buildings?"

Thorax snarled.

"Doors," Gurding offered.

"Furniture," Kravel suggested.

"Maybe—"

"Gentlemen," the Undead King said, even closer than before. "Please allow Edmund to continue. This is his moment. Continue, Master Scholar."

"A 'b' is in buildings."

"A bee?" Gurding repeated. "Why would there be a bee in buildings of wise men?"

"Mr. Gurding." The Undead King's voice grew irritated.

Gurding closed his mouth.

"Doubly so in 'optimism.'" Edmund glanced at the arc of black liquid on the floor. "And in 'knowledge.' B . . . o . . . o . . . k. Book. The answer is a book. Specifically, this book." Edmund pulled Iliandor's diary from his pack and flung it at Kravel's feet. "In it, I found this." He shook the sheets of vellum. "The formula for making Iliandor's indestructible weapons and armor."

The silence felt electric.

"What a stupid riddle," Gurding grumbled to Kravel.

"Very good, Master Edmund," the Undead King's voice said as if it could finally breathe. He was close. Edmund felt his presence like the tingling before a lightning strike. "Very good, indeed. I knew you were extraordinary."

"Now let us go," Edmund demanded.

There was a chuckle. Gurding and Kravel smiled, the same smile they wore before they burnt out his eye.

Edmund grinned back. He held aloft one of the sheets of vellum.

"*Fyre av nå!*"

There was a pop and a spark. A tiny blue flame appeared along the edge of the page.

"He's a Maûa!" Kravel said, his evil face showing fear for the first time.

Gurding withdrew a pace.

"Put out the fire, Edmund," the Undead King said, his voice rising to a shout. "Put it out!"

Edmund pointed to his friends. "Let them go! I know there's a s-s-s-secret door in here somewhere. Where is it?"

The flame crept higher, crackling as it consumed the edge of the vellum.

"All right! All right!" the Undead King said. "Put it out, and they shall go free."

Edmund smothered the fire.

Ripples appeared in the black fluid on the floor. Thorax snapped and growled.

There he is.

"Any closer, Kar-Nazar, and I'll b-b-burn it all." Edmund crumpled the partly burnt sheet into a ball and held it aloft. "You need every page for it to help you."

"You know who I am?" the Undead King said. "That's unfortunate. Did my brother tell you? And were you the one who killed him?"

Vorn was his brother?

Don't get distracted!

"Very well, Master Edmund," the Undead King said. "I was right about you. There's a great deal we have in common."

"The exit!" Edmund shook the vellum again. "Where's the exit?"

A goblin with a crossbow appeared in the doorway behind Gurding. Edmund dove behind a bookshelf.

"*Fyre—*"

"No!" the Undead King said. "Everybody but Kravel and Gurding leave! Now!"

The guards slowly withdrew to the King's bedroom. Kravel and Gurding stayed, standing by the library door. They watched Edmund with growing apprehension.

"All right, Edmund," the Undead King said. "You win. Behind the second bookcase to Molly's left is a door. Beyond it is a staircase. It descends to a passage leading out of the mountains."

"Pond—" Edmund said.

"I'm on it." Pond tugged at the bookcase.

"He's a liar!" Molly screamed from behind Norb. "He wouldn't let us go. He'd never let us go!"

"Molly," Edmund said. "I have what he wants. He doesn't care about you or anything else."

Molly clutched Norb's arm and sobbed.

The bookshelf swung outward.

"There's nothing behind it," Pond called to Edmund.

"There is a small square stone in the wall about waist high for you," the Undead King said. "Push it."

Pond looked at Edmund, uncertain what to do.

"Go ahead, Pond," Edmund said. "He knows what'll happen to his precious formula if he tries to trick us."

Pond pushed the stone.

A metallic click rang out as part of the wall gave way, revealing a narrow stairwell descending into darkness. Stale air enveloped them.

"Your friends may leave," the Undead King said. "You have my word they won't be harmed."

Your word doesn't mean a damn thing to me. But at least they'll have a chance to get away.

Pond, Norb, and Molly stared at the stairs and then at Edmund.

"Pond, take Norb and Molly and go!"

"Ed..." Molly said.

Watching Molly cowering behind Norb, Edmund's fingers tightened around the crumpled pages.

She should be hiding behind me.

She moved on.

Moved on . . .

"Ed," she repeated tenderly.

"Molly, we don't have time. You kn-kn-know how I feel." He forced a smile. "You and Norb go to Rood . . . and have a good life."

Norb and Molly . . .

She took a half step toward him and then stopped. She looked at the stairs.

"Norb," Edmund yelled, "get her out of here. Go on! Go! All of you. He wants me. Go, damn you!"

"Thanks, Ed," Norb said. "And I'm sorry about what I said behind the Rogue. I take it all back."

"Go!"

Molly beheld Edmund one last time. Then, with Norb leading the way, she ran into the blackness beyond the secret door.

Pond appeared torn.

Swearing, Edmund pointed to the stairs. "Damn it, Pond. Go!"

"I'll see you at the bottom," Pond said.

"No! Don't wait. Go! Run! Run to Rood. Run anywhere. Just get the hell out of here."

Pond nodded. "Okay. But remember, everything always works out in the end!"

Not all stories end happily.

"Go!"

Pond disappeared into the darkness.

"You too, Thorax." Edmund pointed to the secret door. "Go! Go with Pond. Okay, girl? He'll take care of you. Go!"

Thorax sat next to him.

I could always count on you.

"Very touching," the Undead King said. "My people had an expression: 'You can always tell who your friends are, for they are the ones standing with you when the fields need to be plowed.'"

"Oh, shut up! I'm tired of hearing what you have to say."

"Are you? Very well. Then give me the document."

What now? He'll never let you leave.

If I reach the stairs, perhaps I can enlarge the secret door so they can't follow me.

"Edmund," the Undead King said with a gentle urgency, "give it to me."

Edmund threw the wadded-up sheet of vellum between two rows of bookshelves. As Kravel and Gurding watched it bounce toward them, Edmund inched toward the secret door.

"Don't be difficult," the Undead King said, annoyed. "And please do not damage the document any more than you have. I am surprised an antiquarian would behave in such a manner."

Edmund tried to get Thorax's attention. But she was sniffing the air.

"Mr. Kravel," the Undead King said. "If you please . . ."

Kravel stepped into the room. Keeping an eye on Edmund, he picked up the wadded paper and unraveled it.

"I can't read this," Kravel said.

"No. But I can." The Undead King's voice lightened. "Well done, Master Scholar. You are one of the greatest in your profession! History books will remember you far longer than Iliandor. And with kinder words. I will see to that."

Edmund crept closer to the open secret door. "Thorax."

She didn't come.

"Now," the Undead King said, "give us the rest of it."

Buy time.

"Remember our deal. You said if I solved the, the, the . . . the riddle, I could go home."

"I'm afraid that will not be the case now."

That's exactly what I thought.

"You know who I am," the Undead King said. "And I'm quite sure you know who I was ages before I killed your precious Iliandor."

Keep him talking.

"You're Kar-Nazar, the elven lord in the faerie tales who caused the civil war between your people." Edmund took another step toward the secret door. "You killed off nearly all of your kind."

"I?" the Undead King said, his fury building. "I killed off my people?"

Thorax snarled.

"I didn't kill my people," the Undead King thundered. "It was you!"

"Me?" Edmund scoffed.

That's it. Every minute he talks gives them time to get away.

"You miserable human," the Undead King bellowed. "For eons, my people were content, joyously basking in the fruits of our intellectual pursuits, living in the heaven we labored so long to create."

To Thorax's right, the black fluid on the ground rippled. She snapped at the air.

"Then you humans infiltrated these lands, bringing with you your filth and disease. It was you who killed us. You! And soon, my people will be avenged!"

Keep him talk—

Suddenly, something smashed into Edmund's left side. He slammed to the floor, his head bouncing off the stone. Something latched onto his throat—an unseen hand, wide and muscular. It lifted Edmund off the ground. Something grabbed the hand holding the rest of the vellum pages. It squeezed.

Kravel and Gurding rushed forward, swords ready. They wavered, apparently unsure of what to do.

Thorax barked at the invisible foe. Then, as if kicked, her head cracked to one side. She skidded along the floor, rolling through the liquid Pond and Norb had cast about in a wide semi-circle.

"*Fyre—*"

The invisible hand around Edmund's throat tightened, choking off the rest of the spell.

Edmund couldn't breathe. His lungs burned. His eye bulged.

"Drop the formula, Edmund," the Undead King said. "Drop it!"

Getting to her feet, Thorax sprang and grabbed a hold of something. The fur around her muzzle turned red. Blood dripped from her teeth. There was a cry of pain as Thorax thrashed in midair, tearing at whatever she latched onto.

With superhuman strength, the Undead King flung Thorax across the room. She crashed into a bookshelf and plummeted to the ground, heavy tomes toppling on top of her.

"*Fyre av—*"

The unseen hand around Edmund's throat reasserted itself. Edmund kicked, his foot striking something invisible.

"Drop it!" the Undead King repeated.

Yelling like a lunatic, a figure bounded out of the darkness beyond the secret door. It lunged forward, stabbing his rapier blindly in front of him.

There was another screech of pain.

Pond's thin blade dripped blood.

Edmund fell to the floor, gasping.

Pond pulled his rapier back for another blow, but Kravel and Gurding were on him. Kravel tackled Pond and hurled him to the ground. Gurding's knife plunged into Pond's stomach. Pond screamed, his midsection awash in crimson.

"*Fyre av nå!*"

There was a popping sound.

The Undead King cried, "No!"

Sprawled on the floor, Edmund threw the burning vellum sheets as far as he could. Several landed in the oil Pond and Norb had thrown about the library. A wall of blue flame erupted.

"No!" The Undead King cried again.

The flames flew around them in a wide arc, racing along the rows of wooden bookshelves. Black smoke billowed to the ceiling. Fire crackled as it consumed the ancient tomes.

A monstrous figure appeared, silhouetted by the hungry flames. Tall and foreboding, the Undead King's shadowy shape dashed after the pages.

"Get the formula!" the Undead King shouted. "Hurry!"

Kravel and Gurding sprang into the fire, snatching all the pages they could reach. Ashes, like smoldering rain, swirled about them.

"Pond!" Edmund crawled toward his pit mate.

Dark blood seeped out between Pond's fingers. He struggled to breathe. "I, I think I hurt him."

"Don't talk." Edmund put his hands over Pond's stomach and took a deep breath.

You're too tired. You can't cast that spell now. Wait a few minutes.

He doesn't have a few minutes.

Edmund closed his eye and concentrated. "*Smerte av reise!*"

His mind went blank, his skin cold. Edmund swooned as the ugly wound in Pond's belly closed.

Kravel and Gurding sped around the room, diving for the papers as their edges blackened and curled. Many were already half-devoured.

The shadowy figure in the middle of the flames lifted the charred remains of Iliandor's formula.

"Damn you, you miserable little human!" the Undead King cried.

He stalked through the inferno as if it were merely scarlet fog. The flames parted and swirled around him, giving form to his ghastly shape. He reached for Edmund's throat.

"I'll show you what an eternity of torment feels like!"

Crawling out from under the books, Thorax limped toward the specter. With a tremendous effort, she leaped and latched onto his outstretched arm.

A piercing shriek shook the chamber.

Flames vaulted from bookcase to bookcase. Blinding smoke filled the library.

Roaring, the Undead King fought to pry Thorax's jaws from his forearm. But she wouldn't let go.

A smoldering cinder landed on her, igniting the oil she rolled through. Flames engulfed her fur.

Edmund opened his eye.

"Thorax!"

The Undead King beat Thorax against a crumbling bookcase as she blazed like a torch. The scent of scorched hair and roasting meat mingled with the aroma of burning books and oily smoke. But still, Thorax held on.

Choking on smoke, Edmund crawled toward them.

A hand grabbed his calf.

"Come on." Pond pulled Edmund toward the secret door.

"No." Edmund staggered to his feet. "I have to save—"

Thorax hit the wall next to the secret door and toppled to the floor. Edmund staggered to her and smothered the flames dancing over her blackened body.

Thorax!

He scooped her up in his arms.

Her brown eyes opened. She licked his face and then went still.

Pond grabbed Edmund's shoulder. "Hurry!"

Crying, Edmund hobbled after Pond, Thorax's head flopping lifelessly against his chest as he fled.

Chapter Sixty-Six

"I'm sorry," Pond said. "I know how much she meant to you. But, if it helps, she's in a better place."

It doesn't help.

Edmund wiped his eye again as he huddled over Thorax's burnt body.

She smells like that damn dog they roasted in the pit.

I'll never eat meat again.

"Ed . . . Your enlargement spells won't last for long."

Edmund stroked Thorax's head, her black skin cracking. "I'm sorry, girl. I'm so sorry."

"Ed . . ."

Edmund gently laid Thorax under a cedar tree and covered her with his cloak.

Perhaps if you studied more when you were younger, you could've saved her.

He wiped his nose on his sleeve and sobbed.

"Ed . . ."

Edmund nodded. "I'll come back. I'll, I'll come back someday, girl. I'll visit you. I promise."

Remember this spot.

"I love you."

Crying, he retreated a step, lifted his hand in a farewell, and ran westward with Pond.

They sprinted down the hills, leaping over boulders and ducking under low branches. When they reached the bottom of the valley, Edmund slid to a halt.

"What is it?" Pond asked. "Why did you stop?"

Placing a finger to his lips, Edmund beckoned for Pond to follow. As he snuck forward, he reached for his scimitar but found it wasn't in its scabbard.

You're weaponless. Get the hell out of here. Run!

No. It might be . . .

Edmund peered between two trees.

Leave them be.

"What is it?" Pond looked over Edmund's shoulder.

There, a couple of hundred yards away, were Norb and Molly. Norb had his arm around Molly's waist as she hopped on one foot.

They aren't worth the effort.

Feeling every stab of her pain, Edmund watched as Molly limped westward. Norb urged her to go faster.

"Don't think about it," he told her. "Ignore the pain."

They deserve what they get. Besides, it'd be better if the goblins had multiple trails to follow anyway.

As Molly struggled, a long-forgotten memory came to Edmund's conflicted mind. In it, a ten-year-old Molly had sliced her finger to the bone on a sharp knife. Edmund carried her through the streets of Rood to his mother's apothecary shop. As his mother bandaged Molly's hand, she gave Edmund a sidelong glance—a glance only a knowing mother could give.

Even then, she knew I loved Molly.

And she approved. She always encouraged you to court her.

But I didn't. Not in the proper way.

Edmund took a deep breath.

Are you sure this is what you want to do?

Stepping out from behind the trees, Edmund called for Norb to stop.

"Ed!" Norb said. "How, how did you—?"

"Are you okay?" Edmund hurried to Molly.

Breathing hard, Molly looked at him—fear, guilt, and pain filling her beautiful green eyes. "I fell. I . . . I can't run."

Edmund knelt by her side. "Here, let me help." He touched her swelling ankle. She whimpered and pulled it away. But Edmund gently held her foot in his callused hands.

"Smerte av reise."

The swelling subsided. The purplish hue faded.

"How, how . . . how did you . . . ?" Molly gasped. "Are you a, a . . . a witch?"

Terrific! Soon, everybody will know. Goblins and witch hunters will both be after you.

"I know a few things," he said. "B-b-but, but it's best if you don't tell anybody."

"I won't. I promise."

"Thanks."

Molly hemmed and hawed, then said, "Look, Ed . . ."

Edmund shook his head. "We don't have time. And everything is fine. You didn't know how I felt."

"Actually—" She bit her bottom lip. "I did." She blushed. "I'm sorry. It's just that . . . well, I always thought of you as a really good friend, you know?"

Edmund blinked at her.

I'd rather have my other eye burnt out than to hear that again.

"I want to thank you." She touched his forearm. "For the money and everything. It's wonderful."

Edmund imagined her and Norb sleeping in his bed and spending his family's fortune. He wanted to scream.

"The goblins?" Pond reminded them.

"Right." Edmund forced himself to breathe. "D-d-don't, don't head this way. Head northwest instead. Follow us."

"We need to head southwest," Norb said. "Rood is that way."

"That's what they'll be expecting. We have to head northward and hide in the hills until they lose track of us."

Norb appeared doubtful.

"He got us in and out of the tower," Pond said. "I suggest you listen to him."

"We'll go north." Molly tested her weight on her injured leg. "Show us the way to go."

*****

They continued for several hours, hurrying northward through the dense forest and into the barren foothills of the Haegthorn. There, they camped in a shallow cave.

Norb climbed the hill where Edmund kept watch. "Hey, Ed?"

From his hiding spot, Edmund scanned the valley below them. Over the past hour, he'd seen considerable movement. Hundreds of dark shapes swarmed from the mountain and disappeared under the sea of green trees. Far off, flocks of birds took to the air. However, nothing seemed to head in their direction.

"Ed," Norb repeated.

"I know what you want to say," Edmund said. "But you don't need to. I . . . I left. She moved on, like you said. Besides," he added with some bitterness, "we were just friends."

Norb thrust his hands deeper into his pockets. "I want you to know that I didn't ask Mol to marry me . . ."

Married. My god, how much pain can one man endure?

". . . because of all the money you gave her."

Then give it back. It wasn't meant for you.

"I've always cared for Mol," Norb went on. "You know that."

Then why didn't you ask her to marry you before?

Why didn't you?

"Ed—?"

"Norb," Edmund said with some anger. "I've been through a lot today. Let's focus on getting Molly to safety. Okay?"

Frowning, Norb nodded, then headed down the hill.

"Norb," Edmund said.

Norb stopped.

"Get some rest," Edmund said. "Once it gets dark, we'll head west along this ridge and find a better hiding spot."

Chapter Sixty-Seven

For many days, they traveled by night and hid themselves while the sun was up. The darkness and rocky terrain slowed their going. But Edmund hoped to remain undetected as they snuck farther westward from the reaches of the northernmost portions of the mountains.

Soon, the hills gave way to the muddy Battle Plains where, in tales of old, Iliandor drove his knife into the Undead King's throat. Occasionally, they found relics rusting in the bright spring sunlight. Many of the goblin weapons and armor were hewed cleanly in two. However, despite his quick searches, Edmund found nothing made of Iliandor's steel.

By the time they reached the River Bygwen, the fear of goblins had left them, having seen nothing more fearsome than a few wolves and the occasional black bear. They turned south and followed the river until it flowed into Lake Nuvelle. Here, they rested for two days, fishing and scrubbing the filth from their bodies in the cool water. But Rood was close at hand, and Molly was anxious to return home with her husband. So, they left the sandy beaches and journeyed in daylight to make quicker time.

Days later, weary and hungry, they approached Rood from the west. A faint hint of wood ash lingered in the evening air. Molly inhaled deeply. Smiling, she squeezed Norb's hand. Walking behind her, Edmund scowled.

"It smells like somebody is cooking something wonderful," she said. "I'm starving."

But her expression quickly changed when they came around the last hill.

Hanging from Rood's western gate were eight bodies, their hands tied behind their backs, their heads rolled unnaturally to one side. Other bodies lined the streets. Some hung from trees, jagged hooks embedded under their jawbones. Many more lay on the ground, hacked to pieces or partly burned.

Molly covered her mouth. "Oh my god."

They're all dead.

Everybody is dead.

They stumbled into Rood. All around them was death and ruin. Familiar faces of men, women, and children stared lifelessly at them. Poles with severed heads lined the town square. Ravens picked at their film-covered eyes.

A dozen knights hung from a broken statue of Iliandor. Arrows stuck out of them as if they were used for target practice. Below their dangling feet, stacked like kindling wood, lay the corpses of their young squires.

Norb stared at the bodies. "The assholes deserved it."

But Edmund wasn't too sure.

"They did what they thought was right," he said. "They protected the town."

Who's going to protect it now?

What's left to protect?

They turned in unison, examining the carnage around them, unable to look away or even to cry. The bakery where Edmund used to beg for cookies as a child had collapsed. The Wandering Rogue, where he had spent countless evenings watching Molly from the corner of his eye, was a black skeleton. Burnt boards banged in the wind. His mother's cherished apothecary shop was a pile of smoldering ash.

All those books . . .

It doesn't matter anymore. Nothing does.

"It looks like you have a lot of work to do," Pond said. "You being the lord of this region and all."

Edmund stirred. "I'm not lord here or anywhere else."

He withdrew the Star of Iliandor from his pocket. The failing evening light reflected dully off its blue gem. It felt cold and heavy, like his heart.

"Here." Edmund handed the Star to Norb. "Bring this to the King in Eryn Mas. If he asks, say you found it on my dead body or something. And whatever you do, don't m-m-mention anything about goblins."

Norb inspected the Star. "Why should I give this to the stupid King? His stinking knights wouldn't even help us."

"Because whoever turns this in will become the Lord of the Highlands. And somebody needs to rebuild the town. I can't do it. The goblins will be hunting for me. It'll have to be you."

Norb's eyebrows arched. "Lord of the Highlands?"

"But there is one thing, Norb." Edmund's expression turned hard. "Treat Molly like the lady she is—or you'll have me to answer to."

EPILOGUE

Far from Rood, Edmund stood on a dirt path bisecting a nameless settlement of perhaps thirty ramshackle buildings, scanning the horizon for any signs of Kravel and his goblin hunters. He thought he had a two-day lead on his pursuers, but he wasn't sure. Goblins could travel as fast as hungry jackals when they smelled blood. And somehow, no matter where Edmund and Pond went, Kravel and Gurding were always a step behind them.

He tapped his foot impatiently.

Hurry up!

To his right, a traveling merchant unloaded another box from his cart and set it on the ground with the rest of his wares. From inside came soft scuffling sounds and a few birdlike cries. The head of a grey puppy appeared, followed by a brown one, a mostly white one, and two black ones.

The grey puppy scrambled on top of her littermates, fell, scrambled back up, and pulled herself to the edge of the box. She teetered for a moment. Then, leaping, she landed in the dirt, her little legs pointing in four different directions. Pushing herself to her feet, she romped over to Edmund.

"You should stay with your friends," Edmund told the puppy. "It's much safer there than out here."

The puppy tripped over Edmund's boot, got back up, and wagged her tiny tail.

Coming out of one of the nearby buildings, Pond hoisted his pack onto his shoulders. "All righty. I'm ready. Where to now, Captain?"

Edmund gestured up the road he'd been studying. "They said this eventually leads to Dardenello. That might be a good place to hide for a while. You'll like it. It's by the sea."

And it's as far from the mountains as humanly possible.

The puppy scampered around them.

"Warm or cold?" Pond asked.

"Warm," Edmund said. "At least in the summers. In the winter, the weather is mild."

"Good. If I ever see snow again, it'll be too soon."

The puppy tripped over Edmund's boots again.

"Remember," Edmund said, "we have to change our names."

"Could I be Lord Horgenswagel?"

Laughing, Edmund patted Pond on the back. "You can be anybody you like."

He walked along the road, a whistling Pond by his side.

"Have I thanked you today for coming to my rescue in the library?" Edmund asked.

"Not today."

"Well, thank you for saving my life."

"Thanks for saving mine."

Standing in the middle of the dusty road behind them, the grey puppy yipped.

Edmund looked at her and sighed.

"Are you sure?" he asked. "It won't be easy. You'll be better off here, trust me."

Her tiny tail wagged so that her entire rear end whipped back and forth. She yipped again.

"Okay." Producing a coin from his pouch, Edmund tossed it to the merchant. "But you'll have to walk. I'm not going to carry you. That's rule number one."

The puppy bounded after them.

"Who's this?" Pond grinned at the little ball of grey fur prancing around them.

"Our new guard dog," Edmund said. "She certainly has big shoes to fill."

Pond scanned the bleak horizon behind them. "Do you think the goblins will keep hunting us?"

Edmund resumed walking.

Until I'm either dead or captured . . .

"Are we … are we almost there?" Pond asked, panting as he scrambled up the hill.

Edmund labored around another tree, sweat trickling into the hole where his left eye used to be. In the shadows caused by the moonlight, he could only see a few feet in front of him, making his progress slow and often painful. Fatigue, however, was his biggest concern. Soon, he would have to stop, whether he wanted to or not, and he knew at least twenty goblin hunters weren't far behind.

"Almost." He ducked under a low branch. "I think I can hear it up ahead."

"Hear what?"

Veering to his left, Edmund set off for a gap between two jagged hills looming in the blackness before them.

The sound of rushing water grew louder.

This better not be another dead end. If we get trapped …

"There's a river around here," he said over his shoulder. "The River Celerin. It's nearby. It'll … it'll … it'll hide our tracks."

"Celerin?" Pond repeated. "That's … that's a big river, isn't it? I mean, it … it isn't a small stream, right?"

Edmund's pace slowed to a limping jog and then to a walk. He stopped and doubled over, sucking in the smell of dry autumn leaves in great, gulping swallows.

His puppy, Becky, leaped from his arms.

"I … I don't know if I can keep this up much longer." Pond collapsed onto the ground next to him. "I can't keep running."

"Do you want to end up in the pits again?"

Pond shook his head.

"Then we either run or we die. It's that simple."

Edmund took a drink.

"I'm … I'm sorry." He handed the waterskin to Pond. "But, but we … we have to keep running. We have no other choice."

Pond took several quick sips and then poured some of the water over his sweaty face. "We could hide."

"They keep finding us. I don't know how … but … but they always do."

They probably smell you. You stink!

The river will take care of that.

Becky danced on her hind legs, begging to be picked up.

"The river," Edmund said, trying to slow his pounding heart. "The river is our only hope. We … we have to put some distance between us and them. The river will help."

Without warning, Becky pounced on one of Pond's boots, latching onto it as though it were a deadly enemy.

"For the love of—" Pond pried her off his ankle.

"You were saying?" He held the writhing puppy in his outstretched arms, her sharp teeth flashing in the moonlight.

"I'm not sure how Kravel keeps f-f-find, finding us," Edmund stammered. He arched his aching back. "Maybe he's … maybe he's tracking us by scent. Maybe by—"

Pond cried out. Becky had found a way to bite her captor.

She sprang free and raced in frantic circles around them, kicking up dead leaves in her wake.

"Damned dog." Pond flexed his bleeding thumb. "I say we tie her to a tree and leave."

Becky jumped on Pond's shin, growling as she pulled at his pant leg.

"Could you please do something about her?" Pond asked.

"Here." Edmund tossed him the knotted remains of a cloak she had already defeated. "Have her play with this."

Pond dangled the tattered cloak in front of Becky's nose. She stopped pulling, her eager eyes following the swirling olive-green fabric. Pond threw it as far as he could. Becky bounded down the hillside, flying after it with reckless abandon.

"Honestly—" Pond examined the holes in his pants. "I don't understand what you see in the little monster."

"I like dogs," Edmund said. "Remember what Thorax did for us? We wouldn't be alive if it weren't for her. Or worse, we'd be living in Kar-Nazar's wet cells with our hands and feet cut off."

"Thorax was well-behaved," Pond said. "This one is crazy. Seriously, there's something wrong with her. It's like she's part demon."

Becky pranced up the incline, thrashing the cloak from side to side.

"I'm sorry she's such a p-p-pain," Edmund said, trying not to stutter. "I'll … I'll make it up to you, I promise. But with her quick ears and keen sense of smell, we can rest easier at night. She's saved us more than once already."

"Sleep easier? Not with her springing on me every few seconds. I haven't slept since you got her."

"She only attacks when you move. So don't move."

Pond snorted. "Don't move, you say."

Behind them, on the crest of a distant rise, a black shape appeared, its humanoid form silhouetted against the bluish stars. Two more became visible, followed by at least another score.

Edmund grabbed Pond's arm. "Hurry!" He yanked Pond to his feet. "They're coming."

They tried to run, but their bodies would only allow a lurching stumble.

Becky bounded after them, still growling and thrashing the cloak about.

"What's your plan exactly?" Pond asked as he forced himself up the incline. "With the river and everything, I mean."

"I figure we can use its current to float downstream." The muscles in Edmund's legs were tightening. In a few minutes, he wouldn't be able to move at all. "We can float toward the lowlands. It'd be f-f-faster, faster than running, and the goblins won't be able to follow our trail." He added, "If we can reach one of the logging camps or mining towns to the south, we might finally be safe."

Pond appeared visibly shaken.

"What?" Edmund asked.

"Well, I'm not a terribly strong swimmer."

"You don't have to be an expert or anything," he said, praying the river wasn't far away. "All you'll have to do is float. The current will do the rest. You'll be fine."

Pond's sour expression worsened.

"You don't know how to swim, do you?" Edmund said. "Pond! You're from sea-faring people!"

"I sold textiles. I'm a merchant, not a sailor."

"Pond!" Edmund tossed his hands in dismay. "Can you at least tread water?"

"Not really. No."

Shaking his head, Edmund stared at the moon in desperation. The night was growing old, and the goblins could move quickly in the dark. They'd be on them within the hour.

Stay and fight or run. Those are our only options.

Next to him, Pond was still catching his breath. Even if it were daylight and they were both fully rested, they couldn't fight twenty goblins and survive.

"We can't stay here," Edmund said. "The river is our only hope."

"Well then, let's give it a go," Pond said. "Who knows, maybe I'm a natural swimmer."

Death by goblins or by drowning ...

At least you'd have a chance in the water.

I do. Pond doesn't.

The night breeze shifted through the forest, rustling the leaves at their feet. It also brought with it a pungent odor of rotting meat.

Edmund sniffed, trying to recall what the stench reminded him of. Then he remembered.

He dropped to his knees. "Get down!"

"Why?" Pond asked. "What's wrong?"

Edmund waved for him to be quiet. He crept to the hill's summit. Peering down the other side, he almost gasped.

In the valley below, he saw the River Celerin shimmering in the moonlight. Striding through its white water stalked a massive figure, a spear the size of a sapling in his hand.

"What is it?" Pond crawled next to Edmund. Through the trees, he saw the problem. "A troll? Oh, well, that's not good."

"Not just any troll." Edmund watched the hideous monster push through the surging current. "That's the same troll who tried to bury me alive under the tower of Tol Helen. We must be farther north than I thought."

He retreated from the ridge and moaned.

"Caught between a troll and goblins."

"What now?" Pond asked.

Edmund thought for a moment.

"We'll be fine," he whispered, not believing a word he was saying. "We'll swing around to the south. The wind is coming from the east, so he won't smell—"

Shrill barking rang out into the night.

Oh no!

Edmund lunged for Becky. But she darted out of his grasp, yipping and snarling.

The troll hesitated midstream, searching for the source of the commotion in the hills to his right. Then he spied the small bundle of grey fur sliding down the slope.

"Becky!" Edmund shouted.

The troll gazed at the patch of trees where Edmund and Pond hid.

"Quick," Edmund told Pond. "Gather those rocks together. Get anything you can throw!"

"Why?" Pond asked.

"Just do it! Hit him when he comes within range."

"What're you—?"

Edmund threw himself over the ridge and plummeted after Becky, who had stopped mere inches from the river's rumbling current. Ears pulled back and front legs lowered like a miniature bull, she barked at the colossal figure in the water.

Laughing, the troll considered the puppy and then Edmund as he half-slid, half-fell down the nearly vertical incline. Edmund tumbled to the riverbank, got to his bloodied knees, and drew his notched and slightly bent sword.

Grinning, the troll waded to shore, his spear at the ready.

What the hell are you doing?

Saving Becky!

You're going to die. You can't fight a troll. Not by yourself!

Shaking, Edmund pointed his sword at the approaching troll.

"Do you know how to use that meat cleaver?" the troll asked, stepping onto the riverbank.

"W ... w ... well, well enough." Edmund's hands tighten around the sword's rusty hilt. "B-B-Beck ... Becky, come!"

Becky retreated a few paces as the dripping troll lumbered closer. Her entire body vibrated with every high-pitched yap and snarl. But she didn't come.

What are you doing? Get the hell out of here. Run!

Run where? Kravel is right behind us. We can't go back.

"Becky," Edmund repeated louder. "Come!"

Becky let loose another deluge of barks, her hackles raised.

"It's either feast or famine in these hills." The troll grinned at Edmund. "It looks like a feast tonight!"

"M-m-m-maybe." Edmund brandished his sword in front of him. "But I'm n-not, I'm not cooked yet. You'll have to catch me first. Becky … come!"

Becky still didn't come.

She craned her neck upward as the troll closed in, the riverbank shaking with each of his pounding strides.

The troll hefted his crude spear. Thirty feet from Edmund, he couldn't miss.

"Oh, I won't cook you," the troll said. "I'm going to eat you alive. Bit by bit. Like a rat nibbling on your bones."

If you're going to fight him, get closer! You can't do anything from here. Make him use that spear for thrusting. At least then, you can parry it.

Edmund inched forward.

"I'm going to tear your fingers off," the troll said. "Then your stubby little arms."

I have to get out of here.

Focus. Don't let him distract you. You won't get many opportunities. When he attacks, block the spear and stab him. Keep your feet under you. Move!

Edmund circled a few steps to his left.

"I'm going to use your skull as a cup," the troll said. "Why don't you run and give me some sport?"

Yes, run!

Edmund wiped the sweat from his hands. "It's too dark. I'd r-r-run … I'd run into a tree."

"You aren't as stupid as you look."

The troll jabbed its spear at Edmund's head.

Edmund dodged the sharpened point. Becky nipped at the troll's toes. But a flick of his foot sent her flying off into the darkness with a yelp.

Do something!

Edmund darted forward and swung his short sword. He missed the creature by at least four feet.

The troll laughed at him.

You're never going to touch him from back here. Get closer.

If I get closer, he'll skewer me.

Edmund took a step closer.

"How did you lose your eye?" the troll asked.

He feigned a stab of his spear. Crying out, Edmund hopped back.

Be calm. Buy time. Look for an opening.

"Goblins burnt it out," Edmund said. "Actually, you, you … you met them a while back. Kravel and Gurding?"

At this, the troll straightened, his expression a mixture of astonishment and trepidation. Edmund shot forward, swinging his sword. The troll blocked Edmund's blow with the shaft of his spear.

Edmund scurried out of the troll's long reach.

"Kravel and Gurding?" the troll asked, unnerved. "You're joking."

Becky reappeared from the darkness, leaves and thorns sticking in her muddy fur. She snapped at the night air.

"Not at all," Edmund said. "A … a c-c-c-couple, a couple of years ago, they spoke with you about me. Something about a weapon made of a bluish metal, I believe."

The troll flinched.

"You stutter," he said, putting together distant memories. "And you have a dog."

Get him in the knee. If he can't run, you might be able to get out of here alive.

Edmund lunged again, jabbing at the troll's elephant-like leg. The troll parried with a swipe of his spear, the force of which nearly wrenched the ringing sword out of Edmund's hands.

A cloud passed over the bright moon, plunging the valley into deeper darkness.

The roar of the river continued unabated.

"If you know Kravel and Gurding," the troll said, "tell me this. Which is the smart one?"

Force him into the river. Perhaps he'll slip on the wet stones.

You're as good as dead if you stay here. You can't fight a troll by yourself. You're just a stuttering fool of a librarian!

"Kravel." Edmund slid to his left. "Kravel was the smart one. Gurding was an idiot who did what he was told. But they didn't have a brain between them."

The troll withdrew a step, keeping Edmund in front of him. "What do you mean, 'didn't'?"

"I killed them," Edmund lied.

He sprang forward, the tip of his sword coming within an inch of the troll's left knee.

Damn! You're never going to stab him with this tiny sword. You need something bigger.

The troll laughed. "You're a fine liar. I spoke to them a few days—"

Suddenly, something the size of a bat flew through the dimness. It sailed behind the troll's head and splashed into the river's foamy current. As the troll spun to see what it was, Edmund drove forward again. This time, his short sword pierced deep into the troll's enormous thigh. Black blood spurted, sizzling as it hit the damp ground.

Howling, the troll whirled around, his spear connecting with Edmund's ribs. Edmund flew backward, bouncing to a stop a dozen strides from where he'd been. Becky launched herself at the distracted troll and bit his ankle.

Holding his aching ribs, Edmund scrambled to his feet and charged. He was about to impale the troll through the creature's unprotected belly when something cold smacked against his temple. He fell sprawling to the ground.

"Sorry!" Pond yelled from the ridge high above them.

On his back, head swimming, Edmund felt blindly for his weapon.

"There's a reward for you," the troll said, ignoring Pond's volley of stones and the growling puppy tugging his leg. "A huge reward!"

Edmund's fingers wrapped around the mud-covered hilt.

If only I had a lance or —

A longer sword? Your spell! Your spell! Use your spell!

Bending over, the troll reached for Edmund. "You, little fella, are going to make me very, very wealthy."

Hand trembling, Edmund pointed his sword at the troll and uttered the incantation his father had taught him when he was a child.

"Forstørre nå!"

Suddenly, the sword doubled in length, piercing the troll between his eyes and popping out through the back of his skull with a bone-splitting crack.

The troll shuddered and then toppled forward. His immense, leathery torso crashed onto Edmund's face and chest, pinning him to the rocky ground. He screamed for Pond as the troll's hot blood coursed over him, burning his skin.

Then he saw no more…

AVAILABLE

APRIL 24, 2026